He liked watching her like this, all soft and vulnerable.

That she trusted him enough to sleep under his watch shifted something in his chest. He'd never met a woman like Olivia. Whatever he was feeling toward her, he wanted it to last.

The urge to climb into that bed with her and make love was powerful. No sooner than he settled in next to her did she start to flail and cry out. She was having another nightmare.

"Olivia." He shook her gently, but she fought him off. "Olivia, wake up."

Her eyes flew open and she screamed.

"Olivia, it's me. It's okay. You were dreaming."

She blinked, inhaled a ragged breath and scrambled away from him. Her eyes looked crazed when she looked at him. "Bad things happened there, Russ. Things we don't even know yet."

Dear Reader,

The first COLBY AGENCY book, *Safe by His Side,* was released by Mills & Boon® Intrigue. Time has flown and the stories featuring Victoria Colby and her esteemed team of private investigators have stolen my heart.

You journeyed with Victoria through the painful memories of having lost her first husband and her son. You held your breath as her son returned a broken man determined to take his life back. You cheered for Victoria when she allowed herself to put the past behind her and love Lucas Camp, the man who had been there for her through it all. You have shared the danger as evil has tried repeatedly to destroy the Colbys and the triumphs of new love and the birth of children and grandchildren.

Most important, you have taken this journey with me every step of the way. I cannot thank you enough for helping me to make the Colby family a great success. As I faced my own personal challenges, your outpouring of support and concern has helped me rise above the pain and defeat it to write that next story and to keep believing in myself and the work. Please know that I read every letter and e-mail that you sent. I look forward to many, many more years of writing the stories I love and sharing those journeys with you. I hope you enjoy this fiftieth COLBY AGENCY story. Never fear, more Colbys are on the way!

Very best!

Debra Webb

COLBY ROUNDUP

BY
DEBRA WEBB

First published in Great Britain 2012
by Mills & Boon, an imprint of Harlequin (UK) Limited,
Eton House, 18-24 Paradise Road, Richmond, Surrey TW9 1SR

© Debra Webb 2012

ISBN: 978 0 263 89581 0
ebook ISBN: 978 1 408 97258 8

46-1212

Harlequin (UK) policy is to use papers that are natural, renewable and recyclable products and made from wood grown in sustainable forests. The logging and manufacturing processes conform to the legal environmental regulations of the country of origin.

Printed and bound in Spain
by Blackprint CPI, Barcelona

Debra Webb wrote her first story at age nine and her first romance at thirteen. It wasn't until she spent three years working for the military behind the Iron Curtain and within the confining political walls of Berlin, Germany, that she realized her true calling. A five-year stint with NASA on the space shuttle program reinforced her love of the endless possibilities within her grasp as a storyteller. A collision course between suspense and romance was set. Debra has been writing romance, suspense and action-packed romance thrillers since. Visit her at www.debrawebb.com or write to her at PO Box 4889, Huntsville, AL 35815, USA.

Chapter One

Olivia Westfield paced the stark interview room to which she had been sequestered. She paused long enough to take a breath and reminded herself that she needed to remain calm. Any visible sign of anticipation or anxiety would be a mistake. Though she was not an attorney, she had sat in enough courtrooms with her boss, who was the best criminal attorney in San Antonio, to know how to lead a witness, especially a potential hostile witness. During the next few minutes, it was immensely important that she lead.

It had taken her a week to get this interview, and then the warden had only been persuaded by her boss's connection to an esteemed Texas senator with the right amount of clout. The prisoner Olivia was here to see was the most infamous death row inmate in Texas's history. Since she was not his attorney, the interview had been extremely difficult to secure. The opportunity both terrified and exhilarated her.

Raymond Rafe Barker had spent twenty-two years in prison, seventeen on death row. In all those years he had not provided the locations of all the missing bodies of his many alleged victims, including those of his three young daughters. In a mere seventeen days he would be executed by lethal injection for his alleged heinous crimes. Olivia wanted his story—the whole story.

But what if he was innocent?

The tangle of nerves that had been twisting inside her for days tightened to a hard knot. Was she making a mistake doing this? Revealing herself to the man who could very well change the course of the rest of her life? Only her boss knew the reason for her need to meet the convicted murderer and learn the real story of what happened all those years ago in a small Texas community. Eventually the world would know; it was inevitable. The ramifications were immense, the impact potentially widespread.

Mistake or not, ultimately she had to do this. Whatever the consequences, living the rest of her life without knowing the truth was something she simply could not do. The past twenty-plus years of her life had been built on too many deceptions. From this moment forward she wanted the truth, the whole truth and nothing but. Want didn't begin to describe what Olivia felt. She *needed* the truth; she needed answers.

The door of the interview room opened. Olivia snapped from her disturbing thoughts. She mentally and physically braced for the impact of meeting the man who was a convicted serial murderer, a coldhearted sociopath according to the law. An inmate who had maintained his silence all this time as to what really happened so many years ago. This man, who held the key to those answers, was also her biological father.

That reality stole her breath yet again.

Two prison guards escorted Rafe Barker into the room. The leg irons around his ankles and the belly chain coiled about his waist rattled as he was ushered to a chair at the table in the center of the small interview room. One of the two chairs stationed around the table was drawn back.

"Sit," one of the guards ordered.

Unable to drag in a gulp of air even now, Olivia watched

the prisoner's every move. He hadn't looked at her yet. She wasn't sure how to feel about that or the possibility of whether or not he would recognize her, for that matter.

It had been twenty-two years since he'd last seen her.

For God's sake, what had she been thinking coming here?

Barker glanced at the guard on his left, then followed the instruction to be seated. He settled into the molded plastic chair. The second guard secured the leg irons to the floor and the ones binding Barker's hands to his waist to the underside of the sturdy table.

"We'll be just outside, Ms. Westfield," the first guard said to Olivia. "Just knock on the door when you're finished here." He shot a glance at the man he obviously considered a monster before meeting her gaze once more.

"Thank you." Her voice was a little shaky and she regretted that outward demonstration of apprehension. *Be strong, Liv.*

When the door had closed behind the guards, Olivia drew in a deep, steadying breath and crossed to the table. She sat down and met the gaze of the man now studying her intently. From what she understood he spent twenty-three hours per day confined to his cell and it showed in the pale skin stretched across his gaunt face; a face that narrowed down to slumped shoulders and a rail-thin body covered by generic prison garb. But the most startling aspect of his appearance was the faded brown eyes. Eyes that perhaps had once been the more vivid chocolate color of hers. The high cheekbones and slim nose were as familiar as the reflection she considered in the mirror each morning.

Genetically speaking, this was her father. No question. No doubts. Her heart pounded with the rush of emotions she couldn't quite define. Anger, defeat, regret…one, or all, maybe.

"Why are you here?" he asked.

The rustiness of his voice made her flinch. His speech

croaked with disuse and age that belied his true years. The warden had told her that Barker rarely spoke to anyone. He had refused to grant a single interview with reporters or cold-case investigators or to cooperate with the doctors who'd attempted to analyze him during the past two decades.

His question—four little words—churned those already turbulent emotions, making her quake inside with a vulnerability she wanted desperately to deny. "That's a good question." She cleared the rasp of uncertainty from her own voice. "I suppose I felt compelled to see you before it was too late."

In seventeen days he would be dead. More of those troubling emotions stirred deep in her belly. Emotions she shouldn't feel for a stranger...a convicted killer. The faint idea that he might not be guilty toyed with her desire for justice...for hope that he was not that heinous monster.

"Do you know who I am?" he ventured, his eyes searching hers for any indication of what she was thinking beyond her vague response. Obviously he felt something, curiosity maybe. Was it even possible for him to feel anything else?

This man who had been labeled pure evil was her *father*. Dear God. He *was* her father. Sitting face-to-face with him, she could not deny that glaring fact. Part of her had wanted to latch onto the idea that it could be a mistake. The photos she had seen from the trial more than twenty years ago had not adequately prepared her for *this*. She hadn't seen him like this, in person, since she was five years old. Basically, she remembered nothing from that time...except in her dreams.

As far back as she could recall, the nightmares had haunted her sleep. The screaming...the blood. The darkness and then the soothing humming—a tune she hadn't been able to identify. Not that she'd really tried. She shook off the images and sounds that tried to intrude even now. Her adoptive parents had blamed the images and sounds on a scary movie she'd watched with a cousin. Another of their well-meant deceptions.

So many, many lies.

"I know who you are." She clasped her hands in her lap to prevent him from seeing the shaking that had overtaken her body. As hard as she tried, she couldn't make it stop. Good thing she wasn't in a courtroom right now. Prosecutors ate nervous defense attorneys and their assistants for breakfast.

Raymond Barker was the Princess Killer. The man charged and convicted of the murders of more than a dozen young girls. The man who had been charged with murdering his own daughters. That was the real reason Olivia was here. She'd had no choice in the matter. The media had gotten it wrong. The police who investigated the murders had gotten it wrong.

Olivia was this man's daughter. If Rafe Barker hadn't killed her, was it possible he hadn't killed anyone? Made sense that if she was alive, her sisters would be, too. She needed an answer to that, as well. Olivia had studied the case. She knew the details, at least the ones that had played out in the media. She had interviewed the detectives who investigated the case, but she had not been allowed to see the actual case files. The detective who'd been in charge, Marcus Whitt, had told her straight up that he didn't appreciate her nosing around.

Giving herself grace, she had only just learned the identity of her biological parents two weeks ago. Before she'd gotten to the point of actually moving forward, Clare Barker had been released from prison—her conviction overturned—and that had changed everything in her opinion. Olivia had tried unsuccessfully to find her.

Her mother. The woman who had professed her innocence for more than two decades. If she was innocent, why hadn't she come to Olivia? Had she contacted the other two women? Sarah, who had been named Sadie by her adoptive parents, and Lisa, named Laney by the folks who adopted her? Olivia had no idea where her sisters were but she intended to find them. The three of them needed to face this challenge together. Time was running out and desperation had lodged deep in her soul.

But what if her sisters didn't know? Olivia's adoptive parents had kept their secret for twenty-two years. As much as she loved the people who had raised her, that decision had been the wrong one. She should have known the truth long ago. What if her sisters didn't want to know? Was it fair for her to impose her personal quest upon their lives?

Rafe cleared his throat, the saggy muscles there working as if the words he intended to utter were difficult to impart. "Whatever you believe about me, I'm thankful you came."

The air she struggled to draw in trapped beneath her breastbone. The ache it generated made speaking as hard for her as it appeared to have been for him. "I need you to tell me the truth about what happened when I was a child."

The prospect carried monumental implications even beyond the potential added pain to the families of the victims. Her chest tightened at the conceivability of what his long-awaited words might mean for all those damaged hearts... what they might mean for her. For her sisters...women she didn't even know.

He had refused to talk from the moment he and his wife—Clare, her mother—were arrested. Today, he had just over two weeks to live. Why not tell the world the truth? Unless, of course, the truth was that he, in fact, was the heinous killer society thought him to be.

Clare Barker had relentlessly stood by her story that she was innocent. According to what Olivia had gleaned, as the investigation of the case had progressed, the bodies of eight young girls, ranging in age from twelve to seventeen, had been recovered but several others remained unaccounted for. Clare insisted that she knew nothing about any of the abductions or the murders. Both Clare and Rafe had been respected members of the community of Granger. No one had suspected either of the slightest legal infraction...yet numerous sets of remains had been exhumed from the woods just beyond their own backyard. A backyard where their daughters, including Olivia, had played.

The reality of that fact made her sick to her stomach. But who was the killer and who was the oblivious bystander? Someone was lying, because Olivia was alive. That had to mean one story or the other was wrong, at least to a degree.

He studied her for a long moment with those too-familiar brown eyes. "The truth you seek will not ease the torment your soul suffers, I fear." He looked down as if he also feared his eyes would give away his true thoughts.

How dare he make such a statement! His suggestion that he had even the most remote concept of what she might think or feel infuriated her. "What about all those other families who want nothing more than to bury their dead? Will you take your secrets to your grave and twist the dagger once more?" She shook her head. "Maybe you are the monster they say you are. Whether you are or not, the truth can't hurt you now. But it could help others." Including her. Her whole life felt out of sync.

He inhaled a sharp breath. "I'm no monster. What I am is a fool. I slept in the bed with her every night and never had the vaguest idea what she was doing right under my nose. I don't deserve to live. My blindness is inexcusable." The craggy features of his face tightened as he visibly fought for composure. "I can't do a thing to bring those girls back and I don't know that the truth, if I had it to give you, would comfort their families. Dead is dead. The only good thing I accomplished was to get the three of you to safety. I wanted you to have a normal life. I didn't want my legacy to haunt your life." He moved his head side to side. "That may be impossible now. You shouldn't have come here. You took too great a risk."

Her fury exploded with a ferocity she could scarcely contain. "How can you pretend to know what's best for me? You have no idea who I am. What about the others? My sisters. Where are they?"

"They're alive and well," he assured her. "Whatever you believe," he said, his eyes watery, "my only concern is for your continued safety. That's why I called the Colby Agency. They're supposed to be protecting my girls."

This announcement startled her, momentarily shoved aside the fury and the tangle of emotions funneling inside her. "What're you talking about?" She'd sensed someone following her the past few days but she hadn't spotted anyone. Finally, she'd decided it was her imagination. With the life-altering discoveries she'd made over the past fourteen days, she couldn't trust her judgment or her instincts. "There's no one protecting me." She was perfectly capable of protecting herself.

"The only thing I ever wanted was for the three of you to be safe and happy." The sadness in his eyes looked convincing enough. "She would've killed you, too. I made sure you were out of her reach. Until now. When her sentence was overturned, I had to do something. I reached out to the only people I felt could be trusted. The Colby Agency. Their reputation speaks for itself."

A barrage of questions whirled like a cyclone inside her head. "I haven't heard from any Colby Agency." How could he sit there and pretend to care about her welfare?

"They're watching you," he promised. "Protecting you from her. Her release is the only reason I broke my silence."

Don't get distracted, Olivia. Don't let him lead. Read between the lines. "You're saying you're innocent, but unless you have proof of that claim—"

He shook his head again. "Don't need any proof. I'm reconciled to my fate. It's nothing more than I deserve for being a fool. As long as my girls are safe that's all that matters to me. I can leave this world satisfied."

His suggestion that Clare would come after her daughters with malicious intent stretched the boundaries of credibility. "Why would she do this? Clare, I mean. She's free. No one can touch her now." She had nothing to gain and everything to lose.

He leaned forward. Olivia instinctively reared back before she could prevent the reaction. "She will do anything to hurt me. When she figured out I'd hidden the three of you away, she began her battle to gain her freedom. Took her twenty-some years, but she did it. Now none of you are safe with her free."

"If she's trying to get to me, she's not very good at it." Maybe Clare had been following her instead of the Colby Agency. Could a woman in her mid-fifties fresh on the street from an extended death-row confinement be that stealthy?

"If you believe nothing else," he warned, "believe me when I say she will find a way. You're the oldest. Find your sisters. The Colby Agency knows where they are. Do what you can to help keep them safe...like you used to do."

Olivia went completely still inside. More of those images and sounds from her dreams surfaced.

"Don't let her do what she tried to do when you were babies. She's evil. Pure evil, Olivia. She won't stop until you're all dead and I'm in hell where she wanted me all along."

Chapter Two

Russell St. James waited well outside the long entry and gate that barred admittance to Polunsky Prison. He'd left his car a considerable distance from the entrance to avoid being spotted by Olivia Westfield, aka Olivia Barker. Based on her movements the past twelve days, she clearly sensed she was being followed. He'd had to take extreme care with his surveillance. The woman was no fool. At least, he'd thought she wasn't until now.

This latest move was troubling. He'd already informed Victoria Colby-Camp and Simon Ruhl, head of the Colby Agency's Houston office. All were braced for the impact of what Olivia's visit to Rafe Barker might mean.

She had no idea the kind of danger she was in. Clare Barker and her apparent partner were now wanted as persons of interest in the murder of the ex-boyfriend of Laney Seagers, aka Lisa Barker. As well as the attempted murders of both Lucas Camp and Colby investigator Joel Hayden. Clare's partner, Tony Weeden, would likely be deemed the prime suspect in that ongoing investigation any time now. The two were also under investigation for the abduction of Laney's five-year-old son. Though the boy's father, Laney's ex-boyfriend Terrence Kingston, took the boy initially, Clare and Weeden grabbed him after the murder. The unknown variable was which of the two committed the murder. The likelihood of Kingston having been murdered before Clare and Weeden found him was highly unlikely since the child had survived the event. This was a very dangerous scenario and growing more dangerous with each passing day.

The actions of Clare and Weeden indicated a building level of desperation. That was never good. The two were obviously capable of anything and the Colby Agency could only guess at the ultimate goal of one or both.

Russ's initial assignment had been to watch Olivia while keeping his distance. Disrupting her life had not been on his agenda. That had changed now. The risk was too great to remain at a distance. Depending on the outcome of Olivia's abrupt visit to her father, which the agency had only confirmed was going down two hours ago, Russ was prepared to intercept Olivia and spell it all out for her. She knew more than her sisters had. Neither Laney nor youngest sister Sadie Gilmore, aka Sarah Barker, had known they were adopted.

Yesterday, Russ had followed Olivia from her home in San Antonio to just outside Livingston. She'd spent the night in a modest motel with the briefcase and one small bag she'd carried into her room. He'd gotten the adjoining room and spent several hours listening to her cell phone conversation with her boss, attorney Nelson Belden. The lady had discovered about two weeks ago that the Barkers were her biological parents. That part saved Russ the uncomfortable task of relating the news. The other side of that scenario was that she appeared bent on finding the truth about the Princess murders.

Russ removed his hat and ran a hand through his hair before settling the Stetson back in place. No question that all three of the Barker girls deserved the truth. Trouble was, right now was not a good time to start digging into the past. At least not until the danger was under control.

Denying the lady had an understandable agenda wasn't possible. She had just learned her existence up to now was built on a foundation of untruths. Equally understandable was her adoptive parents' reasons for keeping the ugliness of the past from her, at least in the early years. Based on the conversation he'd overheard last night Olivia was on the outs with the folks who had raised her over the well-kept secret. Oddly, she hadn't mentioned this visit in the conversation with her boss. Whether she'd been waiting for approval or keeping it from Belden, which didn't add up, was yet to be seen. Whatever she hoped to gain with a face-to-face with Rafe Barker, Russ feared she would be vastly disappointed.

This was a volatile state of affairs and after her meeting with Barker it was only going to grow more unpredictable.

The cell phone in his hip pocket vibrated. He dragged it out and accepted the call from his boss, Simon Ruhl. "St. James."

"A doctor's office in Brenham was broken into early this morning. We believe Weeden may have been involved since the items taken would be useful for his gunshot injury and his white sedan was found in the area. We're hoping to get a confirmation from the prints lifted at the scene. Neither he nor Clare has been spotted in the area and we have no reports of stolen vehicles. Either the two are laying low nearby or have *borrowed* a vehicle that the owner hasn't yet reported missing. Judging by the distance and direction traveled, we feel he and Clare may be headed back to the Houston area or perhaps to Livingston."

"I assume that means I should intercept Ms. Westfield and lay out the situation." Sounded like the next step to Russ. Waiting any longer would only make his job more challenging. He needed to be as close to Olivia as feasible, particularly if Clare and Weeden were headed for her. The two had attempted contact with Sadie and Laney. Logic dictated that a crack at interacting with Olivia would be next.

The trouble was no one on the Colby team could guess the motive. If a simple reunion was the goal, why go about it so covertly and with the collateral damage of the past few days? From the fire at Clare's apartment building in Copperas Cove shortly after her release, to her activities related to connecting with her two younger daughters, not the least of which was kidnaping the Laney's son, a simple, peaceful reunion appeared to be the last thing on the woman's mind.

"Keep your distance until she reaches her next destination," Simon advised, hauling Russ from the worrisome musings. "Move in at that point. We need to see where she plans on taking this new step. I'll keep you informed of what we learn here."

"Will do." Russ tucked his phone back into his pocket. He took one last look at the ominous gray buildings that represented the Polunsky Prison unit where Texas's male death row inmates resided until their number was up.

He hoped Olivia understood that the man inside those walls was capable of most anything at this point. Though it appeared Weeden was working with Clare and represented the biggest threat, in reality, Weeden had served as a prison nurse and Rafe Barker had been one of his patients. The two had apparently formed a bond. It was not outside the realm of possibility that Weeden was following a plan he and Rafe had devised and Clare was nothing more than a foolish pawn. The psychiatric analysis from her prison medical records indicated the woman was not genius material but she was of average intelligence. Despite a college education, Clare Barker had been a simple woman. One whose neighbors had once thought to be kind and generous. Nothing in her psych evaluations suggested serious mental deficiencies. Withdrawn, secretive, with glimmers of paranoia. Nothing overtly violent or dramatic.

But that didn't make her innocent. It made her a total unknown variable with an agenda that somehow involved her daughters. If Rafe could be believed, she wanted all three dead before his execution just to spite him.

Bottom line, Rafe was the one with nothing to lose. In seventeen days he would be dead. Russ hoped his goal was not to take his daughters with him using Weeden or Clare or both. And the Colby Agency.

Whether it was Rafe or Clare who represented the threat, the situation was building and an explosion was inevitable.

Russ returned to the residence where he'd parked his SUV and waited, thankful that no one was home to question his hanging out in their driveway. Every advantage was crucial.

Using compact binoculars, Russ watched the prison's entry gate. He didn't have to wait long until the towering blockade moved to allow a single vehicle to exit. Tan sedan. Olivia Westfield was coming out.

"What're you going to do now, little lady?" he murmured.

Russ put the binoculars aside and started his SUV. He'd give her a few seconds' head start and then he'd follow. A tracking device tucked beneath her rear bumper prevented any real concern about losing her. The device fed to his cell, providing her every turn as long as he didn't allow too much distance between them. As a former Dallas cop, he'd done his share of surveillance duty. He had to admit, this was the first time he'd been detailed to watch a person of interest before the crime occurred. Most of his experience had been clocked tracking down criminals, not protecting the innocent before a threat was identified and confirmed.

He pulled out onto Farm to Market Road with her in the distance but still visible. Since she hadn't taken her suitcase from the motel, it was a safe bet that she would return there at some point in the evening.

The distance between their vehicles diminished and he slowed accordingly. As she continued to slow a frown furrowed an annoying path across his brow. Her driving pattern thus far had been relatively fast and furious but she apparently didn't want another speeding ticket like yesterday, because she was driving well under the speed limit.

Following her lead, Russ slowed again. What was she up to? Was she forcing him to draw closer and closer?

Then she sped up. He applied a little more pressure to the accelerator to avoid the gap between them from widening beyond a comfortable span. She surged forward, moving well past the posted speed limit. Apparently she wasn't concerned about another speeding ticket, after all.

No more speculating, she knew he was tailing her and she wanted him to know it. Fortunately the highway was deserted save for the two of them. If the lady wanted to outdrive him she was going to have to do better than this. Flooring the accelerator, he urged his SUV forward, preserving a visual on the tan sedan. His grip tightened on the steering wheel as he barreled along the road in her wake. There was no traffic for her to get lost in…no turns onto crowded streets. Just open road and the question of who would give in to the inevitable first.

Red flashed a warning. *Brake lights.* His right foot went instinctively to the brake pedal, applying considerable pressure without sending his SUV fishtailing.

She hit her brakes again, harder this time. The sedan slid to a screaming crossways stop in the road.

He rammed his brake harder, burning rubber to a stop some three or four feet from the driver's-side door. She was out of the car and stalking toward him before he'd shifted into Park.

The lady was not happy.

Russ climbed out, keeping his movements slow and steady. She wasn't armed with firepower but she carried a canister that he suspected was pepper spray or some other unpleasant deterrent he would prefer to avoid.

"Who the hell are you?" She stopped well within range of showering him with the weapon she wielded. As if she was considering acting first and getting answers later, the fingers of her right hand tightened around the black canister.

Holding up his hands in the classic gesture of surrender, Russ offered her a congenial smile. "May I remove my ID and show you?" A smart lady wouldn't simply take his word for it. And this one was definitely smart.

Her gaze narrowed with suspicion. "Answer the question. Who are you?" she repeated, not giving an inch and certainly not smiling. She intended that he do this her way. Smart and sassy.

"Russ St. James. I'm with the Colby Agency, a private investigations firm out of Houston." No reason to complicate the matter with details. Simon had given him the authorization to approach, not that he'd needed it as it turned out.

The suspicion didn't fade completely but she visibly relaxed her battle-ready stance. "I'd like to see that ID now."

Russ removed his wallet from his hip pocket and held it out to her. "Be my guest. Make a call if you need confirmation."

She inched close enough to snatch the wallet from his fingers. Her chin-length blondish-brown hair fell around her face as she opened his wallet and studied his credentials. Her hair a little darker than sister Laney's, the lush brown color was accentuated with strands of gold, giving her hair a sheen most women paid big bucks for at their favorite salons. But not the Barker girls. Sadie, the youngest, was blonder than her older sisters. They all had lavish, eye-catching manes that even cut as short as Olivia's would not be ignored. All but Sadie had deep, rich brown eyes. Whatever warped genes carried by one or both their parents, the girls had gotten all the best traits in the looks department. All three were smart and independent.

Unlike her younger sisters, Olivia was a white-collar professional, a paralegal at a prestigious San Antonio law firm, with a wardrobe that shouted success. No jeans and cowgirl boots for her. Elegant pencil skirts and spiked high heels all the way. As conservative as her taste in clothing appeared to be with those long skirts and high-collar blouses, the way the fabric molded to her figure rocked with sensuality.

"You needn't waste any more of your time." She shoved the wallet back at him. "I don't need your protection, Mr. St. James. I can take care of myself."

Russ accepted his wallet and tucked it away. Seemed Rafe Barker had told her about his request for protection from the Colby Agency; otherwise, she would certainly have had more questions. "We should talk about that before you make your decision, Ms. Westfield," he suggested.

She shook her head, folded her arms over her chest in finality. "I'm afraid that would be impossible. I'm not at liberty to discuss a case I'm investigating with you or anyone else."

His instincts perked up. "You're looking into the Princess Killer case? If so, I definitely have information you need to consider before moving forward."

Those brown eyes narrowed once more. "I'm relatively certain you don't have anything I don't already know. I appreciate the offer, but I have things to do." She squared her shoulders. "If you persist in following me, I will have no choice but to take out a restraining order. So back off."

Well, there was that. Russ had one ace up his sleeve. "I have something for you that may facilitate your investigation. If you're willing to give me a few minutes of your time, we can—"

Her eyebrows raised in blatant speculation. "I did an internet search of your agency before driving out of the prison parking lot. I wouldn't have thought an investigator from such an esteemed agency would carry around blackmail in his bag of tricks. If you had something of interest you surely would have said that up front. We're done here, Mr. St. James."

"Ms. Westfield," Russ said, reaching for patience, "I'm not the enemy. Mr. Barker sought out my agency to protect you. I would be remiss if I didn't at least attempt to satisfy his request."

"Fine. Let's not waste more time. What is it you have that you believe will interest me?"

Nothing like getting straight to the point. "I have a photo album from…" How did he explain? "From your early childhood. There are newspaper clippings related to the Barkers' arrest and trial, as well."

A car rolled up, drawing their attention to the road behind her sedan. Russ tensed. Gray in color. Four doors. Two occupants in the front seat. One male, one female. The driver's-side window powered down. Russ's right hand went instinctively to the small of his back where his weapon rested. Clare and her accomplice, Weeden, could be watching Olivia the same as he was.

The driver, the male, poked his head out. *Not Weeden.* "You folks need any assistance?"

"We're fine. Thank you." Olivia moved toward her sedan. "I must have hit a slick spot in the road."

The man nodded, powered his window back up and drove around, using the shoulder of the road to avoid her front bumper.

Olivia glanced back at Russ. "Follow me."

Before he could ask where to she climbed back into her car and started the engine. Russ did the same. Just his luck. Ms. Westfield was going to make his job even more difficult than he'd anticipated. All he had to do was stay one step ahead of her excuses for not needing him.

Five seconds later they were exceeding the speed limit and heading to her destination of choice.

Chapter Three

Victoria Colby-Camp considered the curtains in her new living room. The small beach cottage half an hour from Houston had been a whirlwind weekend purchase. On Saturday, she'd left Lucas resting in the Beaumont hospital and viewed the cottage her Realtor had called about. She and Lucas had leased a condo several months ago and had been happy there while they searched for a permanent home in the Houston area.

The timing of the call from her Realtor had been perfect. Since Christmas last year she and Lucas had been waffling about the decision to retire completely. This investigation had made up Victoria's mind for her. Lucas had almost lost his life just three days ago. She would not allow that to happen again. It was time they moved on and focused forward.

The main Colby Agency offices in Chicago were in good hands with her son Jim and Ian Michaels, a long time second in command for Victoria. Simon Ruhl, another of her seconds in command, had relocated his wife and children to Houston and had the Texas office well underway. It was no longer necessary for her or for Lucas to be involved with the daily operations. They had often talked about taking a winter home. Actually, the plan was to spend as much time at one as

the other, depending on the weather and circumstances with
the grandchildren.

Victoria smiled as she thought of her grandchildren spending weeks on end with her and Lucas here on the beach.
This choice was the perfect balance. Once she had seen this
lovely cottage, she had returned to the hospital in Beaumont
with pictures for Lucas. He had agreed that it was the perfect second home. The transaction had been a simple matter at that point.

Since the cottage was furnished there was no reason not to
move in immediately. She'd brought Lucas here this morning
upon his release from the hospital. Victoria wandered over to
the French doors that overlooked the terrace. She smiled as
she watched her husband flip through the morning paper. He
looked right at home lounging in that comfortable chaise. The
bandage on his forehead would be gone soon. He would be
wearing the walking cast for several more weeks. The sling
for his arm wouldn't be necessary for quite so long. Thankfully his shoulder would heal without surgery. She felt certain
that good fortune was wholly related to how very physically
fit he remained when most men his age fell victim to sed-
entary work and activities. Not Lucas. He was strong and
healthy. Despite the loss of his left leg during that awful war
so many years ago, he had never allowed the awkwardness of
a prosthesis to keep him from a fitness regimen. She wanted
him to stay that way so they could enjoy their golden years together and with their growing family. Now that Slade, Lucas's
son, and Maggie were married and had their precious baby
girl, they would be visiting, as well. Slade would enjoy the
quiet solitude here. His life had been challenging until now.

Beyond the patio and a small landscaped patch of lawn,
the dazzling water lapped at the sandy shore only yards from
their back door. Yes, she decided, they would be happy here.
Victoria turned around in the spacious room. She adored the

open floor plan. There was some redecorating to do. The furnishings weren't precisely suited to her and Lucas's taste, but that would be easily remedied in time. Those decisions could wait until they could shop together.

The sound of her cell chiming disrupted her leisurely daydreaming. Her heart stumbled into an awkward gallop. Though she knew Joel Hayden was well on his way to a complete recovery and safe with Laney Seagers and her son, Buddy, worry tugged at her. Sadie Gilmore and Lyle McCaleb were safe and making wedding plans. But Olivia Westfield remained in a place that was far too precarious. Simon had relayed the news to Victoria that Olivia had garnered a meeting with Rafe Barker, her biological father. This call might be regarding that meeting, which could prove detrimental to the agency's attempts to keep all three of the Barker girls safe. Olivia would be the most challenging. Her background in the legal field indicated she never settled for the status quo.

Knowing she could not ignore the call, Victoria moved across the room and picked up her cell. Simon's name appeared on the screen with the next chime.

"Good afternoon, Simon." She held her breath and hoped the rest of the afternoon wasn't about to be launched into chaos.

"How is Lucas handling a quiet day at home?" Simon inquired.

Disturbing news. Whenever Simon avoided a simple greeting and moved directly into neutral territory, he was preparing to deliver a less-than-pleasant update.

"He's skimming through the paper, having a drink fitting a leisurely afternoon on the beach. I should snap a photo and send it to you. I'm certain you would be amused. Do you have news about Olivia?" Victoria placed a hand on the island counter and held her breath.

"Warden Prentice indicated that nothing Barker said to

Olivia was new. He urged her to find her sisters and informed her that he had hired the agency to provide protection."

Victoria tried unsuccessfully to restrain the fury that sparked to life inside her. Rafe knew far more than he was sharing and his insistence on keeping aspects of the past to himself greatly hindered the agency's efforts. He was playing a game, she was convinced.

"What was Olivia's reaction?" Victoria could only imagine the emotional state the young woman was in since learning the news that her parents were not her birth parents and, even worse, that her biological parents were convicted murderers. She could not be in a rational place, making her far more susceptible to the danger circling the three Barker girls.

"St. James hasn't been able to gauge her reaction as of yet. Olivia confronted him shortly after leaving the prison and as we speak they're having a sit-down in a café in Livingston."

"Let me know as soon as you have an update from Russ." Victoria would feel much better when Olivia was reconciled to having round-the-clock protection.

"There's another development, Victoria. If I didn't know how much you want this case solved in a timely manner—" he sighed "—I wouldn't even pass this information on to you. With Lucas's injuries, I know your attention is needed there. But I am all too aware of your feelings on this case."

The hair on the back of her neck stood on end. This was the part she had sensed was coming. "I'm listening."

"Barker wants another meeting with you. Tomorrow morning, nine o'clock. He says he has additional information he is now prepared to share but he will only share it with you. I pushed the issue of taking the meeting personally but he refused."

Equal measures anticipation and anger fired along her nerves. "If this information is so compelling, why can't he share it now? Today? I can be in Livingston in a couple of hours." The bastard liked playing games with her. With all of them. Whether he was innocent of the crimes with which he was charged or not, he was a twisted soul.

"He refused to negotiate his terms. Nine tomorrow morning, you and you alone. What should I tell the warden?"

Victoria wished she could tell Barker to go to hell. She trusted nothing he said. But her hands were tied. No risk could be taken until they ascertained the true source of the danger to these women. "Tell him I'll be there."

"I'll accompany you," Simon offered.

"No. I can do this alone. Your efforts are needed elsewhere."

"Very well. I'll let Warden Prentice know to expect you."

Victoria ended the call and set her phone aside. She moved back to the French doors and watched her husband fold the paper and set it aside. Part of her wanted to simply stay right here and bar the world from her door. But that was impossible. Lucas would never run away from a challenge any more than she would. Her emotions made her vulnerable just now.

More than twenty-five years ago her son had been taken from her by one of the most evil men who had ever lived. He had tortured and brainwashed Jim for nearly two decades. If Rafe was lying, he had taken Clare's children from her and ensured she was charged for his heinous crimes right along with him. Victoria knew how that kind of loss and betrayal felt.

Yet Clare's actions since her release went against the idea that she was innocent and deserving of a reunion with her daughters. Victoria needed to ferret out the truth here. To reunite this family if possible.

She could not walk away until that was done.

Eventually the case would be solved one way or the other and her emotions would settle down. She would feel herself again. She and Lucas were safe and the Colby team investigating this case would be triumphant. Until then, their choices were sorely limited. She had to do her part.

Lucas reached for his cell lying on the table where his now-empty glass sat. She didn't have to ask to know the caller would be Simon making sure Lucas was aware of Victoria's appointment tomorrow morning.

The men in her life worked overtime to protect her. Rafe couldn't touch her. He could only play with her emotions. Clare and her partner, however, were a different story. Victoria wondered if Clare Barker was the entity of evil that Rafe insisted she was. Or was she a battered and neglected wife who had been used as a scapegoat by the most horrific of evils?

Victoria would know soon. Very soon.

Chapter Four

Olivia stared at the photos of her and her sisters as small children. She recognized the images of herself. Her adoptive parents had many photos taken during these same time frames, only Olivia was alone in those. She realized now, looking at this album, that none of the photos of her as a baby or small child back home had included her parents. Of course not. She had only come into their lives at age five.

But why were most memories before that time so completely lost to her? The average person remembered some part of their pre-school days. Olivia recalled very little. She had learned two weeks ago that her adoptive parents had worked hard to instill in her false memories that included them. She supposed that was why those years were so muddled. They had tried very hard to mesh her fully into their lives. To wipe away the ugliness of her early years.

The most disturbing part of this collection in front of her was the pictures from her life after the age of five. Several from each year. Every major event in her life was captured. Senior prom, high school graduation, college…everything.

"How is this possible?" Her head moved side to side as she stared at the captured moments to which whoever created this album should not have had access. "Who did this?" Her gaze connected with St. James's.

"You two ready to order yet?" The waitress who'd stopped at their booth three times already paused once more.

Olivia blinked. She couldn't think of food right now. This was...unsettling. Just when she thought the bizarre puzzle couldn't get any more twisted, something new and totally warped got thrown at her. Like this photo album of her life.

As the waitress hovered, St. James looked to Olivia. "Something to drink at least?"

The impatience emanating from the waitress was hard to ignore. "Water." Olivia exhaled a shaky breath. None of this made sense. This part of her past was like watching some sort of surreal reality series.

"Two waters." St. James offered the harried lady a smile that was oddly distracting.

Olivia blinked again, tried to find her mental bearings. Had her parents provided snapshots from her life as part of the original adoption agreement? A question she intended to add to her "need to know" list when she was speaking to them again. Deep down she felt guilty for being on the outs with the people who had raised and cared for her as their own. They had been good parents. Still were. She loved them and understood without reservation that they loved her.

"We aren't certain about that part," St. James said in answer to her question about how the more recent parts of the photo album came to be. "But we do know that at the time of the adoption each family was provided with photos of the early years to allay questions later."

Questions from her...and her sisters. Olivia shook her head again. "Why didn't they tell me?" She was an only child—at least she'd thought she was. She and her parents had always been so close. How could they have kept this from her as if the information was irrelevant?

"That was a condition of the adoption. The secret was to be kept at all costs by all parties involved. Your parents were merely fulfilling their obligation to the legal contract they signed twenty-two years ago."

He made it sound so rational, so reasonable. As a paralegal, Olivia knew all about contracts. But this was morally wrong on so many levels. So, so many levels.

"Is your agency investigating Rafe Barker's claims of innocence?" Rafe's roundabout way of suggesting he was innocent had startled her. It shouldn't have. Most prison inmates would claim innocence, whatever their crimes. The fact that she was alive, as were her two sisters, lent credence to his claim to a degree that could not be ignored.

St. James considered her question for a moment. His pause made her want to squirm. Was there more she didn't know? She held his gaze, refusing to back off. Not an easy task. The man had amazing blue eyes, penetrating, hypnotic. He actually looked nothing like her idea of a private investigator. Thick blondish-brown hair that hugged the collar of his shirt. He dressed like the quintessential cowboy: well-fitted jeans, button-down cotton shirt, boots and hat. As handsome as he was, nothing about his appearance suggested skill as an investigator. He looked more like a celebrity cowboy— too well dressed and handsome to be a slave to a ranch or anything else. Didn't help that his voice was whiskey smooth and dark water deep.

Way off subject, Liv. Focus.

"We are looking into his claims," he finally said as if he'd waited for her to complete her mental inventory of his physical assets before interrupting.

Was that it? "Have you reached any conclusions?" Did she need to draw him a map to what she wanted? Why was it that everyone around her at the moment seemed determined to protect her by holding back? She was a big girl and the sooner he understood that the better. This was a pivotal moment in her life. There was so much she needed to know. And no one was cooperating.

"Mr. Barker claims he had nothing to do with any of the murders," St. James went on. "I don't have to spell out the ramifications of what that could mean."

That part she knew. Was everyone two decades behind the curve on this case? "Does your agency have reason to believe his claims have any merit? Is that why you took his case?"

Another of those pauses. "We didn't exactly take his case. His suggestion that you and your sisters are in danger prompted the head of the Colby Agency to take action to ensure your safety. That is our primary objective."

Olivia felt taken aback. "Does your agency make it a habit of taking up causes that don't feed the bottom line?" She had thought that perhaps notoriety was the motive. If the Colby Agency proved Rafe Barker's innocence in the eleventh hour, priceless publicity would be the payoff. Of course, there would be some unpleasant aspects to such a move but if true justice prevailed, the acclaim would be incredible.

The change in his eyes was unmistakable. Her suggestion that the agency might have a motive beyond doing the right thing didn't sit so well. Maybe she had grown accustomed enough to the dog-eat-dog world of the criminal justice system that her skin was thicker than most. Clearly his was not.

"We made a decision based on protecting lives," he informed her with a tone that broadcast loudly that her assumption had been correct. He was offended. "Rafe Barker made a decision about his future, but Clare is another story. If she's guilty then she represents a threat to you, your sisters and society."

"You have proof that she's committed any crimes?" As best Olivia could determine, there was every reason to believe the man with whom Clare was traveling was the guilty party in the criminal events since her release.

St. James shook his head. "None specifically. In fact, when Laney Seagers got her son back during the showdown at the old Barker home place in Granger, she felt certain that Clare helped the boy find his way back to her through the woods. Weeden appeared to be the one determined to inflict harm on anyone who got in his way of escaping."

Olivia frowned as she stared at the photos of Clare, her biological mother, posing with her three little girls. "But she's the one who only recently walked out of a maximum security prison. Weeden's history as a nurse would seem to indicate he's the selfless one." The scenario didn't fit...unless there were hidden secrets related to Tony Weeden she didn't know about. About any of the people involved, for that matter.

No question there. With the exception of fourteen days less leave time in her vacation account, she had nothing to show for two weeks' work on this case. Apparently neither did the Colby Agency.

"Beyond being a nurse and having had access to Rafe, who is this Tony Weeden?"

"We're still working on confirming certain details of his background," St. James said, his tone careful, his words well chosen. "We believe there's a connection between him and Clare beyond the obvious, but that scenario hasn't been confirmed."

In other words, she wasn't getting an answer. Until the news hit this weekend, Olivia had never heard the guy's name. According to St. James, Weeden was the one to smuggle the initial letter from Rafe to the Colby Agency. That was basically all she knew.

The waitress arrived with two glasses of ice water. St. James gifted her with another of those dazzling smiles and ordered a couple of burgers. Olivia wasn't sure she could eat but it was well past lunchtime and she recognized she needed to try. The mass of emotions and confusion just kept twisting tighter and tighter in her belly.

She didn't know how to feel about the Barkers. Her legal training warned that where there was this much smoke there was fire. Olivia had no reason to trust anything Rafe said... no reason to believe Clare was innocent based on her recent release or her actions since. The police had been no real help. The case was closed and they wanted to keep it that way. Unless Olivia could offer information on the missing bodies, they didn't want to hear what she had to say. To them, her digging screamed of reopening the case and trying to clear Rafe Barker of multiple homicides, and no one wanted any part of it. The community of Granger was already unsettled over Clare's release. Any suggestion of Rafe Barker's innocence was too much to tolerate.

Olivia had had no reason to consider trying to prove his innocence...at least not until now. He claimed he hadn't killed anyone and that his only responsibility was his ignorance of Clare's heinous deeds. Olivia was alive, her sisters were alive...did that mean he was telling the truth? Clare hadn't contacted anyone about protecting her daughters. She had taken several steps indicative of past or present criminal activity. Conversely, according to St. James, she had helped Laney Seagers find her son. Her activities since her release continued to send mixed messages as to her intent, which might make sense if the steps had been orchestrated by Weeden. Did that alone suggest she was innocent?

Not in a court of law...but then the Texas Supreme Court had made the decision that she was innocent based on the fact that no evidence had actually pointed to her. Twenty-two years ago the need to ensure the culprits responsible for such horrific murders were identified and punished had hastened the police's efforts and guaranteed the case had been pushed through trial despite the lack of tangible evidence against her. Charge and convict them both and the real killer got his or her just desserts. Didn't matter if the other was innocent. Too many innocent young lives had been taken for anyone to feel compelled to extend mercy. Clare had spent her entire sentence seeking out lawyers to take her case to one appeals court or the other. After the last appeal was lost, it had taken six years for Clare to find a legal team with the ability to get the job done. The woman hadn't given up.

Her tenaciousness reminded Olivia far too much of herself.

"Surely you can see our dilemma," St. James proposed. "No one wants an innocent man to be executed. Yet, we have no evidence that he is innocent. What we do know without doubt is that you and your sisters are at risk. As I said, our primary objective is to ensure your safety."

The circumstances cleared completely for her then. Raymond Rafe Barker had seventeen days to live and no one—*no one*—was focused on determining if he was guilty as convicted. There was only one thing Olivia could do.

The right thing.

"Has your agency explored the possibility of petitioning for a stay of execution until these questions can be answered?" It wasn't until just this moment that she grasped the concept that time was really slipping away. That he was her biological father was irrelevant in all this. Truth and justice were the only pertinent elements and no one appeared to be focused on those points. Not even the prestigious Colby Agency.

"The state district attorney is not prepared to take that step at this time. If we can bring him evidence beyond Barker's word he will entertain the possibility then and only then."

Indignation ripped through the more fragile emotions she'd been experiencing for days. "You have no evidence that he's innocent, that's true, but you do have new compelling evidence that the investigation twenty-two years ago was mishandled to some degree. That alone would likely persuade the governor to stay his execution pending further investigation."

St. James knew exactly what she was talking about. His expression closed her out as tightly as an isolated witness. "Mr. Barker specifically asked that your existence not be made public knowledge for your own safety."

Did he understand what he was saying? "Do you know the odds of getting a last-minute stay? These things take time and that's something we have very little of." Dammit. Did no one care if he was innocent or not?

"Typically we attempt to work within the client's wishes."

"Client? So you admit that he is a client?" Olivia reined in the cross-examination instincts. She held up her hands and waved them side-to-side as if she could erase the question. "Whatever your agency considers him, I would think that at the very least you have an obligation to bring this new evidence to the D.A.'s attention immediately."

His expression still closed, St. James eyed her cautiously. "We've already done that and he has chosen to wait it out and see what we find. Until we have something compelling he's not budging on his position."

"Unbelievable."

The burgers were delivered then but there was no way Olivia could eat. She clamped her mouth shut until the waitress had gotten another smile from St. James and scurried away.

Olivia pressed the issue. "He's aware that three of the murders charged against Barker were bogus and he wants to wait this out?" Incredible. It was men like that who had prompted her to go to law school to make a difference.

And that went well, didn't it, Liv?

"We have a whole team working on this, Ms. Westfield. We will find the truth."

"You are investigating his claims, then?" Why dance

around the admission. A whole team was working on the case and this guy wasn't owning up to what that meant?

"There was never a choice in the matter."

Ah, a man with an honorable spirit. He was either a former cop or soldier. Definitely not from her side of the law. "In my experience, Mr. St. James, good intentions are not always enough. Steps have to be taken now." Two calls were all she needed to make. She'd laid the preliminary groundwork already, even before she had any idea how this would shake down. Two simple phone calls would set the necessary actions in motion.

"If you submit the petition," St. James reminded her unnecessarily, "it becomes a matter of public record. How long do you think it will be before the press splashes your name as well as your sisters' across every headline in the state if not the country?"

Olivia ignored a prick of guilt. "Clare and Weeden have already made the news. It's only a matter of time before some ambitious reporter follows Clare's trail to us—if finding her daughters is her goal. This secret won't keep, Mr. St. James."

"I can see that you're concerned as to whether or not we can find the truth in time, which is completely understandable," he offered. "If you're open to suggestions, we could work together toward that end."

A frown tugged at her brow. What was he proposing? Wait, she got it. "Forming an alliance would provide you with the opportunity to keep an eye on me, is that it?"

He inclined his head and gave her one of those smiles he'd been flashing for the waitress. "That would square away both our quandaries as we move forward toward the same goal."

For the first time in a really long time, some random female chromosome that had gone into hibernation too long ago to remember abruptly hummed to life. That he had managed to resurrect such long-buried sensations startled her.

"You won't get in my way?" She knew what she had to do and she needed to be sure this man and his celebrated agency wouldn't try to stop her when they learned her intentions.

She was about to stir up a hornet's nest and no one, not even the Colby Agency, was going to like her methods. But Olivia was no fool. She could use all the help she could get. The Colby Agency likely had valuable connections that could serve her purposes. And she could use a team on her side.

"I will only get in your way if it's necessary to save your life. I presume you can understand that condition."

Another of those unexpected shimmers of attraction sizzled through her. "You've been watching me twenty-four/seven?"

"I have."

She'd suspected someone was following her. But day and night? "Is that the schedule you plan to keep?"

"Until Weeden is contained and we understand Clare Barker's intentions, that's the plan."

"You'll share your agency's findings?" That was key if he expected her cooperation.

"As long as you share yours." He draped a paper napkin across his lap, grabbed his burger with both hands and bit off a chunk of beef embellished with bun and fixings.

Olivia watched as he licked his lips and savored the explosion on his taste buds. Her stomach reminded her that she hadn't eaten since grabbing a two-day-old doughnut in the shabby motel lobby that morning. She chewed her lower lip and tried to recall the last time she'd enjoyed watching a man eat. Never came to mind.

He downed half the glass of water, and this, too, mesmerized her. The way the muscles of his throat worked and his fingers curled around the glass as it settled on the table once more. He licked his lips and she suffered a little hitch in her respiration. *Back up, girl. Back way, way up.*

"We have a deal, then?" he asked.

"Absolutely." She moistened her lips and braced to watch him dig into the burger once more.

He hesitated, the sandwich halfway to his mouth. "You skipped lunch. You should eat."

Olivia gave herself a mental shake. He would know what she'd eaten and where. "Sure. Right." She grabbed her burger and managed a nibble. Gave her something to do besides stare at him.

He flagged the waitress down and ordered a couple of colas. Olivia told herself not to stare at his mouth as his lips spread into another wide smile but the feat was impossible. That smile was fascinating. She worked with men in suits every day. Handsome, sophisticated men. Dressed in elegant attire. Men who lived in mansions and drove foreign sports cars that cost five times her annual salary. Not once had a single one ever muddled her ability to concentrate this way. She held her own with their impressive law degrees and their enormous egos. The few with the courage to make a pass or toss out a pickup line never made the same mistake twice.

This guy swaggers up to her in his tight jeans and well-worn boots and she turns to jelly? Had to be the emotional turmoil of the past two weeks. She wasn't herself. Ha! Of course she wasn't. She had just learned her entire history was made-up. She wasn't the daughter of Vincent and Nancy Westfield. She was the spawn of convicted serial murderers. Her biological father skated all around the idea that he was innocent while her mother flitted around setting fires and fleeing crime scenes. Evidently, any or all of those tainted genes she'd inherited were playing havoc with her logic and training.

The colas he had ordered arrived and he relished a long drink that once again fascinated her. "You have a plan of action in mind?" he asked.

Olivia swallowed at the lump the bite of burger had become, washed it down with water and cleared her throat. "The attorney I work with will file a petition for a stay of execution based on this new evidence." As she spoke she sent a text telling Nelson, her boss, to move ahead, focusing on the steps rather than the face of the man seated across from her. His eyes were a trap and she needed to avoid looking directly into those analyzing pools of blue. "Meanwhile, I'll start a press initiative in hopes of drawing out anyone who might know details not discovered twenty-two years ago."

"You hope to find information the police didn't find back then? It's been a long time, ma'am. People forget. You might come up empty-handed."

People did forget many things but few failed to recall murder. Especially in a small town like Granger. "Someone knows something. It's impossible that not one person in that small, close-knit community ever noticed anything peculiar about the two serial murderers living in their midst."

"Why wouldn't they have come forward before? It's doubtful that anyone wanted to see a murderer go free. Or an innocent man falsely accused. It goes against human nature."

"Maybe they were afraid or didn't realize the relevance of what they knew." She shrugged. "Or maybe they did come forward but the information was ignored or suppressed. Set aside for the greater good." Eight bodies had been exhumed from the Barker property. The police believed they had their killers. Why look anywhere else? The whole community if not the state had been screaming for justice.

"What if you don't find what you're looking for? Can you come to terms with that?" He pushed his plate aside, braced his forearms on the table and leaned toward her. "If some part of you is hoping this will have a happy ending—that maybe Rafe or Clare or both were falsely accused—you may be in for a major letdown, Ms. Westfield."

"Either way," she argued, "then I'll know, won't I?"

Chapter Five

5:30 p.m.

Clare peeled away the tape that held the bandage on her son's arm. He'd instructed her on how to remove the bullet and suture the wound at their last stop. Her hands had been a little shaky but she'd gotten the job done.

"Have I told you how proud I am of you, son?" She smiled down at him. He was perched on the edge of the bed and had been very patient with her slow, arthritic hands.

He glanced at her and made a sound that was mostly a grunt. She imagined that praise was not something he'd received a lot of in his life. That, too, was her fault. She had made many mistakes in her time on this earth. Her decision to entrust to her evil sister the child born out of wedlock and as a result of a vicious rape was the first mistake. Janet had been born evil but like the devil himself she had returned to Clare's life after the death of their parents and presented herself as an angel of light. She wanted to help…to be friends.

How could Clare have been such a fool? And why hadn't that mistake made her smarter?

"You survived that evil witch and went on to become a nurse. That required hard work and much determination. That *is* an outstanding accomplishment." Particularly with one arm. That part she kept to herself.

Clare applied the antibiotic cream and clean bandages. There were things she needed to ask her son. Some more pressing than others. "Tony, did that awful man who took Lisa's little boy force you into killing him?" Her heart started to pound even as the words echoed in the cheap motel room. Their names and photos were all over the news. They were wanted as persons of interest in the murder of that terrible man who had taken little Buddy. This dump was the best they could hope for by way of a hiding place and still they would need to move soon.

"He was dead when I found him," Tony said, his words low, quiet, as always.

Clare's spirit lifted. "But the killer didn't harm the little boy. That's a blessing." Deep down that notion felt wrong to her. But she wanted to believe him.

"I think it was a drug deal gone bad. The boy was hunkered down in the backseat. The shooter might not have seen him. Probably saved his life."

That was a reasonable explanation. "I'm glad you were able to rescue him before anyone else got to him."

Silence settled around them as she taped the bandage into place. They were tired from running. Hungry. Stopping for food had been too risky. They'd had to hide the car Tony had bought in Brenham. They would retrieve it when it was time to move again.

"I checked with the hospital in Beaumont. Both that Mr. Camp and Mr. Hayden were released. I imagine that means they'll both recover from their injuries."

Her son grunted again. He hadn't meant to hurt either one of them. Over and over as she drove away from Granger and he huddled in the passenger seat he had assured her that he'd only been trying to protect her. She had been angry at what she had seen. Angry and fearful. She didn't want him to be like Janet…like Rafe.

His sincere insistence had calmed her. Sometimes extreme measures were necessary, she supposed. She had decided not to hold it against him. She was his mother; of course he would try and protect her the only way he had at his disposal.

"Have I told you how sorry I am that this happened?" She trailed her fingers along his right shoulder to the stub that was all that remained of his right arm. It pained her to think how he must have suffered losing a limb.

He turned to her, the gray eyes of his no-good father staring directly into hers. Thank God that cunning bastard had gone to hell just a few years after what he had done to Clare. A heart attack had been too good for him, but at least it had taken his rotten life and perhaps saved another young girl from such a travesty.

"I lied to you before," Tony admitted.

Clare had suspected as much. "You weren't injured in an accident when Janet was chopping wood?"

He shook his head. "I don't think you want to know the truth. It would be painful for you."

Clare blinked back the tears that burned her eyes. "Yes, I do." Her response was scarcely a whisper. Fear tingled up her spine. *Dear God, please don't let it be too horrible.*

"Janet sold me to the Weedens. They were old and didn't have any children of their own. They needed someone to do the work around their place and she needed money. Like always. Besides, she had her eye on an old man who had the money to give her the life she wanted. She didn't want me in the way."

Clare told herself to breathe but she couldn't draw the air into her lungs. She had learned the Weedens, both dead now, had been bad people. No friends. No connections in the community where they lived. Just plain old mean. Janet had relished in telling her that all those years ago...but Clare hadn't gotten the chance to do anything about it.

"When I was eighteen I tried to run away. They beat me. They always beat me and I never fought back. Not until that last time. I guess they knew they wouldn't be able to count on me after that. So they decided that if I wasn't going to be their workhorse I wouldn't be anyone else's, either."

"They did this to you?" Disbelief tinged her words.

"That day at lunch the old woman put something in my food. A sedative of some sort. It knocked me out." He stretched his back. "When I woke up they had me tied down and the old bastard had chopped off my arm with an ax."

The horror she had feared bloomed into a pain that cracked open her chest and ripped at her heart. "How did you survive?"

"I guess the old woman grew a conscience or worried they'd go to jail if I died. She tied a tourniquet around what was left of my arm and told me I'd better run. I got as far as town before I ended up in the hospital. Once I was recovered enough, I left the hospital and made a new life." He shrugged his uninjured shoulder. "End of story."

The weight of the decisions she had made back in college settled more heavily onto her shoulders. "I'm so sorry. This should never have happened to you."

He looked away. "You were raped. That shouldn't have happened to you. You did what you thought was right at the time. Janet took advantage of you. She took advantage of all of us."

Clare had done what she thought was right but she had been young and emotionally damaged. Otherwise she might not have made two mistakes so close together. "You did well for yourself in spite of my failure on your behalf." The terrible tragedy he had suffered was as much Janet's fault as hers. That brought Clare to yet another question she needed to ask. "How did you discover the truth about who you were? Did Janet seek you out?"

He shook his head. "It was easy enough."

When Janet had come back into Clare's life twenty-three years ago, Clare had asked her about her son and Janet had insisted he'd been adopted by a fine family who adored him. Lies, all of it. She had ruined Tony and then she'd shown up again to ruin Clare's husband and daughters. Janet'd had no one, evidently whatever man she'd gotten her claws into had either died or dumped her. Never one to go for long without someone to take advantage of, she had taken everything from Clare. Just before the arrests Janet disappeared but not before telling Clare that one day she would know how much her son had suffered with that *fine* family. Clare had had two decades to think about that…to think about all of it and to worry if her daughters were dead or alive.

Her hands shook with the fury that roared through her. Clare was glad her sister was dead. She hoped Janet Tolliver was burning in hell right this minute.

Clare cleaned up the mess she had made and turned to her son. "I'm going out to get us some food."

He tensed visibly. "That's not a good idea."

"It's safer for me than for you," she insisted. With his missing arm, he would be noticed by anyone he passed. She still had a chance of blending in, of being overlooked.

"I don't like it." He stood. "We'll go together."

Clare had to stand her ground here. Things had gotten out of control and she needed to try and regain some kind of order. Her quest was far too important to make any more mistakes, especially any involving the law.

She could not fail.

"Stay here, Tony," she said more firmly. "I will bring back supplies. Stay in the room."

He stood there for a moment that felt like an hour. "You won't leave me this time?"

Lord have mercy. She put her arms around him and held

him tight. The tears streamed from her eyes and she had no hope of stopping them. "I am so sorry I left you before. I swear I will never leave you again."

His arm settled around her in a loose hug. "All right, then. I'll be waiting."

Clare drew back and swiped her eyes. "Never doubt me again, son." She gave him her best smile. "I won't let you down."

Chapter Six

In the Livingston café, Russ listened closely as Olivia made an appointment for eight this evening with a *Houston News* reporter. This television reporter, Keisha Landers, had earned first choice at an exclusive by virtue of being the daughter of the only reporter who had dogged every step the cops made during the Princess Killer investigation more than twenty years ago. Keisha's father, now deceased, had left all his notes with his daughter. Keisha had promised to share those with Olivia if she got an exclusive.

As relieved as Russ felt that Olivia had agreed to cooperate with his protection efforts, breaking the news about the Barker children being alive and well would likely turn this case into a circus. He'd warned her about that, but she insisted her way was the only way to prompt reactions in a timely manner.

He hoped she understood that the reactions she elicited might not be what she'd bargained for. Since there was no changing the lady's mind he had no alternative but to go with the flow. Making sure she stayed safe was his job.

They would both know soon enough. He had sent Simon a text warning him that the storm was about to hit. By noon tomorrow the petition for a stay of execution would be national news. The first interview of one of the Barker daughters, long thought to be dead and buried, would be hot on the same track.

"I'm meeting Keisha Landers and her cameraman at eight," Olivia informed him when she closed her phone. "I won't mention your agency. If she has questions about your presence, you're my personal security."

"This is your show." Whatever she thought, this was never going to go as smoothly as she hoped. The Colby Agency had already approached Landers about her father's notes. Anyone involved or closely associated with the original investigation had been contacted. Landers had suggested she intended to write a book about her father's documented journey following the case and she was not interested in sharing information. Russ couldn't imagine that her game plan had changed that much. The opportunity to capitalize was too appealing.

Olivia stood and picked up her bag. "I'd like to contact Sadie and Laney to see if they're interested in being a part of this. I assume you can assist me with that."

Russ slid from the booth and grabbed his hat before tossing a couple of bills on the table. "I'm waiting for word back from my superior. He notified the investigators providing protection to your sisters. I'll have a decision for you soon."

Olivia stared at him for a moment, those deep brown eyes searching his. "You don't trust me at all, do you?"

He was surprised to see regret in her eyes. They'd come a long way over burgers and colas. Her eyes gave him a peek beyond the tough-lady exterior she wore so proudly. "I want to trust you," he confessed. "I know your intentions are good. That said, I will admit that your take-the-bull-by-the-horns attitude is risky from my perspective."

"It's the only way."

Apparently done with talking, she did a one-eighty and headed for the exit. Russ followed. He'd given Simon a heads-up; there was little else he could do to waylay this collision course. Trying to keep the fallout minimal was the best he could hope for.

The bell over the café door jingled as he opened it for her to exit. The parking lot had been jam-packed when they arrived, forcing them to park on opposite sides. The trip to Houston would take no more than ninety minutes. Sufficient time for Simon to brace Sadie and Laney for the news that their older sister was going public.

"We could always leave your sedan at the motel," Russ suggested. "I'm happy to assume the role of chauffeur, as well." He sweetened the offer with a smile. Not that he was afraid of her giving him the slip, but it would allow him to stay abreast of any phone conversations. He hadn't had the opportunity to leave a listening device inside her sedan. Not to mention that sharing close confines with her wouldn't be a hardship. It would give him a chance to get a better handle on the lady. He'd been watching her for days on end. There was a lot he already liked about her.

She shrugged. "Works for me. That'll give me a chance to go over my own notes before the meeting."

Surprised that arm-twisting or further negotiations hadn't been necessary, he settled his Stetson in place and gave her a nod. "I'll follow you to the motel."

"Once we're on the road to Houston you can explain these unconfirmed details about Tony Weeden" She fished the keys from her bag. "I don't want to be hit with any surprises from Landers. Especially if it's information you already know."

Sensitive territory for sure. The way she looked at him warned she suspected he knew a lot more than he was sharing. "As long as you bear in mind that what we have so far is to a large degree speculation and that it's all off the record."

"I know. I know. I won't say a word to Landers." She

turned in the direction of her sedan. "You can trust me on that."

An explosion thundered in the air, and the ground shook with the blast that sent Olivia hurtling backward into Russ. His arms went around her as they were thrown to the ground. He rolled on top of her and shielded her body as debris showered onto the ground.

"You okay?" he demanded. Her face was pale. Her lips were moving, but he couldn't hear a damned thing she said. Instead of trying to make out her words he checked her body. No blood. No obvious injury.

He scrambled to his feet and checked the parking lot. Remnants of her tan sedan were scattered. The vehicles that had been parked on either side of it were damaged; one lay on its side. Thank God the lot had been empty of people save for the two of them.

The sound of screams and shouting echoed around him as patrons flooded out of the diner. He reached down and pulled Olivia to her feet. She stared at the mangled parts that used to be her sedan and then at him. For the first time since they'd officially met she was speechless.

"You two okay?" asked a tall, thin man wearing a white shirt sporting a name tag that identified him as Larry. He surveyed the parking lot and shook his head. "Oh, my God."

His ears were still ringing but at least Russ could distinguish the words being spoken now. He looked to Olivia and she gave a vague nod. Russ shifted his attention back to the man who had asked. "We're okay. Just a little shook up."

"I'm the manager," Larry explained. "I've got nine-one-one on the line and they're asking if we need medical assistance."

Russ turned back to Olivia. "You sure you're okay?"

She dusted off her skirt, her hands shaking. "The only

thing I need is a new car." She stared at what used to be her car, her expression a little shocky.

"We're good," Russ assured the manager.

From in front of the café door, a kid broke loose from his mother's tight grip and made a dash for Russ's Stetson. While the mother chased after her son, the manager inquired, "That your car?"

"Mine," Olivia answered. Using both hands, she reached up and tucked the hair behind her ears. She was steadier now but her face remained pale. She grabbed her purse and clutched it close as if she feared it, too, might be taken from her.

Russ surveyed the crowd around the diner entrance. "Might be a good idea to keep these folks inside," Russ suggested, "until the police determine there's no other danger." The property was bordered by businesses on either side but there didn't appear to be any damage beyond Olivia's car and the others parked nearest it. Like the diner's patrons, people had poured out of the other stores.

Larry's eyes widened as he realized the implications of Russ's words. "Come on, folks. Let's get back inside." After the promise of free dinner coupons for their next visit, the patrons filed back inside.

"Here's your hat, mister." The kid who'd escaped his mother beamed up at Russ as he held out the Stetson.

"Thanks." Russ claimed his hat and gave the kid a nod of approval before his frazzled mother dragged him back inside.

Olivia started toward where her car had been parked. He snagged her by the arm. "Whoa, there. You should wait inside until the police check things out."

The pale face was gone now, replaced by the flush of anger. "Someone blew up my car!"

Sirens wailed in the distance, the sound a welcome respite. He didn't want her attempting to rummage through the remains of her car. "That's a fact, but until the police do their thing, there's nothing we can do to figure out who or why. It'd be best if you wait inside."

Her brow furrowed into a frown. "I'm not going anywhere. If you can wait out here, so can I."

Since one of them had to speak to the police, he opted not to argue with her. "Just let me do the talking." Otherwise they would be here all night.

She glared at him but didn't disagree. Mostly, he decided, because her cell phone rang and distracted her. Four police cruisers barreled into the parking lot and Russ waited to see who was in charge. A detective would likely be en route. Bomb squad, as well.

"Are you serious? When did this happen?"

As she spoke into the phone, Olivia's face went pale again. Apparently there was more bad news. He had a feeling that she was going to need to reschedule her appointment in Houston.

When she ended the call, she looked from the uniforms approaching to Russ. "My motel room burned. Like twenty minutes ago." She shook her head. "My luggage was in the room." She stared at the spot where her sedan had been parked. "My briefcase was in my car."

Someone was not happy with Olivia Westfield.

9:20 p.m.

THIS WAS UNBELIEVABLE!

Olivia watched as the last piece of her car was loaded onto the truck that would haul it to the county crime lab for further analysis. The bomb squad had determined there was no further danger and the diner's patrons had been allowed to leave. No one had seen or heard anything other than the explosion. The remains of a homemade explosives device had been found. Not a totally rudimentary device, but not state-of-the-art, either. The detonator had been remotely controlled, which meant that whoever had set off the explosion had been watching and waiting for just the right moment.

She stood inside the diner and watched the final cleanup efforts. She had given the owners of the other two vehicles her insurance information. Whether or not her automobile policy covered this kind of thing, she had no idea.

"Would you like some more coffee, Ms. Westfield, before I shut down the coffeemaker?"

She glanced at the manager who had toiled away behind the counter for the past two hours. He'd served coffee and pie to the restless diners and to the policemen. Olivia imagined he was anxious to close up for the night. Thanks to her it had been a long one.

"No, thank you." She forced a smile on her lips. "I appreciate your patience and hospitality."

"No trouble, ma'am," he assured her. "I'm just grateful no one was hurt."

"Me, too." Whoever had done this had tried to get to her. If anyone had gotten hurt...

Was she doing the right thing going after this case, her past, with such a vengeance?

Olivia turned back to the scene transpiring beneath the parking lot lights before her lips started that telltale tremble and gave her away. She was so glad no one had been hurt. This was her fault. That part she understood completely, though no one had said as much. But she had seen the way the detective in charge had looked at her when she'd told him the only reason anyone would want to do such a thing was because of her looking into the Princess Killer case.

No one wanted her digging up that ugly past. Not even the cops, and they should want justice every bit as much as she did. She hugged herself and silently repeated the mantra that had gotten her this far. *It was the right thing to do*.

But was it?

St. James had gotten three calls from the Colby Agency following up on this development. He didn't say as much but she understood that no one was happy with her decisions. Olivia closed a hand over her mouth and stifled the urge to sob. Dammit, she was right to do this.

This had to be done. And there was no one else. Whoever had murdered those poor girls, whether Rafe or Clare or both, the world needed to know for sure once and for all. *She* needed to know. His eyes and that face…she closed her eyes and tried to put his image out of her mind. He just kept haunting her. Not one specific detail was familiar to her and yet there was a vague recognition of some sort. A knowing. Maybe it was more the sound of his voice. The voices from her dreams kept trying to surface.

Was she remembering ugly events from that terrifying time? She wanted to try to remember more…but the idea flat-out terrified her. She hadn't told a soul how much she feared those repressed memories.

She knew what they were. A visit to a shrink when she turned twenty-five and a particularly chilling dream had given her an answer. Whatever happened when she was a kid—and it was no movie—had been a true nightmare.

If Clare Barker had any motherly instincts at all she would have come to her daughters immediately upon her release and tried to set things to rights. She would have explained what the voices and the images meant. Was Olivia the only one who remembered? As the youngest, Sadie probably didn't remember anything from that time. But Laney was only a year younger than Olivia. Would she remember those awful sounds? The darkness? And those creepy feelings of terror?

Maybe she should meet with her sisters before she moved

forward with the meeting with Keisha Landers. The reporter was so anxious she had agreed to meet Olivia at whatever time she and St. James could get there—no matter the hour. Olivia sensed there was something the reporter felt needed to be discussed face-to-face. With all that had happened today, Olivia had to admit, even if only to herself, that she was a little anxious about all this, too.

St. James and the detective were talking again. She really should go out there and see if there was anything new. Mainly she just wanted this to be over. But they couldn't leave until the detective-in-charge gave the word.

What if the person responsible for the bombing had wanted to kill her? Would this quest she had set out to accomplish, no matter how much it hurt her adoptive parents, really be worth the steep price? Good grief, she should call them before they heard about any of this on the news.

She stared at her cell phone and tried to work up the nerve. Not happening. She told herself she needed to conserve battery power until she got another phone charger—since hers had gone up in smoke with the motel room. Later, when she'd picked up a few necessities, had her meeting with Landers and settled into a nice hotel in Houston, she would call home.

Except then it would really be late and her parents would be in bed. Maybe in the morning. Her name wouldn't be connected to anything before then. No reason to be hasty in making that call. They'd only worry more.

"Looks like they're wrapping things up."

Olivia started. She pressed her hand to her throat and felt instantly contrite. Larry, the diner manager, had moved up beside her at the window. "I'm sorry. I'm holding you up." She turned to him and extended her hand. "Thank you very much for being so kind through all this. I'm genuinely sorry for the trouble."

He gave her hand a shake. "You be safe, Ms. Westfield. Looks as if you have some bad people out to get you."

He had no idea. And she doubted he would be at all concerned with her safety once he learned who she was and what she was attempting to accomplish. She thanked him again and headed out to the parking lot to join her new partner.

Speaking of partners, Nelson had called. Everyone at the firm back home was worried sick about her. He would file the petition first thing in the morning. It had been too late to get it done today by the time she'd sent him the go-ahead.

St. James met her gaze as she moved closer, then he flashed her one of those killer smiles. Her heart skipped a beat. She told herself it was all the excitement and the emotional turmoil but she wasn't so sure.

"The detective says we're free to go," he told her in the deep voice that sent goose bumps tumbling over her skin. "As soon as they have anything on the forensics they'll let us know. I wouldn't count on anything that'll tell us who did this, but you never know."

Unless the forensics could tell her who had done this and put that person behind bars, anything else learned would be pointless to her. Her car was dead. Thankfully no one was hurt. Not much else mattered. She really would, however, like to know who wanted to stop her that badly.

"At least we can be in Houston before midnight." The possibility that Landers had information that would be useful to her investigation had Olivia ready to get on the road.

"The bomb squad checked my SUV," St. James told her as he gestured for her to precede him in that direction, "just in case. It's clean as far as explosives go. Other than the unavoidable signs of twenty-four/seven surveillance, I'm sure you'll find it an acceptable ride." As he opened the passenger-side door he flashed her another of those smiles that possessed the power to make her hormones sit up and take notice even at a time like this.

He hastily moved a battery-powered shaver and a bottle of aftershave from the front passenger seat. Tossed them into the backseat between a bag, probably carrying his clothes, and a backpack. An empty foam coffee cup and a half-empty bottle of water waited in the cup holders. The interior smelled of coffee and whatever aftershave was in that bottle and on his handsome face. The SUV was nice. Comfortable. Like him.

Olivia had no idea how exhausted she was until she fastened her seat belt and reclined in the leather seat. He was right. This would be a very acceptable ride. Maybe the bomber had done her a favor. Now she no longer had an excuse to avoid buying a new car.

Once they were on the highway, he interrupted the silence. "I'd like you to compile a list of the names of anyone you've spoken to about Rafe and Clare Barker and their case."

"You believe someone I've spoken to is responsible for destroying my car?" She figured as much herself. "Trying to scare me off?"

"That's exactly what I believe. The sooner we narrow down the possibilities, the more likely we are to head off another attempt at discouraging you."

"Besides you," she said pointedly, "there's my boss, Nelson Belden, the reporter we're going to meet, the detectives who investigated the case in Granger twenty-two years ago and about half a dozen former friends and neighbors of the Barkers. In my opinion," she said as she snuggled more deeply into the soft leather, "we should start with the minister of the small church they—we—attended. He was a little strange. There was one lady who used to help out with the animals from time to time at the vet clinic the Barkers operated in that barn on their property. She actually threw rocks at me as I ran back to my car after asking my first question at her door."

He laughed. The deep rumble seemed to close around her in the darkness, made her feel warm and safe. *Silly, Liv. So very silly. You don't even know this man*.

"She actually threw rocks at you?"

"Yes. She chased me off the porch and as I ran across the yard, she threw those white stones she'd used as a sort of mulch in her flower bed."

Another deep chuckle. "We'll definitely put her on the list. Right under the investigating detectives."

If he hadn't said the last so soberly she might have thought he was kidding. "You want to start with the cops?"

"If a mistake was made in the investigation, they have the most to lose."

Neither she nor he laughed this time.

Chapter Seven

Houston News, 11:55 p.m.

Keisha Landers wasn't exactly happy to have a third party present during the interview. Russ wasn't surprised by her reaction, but Olivia convinced the lady to permit him to stay. Thankfully Olivia hadn't mentioned the name of his employer, which was good since he knew the agency had contacted Landers to no avail. If the television reporter had something significant to bring to the table, they would know soon enough. If her anxious demeanor was any indication, this could be the break Olivia and her sisters needed. The one that could solve this puzzle, finally.

Twenty-two years was a long time for anyone to wait. Even if they hadn't known they were waiting for this moment until very recently.

The *Houston News* conference room wasn't as large as the one at the Colby Agency but it was big enough for staff meetings and morning briefings. Olivia sat next to him, the reporter seated on the other side of her. Coffee had been brewed and all three had a fresh, steaming cup. Russ suspected they would need a second before the meeting concluded. Mostly he was thankful Olivia hadn't put up a fuss when his boss made the decision that under the circumstances it was too dangerous to have the Barker girls meet. To Russ's surprise, Olivia had agreed for now. She would meet her sisters at a later time.

Landers had sent her cameraman home after he set up the camera. She had decided this interview needed complete secrecy. Now, as they got started, she sat a box of material on the table. A standard-size cardboard file box the average person used for storing papers and receipts from the previous year. The once white box was yellowed with age and the corner creases weren't so sharp anymore. The reporter removed the lid and set it aside.

"After Clare's release," Landers began, "I recalled my father working endlessly on the case." She smiled sadly. "I was just a kid and every night during the investigation and then the trial I would ask my mother when my dad was coming home. She would always say that he was trying to help the missing princesses." Her expression grew distant. "I didn't understand what she meant at the time, but later, after his funeral, she mentioned that he always regretted not being able to do enough on that one."

"Your father was a newspaper man his whole life?" Olivia asked.

Landers nodded. "He started out as a delivery boy at the age of ten and came home with ink on his hands until the day he died." Her smile brightened. "He insisted that a good reporter was only as good as his next story. Didn't matter how great the last one was, it was the next one that defined you."

Russ sipped his coffee and analyzed the woman's voice. It was thick with emotion. There was something big in that box. Her anticipation was as palpable as her respect and fondness for her father's memory.

Landers removed bundle after bundle of photos and notes from the box. She unwrapped each, one by one, then began to pass them to Olivia. "The story was never going to be a routine homicide piece." She laughed dryly. "Not that there's ever anything routine about homicide. According to his notes, my father grew more and more disturbed by what he didn't find in the police reports."

"You have copies of the police reports?" Olivia asked, clearly surprised. "I asked to see the files and they turned me down flat. When my boss, Attorney Nelson Belden, followed up with a written request, he received a letter stating the case files had been misplaced."

"My father had friends," Landers explained. "One of his buddies in Houston P.D. got copies of everything for him." She passed the next bundle to Olivia. "Crime scene photos, lab results, interviews with friends, neighbors, anyone and everyone who was interviewed."

"This is incredible." Olivia moved the photos and papers closer to Russ so that they could study them together.

Some of the photos he would have preferred she not see. Blood on the sheets of the bed she and her sisters had shared. Blood in the closet and in the bathroom. A booking photo of Clare looking frazzled and wild-eyed with fear, or something along those lines. Rafe's booking photo with him appearing calm and composed. The stark difference had Russ taking a second, longer look. What kind of man looked so cool at a time like that?

More photos of the numerous digging expeditions in the woods on the Barker property. Olivia stared long and hard at the images of remains.

Finally, she moved on to the official scene investigators' reports and the interviews. They must have read for a half hour or more and were scarcely through half the neatly typed forms when Russ recognized what Landers's father had seen more than two decades ago.

Every single person who had known the Barkers described Clare as a quiet, obedient woman. She did exactly as her husband told her and never dared defy him. Several stated in no uncertain terms that Rafe ruled her and the children with an iron fist. The minister Olivia thought to be odd even said as much. Clare was kind and generous and quiet, he'd said. A good, obedient wife and loving mother.

The physical evidence all pointed to Rafe. The connection between the physical evidence and Clare was negligible to the point of being nearly nonexistent. Each detective concluded that the evidence was such that Clare couldn't possibly have been oblivious to the heinous deeds, thereby making her complicit.

Russ read copies of letters the victims had sent to Rafe thanking him for his wonderful work rescuing pets. The Barkers had been known far beyond the boundaries of their community for their animal rescue work. Veterinarians from many surrounding counties had sent folks there to view the many animals up for adoption. Grateful kids, most often young girls, sent letters thanking Rafe for their new pet. The letters were placed on a bulletin board, some accompanied by a photo of the girl and her pet. The bulletin board was labeled "the princesses." All the victims' photos were there, the ones found as well as the ones who remained unaccounted for. That was how the case had gotten its moniker.

"Do you see how it all points to Rafe until that final morning before the arrest?" Landers queried.

Olivia nodded. "The blood the police suspected came from my sisters and me was the only actual physical evidence that tied Clare to anything. And since we're all three alive, we know that was planted."

"The blood," Landers countered, "and the fact that several of the murdered girls were buried on the property."

"But that doesn't prove Clare helped murder or bury a single one," Olivia insisted. "There was no conclusive evidence that she was involved."

"The consensus," Russ felt compelled to add since the two

appeared at such odds on the issue of Clare's involvement, "was that Clare and Rafe worked as a team. It was difficult for most to accept that Clare had no idea what her husband was up to considering how close the two appeared to be. Where one was seen, the other was always nearby. That she was so submissive to him makes the idea far less acceptable, as well. In my opinion, her conviction was more about perception and possibility than evidence."

"Agreed," Landers said. "Those very elements, though not evidence themselves, speak to motive and opportunity. That conclusion, whether biased or not, and the blood confirmed to be you and your sisters' type were instrumental in Clare's conviction and, as we all know, in the overturning of that conviction. The evidence was circumstantial at best and the Texas Supreme Court recognized that reality."

Olivia lapsed into silence for an extended period. Russ wondered if it was more than she could absorb in one sitting.

"We should finish this tomorrow," he offered. "Today has been a hell of a ride and it's late."

Landers put her hands up in a show of no protest. "I do understand. We can start fresh in the morning."

For an ambitious reporter she was far more reasonable than he'd expected. Five or six years older than Olivia, she had followed in her father's footsteps only she'd chosen television over newspaper reporting, making quite the name for herself in Houston. It was obvious to Russ that this case had thrown her for an emotional loop, as well.

But no one was more emotionally slammed than Olivia and her sisters. This was a test of will for Olivia, but the waiting and not knowing had to be difficult for Sadie and Laney, too.

"If Clare wasn't involved," Olivia said, finally breaking her silence, "maybe there was someone else." The pitch of her voice rose with each word. "Someone who was right there all along that no one knew about."

Russ wondered where that had come from. Something she remembered or wishful thinking? Maybe Olivia just needed one of her biological parents to be a normal person.

"There's no mention of close family in any of the interviews," Landers pointed out. "No friends who visited. Just Rafe and Clare and their daughters. Do you remember anyone else frequenting the house or the clinic?"

Olivia considered the question for several seconds before shaking her head. "I barely remember anything. Mostly what I recall comes in the form of nightmares and none of it is clear. I just feel like there's something we're missing. Something or someone." She shook her head. "I don't know."

"Have you ever considered regression therapy?" Landers asked her.

Russ had wondered the same thing. Olivia had been old enough to have more substantial memories than her younger sisters. But regression therapy was not for the faint of heart. And sometimes there was nothing gained.

"I never had any reason to consider it until now." Olivia stared at the mound of documentation. "The only people who know the whole truth are Rafe and Clare. He's either lying or she's keeping a secret that could have cleared her during the trial."

Olivia was right on both counts. "If anyone else was involved, Clare would have known that person," Russ said, voicing what Olivia hadn't. "She and Rafe were together all the time." He gestured to the documentation on the table. "Wherever those interviewed saw one, they saw the other. But if Rafe pulled disappearing acts to assuage his dark urges or went off with some other person to do the same, why didn't Clare say as much at trial?"

The first person who came to his mind was Clare's sister, Janet Tolliver. Janet had arranged for the secret adoptions of the girls. She had kept the photo albums all those years.

And she'd taken care of Clare's son, Tony Weeden, they suspected, after Clare's rape in college. Why had she never been seen by any of the folks in Granger who knew the Barkers? Surely she had visited her sister at some point, unless they were estranged again by then. Either way, why hadn't Janet been at the trial?

And why the hell had she been murdered shortly after Clare's release from prison?

"Maybe Clare was protecting someone," Olivia offered. She turned to Russ. "But why do what she's been doing since her release? If she was wholly innocent, why behave guilty now? What's the point?"

"I think you need to ask her that." This from Landers.

"That could pose a risk to her safety." Russ made the statement a little more forcefully than he'd intended, but he didn't want Landers putting any ideas in Olivia's head. She was already plotting enough strategies that had garnered her the wrong kind of attention.

"Besides," Olivia mentioned, "it's doubtful that she would come forward at this point and chance being arrested."

"Basically," Landers summed up, "Clare Barker is in the same position now that she was in twenty-two years ago. Whatever she knows that would clear her name, she can't share because coming forward would pose an equally unwanted effect on her future as a free woman."

Russ suspected the reporter was far more correct than she knew. "We've completely ignored this newest development." When he had their attention, he went on. "Someone sent Olivia a very powerful message this evening. Frankly, it's doubtful that the bombing could have been carried out by Clare or Weeden. He was injured in the shootout in Granger this weekend and there is absolutely nothing in his background that indicates he has any explosives experience or that he has attempted to learn the basics via the internet. The police have gone over his home and computer. There's nothing that would suggest he had the skills or the inclination for a move like this."

"Doesn't mean he didn't use someone else's computer or a public access computer," Landers argued. "There are ways of getting information without the trail leading back to you."

"Bomb making can be tedious work," Russ countered, "and would be best accomplished with two hands." Tony Weeden only had one, which Russ didn't need to point out.

"Clare may have helped him," Olivia tossed out.

"Like she helped Rafe?" Russ was leaning toward the idea that Clare was a pawn in all this. Maybe not an innocent pawn, but a pawn nonetheless.

Olivia rubbed at her temples with her forefingers. "Maybe. I'm beginning to wonder if anyone in this nightmare could be innocent in the true sense of the word."

"Tony Weeden served as Rafe's nurse for several years," Landers said. "Is it possible he's following Rafe's orders to draw Clare back into a trap that will somehow frame her for something unthinkable all over again? Rafe only came forward after she was released. Unless you actually believe his motive in doing so is sincere."

Olivia laughed but the sound was far from amused. "I have no idea what his motive is. I can see the validity in your point in terms of his intentions toward Clare." Olivia turned to Russ once more. "Like ensuring she was charged with killing her daughters for real this time or at least attempting to. But why would he do that? Why not just have Weeden or someone else kill Clare if he wants revenge against her for some reason we can't see? Since we have no idea what the truth is, we have to consider that Rafe could be correct and that wanting her daughters out of the way is what Clare wanted all along. But why? What's her motive? How can we possibly hope to know one way or the other if we don't find Clare and persuade her to talk to us? We need more than Rafe's side of the story."

"Finding her might be within our power," Russ reminded her, "but we can't persuade her to tell us anything she doesn't want to share. And if Rafe is behind all of this, Clare may be as much a target as you and your sisters."

Landers picked up on his reasoning. "To go there, Mr. St. James, you would have to presume that she had been the one to hide her daughters away and that Rafe is now attempting to punish her since she got to go free and he didn't. You looked him in the eye today, Olivia. Do you believe the man you spoke to is capable of going to those extremes?"

Olivia shook her head. "I don't know. I was so taken aback by the reality that he was, in fact, my father that I can't trust any conclusions I formed."

Landers gathered several of the reports, tucked them into a folder and handed it to Olivia. "Start with the detectives who investigated the case. My father had another adage that he shared with my mother and me regularly. The one thing you could always count on in an investigation was that the cops would put on paper what they wanted you to know and nothing more. Whatever they left out is the part you need to find."

Olivia felt numb as she left the *Houston News*. It had been almost twelve hours since her meeting with Rafe Barker and she was more confused now than she had been when she walked out of that prison. Could she force the investigating detectives to discuss the case with her now that she had copies of their interviews? Or did she go straight to the sources and see if anything new came of her questioning, as she'd planned to do before meeting with Keisha Landers? Not that her first attempt had garnered her any information. But she had their signed statements now. That might make a difference.

She waited while St. James checked his vehicle for tampering. The sounds from the explosion kept haunting her.

That deafening boom, the screams…the falling debris. Her hearing had scarcely returned to some semblance of normal when they reached Houston. There was still a little ringing but she could hear fine. Had that explosion been intended to kill her? Had it gone off too early? No wait. That couldn't be right. St. James had said the explosive had been remote detonated, which meant whoever set it off had been watching her. If he'd wanted her dead she would be dead.

"You can get in now."

Olivia snapped from her worrisome thoughts. He'd already opened the passenger-side door and was waiting for her to move. "Thanks." She climbed into the seat and tried to go over what she'd learned tonight in a more logical manner, without all the emotions she'd suffered as she'd heard and read the information for the first time.

When he'd settled behind the wheel she made a decision, but she waited until he was out of the parking lot and rolling along the deserted street before making her announcement.

"I need to see my sisters." It was the only way. Between the three of them perhaps they could remember something relevant. Whether they did or not, Sadie and Laney needed to know what was going on and Olivia wanted to tell them face-to-face.

"We discussed that already. That would be a strategic error."

"I understand there's danger but they need to know about this. What on earth do you mean strategic error?" Was he talking about the danger? What? After all she'd been through today, she didn't want any more cryptic statements from him. She wanted straight answers. There was no reason for him to try and keep her from her sisters.

"The best way to keep the three of you safe is by keeping you apart. You said you understood that reasoning."

That made no sense to her now. None at all. "Explain how

that helps, if you don't mind. You said we had to find the truth. At this point, I can't see that happening without the three of us putting our heads together."

They were supposed to be cooperating. She had taken him into her meeting. She had convinced Landers to share what she had with him. Why wasn't he doing his part by rethinking this issue?

"If the ultimate goal is to take the three of you out," he said as he slowed for a turn, "having you together in one place makes the job a lot easier."

She wanted to rant at him but the truth was, he had a point with that one aspect of her request. "Whoever is following me would be led to the others—that's what you're saying. I get it."

"That's what I'm saying."

Dear God. Rafe Barker was in prison. Clare was God only knew where with her wounded accomplice. Who did that leave to put them in danger?

One or more of the detectives who had conducted the original investigation? A surviving family member of one of the victims? Who? There was absolutely no way to know.

And what about the theory that someone else was involved? Was that person still out there, praying the truth would not be discovered and out her or him?

"And if we run out of time without finding the answer?" Rafe Barker had just over two weeks to live.

"We won't," he said with complete certainty. "We will find the truth without putting you and the others in more danger."

St. James was right. There was no point arguing the issue. She couldn't go near her sisters until they knew the answer to who killed all those little girls. Since Rafe did nothing but speak in riddles, the only other real source was Clare. Whether she would tell the truth—if they found her—was anyone's guess.

"We should go to Granger and interview the people whose

statements Landers feels are the most telling as to how poorly the investigation was handled." Olivia would love another shot at the minister. And the lead detective, Marcus Whitt. If she couldn't meet with her sisters, she could at least do this.

"That we can do," St. James allowed. He glanced her way. "After some sleep."

She couldn't argue with that point, either. The exhaustion had gotten the better of her the past few minutes or the subject of a meeting with her sisters wouldn't have come up again. She wasn't thinking rationally. She needed sleep desperately. The only question would be whether or not her mind would shut down long enough for her to get any.

Her cell rang out and she fished through her bag to find it. Surely Nelson wouldn't still be up at this hour. Her chest cramped with the idea that it could be one of her parents. They wouldn't call this late unless something was wrong. If something had happened after the way she'd left things...

Fear had a choke hold on her by the time she found her phone and managed a greeting.

"Olivia, it's Keisha."

Olivia relaxed. "Is something wrong?" The reporter's voice sounded strained and uncertain.

"I was thinking," Keisha said, "that if you're going to Granger to do some follow-up interviews, I'd like to be a part of that. I believe this story deserves some patience. I'm willing to withhold running my story until we've investigated further. Would that be agreeable with you and your associate?"

They could use all the help they could get. "That would be most agreeable. We could meet for breakfast, discuss strategy and head for Granger. Say nine at the Broken Egg?"

Keisha agreed with the time and her choice of cafés and Olivia thanked her and ended the call.

"I assume that means we'll have company on our field trip?" St. James asked.

"She knows more about the investigation than either of us," Olivia countered, stating her case. "She's a valuable source. Involving her assures continued cooperation."

St. James gifted her with one of those knockout smiles of his. "Smart move."

Maybe they would make a good team, after all.

Chapter Eight

Sleep Rite Inn, Tuesday, June 4, 2:05 a.m.

Russ checked the locks on the door one last time. Taking a room in the rear of this low-rent motel provided protection to some degree against being spotted from the street. He'd made sure they hadn't been followed from the television station but the situation remained less than optimal. Tomorrow Simon Ruhl would arrange for an alternate vehicle, since whoever had followed Olivia and placed the explosive beneath her sedan had no doubt seen Russ's SUV. He'd scanned his SUV for tracking devices and found nothing. Still, he would feel more secure when they had a different vehicle and a safe location to lay low. For now this would do.

He'd considered taking Olivia to his place, but tracking them there would be too simple for anyone who knew his name. That wouldn't take long if their tail had access to the right database for running license plates. As a former cop himself he didn't want to believe any of the detectives or officers involved with the investigation twenty-two years ago would go to these kinds of extremes to scare Olivia off but he couldn't dismiss the possibility. Particularly not after her less than hospitable experience in Granger.

Simon had someone checking into the four cops and the one FBI agent who had served as the primary investigators on the joint task force that worked the Princess Killer case. Most cops had some training when it came to explosives, but the type used on Olivia's car required a good deal more than a basic knowledge.

The bathroom door opened and Olivia peeked out. "You decent?"

She looked young and way too vulnerable in her pink pajamas. Her hair was still damp and her brown eyes looked wide with uncertainty. Definitely not the sharp, don't-get-in-my-way lady he'd met that morning. This was the unguarded Olivia. Weary with emotion. As tired as they both had been when they left the *Houston News,* they'd made a quick run through an all-night superstore for necessities she would need. A woman's idea of necessities was definitely different from a man's. Olivia had required two changes of clothes, pajamas, cosmetics and hair products. He, on the other hand, had selected one item—bottled water.

"It's late," he teased, "any decency I possess goes into hiding at midnight."

She scowled at him as she slipped from the tiny bathroom and padded to the first of the double beds. Her scrutiny quickly shifted to the bed as she peeled the covers back. "I hope they don't have bedbugs."

For a woman who had faced her biological father, the convicted serial murderer, and the total destruction of her car via a homemade bomb, worrying about bedbugs seemed a minor nuisance.

"I hear they never linger in the bathtubs if you'd prefer to sleep there."

She shot him another of those dark scowls. He laughed, couldn't help himself.

"It's not a laughing matter. Those things bite and if you take them home with you they're a big problem to get rid of."

"I would have been more worried about the last place you were staying." Compared to that one, this place was a resort.

"I checked their health department rating and the incident reports," she said as she surveyed the sheets. "No pests reported."

"You can check that?" He should have known the lady would be thorough in whatever she did.

"You can." She collapsed on the bed in a cross-legged position. "You don't do that when you travel?"

"This is my first overnight duty since before the bedbug issue got its own byline." He toed off his boots and stretched out on the other bed without bothering to check for critters.

"You're living dangerously, Mr. St. James," she warned with enough of a twinkle in those big brown eyes that he knew she was teasing. She didn't smile often but her eyes made up for it. She had gorgeous eyes. Wide, dark and infinitely inquisitive.

She frowned. "Actually, I suppose I'm the one living dangerously. It was my car that blew up."

"I was just about to point out that fact." He twisted his lips into a wry smile. "You haven't made any enemies at work, have you?" That was an area he hadn't explored. He doubted her life, beyond the fact that her biological parents were the Barkers, was at play here but asking seemed a logical step.

"None that I know about."

She leaned onto her side and propped herself up on the stack of pillows, stretching her long legs, which would have been a nice distraction had she not been wearing neck-to-ankle concealing flannel. Had it not been for that infernal clearance rack she would be wearing one of those gauzy thin summer nightshirts.

"You were going to tell me about the possible connection between Weeden and Clare your agency had discovered, but we got a little sidetracked."

"We found Clare's college roommate from her freshman year. She claims Clare was sexually assaulted by one of her professors and a pregnancy resulted. She had no proof and a birth was never documented. We're exploring the possibility that Tony Weeden was the result of that assault and maybe Clare gave him to her older sister to take care of, only her sister turned him over to a couple, the Weedens, who had no children."

"Janet Tolliver, the woman who was murdered," Olivia ventured, "is without question Clare's sister? And she orchestrated the adoptions of me and my sisters? That's confirmed?"

"We've confirmed that Janet was Clare's sister. There was an incident when Clare was very young and Janet was sent away to live with another family that eventually adopted her, the Tollivers. Hers and Clare's parents, the Sneads, were murdered several years later when Clare was eight years old. But that's as far as we've been able to substantiate our suspicions. The rest is as much speculation as anything." He sat up and reached for the stack of interview reports Landers had given them. "We're assuming that, since Janet had possession of the photo albums and Rafe named her as his co-conspirator, she was the one who took care of the adoptions, but we have no confirmation other than Rafe's word."

Olivia tucked her hair behind her ear and snuggled into her pillow. Her eyes had grown heavy but she wasn't ready to give up just yet. The need to know more was driving her even as tired as she obviously was. "Why was Janet sent away? Did the family have financial problems?"

That was a fair question. The agency had considered that possibility first since it wasn't unheard-of for a family to make a decision like that back in the day. But that wasn't the case. "When Clare was three years old, Janet tried to harm her. Evidently the incident was bad enough that the parents felt removing her from the home was necessary."

Olivia sat up. "What kind of people are we talking about here?" She pushed to her feet and started to pace. "Janet was my aunt by blood and she tried to harm her own baby sister. My parents are convicted murderers." She stopped and turned to stare at Russ. "My older half brother has probably murdered at least one person." The pacing resumed. "How could anyone in their right mind want to risk passing on those kinds of genes?"

"Some of what I just told you is speculation, some is hearsay. It may not be as bad as you think."

She paused again to glare at him. "Do you really believe that?" A frown tugged at her eyebrows. "Wait. You said Clare's parents—my grandparents—were murdered? How? Why?"

More questions she would regret asking. "When Clare was about eight years old someone came into the house and brutally murdered them...." Russ took a breath. "They used an ax. The killer was never found, but at least one eye witness reported seeing a young girl, a teenager, near the home at the time. Considering what we know about Janet, we think it might have been her exacting revenge for having been abandoned. Again, that's supposition on our part."

"Oh, my God." Olivia wilted back down onto the bed. "That explains the nightmares. I've had them my whole life and now I know why. My aunt was an ax murderer and my parents, one or both, are sociopaths, too."

Russ sat up, dropped his feet to the floor and rested his forearms on his thighs. "Tell me about your nightmares." She'd mentioned them in the meeting with the reporter. Anything she recalled could prove useful to the investigation. And maybe it would get her mind off genetics.

Olivia pulled her knees up to her chest and wrapped her arms around her flannel-clad legs. "They're mostly dark. Creepy. The typical childhood night terrors. My parents— my adoptive parents—always blamed some movie I watched with my cousin when I was five." She hesitated as if she'd just realized the timing. "Of course, they told me that since it was the easiest way to explain any memories that might have surfaced from my life before becoming a Westfield." Her eyes filled with pain. "When I confronted them they told me how bad it was that first year. I was practically catatonic. They held me out of school an extra year in hopes I would be better adjusted before thrusting me into a new stressful situation."

The thought of what she may have witnessed as a child twisted inside him. How could either of her parents have been truly innocent? How could either not have known what the other was doing?

"Do you remember anything at all from the nightmares? Images, sounds or voices?"

"I remember darkness. Always the darkness." She rested her head on her knees. Her voice had turned so low and quiet that he wondered if she was reliving those awful moments. "And the screaming. Lots of screaming."

"Was it you screaming? Or one of your sisters? Were the screams close to you or coming from someplace else? Another room maybe?"

"Not me." She frowned in concentration. "I mean, it wasn't my voice. But it wasn't another child's, either. I think it was an adult."

"A woman's screams or a man's?" Olivia might know far more than she realized, Russ thought. The slightest piece of information, like who was screaming, could make a difference.

"A woman's. Absolutely a woman's." Her expression told him that she was searching the past, seeking those vague nuances from her memory banks. "She wasn't in the room with us." She shrugged. "I guess it was a room but it was small, cramped and very dark. Pitch-black."

"Was there anyone in the room with you?" She had two

younger sisters; chances were they had been with their big sister.

She mulled over that question for a bit. "I think so. There was shaking and soft…" She inclined her head and appeared to concentrate hard. "There were softer sounds, like sobbing or whimpering but so soft I might be mistaken. Maybe it was just me breathing."

"When you wake up from the nightmares are you still in the dark room listening to the screams?"

She gave a slow, hesitant shake of her head. "I'm in a bigger room and there's blood. Everywhere." She shuddered. "I hear this humming. Some tune I should know but I don't. That's when I wake up. Screaming, usually."

She took a big breath. "I don't want to talk about this anymore tonight." Her lips curved into a forced smile. "Good night." She switched off the lamp on her side of the table between the beds and curled up with her pillow.

"G'night." Russ hadn't enjoyed pressing her on the issue but there was something there. If she'd seen blood in the house, then she may have witnessed one of the murders.

Sixteen days was all the time they had left before Rafe Barker would be executed. They needed a break in this investigation. A single scrap of information that would point them in the right direction.

After checking the lock on the door again and the rear parking lot via the window, he grabbed his bag and moved to the bathroom. Too damned tired to do more than strip off his clothes and leave them in a pile, he climbed into the shower and set the spray to hot. He left the door open. Closing it was too much of a risk. Privacy be damned.

The water immediately started to loosen up his stiff muscles. He'd been running on adrenaline for hours now. With a trip to Granger on the agenda in just a few hours, he needed at least a little sleep. Judging by what Olivia had encountered in Granger already, the welcome, particularly from the local authorities, would probably be less than friendly. He needed to be on his A game.

His shower took all of three minutes. He dragged on a clean pair of jeans and a tee, checked the parking lot again, tucked his weapon under his pillow and then collapsed into the bed.

With the bathroom light filtering from the crack where he'd left the door ajar, he watched Olivia sleep. Like her sisters, her life would be vastly different after all this. He hoped she would find the peace she needed to move on from here.

Nothing about it was going to be easy.

THE DARKNESS WAS THICK ENOUGH to touch. She could feel it vibrating around her. And the screams… Oh, the screams were so terrifying. She wanted to scream, too, but she kept her teeth clenched to hold back the fear bulging in her throat. Her heart rammed harder and harder against her breastbone.

Mommy…

Her mommy was screaming. And the crying, softly agonizing. Her sisters were crying and she couldn't help them. She did as she was told. She took them into the closet and they hid. Huddled together in that tiny space, their trembling bodies vibrating like an unbalanced washing machine on the spin cycle.

Bad things were happening and Olivia couldn't make them stop. She could hear the awful sounds. Wailing and screaming. There would be blood. There was always blood. So much blood.

The dogs were barking. She could hear them out in the clinic. They knew something was wrong, too. But they couldn't stop it, either. There was nothing to do but hide and hope the monster wouldn't get them. Mommy always said when the monster came they had to hide and be very, very quiet.

He was here tonight. And this time he might just get them all....

Waking with a start, Olivia bolted upright. The air sawed in and out of her throat even as it tried to close. The nightmare. Just another nightmare. She shouldn't have talked about it. That only made it worse...made it more vivid.

Arms reached around her in the darkness. She screamed and tried to pull away.

"Olivia, it's me, Russ."

The voice sounded familiar and strong. Light chased away the darkness and she saw his face. Russ St. James. The man Rafe Barker had sent to protect her.

Olivia hugged her arms around her knees and fought harder to stop the trembling. "Sorry. It was...the nightmare."

The same old nightmare, this time on steroids. She swiped at her face, only then realizing she had been crying. So much worse this time.

St. James scooted closer, settling on the bed beside her. "You're okay now."

"Of course I'm okay," she snapped. She wasn't a child. She didn't need him taking care of her. "I'm fine."

"Well, I wouldn't go that far." He chuckled softly. "That must've been a hell of a nightmare. If we had any neighbors someone would have called the police by now."

God. She pressed her forehead to her knees. "I'm sorry."

"There's no need to be sorry. You need some water or something?"

A good stiff drink would be more suitable. She lifted her head and sighed. "No. I'll pull it together in a minute."

She wanted to resent that he was so close. Hovering around her with his big strong body all warm and solid. But she couldn't. She actually wanted to lean into him and try to forget. But she couldn't forget. Anything she could remember might help solve this awful mystery.

"Do you feel up to talking about it?"

She dared to meet his gaze. The concern in those blue eyes almost undid her. She had to look away. "It was the same only this time I remember more. It's like you said, my sisters were there with me. In a closet. That's why it's so dark. We would hide in the closet whenever the trouble started. I can hear her screaming. It's her...Clare." Her mother. Screaming her lungs out. At least it was a woman...although maybe it was one of the victims. But the sound was more mature somehow. And she was screaming words that Olivia couldn't make out.

"Why did you hide in the closet?"

She didn't want to talk about it but she couldn't resist answering him. His voice drew her. Made her want to lean into the strength he offered.

"Because it was the only place to hide and she told me to hide there. To take my sisters and stay in the closet until the monster was gone."

"Clare told you to do this?"

He knew the answer. Why did he ask? "Yes. Clare."

"Was Clare frightened when she told you this?"

"Yes..." Olivia's head ached with trying to remember. "She was always frightened of the monster. He did bad things."

That she recalled those sensations so vividly gave her pause. She inclined her head and listened to the voice whispering through her mind. Soft, gentle. And another sound... the humming. Olivia couldn't place the tune but it was so familiar. What was the name of that song?

"Did you see or hear Rafe?"

The question startled her. No, she didn't see her father. He was...he was...she didn't know. There was nothing. No feelings whatsoever. She shook her head. "I don't see or hear him in the dreams. And I don't feel him." She turned to St.

James. "What do you think that means? That I was totally disconnected from him? Emotionally disengaged?" People did that as a self-protection. Could that be why she didn't remember him?

Then again, she didn't exactly remember Clare. It was more a feeling that the woman's voice was her mother's.

"You should try and get another hour's sleep. It's barely four o'clock. It's going to be a long day."

He was right, she knew. But the idea of closing her eyes and going back to the dark place held no appeal whatsoever. "I'm not so sure I can do that. Maybe if you help me relax." There was no way to miss the glint of sexual interest in his eyes. She cocked an eyebrow. "I mean, tell me a story, St. James. About you. I know almost nothing about you." The idea that he was interested warmed her, filled that nasty void the nightmare had left in her chest. God, she hated those damned dreams.

"All right."

To her dismay, which she hoped didn't show, he moved back to his own bed.

"I grew up in Dallas. Studied criminology in college and went on to be a cop. Made it all the way to detective lieutenant before I walked."

She had him figured for a cop. She'd watched enough of them in the courtroom giving testimony. "Why'd you walk away from your career?" Like she had any room to talk. She'd walked away from law school barely a year shy of graduation.

He relaxed against the headboard, his hands clasped behind his head. The position forced the cotton tee to mold to his well-muscled body. "We'd take them off the streets and hotshot attorneys would put them right back on the street. I got sick of it and decided to go where I could do more for the victim, rather than wasting the taxpayers' money."

She shot him a speculative look. His expression shifted to

one of understanding, then contrition. "I work in a law firm that specializes in putting *them* back on the street."

"Sorry about that." He shrugged. "But it's true far too often."

"I know what you mean," she confessed. "Sometimes it's not fair, but it's the way our justice system works." Attorneys had no choice but to represent their clients to the best of their abilities—even when they discovered they were guilty.

"Why didn't you finish law school?"

She shouldn't be surprised he'd asked. He knew everything else about her. "I just decided one day that I didn't want that ultimate responsibility. It's kind of like choosing to be a nurse over being a doctor. You still get to help the sick and injured, but you don't have to carry the load when it comes to the politics and business side of the job. I get to counsel clients to a degree. I do lots of volunteer work. The boundaries are a little different. I have more freedom than my boss." And the truth was she'd chickened out. Deep inside she'd felt she wasn't worthy. Maybe now she understood why.

"You have any siblings? Parents still alive?" she asked him.

"One sister. Two parents. We get together on holidays and birthdays. We're all busy."

The tiniest hint of sadness tinged his voice. "You should make it a point to get together more often." Again, she had no room to talk.

He rolled onto his side and fixed those blue eyes on her. "I'll be sure to do that. You should, too."

"Touché." She managed a smile. "G'night."

He switched off the light. "G'night."

Chapter Nine

Victoria leaned forward and peered at the crowd gathered around the gate of the prison. "Wait before you make the turn, please," she said to her driver.

"Yes, ma'am. It looks as though every media outlet in Texas has descended upon the prison. And those picketers don't look too happy. To make that turn, ma'am, we'd be forced to drive right through the worst of the crowd."

Unfortunately, he was all too correct. Dozens of news vans lined the road. Hundreds of people carrying signs and shouting had crowded the prison entrance. Her cell chimed and she reached into her purse to find it without taking her eyes off the massive crowd. She checked the screen. Warden Prentice. "Good morning. It appears you have an onslaught this morning. What's going on?"

"We believe Rafe Barker got word to a reporter that his case was being reviewed by a celebrated private investigations agency. A reporter from Austin called to demand an interview with me as well as Barker and when I denied his request he went public. This is only going to get worse."

The situation was not a completely unexpected turn of events. Victoria had anticipated the news would leak in time, though she had hoped it would be later rather than sooner.

"How did Barker get word to this reporter?" No mail left the prison unscreened. No calls or visitors got in without the warden's knowledge. After Weeden had smuggled out the letter from Barker to Victoria, all prison employees had been warned again that such behavior would not be tolerated.

Yet, someone inside had to have gotten the word out.

"Have you determined the source of the leak?" she prompted when Prentice remained silent. The prison staff with access to Barker was limited. Learning the identity of the culprit shouldn't prove difficult.

"At first I was certain it had to be someone from your agency. There are only four on staff with access to Barker now. But certain discrepancies in their statements changed my mind. No one has admitted to delivering his message, but we believe it was one of the two guards. I suspect one or the other will confess eventually but the damage is done."

"I'm just outside the gate, beyond the media and protest encampment. Is my meeting with Barker still on?" Whatever Barker had to say to her might or might not be relevant, but Victoria had questions for him. Demands, actually. She refused to play any more of his games. Admittedly, he had her at a disadvantage. It wasn't as if she could walk away from the case. Until this was over, Sadie, Laney and Olivia had to be protected. And the idea that Clare needed help, too, wouldn't be shaken from the fringes of Victoria's thoughts.

"That's why I'm calling you," Prentice explained. "Barker announced five minutes ago that he won't see you."

Victoria absorbed the ramifications of that statement for a moment before responding. "Did he provide a reason for this sudden change of heart? He was the one who demanded the meeting in the first place."

She asked the question knowing there would be no reasonable explanation. Rafe Barker was playing a game and she had just fallen into his trap.

"He refused to say anything more." The warden's hiss of frustration echoed across the line. "He's toying with us all, Victoria. He has what he wants now—whatever the hell that is—and he's going to sit back and relish the show until he's either executed or the governor grants a stay."

Prentice was perhaps more right than he knew. "He has a plan, I'll grant you that," she acknowledged. "But I don't believe that plan involves sitting back and waiting for anything. There's more coming. We simply haven't felt the repercussions of it yet."

"We have him on suicide watch. Not that I feel he intends himself harm. To the contrary. I'm fully expecting a final hoorah of some sort. I just hope it doesn't involve a full-on riot in my prison. At this point, I recognize that Barker, despite his decades of silence, has an influence here I never suspected for a second."

"You're aware, I'm certain," Victoria felt compelled to mention, "that an attorney in San Antonio is petitioning for a stay of execution."

"The state D.A. called me an hour ago. I'm sure it'll be breaking news before noon."

"Please keep me advised of any developments involving Barker." Victoria hoped he'd done all the damage within his power for now. But evil knew no boundaries. And she was fully convinced that Rafe Barker was far more evil than he asserted his wife to be.

Whether Clare was equally heinous was yet to be seen. It would seem, in light of recent events, that she was squarely on that path, whether by her own accord or not. If she was innocent, at least in part, how long would it take her to know she was falling into the same trap a second time?

Victoria ended the call. "You can take me back home, Clarence. My appointment here has been cancelled."

"We may have a problem, ma'am."

An abrupt commotion on the road in front of the car drew Victoria's attention beyond the windshield. A throng of reporters were racing toward them. Just behind the reporters and their cameramen was a crowd of protesters, signs waving, voices raised in demonstration.

"I'm backing up, ma'am."

Victoria braced for the maneuvers she knew would be required to avoid the trouble roaring directly at them.

Clarence slammed on the brakes. Victoria twisted in her seat to see what had stopped his retreat. Another news van had arrived and stalled at an angle across the road, preventing their escape.

"I'm calling nine-one-one, ma'am."

"Unfortunately, that may be the only step at our disposal." Still, time would be required for the appropriate authorities to arrive.

Reporters pressed their faces and their microphones to the windows and shouted questions. Was the Colby Agency supporting a stay of execution for Rafe Barker? Had new evidence indicating his innocence been uncovered? Victoria tried to slow her respiration and to relax. She couldn't respond to their questions because she had no answers. Then came the inevitable angrily shouted slogans of the protestors.

None of that bothered Victoria. It was an unavoidable aspect of having made the decision to look into Rafe Barker's claims. It was the questions that eventually came that clamped like a vise around her heart.

Is it true that the Barker girls are still alive?

Chapter Ten

Broken Egg Café, Livingston, 9:30 a.m.

"Something's wrong." Olivia peered out the large plate-glass window but there was still no sign of Keisha Landers. Their appointment had been for nine and this was the only Broken Egg Café in Livingston so there was no misunderstanding.

"You want to try her cell again?"

Olivia didn't see the point. She'd called both her cell and her office three times in the past half hour. The receptionist had no idea where Keisha was. She hadn't come into the office that morning. Worry dug its claws deep into Olivia's ribs, making it difficult to breathe.

"If we don't hear from her soon," St. James began, "we should speak to her employer and get the number for a family member we can call. Maybe there's been a family emergency."

Olivia knew what he was really thinking but she didn't want to go there. With the bombing of her car, there was no way around considering the possibility that something had happened to Keisha. She could be in a hospital somewhere... or worse.

Evidently noting her distress, he added, "I sent Simon a text and had him check with the local police to see if any accidents or other incidents involving Landers had been reported. Nothing so far."

Olivia appreciated his effort but she still couldn't relax. Not until she knew for certain. The buzz of his cell phone vibrating on the table sounded at the same instant that hers rang. That couldn't be good. Holding her breath, she blurted a hello.

"Olivia, I'm at the hospital."

Keisha Landers.

"What happened?" Olivia's gaze tangled with that of her protector, who was in deep conversation with his caller. Those blue eyes warned that the news on his end was equally grim.

"About three this morning someone broke into my house, set the place on fire and almost did me in. Actually I almost did myself in. The bastard made enough noise getting out of the house to wake the dead. I smelled the smoke and got out of the house immediately but I went back in for my father's papers. Dumb move. I ended up having to climb out a second-story window. The rose trellis didn't make for such a good ladder."

A chill seeped through Olivia. "Are you okay?" Keisha's voice sounded a little rusty and a lot tired but she was alive. Olivia should never have called her. She shouldn't have involved anyone else in this.

"Other than the smoke inhalation and a mild concussion, I'll live." Keisha blew out a big breath. "But my house is done. Worse, my father's papers are gone. Just gone. Everything. All that's left is what I gave you and your friend. Guard it with your life. I can't lose that, too."

"I will," Olivia vowed. "You have my word."

"I had a visit from a man named Simon Ruhl of the Colby Agency," Keisha went on. "Apparently they're investigating this case, too."

Olivia felt contrite that she hadn't been honest with her about St. James. But she'd given him her word.

Olivia didn't ask what Ruhl had wanted. Keisha assured Olivia that she would do as the doctor advised and stay in the hospital and rest. She urged Olivia to be very careful. "Someone doesn't want this investigation reopened badly enough to push just shy of murder."

As Olivia ended the call she considered the way the reporter had put her warning. Keisha was correct. Whoever was trying to stop this hadn't blown the car up while Olivia was inside or while anyone was nearby. He or she had waited for just the right opportunity to levy the most fear without hurting anyone. The same with Keisha's house fire. What perpetrator makes that much noise or forgets to disable the smoke detectors if murder by fire is the goal? Not only had her smoke alarms started wailing but the fire department had gotten a call from someone claiming to see smoke. The caller hadn't left a name.

That was a lot of extra trouble to go to in an effort to avoid unnecessary collateral damage unless the only intent was to destroy records that might confirm the investigation had been mishandled twenty-two years ago.

Clearly the person responsible had no intention of causing physical harm.

St. James ended his call, his attention still focused on Olivia. "The perp is either a cop or an ex-cop. Maybe a family member of one of the vics, but my money's on a cop." He withdrew his wallet and tossed several bills on the table.

Olivia's thoughts snagged on that move. "It's my turn to pay." She pushed his money to his side of the table and reached for her purse.

"Did you hear what I said, Olivia?"

She stared at him, blinked. "Yes. A cop." Apparently Simon Ruhl had gotten the story on the fire. Maybe even more insight from the cops investigating the case. She wanted to ask what he'd learned but she had a bad feeling where this was going.

The man seated across the table from her heaved a frustrated breath. "The only cops who would have a stake in this beyond a basic sense of justice are in Granger. Going there would be a bad move. Your reporter friend is in the hospital. Two of my colleagues just got out of the hospital. Another man is dead. Simon, my boss, has located a safe house where we can lay low until the dust settles."

Fury whiplashed her. "You mean until the next sixteen days have passed and Rafe Barker is executed? Or maybe until Clare and her twisted son hurt someone else? Is that what you mean, St. James?" She slapped her own money on the table. "Because if it is, our deal is off. I want the truth before Rafe Barker is dead."

He reached across the table and took her hand. She tried to pull away but he held on, his grip firm and strong yet gentle and unthreatening. "Listen to me. Just because this guy, whoever the hell is doing this, is playing it safe at the moment doesn't mean he'll keep it that way if he feels cornered or if desperation sets in too deep. Are you really prepared to sacrifice everything, even your life, to know the truth that you may already, in fact, know?"

If he hadn't been searching her eyes with such hope in his own, hope that she would understand he wanted to protect her, she might have grown even more angry. But he wanted to keep her safe. It was his job and that was important to him.

Part of her regretted that the job was likely his primary motive. Foolish. Foolish. "Last night I had that same nightmare I've had a thousand times before. I take my sisters into that closet because that's what our mother told me to do. I can hear her or someone, female and mature, not a child, screaming. I can feel the fear vibrating in my little sisters who aren't even old enough to understand what true fear is. And then when I think it's safe, I open the door and there's blood everywhere." Her fingers tightened around his. "I need to know what happened. Can you understand that?"

He gave a nod of agreement. It was vague, almost nonexistent, but at least he didn't say no.

"Then you won't try to stop me?" Her lungs seized, holding the air inside hostage. She had to do this. If he wouldn't help her, she hoped at least he wouldn't hinder her efforts.

"We had a deal, didn't we?" He gave her a smile, not his usual dazzler but brilliant enough to make her heart skip a beat. "Let's go." He glanced at the cash she'd left on the table lying next to the bills he refused to take back. "Our waiter's going to think you have a crush on him with a tip like that."

Olivia rolled her eyes and took back her hand. "Let's go before something else blows up." Like her libido. It was already smoking with the heat he'd generated just holding her hand. How in the world could she be attracted to a man, even one as good-looking and honorable as this one, at a time like this?

Bad genes. It was the only rational explanation.

Olivia hit the ladies' room first. The westward journey to Granger was well over three hours. If they wanted to arrive by midafternoon, they needed to limit stops. St. James had filled up the gas tank this morning so maybe there wouldn't be any stops at all.

After taking care of business, she studied her reflection as she washed her hands. No amount of concealer would take care of her dark circles. She hadn't had a decent night's sleep in ages. The nightmares had been a part of her life for as long as she could remember but the past couple of weeks they had become a nightly ritual. Maybe something trapped deep in her memory was attempting to resurface. Certainly the details in this latest nightmare had been more vivid.

Olivia supposed the shrink she'd seen two years ago was right. Talking about it had prompted more details. She grabbed a paper towel and dried her hands. It wasn't every night she had a big strong guy to hold her afterward and comfort her fears. That was another thing she decided wasn't so bad, having a partner in this.

Her boss was very supportive but only for the paperwork and the guidance. Nelson wasn't entirely convinced her quest was a good idea but he wouldn't deny her the leave from work to do what she felt she had to do. Funny, no matter that St. James was only doing his job, it felt like he actually cared what happened to her. Then again, she'd never had a bodyguard. Maybe this was the usual routine.

"You really are pathetic, Liv." She shook her head at herself. Had it been so long since she'd had a man, besides her father and her boss, in her life that she was overreacting to the mere presence of testosterone?

Maybe.

St. James waited for her right outside the ladies' room door. "Ready?" he asked.

"Definitely." As they moved toward the café exit, she offered him a piece of advice she had found handy on numerous occasions when time was of the essence as it was now. "Speed limits have a ten-mile-per-hour grace in my experience. No cop is going to bother pulling you over and giving you a ticket for anything less than that."

"That," he said as he opened the door and the bell overhead jingled as if punctuating the word, "is because you're a woman. Trust me, I know."

Outside she sent him an annoyed look.

"And you're cute," he added.

Before she could rail at him for making such a sexist remark, he was striding toward the SUV. She hurried to keep up. "That is absolutely not true."

He performed his usual checks before unlocking and opening the vehicle. "You're right," he said when he at last opened the passenger-side door for her. "You're more than cute. You're very pretty in an uptight kind of way."

She settled into the seat and fumed. Uptight? She was not uptight. Her gaze crept down to the skirt and blouse she wore. Her choices had been limited. The navy skirt was not as tailored as the ones she usually wore. And the blouse was very plain. White, button-up. She never bothered with accessories like jewelry or scarves, and wore minimal makeup. She spent more time and money on her hair than anything else. It was too thick to manage easily. She kept it as short as she dared and still it was a handful. But there was nothing uptight about her.

"I resent your implication that I'm uptight." This she finally announced when they were well on the road toward Granger a full fifteen minutes later. Working up her nerve was not a task she generally had to perform. But everything was different with this man. "And your suggestion that women don't get tickets just because they're women isn't true. I've had lots of tickets."

"Statistics show," he argued, "that women do get fewer tickets than men. I should know, being an ex-cop and all."

"Maybe because we're better drivers."

He ignored the jab. "The other is just a figure of speech," he said, moving into the right lane and settling in to a nice speed just five miles per hour above the one posted.

"I dress and conduct myself in a professional manner. What's wrong with that? People have become far too lax in their manners, business and social."

"You have a point there." He glanced at her. Her cheeks flushed as if he'd stared at her a whole minute. "Do you want to hear what I really think or would you rather I kept my thoughts to myself since these particular ones have nothing to do with business?"

Olivia moistened her lips and ordered her heart to slow. "Why would you speak to me any other way besides frankly? We are a team, after all." Did two constitute a team? They certainly weren't a couple. Perhaps the better term was partnership.

"Whatever you say." He gave her another of those assessing sideways glances. "It just seems a shame to cover up so much of a gorgeous body like yours. The skirt could be a few inches shorter. Two or three buttons opened on the blouse would take the look from stiff and uncertain to relaxed and confident. The shoes are pretty damned awesome just the way they are."

Six or seven seconds were required for her to summon her voice after absorbing his suggestions. "You appear to have spent a great deal of time analyzing the way I look." She wasn't sure whether to be flattered or offended. What she did feel was too warm. She reached out and adjusted the vents and prayed the air coming from them would do the trick of lowering her body temperature.

"That's part of my job, too."

Surprised, she studied his profile. "To what end, Mr. St. James? Unless you'd rather not say. I wouldn't want you to give away any trade secrets." Were all men alike in that respect? They first measured a woman by the way she looked.

He sped up to move around a massive truck. "First off, my name is Russ. When you call me Mr. St. James it makes me feel old." He cut her a smile. "I'm not that old."

"Russ it is, then." Olivia stared straight ahead and wished she could unbutton the top two buttons of her blouse. But she would melt first. Not in a million years would she loosen her collar and have him think his suggestion had prompted the measure. She would be fine in a few minutes when he stopped talking in that deep, rich voice and he stopped sending her those sexy smiles.

"I assess the way people think and react in order to do my job. For instance, I know you get up at six every morning—usually," he qualified with another of those smiles tossed in her direction. "You go for a three-mile run on the same route, you shower for the same length of time, you eat a bagel or a cup of yogurt, get dressed and take the same route to the office."

"It's called a routine," she defended. "All organized people have one. That's why in two years I've never been late for work or court once." It was true. She did take the same route with her runs and her drive to the office. What of it?

"That kind of routine makes you an easy target. Even without a case like this on your plate, there are random assaults every day. Organized people make it easy for the bad guys."

Well, she would certainly never look at her routine the same way again. The idea stunned her. And it shouldn't have. She was well aware of the elements that made victims more vulnerable. But she had never considered herself a victim, which was the average person's first mistake. When had she stopped paying attention to her life to that degree?

"You wear gray on Mondays, navy on Tuesdays, brown on Wednesdays, and black both Thursdays and Fridays."

"I…" She stared down at the navy skirt she had chosen at the store in the wee hours of the morning without thought. "I hadn't really noticed." She was focused. Ambitious. And busy. She worked ten-hour days most of the time. What did he want from her? She was no clotheshorse. As long as she looked professional and well groomed, what difference did it make?

"You're totally different from your sisters."

The silence thickened while she steadied her bearings. Did he think he could make a statement like that and not follow it up with some explanation?

"What does that mean?" She didn't know her sisters. Why would she be anything like them other than in terms of genetics? The concept that she had two sisters and knew absolutely nothing about them still rattled her.

"Sadie runs a small ranch outside Copperas Cove. She

rescues horses. Laney owns and operates a classy saloon in Beaumont. She rescued the place from the wrecking ball and renovated it herself. Her old farmhouse, too. Both are never caught in anything but jeans and boots. I'll bet they don't own a single suit between the two of them."

Country girls. Rescuers. She did her share of rescue work, too. Only it was with legal advice and papers. She wore jeans in her off time. But never boots. She hated boots of any sort.

"What're they like beyond how they dress?" Part of her was afraid they wouldn't like her. That somehow they would blame her for not protecting them. She was the oldest. She should have done more...should have done better.

"They're good people, Olivia." He slowed for a bottleneck in the interstate traffic. "Hard workers, compassionate." He glanced at her, his gaze lingering long enough to send her pulse rate escalating. "Like you."

That his words pleased her so inordinately frustrated her.

"What do they look like now?" Would she recognize either one if she ran into her on the street? The thought tugged at something deep inside Olivia. It wasn't natural not to know one's family.

Russ picked up his cell from the console and passed it to her. "There's a photo of Sadie and Laney as well as Laney's son, Buddy."

"I have a nephew?" Had he mentioned that before? Olivia shouldn't have forgotten that no matter how caught up she was in this insanity.

"He's five. His father was the man we believe Weeden murdered."

He had told her that part, but somehow the fact that she had a nephew had been left out. Or maybe she'd been so caught up in the idea that Clare and Weeden had murdered someone that she'd missed the rest of what Russ said. With all that had happened in the less than twenty-four hours they had known each other it was a miracle they'd stayed on track with any kind of conversation.

She tapped the screen and opened the folder that contained the photos he'd either taken with his phone or that had been sent to him. The most recent photo was of herself going into the motel where she'd stayed her first night in Livingston. She looked tired. The next was of a little boy with brown hair and big brown eyes. He wore a cowboy hat and was all smiles. The woman who appeared on the screen next had the same blondish-brown hair as Olivia and the same eyes. Lisa— Laney, she amended. Her face was as familiar as Olivia's own. Her heart thundered as she moved to the next image. Sadie was beautiful. Her hair was more blond than brown and her eyes were green. She'd been so small the last time Olivia had seen her. But her face was familiar, too.

All these years they had been right here in Texas, only a few hours from Olivia. Anger stirred. Her adoptive parents should have told her. It was wrong that she and her sisters had grown up apart. As strangers.

Dealing with that hurt would have to wait for another time. She'd called her folks last evening and left a voice mail. She'd purposely chosen a time when she knew they wouldn't be home to avoid speaking to one or both. She'd told them she was fine and not to worry and that she would call again in a day or two. She hadn't mentioned the car. For now there was no need. They would worry if they didn't hear from her in any event. Who was she kidding? They were already worried and part of the reason was her fault. They were aware of her determination to understand the past and to find answers.

"May I forward these photos to my phone?" It would be nice to have recent photos of her sisters. At some point they would meet and maybe take the first steps toward a relationship. If either of them was interested.

"Sure." He sent her a telling look but kept the warning to himself.

"Don't worry, they're not evidence. I won't share them with anyone else until this is over." Did he think she was that desperate to prove her case?

Did she even have a case?

If she had deciphered her latest dream correctly, her father was a monster. But there was always the possibility that recent events had influenced her subconscious, causing her to lean in that direction. The only thing Olivia understood with complete certainty right now was that she had to know for sure. No speculating. No assuming. She needed the facts. And those facts would be found in one of three places. With Rafe and Clare, who were beyond her reach, and in Granger.

Someone there had to know something.

And if Russ was correct in his theory, someone there wanted the past and those facts to stay dead and buried.

Chapter Eleven

Granger, 2:20 p.m.
Where history lives...

Granger's town slogan seemed fitting in more ways than one, Russ mused. This was where the Barkers' history lived, buried under decades of pain and hatred. Reopening those old wounds was not going to be a pleasant task or an easy one.

He placed his hand on Olivia's arm and gave her a gentle shake. Her eyes opened, big and a rich brown that was even darker when she was angry or excited. She'd fallen asleep en route. He hadn't wanted to wake her. She'd needed the rest. But now he had no choice. Rest or no, she wouldn't be happy if he allowed her to miss anything beyond the Welcome to Granger sign he'd just passed.

"We're here."

She sat up, the seat belt tightened and she tugged to loosen it. For several seconds she studied the landscape. "Looks even smaller than it did the last time I came."

"Small, quiet," he agreed, "the kind of place where everyone knows each other's names."

"I imagine my name is one they would all like to forget."

The town's population was scarcely two thousand. At one time the area had been the hub of cotton trade with railroads ruling transit. Many of the old historic buildings remained, giving the town a true sense of the Old West.

"Do you want to start with Barbara Samson?" He remembered reading in one of the interview reports Landers had provided that Samson was one of the only two fairly close friends the Barker family had. Mrs. Samson had a daughter the same age as Olivia. The two girls had played together as kids according to the interview report but Olivia had no recall of the other little girl.

"Yes, she's a good starting place." Olivia dug through her bag until she came up with the folder she'd gotten from the reporter. "Maybe seeing her and photos of her daughter will trigger some of the memories I should have of that time."

"What was that address again?" Mrs. Samson still lived at the same address. Her husband had passed away and her daughter lived in Michigan now. If the lady was cooperative she could prove a good source of at least basic information.

"I'll enter it into the GPS," she offered. A few clicks later and they were following the turn-by-turn directions to the Samson home in a small neighborhood on the other side of town, not more than a couple of miles from the old Barker home place.

The small bungalow was surrounded by a yard cluttered with enough flowers to threaten the ability of the white picket fence to contain it. An old car encircled by last year's fallen leaves and looking as if it hadn't been driven since gasoline was under a dollar a gallon sat beneath a shade tree.

Russ parked in the driveway and shut off the engine. "Do you want me to get the lay of the land first?"

Olivia surveyed the home for another second or two. "I'm good." She reached for her door and hopped out. "As long as she doesn't start throwing rocks."

Russ chuckled. "Lucky for us there doesn't appear to be any handy." The lady's flower beds were mostly crowded with plants, no landscaping stones or pebbles in sight. He followed Olivia up the walk, taking it slow and giving her the time she required to absorb the details. The urge to ask if anything looked familiar nudged him but he kept the question to himself. She would tell him when she was ready.

They climbed the steps and crossed the wide porch. A sign warning that solicitors were unwelcome hung next to the door. Olivia glanced at him one last time before opening the screen door and knocking. The quiet inside suggested no one was home, but no sooner had the assessment formed than the knob turned and the door opened a few inches. He removed his wallet from his hip pocket just in case the woman of the house demanded official ID.

"You didn't see the sign?" the woman asked. She looked to be early sixties. Her gray hair was bundled atop her head and pink-rimmed glasses magnified her eyes, making them appear too large for her face.

"Ma'am, we're not selling anything. My name is Russell St. James." He showed her his ID. "I'm investigating a criminal case and I'd like to ask you a few questions if you don't mind."

The woman looked from him to Olivia. When she would have shifted her attention back to Russ, her gaze swung back to Olivia. "Do I know you?"

"My name is Olivia Westfield...." Olivia took a breath. "Barker. Olivia Barker. I lived in Granger as a child. You knew my parents, Clare and Rafe."

For two beats the woman stared in disbelief at Olivia then she promptly closed the door.

Not exactly the reception he'd hoped for. Russ raised his fist to knock but Olivia stopped him.

"Give me a few minutes," she urged. "Wait in the car and just...give me a few minutes."

He'd have a clear view of her so there was no reason not to

do as she asked. If he powered down the windows he could likely hear the conversation. "All right."

Olivia waited until Russ had climbed behind the steering wheel before she knocked again. "Mrs. Samson, I know this is startling but I need your help." Silence. "Please. I really, really need someone I can talk to." Olivia knocked again. "Please, Mrs. Samson, there's no one else. I really need your help."

The knob twisted and the door opened a few inches once more. "You and your sisters are supposed to be dead. Like the others. You show up here like a ghost and you expect me to just say come on in?"

That part was likely more shocking than merely startling to the poor woman. Olivia should have been more diplomatic.

"Yes, ma'am. I know. It was a shock to me, too. I had no idea that I was Olivia Barker until two weeks ago. My adoptive parents never told me. When I found out I was adopted, I launched a search for my biological parents. Imagine my shock when I discovered I was supposed to be dead."

The door opened a little wider. "I heard about your mama's release. You seen her yet?"

Olivia shook her head. "Not yet." She blinked at the burn in her eyes. Her emotions were getting the better of her. "Please, Mrs. Samson, I've come all this way and I'm finding nothing but dead ends. Will you please help me?"

"That your husband? I know you young women don't always take your man's name."

Funny, but Olivia wasn't taken aback by the suggestion of a husband. Russ was a nice guy. He would make a good husband for anyone looking for a mate. But Olivia wasn't in that market. Her personal life was far too screwed up to venture into relationship territory. Not that she'd ever had any luck there, anyway.

"He's a friend who's helping me sort this out." Olivia

glanced at the SUV where he waited. "May we come in and ask you some questions?"

"As long as he's not a reporter, I guess it'd be all right."

Olivia motioned for Russ to join them. "Have you been harassed by reporters about the case?"

"Not recently but back then…" She shook her head, sadness in her eyes. "It was awful around here for months. They were like vultures circling a rotting carcass."

When Russ was at her side, Olivia followed the woman into her home. She offered refreshments but Olivia declined, as did Russ. Forcing anything past the lump in her throat right now would be impossible.

When they were settled in her small living room, Mrs. Samson asked, "What do you want to know? I'm not sure I saw or heard anything that will satisfy you but I'll tell you what I remember."

"You lived here when the Barkers moved to town?" Olivia decided to start at the very beginning.

Mrs. Samson nodded. "They bought that old run-down farm years before you were born. Most folks around here had 'em figured for being a card shy of a full deck, if you know what I mean. It needed a lot of work. But in no time flat they had the old house dolled up and the barn turned into a clinic for animals. Everybody who got to know them liked them both immediately. They were that kind of folks. Kind, generous. We hadn't had a vet in this area before and it beat driving an hour to visit one in Austin. My old collie got sick and that's when I first met them. Your daddy had a knack with animals. Your mama was quieter. She mostly lurked in his shadow, but she eventually opened up around me when we ended up expecting at the same time."

"Mrs. Samson," Russ spoke then, "did the Barkers ever mention any relatives coming for a visit? Or did you ever see anyone else who might have been extended family? What we've been told so far is that they stayed mostly to themselves."

"They didn't bother with friends if that's what you mean. Being the only vet for an hour in any direction kept them pretty busy. And then the three of you," she said to Olivia, "came along. They were always busy. Your mama brought you to church most Sundays, but that's about it. If they had any relatives they never talked about them and none...ever visited. That I know of."

"You said the two of you got to know each other," Olivia reminded her. Her nerves were jumping with anticipation, particularly at her stumbling over the last part of her answer. She knew something more than she was sharing. Gaining her trust would take more time, which they didn't have. Olivia would have to go for persuasion and outmaneuvering. It was amazing what people would say when guided in just the right direction.

"As best anyone knew either of them, I suppose." The older woman frowned. "Clare seemed happy at first but things changed somehow those last few months before their arrests. They both changed. Became more withdrawn. Sort of antisocial."

"Surely," Olivia ventured, "having known them so long, you had your suspicions as to why they changed."

The lady stared at her hands a moment. "It started after... that other blonde showed up." She clasped and unclasped her hands as if the subject made her nervous. "But I didn't get the impression she was your mama's friend or a relative of any sort. Truth is, I only saw her a couple of times and then from a distance."

Olivia exchanged a look with Russ, and adrenaline burned through her veins. "What other blonde?"

"A woman. Looked a lot like Clare, maybe a little older. You might have thought she was Clare if you didn't pay close attention. I asked her about the woman once but she changed the subject. I mentioned it to the police after Clare and Rafe were arrested but they seemed to think I didn't know what I was talking about. Guess it was nothing. Considering what the two of them did, anyway."

"Ma'am, could the blonde woman have been Clare's cousin or sister? Maybe an aunt?" Russ ventured. Olivia understood that he was holding back. Putting words in the woman's mouth wouldn't help them find the truth.

"That was what I thought," Mrs. Samson explained. "Course I never saw the woman up close. The shape of the face was the same. Hair color was the same. About the same height and size as Clare. But Clare wouldn't talk about it so I figured it was one of those things best left alone."

Olivia struggled to control the trembling now rampant in her body. "You thought her presence was wrong somehow is that what you're saying?"

Her eyebrows reared up. "What else was I supposed to think? They'd started keeping to themselves as it was. After that woman showed up, I hardly saw Clare at all. There was never time for you and my Josie to play. It was very difficult for my daughter. Then after the news broke, I was thankful I hadn't let her go over there anymore."

"Your daughter visited the Barker home?" Russ asked for clarification.

Olivia held her breath.

"She played over there on numerous occasions." The woman kept her gaze on Russ as she spoke, carefully avoiding eye contact with Olivia. "The last time I took her over there, that's when I saw that other woman. The place was a mess. Not clean and neat like your mama usually kept it. Smelled bad, too. Like alcohol and cigarette smoke. Josie never went again and your mama never let you girls out of her sight even for a visit with me." Mrs. Samson shook her head sadly. "My Josie suffered terrible nightmares after we discovered what had been happening over there. She won't discuss that time in her life to this day."

"Did she ever mention seeing or hearing anything that made her feel uncomfortable or frightened?" Russ pressed.

Olivia was holding her breath again, leaning forward slightly in anticipation of the answer.

Mrs. Samson cleared her throat. "You understand that I don't want my daughter involved in whatever is going on with that tragedy. This whole community suffered enough." She turned to Olivia then. "I truly do sympathize with your need for answers but if you pursue my daughter I will deny everything I've just told you."

"You have my word," Olivia assured her. "No one will ever know that any of what we discuss here came from you."

"Josie said you showed her the bedroom closet and explained that you and your sisters hid there when the bad things were happening." She clasped her fidgeting hands in her lap. "You showed her how your mother would pray for the bad things to stop. Your screaming and ranting, when you were mimicking her prayers, scared Josie and she didn't want to go back for a long time after that visit. But Clare took that decision out of our hands when she totally withdrew from everyone and everything."

Olivia's heart thudded so hard against her sternum she felt certain it would burst. "I…" She wet her lips. "I can't remember anything. I don't remember Josie."

For a moment Mrs. Samson sat very still just staring at Olivia, then she got up and crossed the room. She removed a photo album from a shelf and returned, but this time she sat down on the sofa next to Olivia. When she found the page in the album she was looking for, she reached beneath a photo and pulled out one that was hidden. She handed it to Olivia.

"I took that the last time the two of you played together.

It was just a few months before the arrests. You may keep it. Maybe it'll help you remember. I'm sorry I can't be of more help. Whatever went on in that house, Rafe and Clare kept their secrets from us all. Made the whole town feel guilty for not knowing what was going on over there."

Russ thanked Mrs. Samson as they moved toward the door. Olivia hugged her and thanked her, as well, but the movements and words were by rote. She felt numb, mechanical. Deeply disturbed. The little girl in the photo, Josie, with the fiery red hair, was a total stranger. Olivia had no recall of her whatsoever, yet they stood side by side, arms looped over each other's shoulders. How could she not remember?

In the SUV, her fingers felt like ice as she slid the buckle of her seat belt into place. Russ backed out of the driveway and rolled away from the house and the woman Olivia could not remember. They drove through the town that she had no memory of seeing prior to her recent visit with the police here.

It was all gone. Vanished. Blocked away as if it never happened. But it had happened. Her parents, one or both, had brutally murdered more than a dozen young girls. She and her sisters had been in the house when those tragic events occurred and she recalled nothing but the darkness...the screaming and some vague humming.

"Take me to the house." She had driven by it the last time but she hadn't possessed the nerve to stop, much less get out.

"It may be sealed as a crime scene after what happened there this past weekend."

Laney/Lisa, her younger sister, had come there to find her son, who Clare and Weeden had taken. There had been a shootout and a Colby Agency investigator had been shot. She'd seen some fleeting mention of the shooting on the news but it hadn't been in the major papers. Russ had told her about it, giving her details the news had not.

"I don't care. I need to see that closet."

He didn't protest further. He drove. Olivia closed her eyes, unable to deal with any more visual stimulation. And she needed to think. Who was the blonde Mrs. Samson had seen? Could she have been Janet Tolliver, Clare's sister? If there had been another woman at the house besides her mother, wouldn't she remember that? Why had this news not triggered anything new? Why couldn't Olivia remember her one friend, Josie? Or her friend's mother, Mrs. Samson? She rubbed her thumb across the images in the photograph she held but couldn't bring herself to open her eyes and look at the smiling faces, the seemingly happy faces. But she hadn't been happy. A happy child remembered her childhood.

Olivia wasn't sure how many minutes passed. One or ten, the time ran together in one clump of misery. When he braked to a stop and shut off the engine she opened her eyes. The big old house loomed before her, its white siding grayed with age and neglect. The house sat a good distance off the road, bordered on either side by massive trees that shaded its rusting tin roof. Beyond the house she could barely see a portion of another roof, its shape barnlike. The clinic.

The sound of his door opening prodded her from the uncertainty paralyzing her. She opened her door and climbed out. The ankle-deep grass rushed across the yard and surrounded the house with its crippled porch that leaned to one side. Most of the windows had been partially boarded up, giving an even creepier feel to the place. The air was still and silent as if it too waited for her next move.

So much tragedy had happened here. It was a miracle the stench of evil didn't linger in the air. She walked toward the porch, dragging the thick, humid air into her lungs. On the porch the floorboards creaked as she followed Russ to the door.

"We should check the back door. Entering from the rear will give us cover from anyone passing by."

She nodded in agreement. His words didn't really penetrate. She was drinking in the details. Abandoned birds' nests and cobwebs decorated the sagging porch ceiling. The posts and rails were in bad need of repair and no longer provided the intended structural integrity.

As they moved around the rear corner of the house, Olivia stalled. An old swing set waited beneath one of the ancient trees. The colors were faded and rust had overtaken parts but it seemed familiar. Laughter whispered through her mind. They had played here, she and her sisters.

The barn-turned-clinic sat several yards back from the house. In between was a rock-skirted well. The old-fashioned sort with a rusty, banged-up bucket and a frayed rope. An old crank handle remained where someone had left it the last time water had been drawn.

Another massive tree had grown up against the house as if it had been small when the house had been built and no one had noticed it taking over. Limbs pressed against the siding. The sound those limbs would make when the wind blew scraped across her mind. The sound had terrified them as kids. An abrupt Texas summer storm would have it rubbing and clawing at the house as if it were intent on getting inside.

His weapon in hand, Russ led the way across a screened-in back porch and into the house through the rear entrance. So far they had seen no sign of the house being sealed as a crime scene. The once boarded up door stood ajar as if no one cared who entered.

Inside there were more cobwebs and dust covered most every surface, including the worn linoleum floor. The table had been wiped free of dust and the remains of sandwiches that would soon be moldy lay on paper plates. A chest-type cooler sat on the floor. Clare and Weeden had been here for more than a simple visit. Apparently they'd been hoping to use the place as a hideout.

"Stay behind me," Russ instructed as he moved forward into the darker interior.

A flashlight switched on. She hadn't realized he'd brought one along. Between the musty smell and the creeps this place was giving her, she was glad at least one of them was thinking clearly. The utter silence was spine chilling. She hugged herself and stayed as close to him as possible.

The hallway from the kitchen led to the front door. Off the hall as they neared the front door were two large rooms, one on either side. The stairs to the second floor looked less than reliable even in the dim lighting.

Russ moved carefully up the stairs, checking each tread as he went. At the top of the stairs was a bathroom. To the right was a single door. Her parents' room. She didn't have to go inside; the certainty was palpable. The sensations of betrayal and deception were nearly overwhelming. She did not want to go in there. To the left were two more doors. One that led to a room on the back side of the house and one that opened to a room on the front.

The room on the front was just a bedroom. A single bed and a bureau. She hesitated before moving back into the hall. For a long moment she stood at what she assumed was a closet door. Her hand shaking, she reached out and opened it. Inside were ropes and chains. Twisted articles of clothing. She closed the door. Didn't want to analyze what that meant.

Down the hall was the final room, the one that backed up to the big tree. She opened the door and sensations and images assaulted her senses. The room was pink. There was one full-size bed, a dresser and toys scattered across the wood floor. Olivia could hear the tree branches rubbing the house…she could smell the scents of the baby shampoo her mother had used to wash their hair and the soap she'd used on their skin.

The bubbles and the splashing water as they bathed together felt as warm and real as if it were happening at that very moment. She could see the images as plainly as if she were watching a movie. Clare would laugh with them, scrub their shivering bodies with a big fluffy white towel. Then she'd dress them in matching pajamas and usher them off to bed.

They would play and giggle beneath the covers until they fell asleep…only to be awakened hours later by the screaming.

Olivia turned to the closet. Their hiding place. The secret place that protected them from the monster. She walked across the room and reached for the knob. Her hand shook.

Russ was suddenly beside her, his hand on the small of her back. "I'm right here," he murmured.

She had never in her life been more relieved to have backup. "Thank you."

Olivia opened the door and Russ ran the flashlight over the small space. Bead board walls and ceiling, like the rest of the house. Cobwebs and dust covered every surface. It was so much smaller than she remembered…cramped.

She turned to Russ. "I need to do something." She moistened her lips and grappled for the courage. "Stay right here, please." The notion of being left alone in this place was abruptly terrifying.

"I'm not going anywhere," he promised.

Olivia stepped inside the closet and pulled the door closed. Total darkness consumed her. She shut her eyes and inhaled deeply. This had been their safe place. The monster couldn't touch them here. It had seemed so big as a child…like a room, but it was nothing more than a closet. A tiny closet where three children had cowered from the danger.

The whoosh of fear came out of nowhere. Suddenly Olivia was five again and her sisters were huddled against her sobbing softly, their little bodies shivering with fear. She couldn't block the screaming…the words of supplication that she now recognized as fervent prayer. The blackness started to spin and spin and spin. Olivia couldn't catch her breath.

She would see the blood when she opened the door. It was always there.... She saw it every time in her dreams. She didn't want to open the door. Didn't want to see the blood. But if doing this would trigger more memories, she had no choice.

Her hand shaking, she reached out and twisted the knob. The latch snapped, the door creaked open and her mother smiled at her. She was wearing a pink dress with little white flowers. Her hair was long and blond, her feet were bare. She looked young and pretty, the way she had when Olivia was five.

"Don't worry, baby, it's okay now."

Olivia's gaze lowered, followed as her mother got down on her hands and knees on the floor. There was a bucket of sudsy, steaming water. Her mother reached into the bucket and pulled out a scrub brush and started rubbing at the blood pooled on the scarred wood floor.

"It was just an accident, baby, don't be afraid."

The room started to spin harder and faster and then it went black.

Chapter Twelve

Russ caught Olivia before she crumpled to the floor. The flashlight bounced and rolled, sending its beam of light circling around the dimly lit room.

"I've got you." He gathered her into his arms, but she stirred and started to struggle. "You're okay, Olivia. We're getting out of here."

Olivia stopped struggling and rested her head against his shoulder. He glanced at the flashlight but decided it wasn't worth the trouble.

He angled and sidled out the door of the bedroom she and her sisters had shared long ago, then he moved more quickly down the hall. The stairs he took more slowly since, under their combined weight, the treads gave a little more than he would have liked. By the time they reached the kitchen he was mentally cursing himself for bringing her here. The dampness of her tears on his neck made him want to drive to the prison and beat the hell out of her monster of a father.

A deep breath wasn't possible until they were safely outside in the fading sunlight. There were still a couple of good hours of daylight left but he had no desire to hang around here a minute longer. Olivia had had enough for one day.

She lifted her head and swiped at her eyes. "I'm fine now."

He settled her onto her feet and she swayed. "You sure

about that?" She looked about as fine as a rosebush after a hailstorm. Shaky, torn and frazzled.

After a deep breath, she nodded. "My mother was cleaning up blood from the floor and she kept telling me it was just an accident and for me not to be afraid." She pressed her hand to her stomach. "The things that happened here..." She stared up at the old house. "I can't remember specific events but even in my five-year-old mind I recognized it was bad... really bad."

She hugged her arms around her middle and turned away. "My mother might not have killed any of those little girls but she cleaned up the mess at the very least. She enabled him and this—this house of horrors."

"You can't be sure of those snippets of memory," he reminded her gently. No matter whether she said it out loud or not, some part of her needed to believe that one or the other of her biological parents was inherently good. No child wanted to feel they'd come from pure evil, and that little five-year-old girl who still lived deep inside Olivia didn't want to, either.

"I'm sure enough," she argued. "I'm certain of something else, too." She fixed a determined gaze on him. "I want to see the place where they found the bodies."

That really was a bad idea. Before he could stop her she was already marching toward the woods. "Don't put yourself through that, Olivia. It won't change anything." It was possible she could remember more but was it worth the torture? Would it change the facts and how those facts impacted her heart and her life?

She whipped around and glared at him. "I don't know why they didn't burn this place down." She shifted her furious look to the house. "It shouldn't still be standing. That's what I know for an absolute certainty."

"The families of several of the victims bought the place

and closed it up so they could ensure no one ever lived here again. Not in this house or one that was built in its place."

"What was the point in that?" She flung her arms upward in frustration. "It's here. A tragic monument to murder. Can't they see that?"

Russ couldn't pretend to know how those families felt so he offered what he could. "Maybe they believe that some part of their children's spirits will forever be attached to this place. Maybe they can't bear the idea of burning down that possibility. This was the last place they were alive. Maybe the survivors need that connection. Or maybe they just hope some kind of answers will eventually be found here about the remains still unaccounted for."

Olivia shook her head and turned to the woods. She was determined to go in there and see what she could find. He didn't try to stop her; the attempt would be futile. Keeping an eye out for trouble, he followed. It was his job to keep her safe but she wasn't making it easy.

The canopy overhead was thick enough to block a good portion of the sun. A few streaks of daylight managed to filter through the mass of trees. The former gravesites were located only a couple hundred yards from the clinic, directly behind the house. But twenty years of underbrush and saplings had obscured them. He felt fairly certain she wouldn't find what she was looking for but she needed to see that for herself.

She wound through the trees, plowing through the brush as if her life depended on accomplishing her goal. Emotion was driving her and nothing he said or did would make this right. As the oldest, the past was a far greater burden for Olivia. Her sisters had accepted what they could not change and appeared to be moving on. The task would be far more difficult for the oldest. She felt a sense of responsibility that wouldn't be shaken quite so easily.

As much as Russ wanted to be sensitive to that, lingering

in the woods this way made keeping her safe far more difficult for him and her safety needed to be priority one just now. As vigilant as his surveillance, there were too many hiding places for trouble out here for his liking.

"Come on, Olivia, too much time has passed. You're not going to find what you're looking for and we need to be on our way before dark."

She turned on him, directing her frustration and her anger his way. "You don't understand how this feels." She started forward once more. "I need to do—" She stumbled, went down face-first.

He cut through the brush and was at her side before she could drag up onto her hands and knees. "We should go now. You've put yourself through enough for today. We'll come back early in the morning if you still feel this is necessary."

Ignoring him completely, she swept the leaves away from the ground in front of her. "I think I found something."

A flat stone, partially buried in the earth, had a kneeling angel carved into its surface. He hadn't read anything about the grave sites having been marked. Maybe one or more of the families had done this later. All the remains found had, of course, been removed and claimed by the families for proper burial. But this place was where their children's remains had rested for months and years.

The reality had his gut churning. All that time those girls were missing, their families and the police searching and searching, hoping against hope they were still alive. And they were right here…in a monster's backyard.

Olivia sat back on her heels. "Oh, my God. This is it." She scanned the woods around her. "The remains were discovered in unmarked graves very close together." She gestured to the area in front of her. "See how there aren't any big trees, just smaller ones? This is it."

On their hands and knees, they prowled through the brush,

feeling for more of the stones. "Found one," he called out to her. Their gazes met across the small span and his heart lurched. Her face looked so pale. Her heart was breaking for the young girls who had been buried here, their lives cut short by an evil bastard.

The evil bastard who was Olivia's father.

It was almost dark by the time they found the last one. Olivia's hands and knees were covered in dirt. The skirt she'd bought last night was ruined and dotted with decaying leaves but she didn't care.

Eight stones for eight little angels who had once rested here.

At some point in the past two decades the families had stopped coming and to this unholy place. They'd been forced to move on. Their daughters were gone and coming back here wasn't going to give them the answers they sought.

Whatever she found, Olivia wondered if it would give her any peace.

She stood and brushed off her skirt and attempted to do the same to her knees. Not happening. The dirt might very well be hiding the fact that both knees were skinned from scrubbing around on the ground.

She should be more like her sisters and dress in jeans more often, she thought. Her hands paused in their work. Had her sisters come here and looked at this place? Laney had come to find her son, but had she taken a long, hard look? Had they studied the sickening details of this rotting monument to their painful history? If they hadn't maybe it was better for them. If they remembered nothing at all about this place and that time they were far better off in Olivia's opinion.

There was nothing here worth remembering.

Russ walked over to her and reached for her hand. His were as filthy as her own but their strength and warmth felt good to hold onto. The knees of his jeans would never be the same. His black shirt hadn't handled the abuse well, either. He'd left the Stetson in the SUV, which had probably saved it from a similar fate.

"I'm taking you out of here even if I have to throw you over my shoulder and carry you."

He meant what he said, too. Her eyes had long ago adjusted to the scant and sporadic sprinkling of light, allowing her to see his expression. "You won't get any argument out of me this time." She was beat. As crazy as it sounded, she felt as if she actually had accomplished something important. She had acknowledged those who'd lost their lives here and she'd needed to do that. She'd needed to feel the dirt between her fingers and to know that despite the insanity of this hellacious place she had survived. Whatever the truth was, she owed it to those who had not survived to find it and reveal it to the world.

He tightened his fingers on hers. "Let's go. It'll be dark soon. We've pressed our luck already."

With him leading, she hung on to that big strong hand of his and lamented her foolish fetish for high heels. Not that she'd exactly planned things this way. The decision to search for those former grave sites had been her going with her heart instead of her brain for the first time in a really long time.

Once they reached the yard she realized how late it actually was. The sun had dipped low in the sky and a crisp breeze had kicked up. Limbs of the old tree at the back of the house were swiping back and forth against the neglected siding, making the sound she knew so well from her dreams. She hadn't precisely known what the sound was until she came here today and saw the tree. Many things about her dreams had cleared in her mind.

But she was no closer to the truth than she had been yesterday. She drew Russ to a stop midway across the backyard. When his full attention rested on her, she asked the question she'd set aside to come here. "Do you think the other woman Mrs. Samson thought she saw was Janet Tolliver?"

"That was my thinking," he offered. "We don't have any photos of Janet when she was young. If the agency had suspected who she was immediately after her murder, we might have been able to get a photo from her great-niece. The house she lived in has been packed up and everything moved to storage so it won't be so easy now. I sent an update to Simon via text. He's going to contact the niece and see if she can help us."

"Could she have been hiding out here? Involved in the murders? Why wouldn't Clare or Rafe mention that at trial?" Of course, Rafe hadn't said a word but Clare had said plenty. Never once had she mentioned another female presence in the house. Olivia had read a copy of the trial transcript and there was nothing there about another woman, blonde or otherwise.

"We may never know. There's always the chance that Mrs. Samson was mistaken."

"Do you think we should go against Mrs. Samson's wishes and contact her daughter?" Olivia didn't want to hurt the woman or her daughter but this was too important to ignore what had been swept under the rug.

"I think we should do whatever we have to do."

Olivia's chest welled with gratitude. As much as she respected her boss, he was a good boss and a friend. But he felt Olivia's digging into all this was a mistake. Having this man on her side meant a great deal. "Thank you."

Confusion lined his face. "What for?"

"Supporting me as well as playing the part of protector. And if," she said before he could respond, "you say it's your job I might just punch you." He had a smudge of dirt on his jaw. His blond hair was tousled. As ridiculous as it sounded, he looked good all messy and unpolished.

"I won't pretend to know how difficult this is," he said in

the gentle voice that was so unexpected from a big cocky-looking cowboy like him. "But I know when a person needs a real friend. Today, you needed a friend. In addition to a bodyguard." That prized grin spread over his face.

She reached up hesitantly. "You have dirt...right here." She wiped it away with the pad of her thumb. "There."

For a long time he stared straight into her eyes. And for the first time in too long to recall she wished for more. Most of the time when she got those stares of longing she just turned away. But not this time. This time she wanted him to look his fill and then she wanted him to kiss her. To put those powerful arms around her and hold her tight the way he had when he'd carried her out of that awful room.

"What I want to do right now is definitely not part of my job," he said softly.

"I'm sure it's after five o'clock." She moistened her lips. That he watched the move so intently had her heart racing. "Even a bodyguard has to have a break."

His arms went around her and his mouth crushed onto hers. She didn't have time to catch her breath but she didn't care. She wanted to feel something real. Something warm and alive. She wanted to feel him holding her this way, his mouth devouring hers with the same intensity she'd seen in his eyes.

When he at last drew his lips from hers, resting his forehead against hers, he whispered, "I'm going to need a lot longer than a quick break to do this right." He inhaled a heavy breath. "And unfortunately now is not a good time to be that distracted."

The way his hands cupped her bottom, keeping her pelvis pressed solidly against his warned that he wasn't happy about the choice but it was the right one to make. The contact also revealed that he wanted a whole lot more than just a kiss. Anticipation swelled inside her.

She licked the taste of him from her lips, couldn't help herself. "As soon as this is done, I expect you to make good on the implication your hips are making, Mr. St. James."

"Count on it."

He dragged his arms free of her body, maintaining the intimate contact for as long as possible before turning to head to the SUV. That he held on to her hand did strange things to her pulse rate.

As they neared his SUV, he stalled. "What the hell?"

Olivia leaned around him and tried to determine the problem. Her gaze latched onto the front tires. She gasped. Both were flat. They walked around the SUV. The rear tires were flat, as well. He crouched down to inspect first one, then the next on the driver's side.

"Someone isn't happy to see us."

"Slashed?" That was her first thought.

He stood, gave her a nod as he withdrew his weapon and took a long look around. "I'll put in a call to my motor club and see if they can get someone out here ASAP."

Ice filling her veins, Olivia turned back to the house. She sure hoped so. Staying here after nightfall was not something she could do. She hugged her arms around herself in an effort to block the cool breeze. Out here in the middle of nowhere it might take some time to get roadside service. Her fingers tightened into fists. Who would do this? Could have been Tony Weeden, maybe. He and Clare could be lurking about. Olivia surveyed the property and then the woods and pastures that bordered the road for as far as the eye could see. They could be watching and waiting for the cover of darkness.

"You think whoever did this is still out there somewhere?" She shuddered. Russ was with her and he had a weapon.

"Maybe." He surveyed the area again. "Depends on if it was Weeden or just some local who wants us to know he isn't happy we're here. One thing you can count on, if whoever did this had wanted to do either of us harm he had the perfect opportunity while we were in the woods. Chances are he did this and got the hell out of here."

Olivia stayed close to him as he made the necessary call. If anyone was watching them they were hidden in the woods. The road was deserted in both directions. Another of those creeping shivers rushed over her skin.

"They can have someone here in an hour," he announced, drawing her from the troubling thoughts. "Give me a minute to check it out and if I don't find any hidden explosives or other anomalies, we'll load up and have some of those snacks and bottled water I have tucked in my backpack while we wait."

Her stomach responded to the suggestion. She hadn't thought of food in hours. "I hope you have potato chips."

"Never leave home without them."

Her lips curved into a smile. How he did that under the circumstances was beyond her. He spent a good long while examining the undercarriage of the vehicle, then beneath the hood. He'd scrounged up another flashlight from beneath the front seat. While he checked the SUV, she kept an eye out for any movement.

When he was satisfied that it was safe, he unlocked the SUV and opened her door. While she made herself comfortable, he opened the door behind her and rummaged through his backpack.

"Just what the lady ordered." He passed her a bottle of water and a bag of chips.

When he'd rounded the hood and climbed behind the wheel, she asked, "Do you think someone followed us here?"

"Don't think so. I kept an eye on the traffic behind us as we neared Granger. No one followed us from the Samson home. My guess is she called someone and mentioned that we were here."

"Someone like a family member of one of the victims?"

She downed a gulp of water to chase the salty chips. "Or someone like a local cop?" Her money was on the cop. The two she'd attempted to interview had let her know in no uncertain terms that they were not happy with her digging.

"Hard to say. Slashed tires are far less troubling than having automobile parts end up all over the yard."

She could vouch for that. "But how would anyone, even the police, know we were here unless they got a call? Mrs. Samson is the only person who knew we were in town."

He reached into his pocket and retrieved his ringing cell. A glance at the screen and he said, "It's Simon."

Olivia found herself holding her breath as she listened to his side of the conversation. Didn't sound like the kind of news he'd wanted to hear. His voice had turned somber. His profile looked grim.

He ended the call and placed his phone on the console. "We're about to have company."

"The police?" How she made that leap based on a call from the Colby Agency, which was in Houston, she would never know.

"Not yet, but they'll be next. Someone leaked to the press that you're here. As in *here*. Several stations from surrounding areas are en route. And we're stranded."

Olivia stared at the house. She would not go back in there. "How do you know the police will be here next?" The salty taste of the chips turned sour on her tongue.

"The petition for the stay of execution just hit the wire. Word is spreading like wildfire. The local cops will feel compelled to intervene in the event that reporters aren't the only folks who show up out here before roadside assistance arrives."

"You mean like protesters?" That was a strong possibility if her presence was known.

"Yep. And irate family members of the victims." He

showed her the depth of his concern with his eyes. "Some won't take this well. You need to be braced for that."

For two weeks she had been certain she was braced for anything. Now she wasn't so sure.

Chapter Thirteen

8:45 p.m.

"She's on the news."

Clare roused from the doze she had slipped into. She sat up on the side of the bed. "What did you say?" She and Tony had driven back to Houston, since fading into the background in a large city was far easier than in a small town. There were many more cheap motels to choose from, as well. No one asked questions in places like this.

"Olivia is on the news." Tony gestured to the television set. "She and the man from the Colby Agency."

Clare peered at the dim screen. The reception was quite terrible, leaving the images snowy and wavy. But he was right. It was Olivia. Her heart leaped. Her oldest.

The breath trapped in her lungs and twisted like a corkscrew. "She's at the house." She leaned closer still to the fuzzy images. "The police are there." Blue lights flashed against the night. "Do you suppose something has happened?"

"Listen and we'll find out," he snapped.

Tony had been very irritable this evening. She supposed his shoulder ached. But that was no reason to ignore her the way he had and then jump down her throat the first chance he got.

He'd been very withdrawn since the shooting. It was as if he blamed her. She hadn't told him to hurt anyone. If he hadn't shot at that man watching over Lisa—Laney, she called her-self now—none of this would have happened. Maybe Clare could have spoken to her daughter and explained how they had rescued Buddy. But as it was Clare hadn't gotten the chance and she'd been terrified that Laney or her precious little boy would be hurt.

She dismissed the disturbing thoughts and paid attention to the reporter. Someone had damaged the vehicle Olivia and the man were driving. The police were there to protect them from further trouble, according to the reporter.

Then the woman launched into the breaking news that her station had learned that all three of the Barker girls were alive. The eldest, Olivia, had petitioned the courts for a stay of execution on her father's behalf.

The rest of the reporter's words were lost on Clare. How could Olivia be so foolish? Rafe should die! He should burn in hell for all eternity! Who had filled her head with such nonsense?

The Colby Agency. Olivia had only done this foolish thing after becoming involved with them. The Colby Agency was keeping Laney and Sadie out of Clare's reach.

She had to do something. Wilting onto the side of the bed, she twisted her fingers together to stop their shaking. How could she talk to her daughters if they were being kept from her? *He* had summoned the aid of this Colby Agency. He did not want her to succeed in bringing her girls together as a family again.

"You see what she's done?"

Clare jerked from her troubling thoughts. Tony was staring at her, his eyes wild with fury. "She's under the influence of that Colby Agency," Clare argued. "She's confused, that's all."

"She wants to hurt you," Tony challenged. "I'm the only one who really cares about you. Don't you see that?"

He had suggested that same nonsense after that man had

shot him. Clare didn't like when he talked that way. "I think we've gone about this all wrong. I should have called each one as soon as I was released from prison and told them the truth."

"How could you?" he mocked. "You didn't even know where they were until I beat it out of that old bitch."

He was right. Clare's hopes fell. Janet had tried to keep the truth from her. If not for Tony she would have had no idea where to look. As soon as she was released he had found Clare. He had known her release was imminent and he had made numerous arrangements. She had scarcely thanked him. How could she be frustrated with him now? He was only trying to protect her. He had told her over and over that none of the trouble in Beaumont had been his fault. Hadn't he gotten her away from that man who had been watching her in Copperas Cove? That Lucas Camp from the Colby Agency. Yes, her boy had helped her tremendously.

He had risked much to help her. He had given up his job and done whatever she needed. He'd had no control over the turn of events in Beaumont when Laney's child had been taken by his no-good father. Tony had rescued the boy.

Then that awful Colby Agency man had tried to cause trouble by interfering. No one would have been hurt if not for him. Tony was right. He had been protecting her. Rafe had hired the Colby Agency. They were on his side, which meant they were against Clare.

No one was ever going to believe the truth. She had no way to prove what really happened. Rafe had turned their home into hell. He and that whore sister of hers.

Rafe would take the truth to hell with him and Janet was already in hell. Perhaps if Tony had been more careful, Janet would still be alive and Clare could get the truth out of her. But he'd had to stop her interference. Janet had intended to warn the girls and threatened to make sure they never spoke to their mother. She would have, too. She would have done anything to ensure Rafe got what he wanted.

She had turned him into the monster he became. Her and her sexual deviance.

Clare wished she had ended her evil existence a long time ago. Before she ruined everything.

It was too late for that now. Clare had to focus on the future. She had nothing to take to her daughters in the way of proof of what she knew. Somehow she had hoped they would remember certain things. Particularly Olivia. She was the oldest and should have remembered something.

But she hadn't so far; otherwise she would not be taking her father's side. Perhaps her memories were blocked... buried. Too painful to look at. But she wanted to remember or she wouldn't have gone to the house in Granger.

She had to be searching for the truth whether she was conscious of it or not.

Clare had read a little about memory triggers. Smells often helped with recalling people and events. Sounds did, as well.

Hope bloomed in her chest and a smile lifted her lips. There might be hope. If only she had thought of this before.

"I want to go back to the house," she announced.

Tony glared at her as if she had lost her mind. "We can't go back there."

She stood, squared her shoulders. "We can and we will. There's something in the house I have to find."

He growled. "I hope it's worth going back to prison for."

He had no idea, but it was worth anything and everything. It might very well be her only chance.

Chapter Fourteen

The Boxcar Motel, Granger, 11:00 p.m.

Russ clicked off the television and paced the small room. His SUV wouldn't be ready until morning. Simon had ensured a rented sedan was delivered to the motel but it was too late to head back to Houston by the time it arrived. Russ didn't like the idea of staying the night in Granger, but it was the most reasonable option.

Tomorrow he was getting Olivia out of here. She'd put on a brave face throughout the ordeal of being bombarded by the reporters. The two police officers who had arrived to make the report had been less than sympathetic because Russ and Olivia had been trespassing. Russ had kept the part about going inside the house out of their statements. Spending the night in lockup for breaking and entering was about as appealing as going head to head with another flock of reporters. The investigating officers hadn't bothered to go beyond the first floor inside the house. Russ would have had a heck of a time explaining the flashlight he'd dropped in that bedroom.

To her credit, Olivia had fielded their questions with strong, noncommittal responses. She hadn't denied having a hand in the petition for Barker's stay of execution but she hadn't confirmed it, either. She'd explained with strength and conviction that she had only just learned she was, in fact, Olivia Barker. Her legal persona had taken over despite the circumstances and their state of dishevelment.

But this was only the beginning. As the news spread, all three women would be hunted down and revealed as the long-lost Barker children. There was no stopping this frenzy. Lyle McCaleb and Joel Hayden were on high alert for the wave to hit them by noon tomorrow. The Colby Agency would be bombarded with calls and protesters. This was going to get ugly.

Russ and Olivia were out in the open, where anyone could reach them. He held the curtain aside and checked the parking lot again. The only available parking was in the front, facing the street. He'd tucked the rental next door behind the pharmacy, which prevented it from being visible from the street. Problem was, this was the only motel in town and anyone looking for Olivia would start here. If they were lucky, most would assume they had left Granger.

Simon had no news on Clare and Weeden. No vehicles had been reported stolen from the area where the abandoned sedan they'd left behind had been found. No one matching their descriptions had taken public transportation or rented a vehicle from any agencies requiring ID. Depending on the funds readily available it was possible Weeden had purchased a used vehicle from an individual. The transaction wouldn't show up in the usual places so long as Weeden didn't attempt to register the vehicle and he wouldn't. With the news of Olivia's presence in Granger all over the airwaves, Weeden and Clare would be well aware of her movements.

Russ checked the weapon in his waistband and turned to consider the bathroom door. She'd announced she needed a long, hot soak as soon as they'd gotten into the room. She'd offered to let him shower first but he'd needed to confer with Simon so he'd passed.

She'd been in there a long time. As much as he didn't

want to disturb her, he needed to see that she was okay. He crossed the room and rapped on the door. "You doing all right in there?"

"I'd be doing a lot better if I were at a spa," she called out, her voice muffled by the closed door. "A good neck rubdown would be perfect right now."

He couldn't turn this into a spa but he'd been known to give a pretty damned good rubdown. His body tensed at the thought of touching her that way. Most likely it would be better if he stayed out here with that door between them. He'd already suffered a lapse in control when he'd permitted that kiss. As much as he understood allowing a personal connection to build, he couldn't regret kissing her.

"Take your time," he said, his voice sounding rusty. He cleared his throat. "Relax and those tense muscles will loosen up." Too bad he couldn't take his own advice. His whole body was rigid with tension that had everything to do with visions of her body.

He turned away from the door, proud of himself for doing the right thing, as challenging as that move was. "Good for you, pal," he muttered. This night was already going to be challenging enough with only one bed. The motel had one kind of room and those rooms had one bed. He wasn't about to let Olivia out of his sight, so sharing a room and a bed would have to work.

"Actually," she called out, "I was hoping you'd volunteer to give me a neck rub. I'm out of the tub now. Everything covered from neck to knee."

He closed his eyes. Wished she hadn't asked. The door opened and steam billowed out around him. A lungful of damp air filled his chest as the cloud dissipated and the image of Olivia, clad in only a towel, filled his eyes. Her hair was damp and clinging to her neck. Her skin was flushed from the warm soak and she looked as soft as smooth-whipped cream.

"I'm sorry." She sighed and ran her fingers through her hair. He tensed, worried or maybe hopeful that the towel would tumble to the floor. "I'm certain you want to have a shower and all I can think about is my own selfish pleasure."

"Trust me," he promised, the words sounding more like a growl, "skipping a shower to give you pleasure would not be a hardship."

Her eyes rounded as if she'd only just realized how her request sounded. "I'm sorry. I…" She shook her head. "I was about to say I didn't think of that, but the truth is that's all I thought about while I was relaxing in that steamy water."

She took the three steps that stood between them and stared up into his eyes. "I kept thinking about the way you kissed me and the idea that I've never enjoyed a kiss more. I'm certain it's the stress and the insanity circling around me right now. Desperation, too. Your kiss felt…real and fulfilling. Is that crazy or what?"

Considering he felt ready to tear off that towel and show her what true fulfillment was, he kept his mouth shut.

His silence did the trick. She stared at the well-worn carpet. "What am I doing? You're trying to do your job and I'm behaving like a teenage girl who doesn't understand the difference between physical attraction and the beginnings of a real bond between two people." She drew in a deep breath and met his eyes once more. "Forgive me, I'm not myself." She rolled her eyes. "With my track record, it's obvious I wouldn't know a real relationship if it hit me over the head with a gavel."

He couldn't let her dangle out there another second. "Relationships are complicated. I've bombed at a few myself."

"I can't even say that."

She went to the closet where he'd stowed their few belongings and rummaged through the bag from the store they'd hit last night. She pulled out a blouse and slacks and undies.

His throat went dry as he contemplated the idea that the tiny scrap of silk she held in her hand would soon be hugging that luscious bottom of hers.

"Turn around," she ordered.

Russ blinked. Tried to formulate a move based on her direction but it wasn't working.

She gave him an expectant look. "Turn around so I can get dressed. It's too humid in that bathroom. The fabric will just stick to my skin."

He turned around, his muscles screaming at the move. If he didn't get the need that she'd aroused under control soon he was going to explode.

"Guys tell me that I push them away." The sound of silk gliding across her skin whispered over his senses. "I've always thought they were just using that as an excuse to move on. But now—" the sound of a zipper skimming upward grated on his oversensitized nerves "—I wonder if maybe they were right. I think it's true. I don't know how to bond that way because of what happened when I was a child."

The closet door bumped to a close and he jumped. His brain kept assimilating images related to the sounds of her movements. He tightened his fingers into fists.

"Personally, I've always thought it was a cop-out when people blamed their issues on their childhoods. I mean, jeez, just because your mom or dad didn't show you any affection, did that mean you were destined to become an addict or serial killer?" The water came on in the sink, which was stationed outside the bathroom door. "Really, isn't our destiny our own to determine? We don't have to choose a certain path."

The swish and scrub of her brushing her teeth had him fighting the urge to turn around. Surely she was dressed by now, but she hadn't given him the okay. Should he just stand here like a statue and wonder?

More running water. More swishing and scrubbing, then

the inevitable whack of the toothbrush against the basin. "Guess I was wrong. I can see now that whatever happened in that house when I was a child has a direct correlation to my ability to trust and form bonds now. No matter how my adoptive parents tried, they couldn't erase the imprint of that horror."

She was opening up, trying to make sense of the emotional battle taking place inside her. He should be saying something. Offering his thoughts, cheering her on for coming to terms with her past…something…anything besides wishing he could strip those newly donned clothes off her and…

"There should be plenty of hot water by now." She touched his arm. He jerked, railed at himself for being so damned selfish. "You okay? You haven't said a word while I went on and on about my problems." She moved around in front of him and searched his face. "I really went off on a tangent, didn't I?" She bit her bottom lip. "Sorry about that. My boss and I carry on conversations like this all the time. It took years for me to feel comfortable having a discussion like this with him. He's probably my best friend as well as my boss. I've known you less than two days and already I feel comfortable."

The words were on the tip of his tongue. A nice, amiable response. A thank you for sharing and feeling able to do so. But none of that came out. "Why don't you take those clothes back off and let me show you just how comfortable things can get, the way I'm feeling right now." The ferocity in his tone startled even him. He wanted her badly…and he wanted her now.

She stared at him for three long seconds before her pupils flared with undeniable desire. "I…" She moistened those soft, pink lips. "I don't know what to say." She looked basically anywhere but at him.

He'd gone too far to back out now. "Don't say anything." His fingers were in her hair before he could stop himself.

Her breath caught as he closed his mouth over hers. The sweet minty taste filled him and he wanted to taste every square inch of her. Her fingers were tearing at the buttons of his shirt. His were fumbling with the hem of her blouse. They worked around each other, the moves seemingly choreographed as her blouse came over her head and off and his shirt was peeled away from his back and arms.

The idea that he should have taken that shower flitted through his head but he couldn't slow down long enough to ponder the notion—not when she wore no bra and her firm, high breasts were right in front of him, the nipples hard with need. His palms closed over the lush mounds and she leaned into his touch. He lowered his head and tasted first one then the other before ushering her down onto the bed. He lowered her zipper and dragged off her slacks, leaving nothing but that scrap of black silk covering her hips.

Russ stood at the foot of the bed and admired her body for a moment. She was trim and athletic with just enough feminine curves to add up to pure perfection. He unfastened his belt, liking that she watched his every move. He placed his weapon on the bed and tugged off his jeans. The condom in his wallet went down next to the weapon. Then he hauled off his stained jeans and tossed them aside. His shorts went next.

She continued to openly study him and he liked it. His body hardened even more as her gaze roved over his lower anatomy. He shucked his socks and reached for the condom. The pulse at the base of her throat fluttered as he watched her watching him tear open the necessary precaution. He skimmed the protection over his arousal and moved onto the bed, crawling on all fours up the length of her.

Belatedly, he grabbed the weapon and put it on the bedside table and reached for the light.

"Leave it on."

Surprised that she wanted the light on, he lowered his

hand back to the bed. In his experience women most often wanted the light off.

"I like looking at you." She reached up and feathered her fingers down his chest. "Your body is amazing. So strong." She stroked his chest again, only this time her hands moved even lower, allowing her fingertips to glide over his length. "You make me want to do things I've never even considered before."

He lowered his face closer to hers. "We'll do whatever you want, Liv." He brushed his lips across hers. "Just tell me what it is you want most and we'll start there." His body was vibrating with the urge to take her hard and fast but he wanted to do this right. To make her feel all those wondrous sensations she'd missed out on before.

She encircled his arousal with her fingers. "I want this now." As if to underscore her demand, she wrapped her legs around his and lifted her hips.

As much as he wanted to grant her every wish, he needed to be sure she was ready. Reaching downward, he trailed a finger down her abdomen, traced those most intimate parts of her and then delved inside. She was ready all right. Hot, slick and undulating invitingly against his touch.

He shifted to his knees and lifted her bottom with one hand while guiding himself into her with the other. Once he was inside her just far enough, he grasped her hips with both hands and held her steady as he slowly thrust fully inside her.

Her fingers fisted in the sheets as her body rose instinctively to meet him. Her cries told him she wanted more so he began to move, ensuring full penetration with each drive of his hips. She climaxed almost instantly. That only fueled the fire roaring inside him. Made him want to bring her to that place over and over again before he plunged over that incredible edge.

To do that he had to slow things down. He started with

her nose, kissing her face…all those features he adored. The dimples that appeared when she smiled, like now. Those long, long lashes that shaded her big dark eyes. Her chin…that long slender neck. And those breasts, man he loved her breasts. Just the right size. He moved down her slender rib cage, paid special attention to her belly button and then he showed her how a man could cherish a woman's most intimate places.

When she screamed with release a second time, it was his turn. He filled her over and over, until she came with him. Then he slumped onto the bed and drew her into his arms. If not for needing a shower so bad, he could have snuggled that way right there for the rest of the night.

He waited until she was sleeping soundly before slipping away. With his weapon in hand, he stalked to the bathroom and climbed into the shower. Leaving the door open to the room and working as quickly as possible, he was in and out of the shower in about three minutes. He tugged on clean jeans and a tee. He had more socks but he'd either have to do laundry or make another hit on a department store for shorts. Didn't matter. The well-worn jeans suited him just fine.

To his surprise, Olivia was not only awake but dressed and sitting on the side of the bed when he came out of the bathroom. He joined her and waited for her to say what was on her mind. He hoped she wasn't already regretting their lovemaking.

Without meeting his gaze, she asked, "Should we talk about this?" She shrugged. "I don't usually get intimate with strangers."

And there came the guilt. He reached over and took her by the chin to turn her face to his. "We've shared too much the last thirty-six hours to be called strangers. What people feel is not always best measured in terms of time. At this moment we need each other and maybe that need won't be as intense tomorrow or the next day but that doesn't change what it is right now."

Her lips trembled into a smile. "Have you ever considered changing career paths? You'd make a very persuasive trial attorney."

"I'm not sure that's a compliment, but I'll take it as one coming from you."

A solid rap on the door had him reaching for the weapon at the small of his back. "Go in the bathroom and shut the door."

He got another surprise when she actually did as he said without a word in challenge.

Russ went to the side of the window farthest from the door and lifted the curtain away just far enough to get a look at the person knocking. The light at the door revealed a man in a rumpled suit. As the guy reached up to knock again, he set his left hand on his hip, pushing his suit jacket aside as he did so. The weapon and badge attached to his belt shouted *cop* loud and clear.

Russ noted only one sedan in the dimly lit parking lot besides the two that had been there when they arrived. Obviously the guy was alone.

The two deputies who had showed up at the old Barker place had apparently informed the detectives division. Judging by the guy's age he was old enough to have worked the Princess Killer case. Gray hair, glasses, lean, wiry frame for a man undoubtedly well into sixty. Time to find out.

Russ tucked his own weapon back into his waistband, in front so the guy could see it, and then reached for the door. When he and the man with the badge stood face-to-face, Russ waited for him to speak first.

"Detective Marcus Whitt," he said without offering any other ID as proof of his word. "Mr. St. James, may I have a few minutes of your time?"

"Sure." Russ stepped back and opened the door wider, then

closed it behind the detective. "Have a seat." There were two chairs flanking a small table in front of the window.

"That's not necessary." The detective braced his hands on his hips and got right to the point. "Ms. Westfield came to see me last week and I told her in no uncertain terms that there was nothing to be gained by digging around in the Barker case. Apparently that message didn't get through to her. I don't know how much you know about this case, but your agency has a reputation for doing the right thing. I'm certainly hoping you'll do the right thing here and take Ms. Westfield home before this gets any worse. She's already caused enough pain to the families of the victims by pursuing a stay of execution for that monster Rafe Barker."

Russ weighed his words for a bit, mostly to keep him calm. The man was more than a little worked up. "I appreciate you stopping by, Detective, but you need to be aware that I work for Ms. Westfield. If she wants to look into the case, then that's what we'll do."

"I'll be calling your superior," Whitt threatened. "One travesty of the justice system has already taken place with the overturning of Clare Barker's sentence. I'm not going to sit back and wait while another killer gets off."

"What is it you plan to do? It's a free country as long as no laws are broken. It's not like we blew up anyone's car or slashed their tires."

"Are you accusing me of something, St. James?" He cocked his head. "I'm not a P.I. like you. I have a sworn duty to uphold the law. The citizens of Granger depend on people like me to ensure the bad guys are taken off the streets and *kept* off the streets. It's people like you and that misguided woman you're with who hurt those who've already been hurt far too much."

"Misguided?" Olivia joined their friendly meeting. "That's what you think I am? Rafe and Clare Barker were charged with numerous murders, including the murders of their three daughters. Clearly mistakes were made. If one or both are guilty, then they deserve the sentence levied by the courts. But the fact that my sisters and I are alive insists that we take a second look. You should be the first in line to ensure that it's done properly."

"The investigation was conducted properly the first time," he argued with fury vibrating in his voice. "Your father murdered those girls. I don't know why or how you and your sisters were spared, thank God you were, but I know what that monster did. I helped bring those remains out of those woods. I know what they did."

"We understand your position," Russ stepped in. "That's why we've been trying to conduct our investigation as discreetly as possible. I don't know who tipped the media off to our presence but this kind of attention was not our intent. My agency felt and still feels that Ms. Westfield and her sisters may be in danger from Tony Weeden and perhaps even Clare Barker. We're doing all we can to keep them out of the media's keen focus."

Whitt looked from Russ to Olivia and back. "I guess we'll just have to agree to disagree on the matter."

"We could work together," Olivia offered. "Go over the details of the case and see if looking back twenty years later we see something that was missed in the heat of emotion. That case was a nightmare for all involved. It would've been easy to overlook something small or to see something the wrong way through that lens of so many volatile emotions."

Whitt's lips formed a grim line and Russ felt certain he was going to blast Olivia for suggesting he'd made a mistake. "All right. Let's do that. If you think you can see something I missed, let's have at it. Then you'll know what I knew back then—that Rafe and Clare Barker are cold-blooded killers."

Olivia squared her shoulders. "I'm ready right now."

Except for her shoes, Russ thought. They were both standing there with bare feet.

"Follow me to my office and I'll show you everything."

Chapter Fifteen

Olivia could hardly stay focused on one single aspect of the case Detective Whitt had laid out on the conference table. The crime scene photos were sickening and there were far more than Keisha Landers had had in her possession. The descriptions of the conditions in the home and clinic were deplorable. What had happened those last few months? The vague memories that had surfaced showed a clean, if not modern, home. Mrs. Samson had said the same. But then it all went downhill afterward.

"We couldn't determine the full extent of the atrocities the girls suffered from their remains," Whitt said. "We would know more now but twenty-some years ago we worked with what we had. The bodies were dismembered and placed in wooden boxes." He pointed to one of the photos. "Then buried in that makeshift graveyard they used for the animals they couldn't save. Back before the arrests, the Barkers had a regular pet cemetery going back there. Folks would bring their deceased pets and Rafe would show them a spot they could use."

"There were four other girls who went missing that you suspected were connected to the Princess Killer case," Olivia noted.

"Four for certain but we suspect there were six or more, but we couldn't connect those with any real certainty. The remains we found were of girls all pictured on Rafe's pet-adoption bulletin board he kept in the clinic. Those victims had been missing for years. Every parent of a missing daughter remembered the seemingly kind veterinarian referring to their daughter as a princess when they visited the clinic. But it was the final victims before he was caught that we never found. Four for sure, maybe more. Those girls went missing very close together, which was a different MO from the previous abductions. With the others it was one a year, then suddenly four or more go missing in the space of as many months. We think that's when he started to unravel and his house of horrors fell in on him, so to speak."

"You were part of a fairly large task force," Russ put in. He'd spent most of the past hour listening. Olivia had spent that same time avoiding eye contact with him. As much as she wanted to be cool with what happened in the motel room, a part of her was mortified at her uncharacteristic boldness with him. She generally reserved that side of her personality for work.

"I was lead, but I worked with four other detectives from surrounding counties and two FBI agents." To Olivia he added, "We made no mistakes. The evidence we used to determine that the three of you had fallen prey to foul play was perhaps minimal but we had every reason to believe you were gone. Clare was hysterical. She kept saying over and over that he had killed her babies."

He surveyed the stacks of interview reports and crime scene reports and shook his head. "Maybe we should have dug further but we had no compelling reason to." He fixed his weary gaze on Olivia. "Looking back, I can say without reservation that you were better off being whisked away from that nightmare. The investigation took weeks and weeks. The trial went on for months and months. It was a legal and moral nightmare for all involved. For the families of the victims and the rest of the community, it was an unparalleled tragedy. The whole town was in mourning."

Olivia couldn't deny he had a valid point but that didn't change what she needed to know. "One of the witnesses you interviewed has told us that there was another woman present in the Barker home for quite some time before the arrests." Olivia didn't want to mention Mrs. Samson's name. "Did anything your investigation discovered suggest there was a third adult in the house?"

"Mrs. Samson, yes." Whitt picked up his third cup of coffee and had a swallow, then grimaced. "She mentioned seeing another woman, who bore a striking resemblance to Clare. But Clare denied another woman's presence. Since she had no living relatives that we could find, we assumed Mrs. Samson was mistaken. The other witness," he hastened to add before Olivia could point it out, "only saw this other woman once and wasn't really sure it wasn't Clare. We found no prints that pointed to anyone else. Of course, our print databases weren't what they are now."

"There was a murder in Copperas Cove a couple of weeks ago," Russ said. "A woman, Janet Tolliver. Is it possible to check any prints you have on file from the Barker home during your investigation to the ones discovered in this recent investigation? Specifically to those of Tolliver?"

"It would take some time." Whitt shrugged. "But if you think it's important I could get it done. Who is this Tolliver woman and how does she connect to the Barkers?"

"She was Clare's sister. She and Clare were separated when Clare was only three, we believe, because Janet had violent tendencies. Later, as adults, the two reconnected and Janet was the one keeping Rafe's secrets about his daughters. She could be the other blonde woman who looked so much like

Clare. And if she was there, you can bet she had a hand in whatever atrocities were taking place."

Olivia's heart bumped her sternum. How would she have gotten this far without Russ? He'd elbowed his way into her life and now she couldn't imagine going through this without him. How would she handle him walking away when his job was done? She suddenly felt completely alone. Her biological parents were killers, or at the very least completely mental. She had damaged her relationship with her family and latched onto a man whose sole purpose was to serve as her protector.

How screwed up was that?

She shook off the painful thoughts and focused on the discussion she'd wanted so desperately to have with this detective. She'd felt certain he was holding something back when in reality he had not. He and the others had done the best they could with what they had. The evidence, though not directly connected to Clare, had been damning. Had Olivia been involved with the case, as she saw it spread out before her right now, she couldn't say that she would have done anything any differently.

Not a single thing.

"Excuse me." Detective Whitt reached for his ringing cell phone and stepped away from the conference table.

"How're you feeling about this?" Russ asked quietly.

She surveyed the mountain of paperwork. "I feel they did everything possible. I was wrong to blame the authorities involved with investigating this case." Her gaze sought his. "Whatever discrepancies...whatever the truth really is...it lies with Rafe and Clare. Janet's dead so she can't tell us anything." Olivia took a breath and said what she knew needed to be on the table with the rest of this monstrosity of a puzzle. "I believe the only way we'll ever get anything else is from Clare. If she survives her partnership with Weeden."

Clare, whether she was innocent of those long-ago crimes

or not, was in danger now. Olivia felt it all the way to the core of her being. Somehow, though he had likely killed her, Weeden had been involved with Janet in recent years. And Janet had no doubt been involved with Rafe. Was it possible that Clare had been an innocent victim? Maybe with a few loose screws? Taking into account her crazy family, that last part was a given.

"I can't let you take a chance like that. Trying to connect with Clare is too dangerous." Russ shook his head firmly from side to side. "Whatever you believe could be gained, it's not worth the risk to your safety. If she would willingly come forward, under the right circumstances, then no problem. But not on the sly. No way."

Olivia crossed her arms over her chest. "You do realize I'm a grown woman," she countered.

He reached out, stroked her cheek with the pad of his thumb. She shivered. "Unconditionally."

"Then—" she cleared her throat of the emotion that tightened it "—you understand I can make that decision without your permission or your approval."

"You can," he agreed, "but you understand that I'm a hell of a lot stronger than you and I will do whatever it takes to protect you from all danger, including any your own decisions pose." He held up a hand to silence her when she would have launched her next objection. "And that part has nothing to do with the job. It's about you and me."

Her heart stumbled and the words she wanted to say wouldn't form on her tongue.

He gifted her with the dazzling smile that took her breath away every single time. "I like it when you're speechless."

"There's someone here who wants to see the two of you if you're willing," Detective Whitt announced.

Olivia whirled to face him. "Clare?" Would she turn herself in like this? "Is Weeden with her?"

"It's not Clare. It's Claude Henson. He's the father of one of the girls who was buried on the Barker farm. He has something to say to you about what happened to your SUV."

Whitt led the way to an interview room where an older man sat at a table with another detective. He reminded Olivia of her adoptive father. She recognized the weary lines that warned he'd worried himself sick about whatever he had to say. In Olivia's case, her father was usually worried about something she had done or planned to do.

"Mr. Henson, this is Olivia Westfield and her friend Mr. St. James," Whitt said, making the introductions.

Henson and the other detective stood. Henson shook his head and stared a moment at the cup of coffee he held in his hand. "I was the one who slashed the tires on your vehicle." He lifted his gaze to Olivia. "A friend of mine over in Livingston called and said he'd heard from a reporter with inside information what you were up to. The petition for a stay of execution and all. He said that his source mentioned you were coming here to look into the investigation." He shrugged. "I drove all over town until I found an outsider's vehicle. Since it was parked at that awful place, I knew it was you." He heaved a burdened breath. "I was wrong. I'll pay for the damages if you'll allow me to." He glanced at the detective who'd been speaking to him. "And I'll face whatever charges are appropriate."

Olivia found her voice. "Sir, you don't owe me an apology. I can't imagine how you suffered at the hands of one or both of the people who are unfortunately my biological parents. I'm the one who owes you an apology." She turned to Whitt. "I owe you one, as well. I came here last week all fired up to prove you hadn't done your job. I convinced myself that because my sisters and I are alive that perhaps my parents weren't the monsters you had painted them to be.

But I was wrong to come with that attitude. All I want is the truth. Whatever that is."

Russ pressed his hand to her back and she'd never needed that kind of support more. The mere touch told her he was not only beside her, he was with her on this.

"I have no desire to press charges," Russ added. "I mentioned that last night when the report was written. My insurance will pay for the damages. Let's leave it at that."

"I guess you can go, Mr. Henson," the other detective offered. To Russ he said, "That's very obliging of you."

Russ gave him an acknowledging nod.

Mr. Henson paused at the door and turned to Olivia. "You look a lot like your mother. She brought you and your sisters to church every Sunday long after Rafe stopped coming. I guess if I'd been the kind of Christian I should have been I would have known something was wrong then. And when she stopped coming at all, every one of us should have noticed and acted. But we let it go. I've had to live with that mistake for more than twenty years. I don't care to live with it anymore."

Olivia touched his arm and managed a faint smile. "Thank you, Mr. Henson. If we learn anything new about what happened we'll be sure to see that Detective Whitt lets you know."

He gave her a nod and went on his way.

Half an hour later Russ had parked the rented sedan behind the pharmacy next door to the Boxcar Motel. Olivia was beyond exhausted. She desperately needed sleep. Without nightmares hopefully.

When Russ was satisfied that the coast was clear he led her to the door of their room. Dawn was peeking through the darkness. It would be daylight soon…barely two more weeks until Rafe's execution. Part of her wanted him to die. He had to have committed those awful kidnappings and murders. But what if she was wrong? What if it had been Clare?

"Hold on."

Russ drew her back when she was only three or four steps from the door. She started to ask why and then she saw the package on the sidewalk in front of their door. Mostly it looked like wadded-up newspaper.

"I want you to move back and get behind that truck on the other side of the parking lot."

"Shouldn't you call Detective Whitt? Nine-one-one or someone?" The concept that it could be another bomb had fear throttling at full speed through her veins.

"I'm going to have a look and see what we have here. Now go," he ordered.

Olivia hurried across the lot and got behind the truck she presumed belonged to the manager or motel owner. She held her breath as Russ approached the door and leaned down to gingerly inspect the clump of newspapers.

When he reached inside she almost cried out his name. And he was always lecturing her about risks.

He studied the object he'd removed for a moment. She tried to make out what it was but she was too far away. A small box of some sort. He opened it and inspected the inside, then closed it again.

"It's okay. It's a music box." He motioned for her to join him.

She hurried over, curious to see the object up close. "A music box?"

He twisted the key on the bottom and opened the lid so the tune would play.

Olivia froze.

That was the tune. The humming she heard in her nightmares. The tune her mother used to hum whenever she was rocking the baby…Sadie.

"That's my mother's music box." The words were hardly more than a whisper. "She knows we're here. She's been here."

7:30 a.m.

RUSS HADN'T SLEPT MORE than a few seconds in the past hour. He scrubbed a hand across his face and considered the newspaper he had smoothed out from the crumpled mess that had been wrapped around the music box.

The stick-figure drawing was the same one Clare had been leaving in her wake. Only this time it was only the mother figure, the three girls and then a small boy figure that represented Laney's son. Tony Weeden was not a part of this drawing as he had been in the ones she had left behind in Beaumont. In the ones that had included Weeden, his figure had been drawn larger than the three girls.

Did that mean she and Weeden were about to have a parting of ways? From what he knew about Weeden, Russ wasn't sure Clare would come out the victor from a battle with her son. Since the stick figures in this drawing hadn't been crossed out with big X's as the ones had in the motel room in Beaumont that Lucas discovered when he suspected Clare and Weeden were watching Laney, did that mean she and Weeden had already parted ways? One thing was certain, she was here in Granger. With Weeden's and her faces all over the news, she was taking a hell of a chance coming here. This was the last place she would want to be captured even if for nothing more than questioning.

What was the point in sending this music box? Olivia had said that she had heard the tune in her nightmares. Was Clare hoping to trigger more memories? Was she that certain that what Olivia would remember would prove to all with doubts that she was innocent?

Once they entered their motel room, Russ made a call to Simon to update him on the tire slasher and the delivery of the music box. Rafe Barker still refused to speak to anyone from the Colby Agency. Simon suspected that he had called

Victoria to the prison at precisely the time that would cause her to be caught up in the protesters and the media frenzy. Like Russ, all at the Colby Agency suspected Rafe was using them for an agenda that was nothing like the one he had presented to Victoria in his letter or at their first meeting.

Detective Whitt would call as soon as he had anything on those prints. It would take some time since twenty-two years ago collection and storage of evidence had been done a little differently. Russ wasn't sure what they would accomplish by confirming Janet Tolliver's presence in the Barker home without Clare to explain what that meant, but it was a detail they hadn't known until now. It was impossible to know which tiny seemingly insignificant detail would matter.

He shifted in the chair to watch Olivia sleep. He hadn't meant to get this deeply entangled, particularly not with a client. But he was squarely there and there was no turning back now. When this was over, they had things to sort out. He wasn't simply going away.

The midst of a stressful and desperate investigation like this was the least desirable launching point for a prospective relationship, but sometimes life sneaked up on a guy like that. He wanted to explore these feelings. Maybe that made him soft, but it was the truth. He'd always found that living by the truth and one's honor was the best way. At thirty-five he wasn't about to change that now.

His lips slid into a smile. He enjoyed watching her like this, all soft and vulnerable. The idea that this woman trusted him enough to sleep under his watch shifted something in his chest. She was no pushover. Definitely no shrinking violet. Gaining her trust and her respect was a big deal and he savored the idea that he had earned that from her. Particularly in such a short time.

She damn sure had earned his respect and trust. He'd never met a woman any stronger. Except maybe Victoria. And his mother. She was a strong woman, as well. The thought of introducing Olivia to his mother had another of those strange little curls of emotion happening in his chest. He hadn't been in love before so he couldn't hazard a guess as to whether this was it or not, but he knew for sure that whatever it was, he wanted it to last.

The urge to climb into that bed with Olivia and make love again was powerful. But she needed sleep and he was fresh out of condoms. He carried one in his wallet at all times. Not that he planned casual sex but it was better to be safe than sorry.

Her respiration grew rapid and uneven and the pained look on her face had him moving to the side of the bed. No sooner than he settled in next to her she started to flail and cry out.

She was having another nightmare. Dammit.

"Olivia." He took her by the shoulders and shook her gently.

She tried to twist out of his hold, tried to fight him off. "Olivia, wake up."

Her eyes flew open and she screamed.

"Olivia, it's me, darling. It's okay. You were dreaming."

She blinked, inhaled a ragged breath. "Oh, God."

Before he could try and calm her she scrambled away from him and off the other side of the bed. A smile tugged at his lips just watching her pace the room wearing nothing but his shirt. Man, she was gorgeous.

"It was her." She turned to him, her body trembling. "Janet. It was her."

He stood and moved toward her. "What do you mean it was her?"

"She was at the house during those final days or weeks." Olivia nodded frantically. "And she was up to something."

"What did you remember exactly?"

"I woke up from a bad dream and I went in search of my

mother." She moistened her lips. "Only when I went into her room it wasn't her in the bed with my father. It was Janet."

Olivia hugged her arms around her middle. "That's why I felt repulsed by the thought of going into their room when we were at the house."

Russ went to her and put his arms around her.

She stared up at him. "Bad things happened there, Russ. Things we don't even know yet."

Chapter Sixteen

8:00 a.m.

Clare had made her decision. No matter what Tony said she was going to see her daughters. All she had to do was get them all to meet her somewhere. Anywhere. The only way she imagined she would be able to do that was to call that woman…the head of the Colby Agency.

Tony would be angry. She glanced at him still covered head to toe in the bed. His gunshot wound was infected. He knew this and still he refused to go to a doctor. Though he was a nurse and he was on the antibiotics he had taken from that clinic, there was a problem.

She had wanted to believe in her son. He was so smart and he had done so well for himself. She had prayed for him over the years. But Janet and those awful people who had adopted him had ruined him.

Clare feared there was no hope for his redemption.

She hadn't driven in more than twenty years when she'd had to race away from her old house with Tony bleeding like a stuck pig. That had proved that driving was like riding a bicycle. One never forgot how.

Maybe she should just slip out while he slept. They had hurried away from Granger after delivering the package to the motel where Olivia was staying. They'd gotten to this small town before Tony had complained that he was too tired to go on. He'd taken some of the pain pills he'd stolen from the clinic, as well, so he might not wake up for a while yet. That would prevent an ugly confrontation. She didn't want to leave him on bad terms. Whatever he had become in his life it was her fault in large part.

God had blessed her with a child after that awful rape. She should have kept her child and faced the consequences like a grown-up. Instead, she'd run to the only family she'd had left. Janet had given her bad advice. She had used the opportunity to hurt Clare yet again. Worse she had hurt an innocent child. She had ruined his life.

Perhaps Clare shouldn't leave him. She could try harder to make him see right from wrong. When this mess was all cleared up maybe they could join a small church and let God cleanse them. And she would have the chance to make up for her terrible mistakes. Tony deserved more from her.

But she had begun to worry that he might hold a grudge in his heart against the girls. Clare could not let him hurt the girls. Like him, they had suffered enough already.

She peeked beyond the curtain and checked the parking lot. It was cracked and weeds had long ago grown up in those cracks. The building was surely on its way to being condemned. But that had made it safe for them.

Only two other cars were in the lot. Old, beat-up cars like the one Tony had purchased from a man with two cars for sale in his front yard. Tony had plenty of money. He would be all right without her. Once this trouble was cleared up he could get another nursing job and all would be well for him. He'd said he didn't kill that man. Surely the police would find the truth.

Like they found it twenty-two years ago?

Clare shuddered. That had been different. There were things she couldn't tell the police. Things that would have made the difference, but her hands had been tied. All she could do was try to convince them that she was innocent and pray that justice would prevail.

But it had not...not for more than twenty years.

Clare dismissed those haunting memories and painful emotions. She couldn't change the past. She had to focus on the here and now. If her being a part of Tony's life was going to cause him pain, perhaps leaving was the right thing to do. But she hated to go without telling him she loved him and appreciated all that he had done. Well, most all that he had done. Some things she wasn't so sure about but she was only human.

She would leave him a note. Then she would drive to Houston and demand to see this Victoria Colby-Camp. As a mother herself, surely she would understand Clare's position.

Clare took her time emptying the paper sack of food supplies she'd gotten from the grocery store. The motel had no writing paper but there was the pen she had used when she'd left that note for Olivia. Well, it hadn't really been a note. More an omen. Even then she had known that this moment was coming. It was time for her to stand on her own and stop depending on her son to take care of her.

She flattened the bag and carefully wrote a note to her son. Taking care to say all the right things, she told him how much she loved him and how sorry she was for not taking care of him as a mother should have. He had deserved better and she had failed him. She hoped he would one day forgive her. She told him of her plan to go to see the woman at the Colby Agency. Clare had as good a chance of swaying her as Rafe had had. Better maybe since they were both women and mothers. Tears welled in her eyes as she told Tony how she wanted to be reunited with her daughters and that this was the only way. When this was over perhaps they could all be together. She signed it with much love and then drew a little heart.

With the note left where he would see it first thing when he woke up, Clare gathered her few items. A change of clothes and a hairbrush. She didn't need anything else. There was a bus station not far from here. The car was Tony's and it would be wrong for her to take it.

She had a small amount of cash of her own. They'd given it to her along with her few earthly possessions when she left the prison. Surely two hundred dollars would be adequate to get her from here to Houston.

Moving quietly, she eased toward the door. Once she reached it she had to carefully remove the security chain and then pray he wouldn't hear the knob turn.

"Where do you think you're going?"

Clare froze. Think! She needed an excuse. "I thought I would go out and get us some breakfast." She pasted a smile on her face and turned around. Her lips dragged into a frown. He held that awful gun aimed right at her.

"Is that right?" He threw back the covers and sat up. "Is that why you're carrying that stuff?"

Fear pumped through her veins. "I was…was going to put them in the car so I wouldn't forget about them. They're all I have."

He snatched the keys up from the bedside table. "Really? How did you plan to unlock the car? I keep it locked, you know."

"I forgot. Silly me." She pushed her smile back into place. "Would you like some breakfast?" His T-shirt was bloody. The wound was bleeding again.

"Sit down over there." He waved the gun toward the chair.

Her body trembling so much she wasn't sure she would be able to walk, she pointed herself in the direction of the chair and moved toward it. "I'm very hungry this morning." Please, please let him believe her.

He got up and started toward the bathroom.

If he went into the bathroom she could still get away without him catching her.

He stopped at the console where the broken television sat and reached down.

Her heart lurched wildly as he picked up the paper sack she'd written the note on.

The seconds ticking past screamed in her ears. Finally, he turned around slowly and aimed the gun at her once more. "Love you, too, Mommy."

Chapter Seventeen

Bay Point, 9:30 a.m.

Victoria sat down on the chair facing the sofa. Her husband was the most stubborn man she had ever met. He absolutely would not listen to reason.

"We have to come to some sort of agreement, Lucas," she argued yet again. "I will not have you taking these kinds of risks anymore. It's far too dangerous."

It pained her to look at the awful bandage on his forehead and the walking cast on his good leg. Dear God, what else did it take for him to see that they were too old for this business? Enough was enough. The Colby Agency was in good hands. Let the next generation take the reins.

Lucas closed the novel he'd been reading and set it aside. He removed the eyeglasses that he never allowed anyone save Victoria to see and put them aside, as well. "We can come to an agreement right now but it would be a wasted effort."

"You're wrong this time, Lucas." She squared her shoulders and lifted her chin in defiance of the little voice his words awakened. "I will not change my mind. We are officially retiring. No more cases. None."

"And what will you do the next time you receive a letter from a desperate client? Or a call from someone in need?"

The man knew her too well. "I won't be receiving any letters or calls because no one, outside of our family and Simon and Ian, will know this address or this number." She intended to do this thing this time. It was well past time they stopped kidding themselves. They should be traveling and enjoying life, not working cases that put them in the line of fire.

He made a harrumphing sound. "All right. Where are we off to first? A cruise? A trip to Europe? Name the place and we'll go. Just leave all the business cares behind and fly off into the sunset."

"We'll need to wait until you're fully recovered first. Then we'll make a list of all the places we've always wanted to visit. We'll prioritize them and start checking off destinations." She smiled, feeling good about making this decision once and for all.

"In the meantime I suppose we can oversee all that redecorating you want to do."

That he made the task sound less than palatable grated on her nerves. Did he truly not want to retire? Had that knock on the head rattled him to the point that he was confused? They'd had this conversation months ago and he'd been all for retirement.

"Don't make it sound like such a dreaded chore. Do you not want to redecorate?" It wasn't absolutely necessary. If he was opposed, that was certainly all right with her.

He patted the sofa next to him. "Come over here and sit by me, my love."

With a dramatic display of reluctance she did as he asked. Once she was seated he put his arm around her and hugged her close. "Victoria, I love you more than you can possibly fathom. As I know you love me."

She rested her head on his strong shoulder. "Then why won't you see reason on this? We've had a wonderful three decades. It's time to move on to that next stage in our lives, like normal people do."

He laughed, the sound rumbling up from his chest. "My dear, we have never been and we will never be normal. Surely you recognize that. There are people who rescue and there are those who get rescued. We're the rescuers. The world needs us."

"We need us." She rose up and looked him in the eye. "I need you."

"Now we get to the true heart of the matter. You're afraid. Not for yourself, but for me."

It was true. She couldn't deny it. "Yes. I want us to take the time we never seemed to have in the past and enjoy each other. We discussed this all before and you agreed that it was the best decision."

"And then you answered Rafe Barker's call to come see him in prison and you were bombarded and harassed by protesters and reporters. It did little good for me to agree if you aren't going to abide by that mutual agreement."

The situation cleared for her. This wasn't about him having second thoughts. This was about him being worried about *her*.

"I'm finished with that case," Victoria proclaimed. "Simon and his staff have it under control. There is nothing else I can do. I'm done, Lucas. I want to begin plans for our first trip."

Her desperation was showing and that was never attractive. The memory of hearing that he had been found in that ravine, half-dead, still haunted her. She couldn't face the possibility of another call like that.

"Very well. You've convinced me." He pressed a kiss to her cheek. "What city is at the top of your list, Victoria? Where in the world would you go first?"

The telephone rang and she sighed. "Hold that thought." Satisfied that she and Lucas were on the same page now, she went in search of the house phone. She checked the screen. The office.

"Hello, Simon, how are you this morning?" This would

be as good a time as any to let him know that she was off the case.

"Victoria, we have a situation."

The seriousness of his tone warned that it was not a good situation. "What's going on?" From the corner of her eye she saw Lucas's eyebrows rear up.

"It's Clare Barker. She just called here and she wants a meeting with you. Today, Victoria. She wants to meet with you today. She says she's ready to give you the whole story on what really happened twenty-two years ago. But she will only give it to you and her daughters. She will not negotiate those conditions."

The certainty that she was finished with this case, that Simon and the others had everything under control, vanished. There was no other option.

"Tell her I'll be there."

Chapter Eighteen

Barker Farm, Granger, 3:30 p.m.

Olivia sat perfectly still for a long moment after Russ parked the SUV. The others were already here. The meeting with Clare wasn't until four o'clock, but Victoria Colby-Camp wanted time for the introductions and for preparation.

Russ, along with the other two Colby investigators who had been protecting the Barker offspring, would have to leave before that time. Part of the conditions of the meet was that all three bodyguards were to stay clear of the old farmhouse.

"You holding up okay?"

Olivia turned to Russ. "It helps that you're here." Just the sound of his voice made her feel safe and strong.

"You know we have backup in position already. Two of my colleagues, including Simon Ruhl, are in the house along with two of Detective Whitt's men. There's a whole army of cops in the woods. They've been there for hours just in case Weeden has been watching this afternoon."

"Clare said she would be alone."

"She won't be alone. She may appear alone, but he'll be here somewhere. You can count on it."

Olivia resisted the urge to twist in her seat to scan the area. She tried to steady herself. Her entire being seemed to quake with uncertainty. "On some level I've wanted this reunion of sorts since the moment I learned I was adopted. But it's a big risk to all of us, isn't it?"

"It is. We don't know what either or both have planned but we're assuming the worst."

"I guess I'll see you later, then." Regret washed over her at the idea that this might be the last time she saw him. If she died today—or if he did—they would never know what might have been. For that she was immensely sorry. She had called her parents and apologized for blaming them in any way for trying to protect her from the past. It didn't excuse what she had done or make up for it but at least the air between them had been cleared.

Russ nodded. "I'll be waiting."

Somehow her lips stretched into a smile. Maybe it was the certainty in his eyes and his voice. He had no intention of losing her to Weeden or Clare or anyone else. Her heart filled to overflowing.

"I'm holding you to that promise, cowboy."

He leaned across the console and kissed her. Not a demanding kiss, just a simple, sweet, more-to-come kind of kiss. When he drew back she had to go. Another second and she'd never be able to walk away from him.

He waited until she had reached the door. It opened and Victoria Colby-Camp waited in the entry hall for her. Olivia didn't look back. Watching Russ drive away was more than she could handle right now. She entered the house that held the secrets of her nightmares.

Olivia had not met Victoria, but she had seen her face in the news and Russ had told her how courageous and strong Victoria was. That she was willing to be here for this meeting, at such great risk to herself, spoke volumes.

"Olivia, I'm so pleased to finally meet you. Your sisters are waiting in the parlor."

Olivia fixed a smile in place. "Thank you." Her heart was

racing and her hands were shaking so she clasped them behind her back as she followed the head of the Colby Agency
into the parlor room on the left.

Laney and Sadie stood in the center of the room, both
looking about as nervous as she did. Laney was taller with
hair the color of Olivia's only much longer. Her eyes were
the same rich brown. Sadie was more petite, tiny almost.
Her hair was a lighter blond, like Clare's had once been, and
she had the green eyes of their mother. Both her sisters wore
their usual cowgirl duds, boots included. They were beautiful. Pride tightened her chest.

Olivia wondered what they thought of her. She felt a little
overdressed in her skirt and blouse. She'd had to buy something to wear today. Maybe she should have bought jeans.
But this was who she was, no need to try and conceal that.
They were all three grown women now with different ways
and thoughts on life. They were strangers, really. An ache
twisted in her heart. No matter what happened today, Olivia
hoped this was the first step toward changing that sad reality.

"Olivia Westfield," Victoria announced, "this is Laney
Seagers and Sadie Gilmore. Your sisters."

Olivia tried to smile but her trembling lips wouldn't hold
the expression. "Hello. I'm glad we're finally together again."

Her sisters stared at her without speaking or smiling or
anything at all. Olivia's heart rammed harder and harder
against her chest. The urge to apologize for not protecting
them came out of nowhere and had her eyes burning like fire.

Suddenly the two were surrounding her, hugging her and
kissing her cheeks. Olivia couldn't help herself. She cried like
a baby. The tears and hugs went on and on until they were
all three emotionally exhausted. And then they simply stood
there in a circle, holding hands and staring at each other.

"You always took care of us," Laney said. She pressed her
lips together for a moment to regain her composure. "Since

I learned the truth about us, I've dreamed about you several times. You were the one we clung to when we were scared."

Sadie nodded. "I've had dreams like that, too." Her voice wavered. "You would hold me and whisper to me. I didn't know it was you until I heard your voice just now. I was so stunned I couldn't move for a second there." She broke the chain for a moment and swiped her eyes. "I can't believe I have two beautiful sisters!"

The hugging resumed. The tears had never stopped. Olivia glanced at Victoria, who was dabbing at her eyes, as well. When Victoria's gaze bumped into hers, Olivia mouthed the words *thank you*. Victoria smiled and gave her a nod.

"We only have a few minutes," Victoria said eventually, "before Clare is supposed to arrive. We are as prepared for the unexpected as we can be and that will have to do. Are there any questions?"

Olivia looked to her sisters. "Have any of you remembered anything about the terrible things that happened here?"

"I remember the crying and screaming," Sadie said with a visible shiver. "Not very much else."

Laney nodded. "Me, too. I remember the screaming and being afraid. And the darkness of our hiding place."

"The closet," Olivia confirmed with a shiver of her own. "We always hid in our bedroom closet." She summoned her courage. Victoria's sudden intake of breath startled her but Olivia ignored the distraction. She had to get this said before she lost her nerve. "There was another blonde woman here near the end. I think it was Clare's sister, Janet. In one of my nightmares, I find her in bed with Rafe. So I think there was more going on here than the police realized." She held her breath, hoping either Laney or Sadie could confirm what she believed.

"There was a great deal more going on than anyone knew."

Olivia whirled to face the voice. Clare Barker stood in the

doorway leading from the entry hall to the parlor. She wore a pink dress, apparently her signature color. Her hair was mostly gray and much shorter than in the photos from the album Russ had given Olivia. She looked old and weary and… defeated. Emotions Olivia couldn't begin to label crowded in on her.

This was her mother.

"Have you come alone, Clare, as you promised?" Victoria asked.

Laney and Sadie moved up to stand beside Olivia. The compulsion to usher them behind her was instinctive. But they were grown women now. Olivia squared her shoulders. They stood together, equally strong and brave.

Victoria stood a few feet away, positioned between Clare and them. She waited for an answer to her question. Her posture as well as her expression unyielding.

"I'm alone. He dropped me off." Tears streamed down Clare's cheeks. "But that doesn't mean we're safe. He has something planned." She shook her head. "I don't know what but I know for sure we're all supposed to die."

Sadie gasped and reached for Olivia's hand. Olivia felt for Laney's. "What can we do?" Olivia asked.

"He forced me to make the call to you," Clare said to Victoria. "He insisted that we meet here, so I fear it has something to do with the house."

Victoria touched her ear. "Evacuate now," she ordered.

No wonder her breath had caught a minute ago. She was wearing some sort of communication device. She must have gotten the warning that Clare was coming inside. Olivia struggled to pay attention to Victoria's words and actions but she couldn't stop staring at her mother.

To Olivia and the others, Victoria said, "We're moving out of here now."

Clare's expression morphed to one of terror. "I don't know what he'll do if we try to leave the house."

Suddenly the room was filled with four more bodies. All men, none Olivia recognized. Russ had told her backup was hidden in the house.

"The woods behind the house are clear," one of the men said. "We can go out the back." He looked at each one of them in turn. "Stay low. If you hear gunfire, hit the ground."

"Could there be a bomb?" Olivia asked, suddenly remembering her car exploding in the parking lot of that restaurant. Terror ignited in her veins.

"We brought the dogs through," another of the men said. "They detected no explosives in the house."

The first man who'd spoken touched his ear. "Copy that." He looked to Victoria. "Weeden has been contained. We can evacuate the house without worry now."

Clare was shaking her head. "Something's wrong. He wouldn't go down that easily unless he had a backup plan." She gave her head another resolute shake. "He must have someone helping him. He swore we'd never leave here alive."

Dear God. Olivia held on to her sisters' hands. What did they do now?

RUSS EXHALED A BIG BURST of relief when Weeden was restrained and in the back of the police cruiser. He, Joel Hayden and Lyle McCaleb had staked out the road west of the Barker house, while three of Whitt's men had watched the east end that led back to town. They had given Russ a heads-up when Weeden and Clare passed en route to the old Barker place. According to the scout hidden in the woods closest to the highway, Weeden had let Clare out and driven on. Straight into their trap.

Russ had an uneasy feeling that taking him down had been too easy. His gut was in all kinds of knots.

"We've got remote detonators in the car!" Hayden shouted from the sedan Weeden had arrived in. "Five in all!"

Fear burst in Russ's chest. He charged forward, yanked the rear door of the cruiser open and dragged Weeden out. He shoved him against the car and jammed the barrel of his weapon into the soft underside of the bastard's chin. "Where are the bombs?" Behind him, Russ could hear McCaleb informing Simon and Victoria back at the house.

Weeden laughed. His bloody T-shirt and wild, bulging eyes gave him the look of something out of a horror flick. "You're too late."

"There were no bombs found in the house," Russ argued, fury roaring in his brain. He jammed the muzzle harder into the man's throat. "Where are they?"

"Doesn't matter," Weeden sneered. "They're going off and you can't stop them."

"We have the remote detonators," Hayden countered sharply, moving in closer. "They're not doing a damned thing without being detonated."

"There are backup detonators on timers," Weeden said with a laugh. "Another minute max and all those devices buried around the house will go boom!" He laughed again. "You can't do a damned thing because you're here with me!"

"HEAD INTO THE WOODS," the man Olivia had learned was Simon Ruhl shouted. "The bombs are buried around the house. We need distance and cover."

Heart and legs pumping, Olivia and her sisters ran for the woods. Hot tears stung her cheeks. What if they didn't make it?

They breached the edge of the woods. Victoria and Clare were right behind them.

"Oh, God."

Olivia stopped and turned around. Victoria was rushing

back out into the open. Olivia's heart seemed to stall. Clare wasn't behind them. She'd fallen to the ground halfway between the house and the woods.

"Victoria! Stop!" Simon rushed past Olivia.

Olivia started after them. To help. She had to help. The men in the woods, cops and Colby investigators, were shouting for her and her sisters to come on. To hurry!

For a moment Olivia was frozen watching Victoria risk her life to save the woman who had been charged with multiple murders more than two decades ago. Another man, this one older and hobbling badly, burst from the tree line on the right. Two others rushed after him.

"We should..." Sadie's voice trailed off.

Her sister's voice snapped Olivia out of the trance. She grabbed her sisters by the hands. "We have to go deeper into the woods."

As they rushed forward, men with guns crowded around them, ushering them into the thickening protection of the trees.

The first blast shook the ground.

"Get down!" one of the men shouted.

They all went flat on the ground, between bushes and saplings, amid the leaves.

Another blast and another... They just kept coming.

Olivia prayed Clare, Victoria and the others were unharmed. *Please don't let anyone die today.*

Finally the violent explosions stopped.

Olivia dared to move up onto her knees. Her ears rung with the silence. Was anyone hurt? Sadie and Laney scrambled over to where she knelt.

"Are you okay?" Laney asked.

Olivia nodded. "You?" She looked from Laney to Sadie and back. Both nodded.

The officers and investigators who had been in the woods

with them started to move toward the clearing where the house was…if it was still there. One of them stopped long enough to say, "You ladies stay put until we assess the situation."

Olivia got to her feet, her legs rubbery. She dusted off her skirt and wished she had her cell phone so she could make sure Russ was okay. If the bombs were here and Weeden was contained, surely Russ was safe. She tried to see beyond the trees. Clare had fallen and Victoria had rushed to help her. The man named Simon and another man who'd been limping had gone back out there. She hoped they were all okay.

"What's this?"

Sadie was kneeling near one of the stones Olivia and Russ had uncovered. Olivia knelt beside her and touched the angel inscribed there. "The families or someone marked all the sites where remains were found."

Laney joined them. "Oh, my God. I knew that from one of the old newspaper clippings I read but it didn't seem real."

"It was real all right." She gathered her courage once more. "And it's time we knew the whole truth."

With her sisters following her, Olivia walked out of those woods. Her heart skipped a couple of beats when she saw that Clare and Victoria, as well as the others, were safe.

But the house…it had collapsed in on itself. It lay there, broken and splintered, and incapable of harboring any more secrets.

8:15 p.m.

NO ONE HAD BEEN INJURED in the blasts. Clare had fallen because she had been weak from the beating Tony Weeden had given her. He'd avoided hitting her in the face. Instead, he'd pummeled her body and banged the back of her head against the floor.

Olivia felt sorry for her. Though she didn't know all the facts, the poor woman had suffered a great deal at the hands of her sister, her husband and then her son.

Laney and Sadie paced the hospital waiting room. Olivia had done that for a while but she was exhausted and her feet were killing her. She considered her high heels and then the boots that her sisters wore. Maybe there was something to be said for Western wear. If invited, she might just spend a few days in the country with one or both and try the cowgirl lifestyle.

She smiled. With her sisters. They were finally together.

Victoria and her husband, Lucas, the man with the cast on his leg, waited with them. Simon Ruhl, Russ and the other members of the Colby team were still at the Granger Police Department where Weeden was confessing his sins. Simon kept Victoria apprised of the developments.

Olivia wished she had been able to stay with Russ, but she'd needed to be here…to hear what Clare would tell them. And to support her sisters. Whatever happened after this, Olivia intended to explore these feelings she had for Russ. Warmth flowed through her, chasing away the awful chills those moments in the woods had generated.

They were all safe. The worst was over.

She hoped.

Tony Weeden had admitted to working with Rafe. Tony had finagled the job at the prison just so he could be close to Rafe. He and Rafe had something in common—they both hated Clare and worshipped Janet on some twisted level. When Rafe learned that Clare's conviction would be overturned, he used Tony's hatred to devise a plan to make her pay the ultimate price.

Rafe had given Tony all sorts of ideas on things to do in order to make Clare look guilty. Like the fire at the apartment complex in Copperas Cove where she'd gone straight from prison. The burning down of Sadie's home and the ugly message that had been left on her door. He'd scared Clare into thinking that the Colby Agency was trying to prove she belonged back in prison and was attempting to keep her daughters from her. He had convinced her that he was the only person who could save her and that Rafe had orchestrated the fire at Sadie's and the one at the complex. He'd convinced Clare that he had saved her.

Weeden had wanted to paint her as totally insane and as a murderer. When first interrogated, he'd insisted that it was all Clare's idea but he'd made one glaring mistake. The ex-con he'd hired to do all the explosives work and the fires, including the one at Keisha Landers's home, wasn't about to leave Granger without payment for the final job so he'd waited at the Boxcar Motel for Weeden to settle with him. In a small community like Granger, every stranger was noticed. With the police on high alert for today's meeting between Clare and her daughters, the stranger at the motel had gotten noticed. All sorts of evidence had been found in his car. He'd given up Weeden before the first question was thrown at him. He'd reminded the cops how he was careful that no one got hurt in any of the fires or the explosions. Of course, the lack of casualties at his final foray at the old Barker house was sheer luck.

Having been employed by the prison system, Weeden had known all sorts of unsavory characters. Those still inside and some out on parole.

Murdering Janet, however, hadn't been a part of Rafe's plan. Weeden killing her had been the result of an emotional scene between two twisted individuals gone completely out of control. She'd feared he might attempt revenge as soon as she learned he was playing the part of go-between for her and Rafe. Truth was, according to Tony, she was jealous of his new standing with Rafe. That was the reason she'd given the photo albums to her neighbor. The locations of Rafe's daughters had given her a certain power that she hadn't wanted to relinquish to Weeden. She'd had a sizable savings stashed in her home and had planned to disappear if things went south where she and Weeden were concerned. And she'd worried that Clare might decide to seek revenge. Janet's one mistake was that she'd trusted Rafe completely until the bitter end. She'd told him about her little nest egg. Weeden had killed her and taken the money. It had provided the funds for his explosives and arson expert as well as the car he'd purchased after the shootout last weekend.

Weeden and Rafe had their revenge against Clare all planned out. Both had wanted her to know she was the reason her daughters had died this day. They were supposed to have died twenty-two years ago as punishment for her tipping off the police. Rafe had discovered that Clare had told the minister of her church everything about what she suspected he and Janet were up to. The minister had made the anonymous tip and he had kept Clare's secret all these years. As Clare's minister he could not divulge the secrets she had shared with him in that capacity.

When Rafe learned what she had done, he tied her up in a closet and had Janet take their daughters away from the house. Janet was supposed to kill the girls and dispose of their bodies. She'd had no qualms about doing the job but she had known the girls would be worth something. So she'd used a lawyer to sell them in private adoptions. She hadn't told Rafe until she learned Clare was going to be released. That was when a new plan had been set in motion. Destroy them all in one fell swoop. He'd hoped to capitalize on the Colby Agency's reputation for compassion and integrity. And that their need to seek out and protect the girls would lead Weeden right to all three.

Janet's greed had put her on Rafe's bad side. The way she had abused Weeden had turned his fear of her as a child to sheer hatred as an adult. He had told the police that she was actually the one to chop off his arm when the Weedens informed her that he'd tried to run away. Janet had reveled in telling him that he was lucky she hadn't chopped him to bits the way she had hers and Clare's parents. He'd vowed to himself that she would one day pay, as would Clare for leaving him with her rotten sister.

But Rafe and Weeden had failed in their ultimate goal.

The double doors marked Authorized Personnel Only swung open and Olivia broke from her disturbing thoughts. Dr. Raby, the E.R. physician who'd been on call, breezed into the lobby for the first time in more than an hour.

Olivia stood as he approached. Her sisters came to her side. The feelings that flooded her at having them with her were nearly overpowering. "How is she?" Her voice trembled but there was no help for that. She was still shaky considering what could have happened at that damned farmhouse and all the wondrous emotions she had been experiencing since.

"She has three fractured ribs and a concussion, but Clare is going to be fine."

Despite scarcely knowing the woman and having thought she was a heinous murderer, Olivia breathed a sigh of relief.

"Can we see her?" Sadie asked.

"Detective Whitt is questioning her," the doctor explained. "He can answer that for you when he's done. There is no medical reason to restrict visitors but I don't know where the police stand on the matter."

"Thank you, Dr. Raby." Olivia produced a smile for him and tried valiantly to stop the trembling in her body.

Victoria and Lucas joined their huddle. "Simon just confirmed that Tony Weeden has been charged with multiple counts of attempted murder as well as murder in the first degree for the death of Terrence Kingston."

Kingston was Laney's little boy's father. Weeden had killed

him and taken the boy. It was a miracle the little boy had been returned to his mother unharmed. Probably only because of Clare's intervention. There Olivia went, giving Clare the benefit of the doubt. Olivia gave herself a mental shake. There were still a lot of unanswered questions from twenty-two years ago. Clare's guilt or innocence, in Olivia's eyes, was still in question.

"That's a relief," Laney said. "No matter that Buddy's father was a jerk, he didn't deserve to be murdered. And his killer definitely shouldn't get away with it."

Olivia hugged Laney. As brave as Laney wanted to appear, Olivia could see that she suffered on the inside with the loss of a man for whom she had obviously once cared.

"Victoria and I are going to the cafeteria for coffee," Lucas said. "Would you ladies care for anything?"

All three declined.

When they were alone, Olivia fixed another, brighter, smile into place. "So, what have you two been up to the last twenty years or so?"

They all laughed and the tension shrank a little. Laney and Sadie filled her in and Olivia had just gotten started when Detective Whitt appeared.

"Clare would like to see the three of you," he announced.

"Is that okay with you?" Olivia held her breath, hoped he wouldn't deny them at least a few minutes.

"It's time the four of you had some time together." Like the rest of them he looked tired and rumpled and relieved. "I've spent the past two decades plus believing that Clare Barker was as guilty as her husband. But it appears I may have been wrong."

Olivia and her sisters waited in stunned silence for him to continue.

"I'll let her tell you her story. I have to hand it to the higher courts, they definitely got it right this time. We made a mistake by coloring her with the same brush we used on Rafe. She has paid a heavy price for that mistake."

"Does that mean she won't face any charges for her complicity in Weeden's actions?" Olivia understood that there were extenuating circumstances. Still, she had been aware that Tony had done certain things that were unquestionably criminal.

"I think I can convince the D.A. to let her off with a year in a recovery center. After what she's been through I suspect some time in real counseling and with structured daily activities will help her to transition back into society. There's a very good place just outside Houston. She'll have her own small apartment and she can have visitors but she'll get the help she needs to come to terms with the bad hand she was dealt in the past. For now, the hospital is keeping her overnight for observation considering what she's been through mentally and physically."

"That's an excellent idea." Olivia was relieved that he had come to that conclusion. "Thank you, Detective." She had been so wrong about him. Justice was often difficult to bring about under such puzzling and emotional circumstances as all involved faced twenty-two years ago.

He gestured to the doors. "Let the desk nurse know and she'll buzz you ladies back."

As they passed through those foreboding doors, the Barker sisters held hands. They would face this together as they would likely face much more together, both good and bad, in the future. It was a genuine relief to know that Clare had not been a part of those tragic murders. But they had a long ways to go before Clare would feel like family.

Clare's eyes were closed when they entered the room. She looked as pale as the white sheet covering her. Soon she would be transferred to a room for her overnight stay. Olivia suspected the observation was more for monitoring her mental state than the concussion.

When the door closed behind them Clare's eyes opened. Her lips trembled into a smile. "I was afraid you wouldn't want to see me."

Sadie and Laney looked to Olivia to speak first. "We wouldn't leave without seeing you first."

"Thank you." She fiddled with the sheet. "I don't deserve your compassion."

Sadie moved to her bedside first. She reached out and took her hand. "Are you comfortable? Did they give you something for the pain?"

More of those hot tears slid down Olivia's cheeks. She and Laney exchanged a look and then they both went to Clare's side. It would take time and there would be many bumps on the road, but they would find their place together.

Clare told them the story of how she'd had no idea her husband was a murderer. He'd always seemed so kind and caring. Until Janet showed up in their lives. She and Rafe would drink and behave badly. Clare looked away when she told them that part. It was still hard for her to believe that he'd been doing those awful things for most of their marriage. She felt like a fool for not recognizing that side of him. Olivia and her sisters didn't ask any questions.

"I don't know," Clare said, "if it was the alcohol or her, but something made those evil urges of his escalate." She looked from one of her daughters to the next. "That's when I knew something was wrong. He and Janet would come home in the middle of the night. They'd have blood all over them. I didn't know what to think. The way they were acting I was afraid to ask. The next morning he would tell me that he'd rescued some animal or done some sort of emergency surgery to explain his bloody clothes. Lies." She shook her head. "All of it. They were out hunting little girls to slaughter. When I tried to question Janet, she warned what she would do if I made trouble for her." Clare's gaze settled on each of her daughter's in turn. "She threatened to hurt you girls. She watched everything I did. I was trapped for those four long months after she showed up. I couldn't run without leaving the three of you behind and that was out of the question. Finally, I took that chance by telling my minister what I suspected and all hell broke loose. Janet had been following me. She didn't know what I told him but she knew I told him something. She and Rafe went into a frenzy." She closed her eyes ad shook her head. "I was terrified for you girls."

Olivia cleared the lump of emotion from her throat. "I saw you cleaning up blood from the floor once." Remembering that scene in a dream had made Olivia believe that Clare had been involved in the murders or that, at the very least, she had known about them.

"Janet got injured somehow on one of their outings. I found her on your bedroom floor the next morning. By the time I got her patched up and in bed in the guest room and returned to clean up the mess, the three of you had gotten up, seen the blood and hidden in the closet. You were scared to death. I tried to assure you everything was okay. But it wasn't. It was never okay. I was just too blind to see it until the end."

"Why did Janet try to hurt you so?" Laney wanted to know.

Clare reached for Laney's hand. "She hated me. When I was born she thought our parents loved me more so she tried to drown me. After several attempts to kill me, my parents sent her away to live with another family."

Clare blinked at the emotion shining in her eyes. "A part of me always suspected she was the one who murdered them, but I couldn't be sure and she never said. When she helped me with Tony, I thought maybe I'd been wrong about her all that time. But I know now that she only did that to hurt me more. She did terrible things to him and the people she sold him to were even worse. He's not entirely to blame for how he turned out. I'm responsible in large part."

She sighed mightily. "When she learned I was happily married with three beautiful daughters she wanted to ruin that, too. Discovering that she and Rafe shared evil urges was just icing on her poison cake. God only knows what they did with the bodies of those girls they murdered. Rafe won't ever tell. I guess we'll never know."

They talked for a long time. Many tears were shed, but in the end it was a new beginning for them all.

And the secrets of the past were finally revealed for Olivia and her sisters. Now they could try to move on with their lives.

It wouldn't be easy. There was a lot of healing ahead of them. But Olivia knew exactly where she wanted to start.

Chapter Nineteen

10:30 p.m.

Russ couldn't sit still. He had paced the hospital lobby for the past hour. McCaleb and Hayden had done the same. They'd driven back to the hospital as soon as Weeden's interrogation and booking was complete. When they arrived, Victoria explained that Olivia and her sisters were talking to Clare. Russ had been losing his mind ever since.

The sinking feeling that had about stolen his legs from under him when he heard the first explosion would haunt him for the rest of his life. They had intercepted Weeden about a half of a mile from the old Barker place and even at that distance they had heard the explosions as if they were right on top of them. Not knowing if anyone was injured had ripped his heart from his chest.

As soon as he heard that Olivia and everyone were safe he'd been able to breathe again. It had taken every ounce of restraint he possessed not to beat the hell out of Weeden then and there.

Now that bastard would end up on death row like his pal Rafe. Only Rafe wouldn't last long enough for a reunion. Victoria had told them that Olivia had called her boss and told him to withdraw the petition, considering Weeden's confession of Rafe's part in this latest travesty. Detective Whitt had spoken to him, as well. The three had ultimately had a conference call with the D.A. and the Governor. Rafe's execution would be carried out as scheduled.

Now Olivia and her sisters could move forward toward getting to know each other without all those questions hanging over their heads. Russ hoped Olivia felt the way he did about his being a part of her future. It was hard to believe they'd only been together a few days. But he'd been watching her a lot longer than that and the truth was he'd fallen for her just a little before they'd even exchanged a word.

As if his thoughts had summoned her she walked right up to him and smiled. His heart took a leap.

"Hey," she said.

"Hey," he said back, his insides shaking with anticipation.

Laney and Hayden were hugging, as were Sadie and Mc-Caleb. Both couples were engaged. Made Russ a little jealous, even though he was happy for them. If he had his way, he would fix that in the very near future.

Olivia looped her arm in his and pulled him close. "We're the only ones out here who aren't getting married," she whispered. "I'm now scheduled to be a bridesmaid twice in as many months. I've never been a bridesmaid before." She smiled again but her eyes told the tale. She was wondering where they went from here, as well.

Russ leaned closer to her, loving the electricity that instantly sparked. "You'll love it. And since I'm a groomsman, we'll have to make sure we get to walk together." Practice, he wanted to add.

She lifted a skeptical eyebrow. "I don't know about the loving-it part. Since both their mothers are gone, I think they're expecting me to be in charge of the wedding plans. I've seen movies about how crazy that can get." She shrugged. "I suppose as long as it doesn't include taffeta I might survive."

They shared a nervous laugh. God, he just wanted to pull

her into his arms and kiss her right there. Instead, he worried about whether or not she had ever considered marriage in her future. "You should be proud to have that honor."

Her cheeks flushed as she chewed on her lower lip. "I guess I am. I just never expected to be in a wedding period."

"Not even your own?" he ventured, his nerves vibrating with uncertainty. He wanted to show this woman just how good the right relationship could be. He wanted that chance more than he'd ever wanted anything.

"Especially not my own." She laughed, the sound as nervous as he felt. "Remember I'm the woman who doesn't know how to have a relationship."

He put his hand over hers and squeezed. It was time to man up and pop the first preliminary question. "I thought we were going to change that."

She smiled up at him, her eyes hopeful. "I was afraid you might have changed your mind now that your assignment is over and things are back to normal. Not that anything about my life will ever be completely normal. I'm fully aware that people do and say things in the heat of the moment that they regret later. If you want to rescind the offer now I understand. I'm not exactly a safe bet in the relationship department."

He kissed her. It was the only way to show her in no uncertain terms that he had no intention of retracting anything. Her arms went around his neck and his went around her waist. It was the perfect fit. He had no intention of letting this lady go. She hadn't been the easiest filly to round up but she was his now.

Applause echoed around them. They drew apart and Olivia's cheeks turned a deeper red as her sisters and their fiancés continued to clap loudly and cheered them on.

"Looks like it's official," Russ warned her.

"What's that?" she asked, that uncertainty still shining in her eyes.

"Your sisters approve. We can't let them down."

"So where do we go from here?"

"My place," he said with a wink.

"And after that?" She toyed with a button on his shirt, still obviously a little skittish when it came to putting her hopes in the future of a relationship.

"We'll work that out as we go. There's no hurry. As long as we're committed, the rest will fall into place."

She turned those big brown eyes up to him and the uncertainty was gone. "I'm definitely committed."

He grinned. "That makes two of us."

She made a face that warned she was worried about how he would take what she had to say next. "I was thinking about going back to law school and finishing that final year."

"If that's what you want, I'll back you one-hundred percent. Never doubt that, Liv. I'm with you, whatever we do and wherever we go."

Her relief was palpable. "My reason for walking away was a cop-out." She shrugged. "Another one of those commitment issues. But I'm not afraid anymore. Not with you backing me up."

"That's my girl."

Olivia rose up on tiptoe and kissed him. More of that zany applause broke out behind them.

Russ intended to take the lady home with him and spend the rest of his days showing her how good life and the right relationship could be.

VICTORIA WAS IMMENSELY thankful they were almost home. She refused to let Lucas drive with that cast. He'd finally stopped arguing and settled in for the three-hour trip.

They'd chatted about how thankful they were that the facts in the Princess Killer case had been brought to light once and for all. They'd even discussed the possibility of Russ and Olivia joining the ranks of the engaged. It seemed that the Colby Agency had facilitated the love lives of three happy couples.

She sighed. She loved it when things turned out exactly right.

"Did I tell you that Casey called?" Lucas said.

He knew perfectly well he had not. "When did he call?" Thomas Casey was one of Lucas's oldest and dearest friends, as well as his former boss from their CIA days.

"Oh, yesterday or the day before."

Lucas was still annoyed that she was pushing the issue of total retirement. The truth was, she loved being a part of the cases that came into the Colby Agency. The trouble was, Lucas too often ended up in danger. She would not allow him to continue to risk his life for anything.

"What did Thomas have to say?" Thomas Casey's niece, Casey Manning, had helped Levi Stark, one of Victoria's investigators from the Chicago office, with an investigation last fall into the troubles with Lucas's son, Slade Keaton. Casey and Levi had fallen in love and had been together since.

"His niece Casey is getting married next spring."

Why hadn't Victoria heard about this? Levi hadn't said a word. Of course, she had been down here in Texas and rather busy. "That's wonderful."

"As soon as the arrangements are final he'll let us know. We're at the top of the guest list, of course."

"Of course."

"He also asked me to consider doing some advising with his team later this year. I told him I would think about it."

Victoria held her tongue until the wave of frustration had eased to a tolerable level. "You worked in an advisory capacity in D.C. for many years, Lucas. I thought those days were over." She wanted him at her side. Safe.

"I can't deny that I miss the fulfillment of helping with a top-secret mission that involves national security."

And there it was. The bare truth. He did not want to retire.

"So you don't want to retire, after all?" She hated that disappointment weighted her words but there was no help for it.

"Victoria, this whole business about retirement has been about you being afraid I would be hurt."

That was true. She couldn't deny it.

"And we both know that could happen getting out of the shower in the morning."

"Let's not compare work with the CIA to getting out of the shower, Lucas."

"It could happen rushing back to help someone who had fallen, despite knowing that bombs were buried in that area."

He had her. "Yes, yes, I rushed back to help Clare with no thought to the danger to myself." It was true and she would do it again. "I know this about both of us, Lucas. And it terrifies me. I just want us to be a normal couple with a normal life."

He laughed long and loud.

"I see absolutely nothing amusing. I'm completely serious."

"Pull over, my dear."

"What? Now?"

"Yes."

Since they had left the interstate behind, his request wasn't a problem. She turned into the parking lot of the next convenience store. She put the car in Park and turned to him.

He leaned over the console and took her face in his hands. "Victoria, we are not normal people. We will never be normal people. We have a calling, and to deny that calling is to live in fear or avoidance and that would only make us unhappy and resentful. It's far better that we embrace who we are and what we do."

"But what about traveling and spending time just the two of us?"

"That we will do, I promise you. What we need in our lives now is balance. We can achieve that without giving up our calling. When we're needed on a special case, like this one, we'll be there. The rest of our time will be ours to do with as we please. Does that sound like an acceptable compromise?"

Victoria smiled. "It's more than acceptable. It's brilliant."

Lucas kissed her and Victoria understood that this was exactly what they were supposed to do for the rest of their lives.

* * * * *

Jordan moved quickly through the gravestones until he found the one stone that was newer than the others, only six years in the ground.

The name on the tombstone read Mary Justice Cardwell.

"Hello, Mother," he said removing his hat as he felt all the conflicting emotions he'd had when she was alive. All the arguments came rushing back, making him sick at the memory. He hadn't been able to change her mind, and now she was gone, leaving them all behind to struggle as a family without her.

He could almost hear their last argument whispered on the wind. "There is nothing keeping you here, let alone me," he'd argued. "Why are you fighting so hard to keep this place going? Can't you see that ranching is going to kill you?"

He recalled her smile, that gentle gleam in her eyes that infuriated him. "This land is what makes me happy, son. Someday you will realize that ranching is in our blood. You can fight it, but this isn't just your home, a part of your heart is here as well."

"Like hell," he'd said. "Sell the ranch, Mother, before it's too late. If not for yourself and the rest of us, then for Dana. She's too much like you. She will spend her life fighting to keep this place. Don't do that to her."

"She'll keep this ranch for the day when you come back to help her run it."

"That's never going to happen, Mother."

Mary Justice Cardwell had smiled that knowing smile of hers. "Only time will tell, won't it?"

Dear Reader,

It was so much fun for me to return to Cardwell Ranch. *Crime Scene at Cardwell Ranch* has been read by more than two million readers, so it was a treat to go back and find out what happened to the Justice and Cardwell families in the sequel. *Justice at Cardwell Ranch* is a story I've wanted to write for a long time.

When I was a girl, we had a cabin just down the road from where these books take place. I have such wonderful memories of the Gallatin Canyon. My brother and I had a fort out in the woods and spent hours exploring in what is now a wilderness area. I skied at Big Sky many times, and have hiked with a friend to Ousel Waterfalls, where part of this story takes place.

I hope you enjoy this return trip to the "canyon."

BJ Daniels

www.bjdaniels.com

JUSTICE AT CARDWELL RANCH

BY
BJ DANIELS

First published in Great Britain 2012
by Mills & Boon, an imprint of Harlequin (UK) Limited,
Eton House, 18-24 Paradise Road, Richmond, Surrey TW9 1SR

© Barbara Heinlein 2012

ISBN: 978 0 263 89581 0
ebook ISBN: 978 1 408 97259 5

46-1212

Harlequin (UK) policy is to use papers that are natural, renewable and recyclable products and made from wood grown in sustainable forests. The logging and manufacturing processes conform to the legal environmental regulations of the country of origin.

Printed and bound in Spain
by Blackprint CPI, Barcelona

This book is dedicated to my amazing husband.
He makes all this possible along with inspiring me
each and every day. Thank you, Parker.
Without your love, I couldn't do this.

Prologue

Nothing moved in the darkness. At the corner of the house she stopped to catch her breath. She could hear music playing somewhere down the street. Closer, a dog barked.

As she waited in the deep shadow at the edge of the house, she measured the distance and the light she would have to pass through to reach the second window.

When she'd sneaked into the house earlier, she'd left the window unlocked. But she had no way of knowing if someone had discovered it. If so, they might not have merely relocked it—they could be waiting for her.

Fear had her heart pounding and her breath coming out in painful bursts. If she got caught— She couldn't let herself think about that.

The dog stopped barking for a moment. All she could hear was the faint music drifting on the night breeze. She fought to keep her breathing in check as she inched along the side of the house to the first window.

A light burned inside, but the drapes were closed. Still, she waited to make sure she couldn't hear anyone on the other side of the glass before she moved.

Ducking, she slipped quickly through a shaft of illumination from a streetlamp and stopped at the second bedroom window.

There, she waited for a few moments. No light burned inside the room. Still she listened before she pulled the screwdriver from her jacket pocket and began to pry up the window.

At first the old casement window didn't move and she feared she'd been right about someone discovering what she'd done and locking the window again.

When it finally gave, it did so with a pop that sounded like an explosion to her ears. She froze. No sound came from within the room. Her hands shook as she pried the window up enough that she could get her fingers under it.

Feeling as if there was no turning back now, she lifted the window enough to climb in. Heart in her throat, she drew back the curtain. She'd half expected to find someone standing on the other side lying in wait for her.

The room, painted pink, was empty except for a few pieces of mismatched furniture: a dresser, a rocking chair, a changing table and a crib.

She looked to the crib, fearing that she'd come this far only to fail. But from the faint light coming from the streetlamp, she could see the small lump beneath the tiny quilt.

Her heart beat faster at the thought that in a few minutes she would have the baby in her arms.

She heard the car coming down the street just seconds before the headlights washed over her. Halfway in the window, there was nothing she could do but hurry. She wasn't leaving here without the baby.

Chapter One

The breeze rustled through the aspens, sending golden leaves whirling around him as Jordan Cardwell walked up the hill to the cemetery. He wore a straw Western hat he'd found on a peg by the back door of the ranch house.

He hadn't worn a cowboy hat since he'd left Montana twenty years ago, but this one kept his face from burning. It was so much easier to get sunburned at this high altitude than it was in New York City.

It was hot out and yet he could feel the promise of winter hiding at the edge of the fall day. Only the memory of summer remained in the Gallatin River Canyon. Cold nightly temperatures had turned the aspens to glittering shades of gold and orange against the dark green of the pines.

Below him he could hear the rushing water of the Gallatin as the river cut a deep winding course through the canyon. Across the river, sheer granite cliffs rose up to where the sun hung in a faded blue big Montana sky.

As he walked, the scent of crushed dry leaves beneath his soles sent up the remembered smell of other autumns. He knew this land. As hard as he'd tried to escape it, this place was branded on him, this life as familiar as his own heartbeat—even after all these years.

He thought of all the winters he'd spent in this canyon listening to the ice crack on the river, feeling the bite of snow as it blew off a pine bough to sting his face, breathing in a bone-deep cold that made his head ache.

He'd done his time here, he thought as he turned his face up to the last of the day's warmth before the sun disappeared behind the cliffs. Soon the aspens would be bare, the limbs dark against a winter-washed pale frosty sky. The water in the horse troughs would begin to freeze and so would the pooling eddies along the edge of the river. The cold air in the shade of the pines was a warning of what was to come, he thought as he reached the wrought-iron cemetery gate.

The gate groaned as he shoved it open. He hesitated. What was he doing here? Nearby the breeze sighed in the tops of the towering pines, drawing his attention to the dense stand. He didn't remember them being so tall. Or so dark and thick. As he watched the boughs sway, he told himself to make this quick. He didn't want to get caught here.

Even though it was a family cemetery, he didn't feel welcome here anymore. His own fault, but still, it could get messy if anyone from his family caught him on the ranch. He didn't plan to stick around long enough to see any of them. It was best that way, he told himself as he stepped through the gate into the small cemetery.

He'd never liked graveyards. Nor did it give him any comfort to know that more than a dozen remains of their relatives were interred here. He took no satisfaction in the long lineage of the Justice family, let alone the Cardwell one, in this canyon—unlike his sister.

Dana found strength in knowing that their ancestors had been mule-headed ranchers who'd weathered everything Montana had thrown at them to stay on this ranch. They'd settled this land along a stretch of the Gallatin, a crystal clear trout stream that ran over a hundred miles from Yellowstone Park to the Missouri River.

The narrow canyon got little sunlight each day. In the winter it was an icebox of frost and snow. Getting up to feed the animals had been pure hell. He'd never understood why any of them had stayed.

But they had, he thought as he surveyed the tombstones. They'd fought this land to remain here and now they would spend eternity in soil that had given them little in return for their labors.

A gust of wind rattled through the colorful aspen leaves and moaned in the high branches of the pines. Dead foliage floated like gold coins around him, showering the weather-bleached gravestones. He was reminded why he'd never liked coming up to this wind-blown hill. He found no peace among the dead. Nor had he come here today looking for it.

He moved quickly through the gravestones until he found the one stone that was newer than the others, only six years in the ground. The name on the tombstone read Mary Justice Cardwell.

"Hello, Mother," he said removing his hat as he felt all the conflicting emotions he'd had when she was alive. All the arguments came rushing back, making him sick at the memory. He hadn't been able to change her mind and now she was gone, leaving them all behind to struggle as a family without her.

He could almost hear their last argument whispered on the wind. "There is nothing keeping you here, let alone me," he'd argued. "Why are you fighting so hard to keep this place going? Can't you see that ranching is going to kill you?"

He recalled her smile, that gentle gleam in her eyes that infuriated him. "This land is what makes me happy, son. Someday you will realize that ranching is in our blood. You can fight it, but this isn't just your home. A part of your heart is here, as well."

"Like hell," he'd said. "Sell the ranch, Mother, before it's too late. If not for yourself and the rest of us, then for Dana. She's too much like you. She will spend her life fighting to keep this place. Don't do that to her."

"She'll keep this ranch for the day when you come back to help her run it."

"That's never going to happen, Mother."

Mary Justice Cardwell had smiled that knowing smile of hers. "Only time will tell, won't it?"

Jordan turned the hat brim nervously in his fingers as he looked down at his mother's grave and searched for the words to tell her how much he hated what she'd done to him. To all of them. But to his surprise he felt tears well in his eyes, his throat constricting on a gulf of emotion he hadn't anticipated.

A gust of wind bent the pine boughs and blew down to scatter dried leaves across the landscape. His skin rippled with goosebumps as he suddenly sensed someone watching him. His head came up, his gaze going to the darkness of the pines.

She was only a few yards away. He hadn't heard the woman on horseback approach and realized she must have been there the whole time, watching him.

She sat astride a large buckskin horse. Shadows played across her face from the swaying pine boughs. The breeze lifted the long dark hair that flowed like molten obsidian over her shoulders and halfway down her back.

There was something vaguely familiar about her. But if he'd known her years before when this was home, he couldn't place her now. He'd been gone too long from Montana.

And yet a memory tugged at him. His gaze settled on her face again, the wide-set green eyes, that piercing look that seemed to cut right to his soul.

With a curse, he knew where he'd seen her before—and why she was looking at him the way she was. A shudder moved through him as if someone had just walked over *his* grave.

LIZA TURNER HAD WATCHED the man slog up the hill, his footsteps slow, his head down, as if he were going to a funeral. So she hadn't been surprised when he'd pushed open the gate to the cemetery and stepped in.

At first, after reining her horse in under the pines, she'd been mildly curious. She loved this spot, loved looking across the canyon as she rode through the groves of aspens and pines. It was always cool in the trees. She liked listening to the river flowing emerald-green below her on the hillside and taking a moment to search the granite cliffs on the other side for mountain sheep.

She hadn't expected to see anyone on her ride this morning. When she'd driven into the ranch for her usual trek, she'd seen the Cardwell Ranch pickup leaving and remembered that Hud was taking Dana into Bozeman today for her doctor's appointment. They were leaving the kids with Dana's best friend and former business partner, Hilde at Needles and Pins, the local fabric store.

The only other person on the ranch was the aging ranch manager, Warren Fitzpatrick. Warren would be watching *Let's Make a Deal* at his cabin this time of the morning.

So Liza had been curious and a bit leery when she'd first laid eyes on the stranger in the Western straw hat. As far as she knew, no one else should have been on the ranch today. So who was this tall, broad-shouldered cowboy?

Dana had often talked about hiring some help since Warren was getting up in years and she had her hands full with a four- and five-year-old, not to mention now being pregnant with twins.

But if this man was the new hired hand, why would he be interested in the Justice-Cardwell family cemetery? She felt the skin on the back of her neck prickle. There was something about this cowboy... His face had been in shadow from the brim of his hat. When he'd stopped at one of the graves and had taken his hat off, head bowed, she still hadn't been able to see more than his profile from where she sat astride her horse.

Shifting in the saddle, she'd tried to get a better look. He must have heard the creak of leather or sensed her presence. His head came up, his gaze darting right to the spot where she sat. He looked startled at first, then confused as if he was trying to place her.

She blinked, not sure she could trust her eyes. *Jordan Cardwell?*

He looked completely different from the arrogant man in the expensive three-piece suit she'd crossed paths with six years ago. He wore jeans, a button-up shirt and work boots. He looked tanned and stronger as if he'd been doing manual labor. There was only a hint of the earlier arrogance in his expression, making him more handsome than she remembered.

She saw the exact moment when he recognized her. Bitterness burned in his dark gaze as a small resentful smile tugged at his lips.

Oh, yes, it was Jordan Cardwell all right, she thought, wondering what had made her think he was handsome just moments before or—even harder to believe, that he might have changed.

Six years ago he'd been the number one suspect in a murder as well as a suspect in an attempted murder. Liza had been the deputy who'd taken his fingerprints.

She wondered now what he was doing not only back in the canyon, but also on the ranch he and his siblings had fought so hard to take from their sister Dana.

DANA SAVAGE LAY BACK ON THE examining table, nervously picking at a fingernail. "I can't remember the last time I saw my feet," she said with a groan.

Dr. Pamela Burr laughed. "This might feel a little cold."

Dana tried not to flinch as the doctor applied clear jelly to her huge stomach. She closed her eyes and waited until she heard the heartbeats before she opened them again. "So everything is okay?"

"Your babies appear to be doing fine. Don't you want to look?"

Dana didn't look at the monitor. "You know Hud. He's determined to be surprised. Just like the last two. So I don't dare look." She shot a glance at her husband. He stood next to her, his gaze on her, not the screen. He smiled, but she could see he was worried.

The doctor shut off the machine. "As for the spotting…"

Dana felt her heart drop as she saw the concern in Dr. Burr's expression.

"I'm going to have to insist on bed rest for these last weeks," she said. "Let's give these babies the best start we can by leaving them where they are for now." She looked to Hud.

"You can count on me," he said. "It's Dana you need to convince."

Dana sat up and laid her hands over her extended stomach. She felt the twins moving around in the cramped space. Poor babies. "Okay."

"You understand what bed rest means?" the doctor asked. "No ranch business, no getting up except to shower and use the bathroom. You're going to need help with Hank and Mary."

That was putting it mildly when you had a four-and five-year-old who were wild as the canyon where they lived.

"I'm sure Hud—"

"You'll need more than his help." The doctor pressed a piece of paper into her hand. "These are several women you might call that I've used before."

Dana didn't like the idea of bringing in a stranger to take care of Hud and the kids, but the babies kicked and she nodded.

"Doc said I was going to have to watch you like a hawk," Hud told her on the way home. Apparently while she was getting dressed, Dr. Burr had been bending his ear, down the hall in her office. "You always try to do too much. With the kids, the ranch, me—"

"I'll be good."

He gave her a disbelieving look.

"Marshal, would you like a sworn affidavit?"

He grinned over at her. "Actually, I'm thinking about handcuffing you to the bed. I reckon it will be the only way I can keep you down for a day let alone weeks."

Dana groaned as she realized how hard it was going to be to stay in bed. "What about Hank and Mary? They won't understand why their mommy can't be up and around, let alone outside with them and their animals." Both of them had their own horses and loved to ride.

"I've already put in for a leave. Liza can handle things. Anyway, it's in between resort seasons so it's quiet."

September through the middle of November was slow around Big Sky with the summer tourists gone and ski season still at least a month away.

Dana knew October was probably a better time than any other for her husband to be off work. That wasn't the problem. "Hud, I hate to see you have to babysit me and the kids."

"It's not babysitting when it's *your* wife and kids, Dana."

"You know what I mean. There are the kids and the ranch—"

"Honey, you've been trying to do it all for too long."

She *had* been juggling a lot of balls for some time now, but Hud always helped on the weekends. Their ranch manager, Warren Fitzpatrick, was getting up in years so he had really slowed down. But Warren was a fixture around the ranch, one she couldn't afford to replace. More than anything, she loved the hands-on part of ranching so she spent as much time as she could working the land.

When she'd found out she was pregnant this time she'd been delighted, but a little worried how she was going to handle another child right now.

Then the doctor had told her she was having twins. *Twins?* Seriously?

"Are you all right?" Hud asked as he placed his hand over hers and squeezed.

She smiled and nodded. "I'm always all right when I'm with you."

He gave her hand another squeeze before he went back to driving. "I'm taking you home. Then I'll go by the shop and pick up the kids." Her friend Hilde had the kids in Big Sky. "But I'd better not find out you were up and about while I was gone."

Dana shook her head and made a cross with her finger over her heart. She lay back and closed her eyes, praying as she had since the spotting had begun that the babies she was carrying would be all right. Mary and Hank were so excited about the prospect of two little brothers or sisters. She couldn't disappoint them.

She couldn't disappoint anyone, especially her mother, she thought. While Mary Justice Cardwell had been gone six years now, she was as much a part of the ranch as the old, two-story house where Dana lived with Hud and the kids. Her mother had trusted her to keep Cardwell Ranch going. Against all odds she was doing her darnedest to keep that promise.

So why did she feel so scared, as if waiting for the other shoe to drop?

Chapter Two

Jordan watched Deputy Liza Turner ride her horse out of the pines. The past six years had been good to her. She'd been pretty back then. Now there was a confidence as if she'd grown into the woman she was supposed to become. He recalled how self-assured and efficient she'd been at her job. She was also clearly at home on the back of a horse.

The trees cast long shadows over the stark landscape. Wind whirled the dried leaves that now floated in the air like snowflakes.

"Jordan Cardwell," she said as she reined in her horse at the edge of the cemetery.

He came out through the gate, stopping to look up at her. "Deputy." She had one of those faces that was almost startling in its uniqueness. The green eyes wide, captivating and always filled with curiosity. He thought she was more interesting than he remembered. That, he realized, was probably because she was out of uniform.

She wore jeans and a red-checked Western shirt that made her dark hair appear as rich as mahogany. She narrowed those green eyes at him. Curiosity and suspicion, he thought.

"I'm surprised to see you here," she said, a soft lilt

to her voice. She had a small gap between her two front teeth, an imperfection, that he found charming.

"I don't know why you'd be surprised. My sister might have inherited the ranch but I'm still family."

She smiled at that and he figured she knew all about what had happened after his mother had died—and her new will had gone missing.

"I didn't think you'd ever come back to the ranch," she said.

He chuckled. "Neither did I. But people change."

"Do they?" She was studying him in a way that said she doubted he had. He didn't need to read her expression to know she was also wondering what kind of trouble he'd brought back to the canyon with him. The horse moved under her, no doubt anxious to get going.

"Your horse seems impatient," he said. "Don't let me keep you from your ride." With a tip of his hat, he headed down the mountain to the ranch house where he'd been raised.

It seemed a lifetime ago. He could barely remember the man he'd been then. But he would be glad to get off the property before his sister and her husband returned. He planned to put off seeing them if at all possible. So much for family, he thought.

WHEN DANA OPENED HER EYES, she saw that they'd left the wide valley and were now driving through the Gallatin Canyon. The "canyon" as it was known, ran from the mouth just south of Gallatin Gateway almost to West Yellowstone, fifty miles of winding road that trailed the river in a deep cut through the mountains.

The drive along the Gallatin River had always been breathtaking, a winding strip of highway that followed the blue-ribbon trout stream up over the continental divide. This time of year the Gallatin ran crystal clear over green-tinted boulders. Pine trees grew dark and thick along its edge and against the steep mountains. Aspens, their leaves rust-reds and glittering golds, grew among the pines.

Sheer rock cliffs overlooked the highway and river, with small areas of open land, the canyon not opening up until it reached Big Sky. The canyon had been mostly cattle and dude ranches, a few summer cabins and homes—that was until Big Sky resort and the small town that followed at the foot of Lone Mountain.

Luxury houses had sprouted up all around the resort. Fortunately, some of the original cabins still remained and the majority of the canyon was national forest so it would always remain undeveloped. The "canyon" was also still its own little community, for which Dana was grateful. This was the only home she'd known and, like her stubborn ancestors, she had no intention of ever leaving it.

Both she and Hud had grown up here. They'd been in love since junior high, but hit a rocky spot some years ago thanks to her sister. Dana didn't like to think about the five years she and Hud had spent apart as they passed the lower mountain resort area and, a few miles farther, turned down the road to Cardwell Ranch.

Across the river and a half mile back up a wide valley, the Cardwell Ranch house sat against a backdrop of granite cliffs, towering dark pines and glittering aspens. The house was a big, two-story rambling affair with a wide front porch and a brick-red metal roof. Behind it stood a huge weathered barn and some outbuildings and corrals.

Dana never felt truly at home until they reached the ranch she'd fought tooth and nail to save. When Mary Justice Cardwell had been bucked off a horse and died six years ago, Dana had thought all was lost. Her mother's original will when her children were young left the ranch to all of them.

Mary hadn't realized until her children were grown that only Dana would keep the ranch. The others would sell it, take the profits and never look back until the day they regretted what they'd done. By then it would be too late. So her mother had made a new will, leaving the ranch to her. But her mother had hidden it where she hoped her daughter would find it. Fortunately, Dana had found it in time to save the ranch.

The will had put an end to her siblings' struggle to force her to sell the land and split the profits with them. Now her three siblings were paid part of the ranch's profit each quarter. Not surprisingly, she hadn't heard from any of them since the will had settled things six years before.

As Hud pulled into the ranch yard, Dana spotted a car parked in front of the old house and frowned. The car was an older model with California plates.

"You didn't already hire someone—"

"No," Hud said before she could finish. "I wouldn't do that without talking to you first. Do you think the doctor called one of the women she told you about?"

Before Dana could answer, she saw that someone was waiting out on the broad front porch. As Hud pulled in beside the car, the woman stepped from out of the shadows.

"Stacy?" She felt her heart drop. After six years

of silence and all the bad feelings from the past, what was her older sister doing here?

"SURPRISE," STACY SAID WITH a shrug and a worried smile. Like Dana, Stacy had gotten the Justice-Cardwell dark good looks, but she'd always been the cute one who capitalized on her appearance, cashing in as she traded her way up through three marriages that Dana knew of and possibly more since.

Just the sight of her sister made Dana instantly wary. She couldn't help but be mistrustful given their past.

Her sister's gaze went to Dana's stomach. "Oh, my. You're *pregnant*."

"We need to get Dana in the house," Hud said, giving his sister-in-law a nod of greeting. Stacy opened the door and let them enter before she followed them in.

Dana found herself looking around the living room, uncomfortable that her sister had been inside the house even though it had once been Stacy's home, as well.

The house was as it had been when her mother was alive. Original Western furnishings, a lot of stone and wood and a bright big airy kitchen. Dana, like her mother, chose comfort over style trends. She loved her big, homey house. It often smelled of something good bubbling on the stove, thanks to the fact that Hud loved to cook.

Dana preferred to spend her time with her children outside, teaching them to ride or watching a new foal being born or picking fresh strawberries out of the large garden she grew—just as her own mother had done with her.

As she looked at her sister, she was reminded of some of her mother's last words to her. "Families stick together. It isn't always easy. Everyone makes mistakes. Dana, you have to find forgiveness in your heart. If not for them, then for yourself."

Her mother had known then that if anything happened to her, Jordan, Stacy and Clay would fight her for the ranch. That's why she'd made the new will.

But she must also have known that the will would divide them.

"It's been a long time," Dana said, waiting, knowing her sister wanted something or she wouldn't be here.

"I know I should have kept in touch more," Stacy said. "I move around a lot." But she'd always managed to get her check each quarter as part of her inheritance from the ranch profits. Dana instantly hated the uncharitable thought. She didn't want to feel that way about her sister. But Stacy had done some things in the past that had left the two of them at odds. Like breaking Dana and Hud up eleven years ago. Dana still had trouble forgiving her sister for that.

Stacy shifted uncomfortably in the silence. "I should have let you know I was coming, huh."

"Now isn't the best time for company," Hud said. "Dana's doctor has advised her to get off her feet for the rest of her pregnancy."

"But I'm not *company*," Stacy said. "I'm family. I can help."

Hud looked to his wife. "Why don't you go. It's fine," Dana said and removed her coat.

"So you're pregnant," her sister said.

"Twins," Dana said, sinking into a chair.

Stacy nodded.

Dana realized Hud was still in his coat, waiting,

afraid to leave her alone with Stacy. "Are you going to pick up the kids?"

He gave her a questioning look.

"I thought you probably had more kids," her sister said. "The toys and stuff around."

Dana was still looking at her husband. She knew he didn't trust Stacy, hated she'd been alone in their house while they were gone and worse, he didn't want to leave the two of them alone. "Stacy and I will be fine."

Still he hesitated. He knew better than anyone what her siblings were like.

"Stacy, would you mind getting me a drink of water?" The moment her sister left the room, Dana turned to her husband. "I'll be *fine*," she said lowering her voice. "Go pick up the kids. I promise I won't move until you get back." She could tell that wasn't what had him concerned.

He glanced toward the kitchen and the sound of running water. "I won't be long."

She motioned him over and smiled as he leaned down to kiss her. At the same time, he placed a large hand on her swollen stomach. The babies moved and he smiled.

"You have your cell phone if you need me?"

Dana nodded. "The marshal's office is also on speed dial. I'll be fine. Really."

Stacy came back in with a glass full of water as Hud left. "I'm glad things have turned out good for you. Hud is so protective."

"Thank you," she said as she took the glass and studied her sister over the rim as she took a drink.

"I would have called," Stacy said, "but I wanted to surprise you."

"I'm surprised." She watched her sister move

around the room, touching one object after another, seeming nervous. Her first thought when she'd seen her sister was that she'd come here because she was in trouble.

That initial observation hadn't changed. Now though, Dana was betting it had something to do with money. It usually did with Stacy, unfortunately.

Years ago Dana had found out just how low her sister would stoop if the price was right. She had good reason not to trust her sister.

"The place hasn't changed at all," Stacy was saying now. "Except for the pile of toys in the sunroom. I heard Hud say he was going to pick up the kids?"

"Hank and Mary, five and four."

"You named your daughter after mother, that's nice," Stacy said. "I thought you probably would." She seemed to hear what she'd said. "I want you to know I'm not upset about mother leaving you the ranch. You know me, I would have just blown the money." She flashed a self-deprecating smile. "And you're pregnant with twins! When are you due?"

"Eight weeks." When she finally couldn't take it anymore, Dana asked, "Stacy, what are you doing here?"

"It's kind of a strange story," her sister said, looking even more nervous.

Dana braced herself. If Stacy thought it was a strange story, then it could be anything. Her sister opened her mouth to say something, but was interrupted.

From upstairs a baby began to cry.

"What is that?" Dana demanded.

"I haven't had a chance to tell you," Stacy said as she started for the stairs. "That's Ella. That's my other surprise. I have a baby."

LIZA PARKED HER PICKUP ACROSS the road from Trail's End and settled in to wait. She had a clear view of the small cabin Jordan had rented. Like a lot of Big Sky, the string of cabins were new. But it being off-season and the cabins' only view being Highway 191, she figured they weren't too pricey. She wondered how Jordan was fixed for money and if that's what had brought him back here.

Pulling out her phone, she called Hud's cell. He answered on the third ring. She could hear the kids in the background and a woman's voice. Hilde, Dana's best friend. He must be at Needles and Pins.

"How's Dana, boss?" she asked.

"Stubborn."

She laughed. "So the doctor *did* prescribe bed rest."

"Yes. Fortunately, I know you can run things just fine without me."

"Probably more smoothly without you around," she joked.

He must have heard something in her voice. "But?"

"Nothing I can't handle," she assured him. "But you might want to give Dana a heads-up."

"Dana already knows. Stacy's at the house right now."

"Stacy?"

"Who were *you* talking about?" Hud asked.

"Jordan."

She heard Hud swear under his breath.

"I saw him earlier on the ranch, actually at the family cemetery," Liza said.

"What's he doing in the canyon?"

"He didn't say, but I found out where he's staying. He's rented a cabin past Buck's T-4." Buck's T-4 was a local landmark bar and hotel. "I'm hanging out, watching to see what he's up to."

"Probably not the best way to spend taxpayers' dollars, but I appreciate it. As far as I know, he hasn't contacted Dana."

"Let me know if he does. In the meantime, I'll stick around here for a while."

"You really need to get a life, deputy," Hud said. "Thanks. Let me know if you need help."

"So Stacy's here, too?"

"We haven't heard from any of them in six years and now two of them are in the canyon? This doesn't bode well."

That had been her thought exactly.

"I don't want them upsetting Dana," he said. "All we need is for Clay to show up next. This couldn't come at a worse time. I'm worried enough about Dana and the babies. I have a bad feeling this could have something to do with that developer who's been after Dana to sell some of the ranch."

"The timing does make you wonder," Liza said.

"I'm going back to the ranch now."

"You stick close to Dana. I'll let you know if Jordan heads for the ranch." Hanging up, Liza settled in again. She knew it could be a while. Jordan might be in for the night.

The canyon got dark quickly this time of year. With the dark that settled over it like a cloak came a drop in temperature. She could hear the river, smell the rich scent of fall. A breeze stirred the nearby pines, making the branches sway and sigh. A couple of stars popped out above the canyon walls.

The door of the cabin opened. Jordan stepped out

and headed for his rented SUV parked outside. He was dressed in a warm coat, gloves and a hat, all in a dark color. He definitely didn't look like a man going out for dinner—or even to visit his sister. He glanced around as if he thought someone might be watching him before climbing into his rental.

Liza felt her heart kick up a beat as she slunk down in the pickup seat and waited. A few moments later she heard the SUV pull out. She started the truck, and sitting up, followed at a distance.

To her relief, he didn't turn down Highway 191 in the direction of the Cardwell Ranch—and his sister's house. Instead, he headed north toward Big Sky proper, making her think she might be wrong. Maybe he was merely going out to find a place to have dinner.

He drove on past the lighted buildings that made up the Meadow Village, heading west toward Mountain Village. There was little traffic this time of year. She let another vehicle get between them, all the time keeping Jordan's taillights in sight.

Just when she started speculating on where he might be headed, he turned off on the road to Ousel Falls. They passed a few commercial buildings, a small housing complex and then the road cut through the pines as it climbed toward the falls.

Liza pulled over, letting him get farther ahead. Had he spotted the tail? She waited as long as she dared before she drove on up the road. Her headlights cut a gold swath through the darkness. Dense pines lined both sides of the mountain road. There was no traffic at all up this way. She worried he had spotted her following him and was now leading her on a wild-goose chase.

She hadn't gone far when her headlights picked up

the parking lot for the falls. Jordan's rental was parked in the empty lot. She couldn't tell if he was still in the vehicle. Grabbing her baseball cap off the seat, she covered her dark hair as she drove on past.

Out of the corner of her eye she saw that the SUV was empty. Past it near the trailhead, she glimpsed the beam of a flashlight bobbing as it headed down the trail.

A few hundred yards up the road Liza found a place to pull over. She grabbed her own flashlight from under the seat, checked to make sure the batteries were still working and got out of the truck.

It was a short hike back to the trailhead. From there the path dropped to the creek before rising again as it twisted its way through the thick forest.

The trail was wide and paved and she found, once her eyes adjusted, that she didn't need to use her flashlight if she was careful. Enough starlight bled down through the pine boughs that she could see far enough ahead—and she knew the trail well.

There was no sign of Jordan, though. She'd reached the creek and bridge, quickly crossed it, and had started up the winding track when she caught a glimpse of light above her on the footpath.

She stopped to listen, afraid he might have heard her behind him. But there was only the sound of the creek and moan of the pines in the breeze. Somewhere in the distance an owl hooted. She moved again, hurrying now.

Once the pathway topped out, she should be able to see Jordan's light ahead of her, though she couldn't imagine what he was doing hiking to the falls tonight.

There was always a good chance of running into a

moose or a wolf or worse this time of a year, a hungry grizzly foraging for food before hibernation.

The trail topped out. She stopped to catch her breath and listen for Jordan. Ahead she could make out the solid rock area at the base of the waterfall. A few more steps and she could feel the mist coming off the cascading water. From here, the walkway carved a crooked path up through the pines to the top of the falls.

There was no sign of any light ahead and the only thing she could hear was rushing water. Where was Jordan? She moved on, convinced he was still ahead of her. Something rustled in the trees off to her right. A limb cracked somewhere ahead in the pines.

She stopped and drew her weapon. Someone was out there.

The report of the rifle shot felt so close it made the hair stand up on her neck. The sound ricocheted off the rock cliff and reverberated through her. Liza dove to the ground. A second shot echoed through the trees.

Weapon drawn, she scrambled up the hill and almost tripped over the body Jordan Cardwell was standing over.

Chapter Three

"You have a *baby*?" Dana said, still shocked when Stacy came back downstairs carrying a pink bundle. "I'm just having a hard time imagining you as a mother."

"You think you're the only one with a maternal instinct?" Stacy sounded hurt.

"I guess I never thought you *wanted* a baby."

Stacy gave a little shrug. "People change."

Did they? Dana wondered as she studied her sister.

"Want to see her?" Stacy asked.

Dana nodded and her sister carefully transferred the bundle into her arms. Dana saw that it wasn't a blanket at all that the baby was wrapped in, but a cute pink quilt. Parting the edges, she peered in at the baby. A green-eyed knockout stared back at her.

"Isn't she *beautiful*?"

"She's breathtaking. What's her name?"

"Ella."

Dana looked up at her sister, her gaze going to Stacy's bare left-hand ring finger. "Is there a father?"

"Of course," her sister said with an embarrassed laugh. "He's in the military. We're getting married when he comes home in a few weeks."

Stacy had gone through men like tissues during a sad

movie. In the past she'd married for money. Maybe this time she had found something more important, Dana hoped, glancing down at the baby in her arms.

"Hello, Ella," she said to the baby. The bow-shaped lips turned up at the corners, the green eyes sparkling. "How old is she?"

"Six months."

As the baby began to fuss, Stacy dug in a diaper bag Dana hadn't seen at the end of the couch. She pulled out a bottle before going into the kitchen to warm it.

Dana stared at the precious baby, her heart in her throat. She couldn't imagine her sister with a baby. In the past Stacy couldn't even keep a houseplant alive.

As her sister came out of the kitchen, Dana started to hand back the baby.

"You can feed her if you want."

Dana took the bottle and watched the baby suck enthusiastically at the warm formula. "She's adorable." Her sister didn't seem to be listening though.

Stacy had walked over to the window and was looking out. "I forgot how quiet it is here." She hugged herself as a gust of wind rattled the old window. "Or how cold it is this time of year."

"Where *have* you been living?"

"Southern California," she said, turning away from the window.

"Is that where you met the father?"

Stacy nodded. "It's getting late. Ella and I should go."

"Where are you *going?*" Dana asked, alarmed, realizing that she'd been cross-examining her sister as if Stacy was one of Hud's suspects. She couldn't bear the thought of this baby being loaded into that old car outside with Stacy at the wheel.

"I planned to get a motel for the night. Kurt's got some relatives up by Great Falls. They've offered me a place to stay until he gets leave and we can find a place of our own."

Dana shook her head, still holding tight to the baby. "You're staying here. You and Ella can have Mary's room. I don't want you driving at night."

LIZA SWUNG THE BARREL OF HER gun and snapped on her flashlight, aiming both at Jordan. "Put your hands up," she ordered.

He didn't move. He stood stock-still, staring down at the body at his feet. He appeared to be in shock.

"I said put your hands up," she ordered again. He blinked and slowly raised his gaze to her, then lifted his hands. Keeping the gun trained on him, she quickly frisked him. "Where is the weapon?" She nudged him with the point of her gun barrel.

He shook his head. "*I* didn't shoot him."

Liza took a step back from him and shone the flashlight beam into the pines. The light didn't go far in the dense trees and darkness. "Who shot him?"

"I don't know."

She squatted down to check for a pulse. None. Pulling out her phone, she called for backup and the coroner. When she'd finished, she turned the beam on Jordan again. "You can start by telling me what you're doing out here."

He looked down at the body, then up at her. "You know I didn't kill him."

"How do I know that?"

True, she hadn't seen him carrying a rifle, but he could have hidden one in the woods earlier today. But how did he get rid of it so quickly? She would have heard him throw it into the trees.

"What are you doing here at the falls in the middle of the night?"

He looked away.

She began to read him his rights.

"All right," he said with a sigh. "You aren't going to believe me. I was meeting him here."

"To buy drugs?"

"No." He looked insulted. "It's a long story."

"We seem to have time." She motioned to a downed tree not far from the body but deep enough in the trees that if the killer was still out there, he wouldn't have a clear shot.

Jordan sighed as he sat down, dropping his head in his hands for a few moments. "When I was in high school my best friend hung himself. At least that's what everyone thought, anyway. I didn't believe he would do that, but there was no evidence of foul play. Actually, no one believed me when I argued there was no way Tanner would have taken his own life."

"People often say that about suicide victims."

"Yeah. Well, a few weeks ago, I got a call from…" He looked in the direction of the body, but quickly turned away. "Alex Winslow."

"Is that the victim?"

He nodded. "Alex asked if I was coming back for our twenty-year high-school reunion."

"You *were?*" She couldn't help her surprise.

He gave her an are-you-kidding look. "I told him no. That's when he mentioned Tanner."

"Alex Winslow told you he was looking into Tanner's death?"

"Not in so many words. He said something like, 'Do you ever think about Tanner?' He sounded like he'd been drinking. At first I just thought it was the booze talking."

He told her about the rest of the conversation, apparently quoting Alex as best as he could remember.

"Man, it would take something to hang yourself," Alex had said. "Put that noose around your neck and stand there balancing on nothing more than a log stump. One little move… Who would do that unless they were forced to? You know, like at gunpoint or…I don't know, maybe get tricked into standing up there?"

"What are you saying?"

"Just…what if he didn't do it? What if they killed him?"

"They? Who?"

"Don't listen to me. I've had a few too many beers tonight. So, are you sure I can't talk you into coming to the reunion? Even if I told you I have a theory about Tanner's death."

"What theory?"

"Come to the reunion. Call me when you get into town and I'll tell you. Don't mention this to anyone else. Seriously. I don't want to end up like poor old Tanner."

"That could have just been the alcohol talking," Liza said when he finished.

"That's what I thought, too, until he wanted to meet at the falls after dark. Something had him running scared."

"With good reason, apparently. Alex Winslow is a former friend?"

Jordan nodded.

"You weren't just a little suspicious, meeting in the dark at a waterfall?"

"I thought he was being paranoid, but I played along."

"You didn't consider it might be dangerous?"

"No, I thought Alex was overreacting. He was like that. Or at least he had been in high school. I haven't seen him in twenty years."

"Why, if he knew something, did he wait all these years?"

Jordan shrugged. "I just know that Tanner wouldn't have killed himself. He was a smart guy. If anything he was too smart for his own good. I figured if there was even a small chance that Alex knew something..." He glanced over at her. "Apparently, Alex had reason to be paranoid. This proves that there is more to Tanner's suicide."

She heard the determination in his voice and groaned inwardly. "This proves nothing except that Alex Winslow is dead." But Jordan wasn't listening.

"Also it proves I wasn't such a fool to believe Alex really did know something about Tanner's death."

She studied Jordan for a moment. "Did he say something to you before he was shot?"

His gaze shifted away. "I can't even be sure I heard him right."

"What did he say?"

"Shelby."

"Shelby?"

He nodded. "We went to school with a girl named Shelby Durran. She and Tanner were a couple. At least until Christmas our senior year."

HUD HAD JUST RETURNED with the kids when he got the call about the shooting.

"Go," Dana said. "I'll be fine. Stacy is here. She said she'd have the kids help her make dinner for all of us."

He mugged a face and lowered his voice. "Your sister *cooking?* Now that's frightening."

"Go," his wife ordered, giving him a warning look. "We can manage without you for a while."

"Are you sure?" He took her hand and squeezed it. "You promise to stay right where you are?"

"Promise."

Still, he hesitated. He'd been shocked to walk into the house and see Dana holding a baby. For a few moments, he'd been confused as to where she'd gotten it.

"Has Stacy said anything about where she's been?" he asked, glancing toward the kitchen. He could hear the voices of his children and sister-in-law. They all sounded excited about whatever they were making for dinner.

"Southern California. She's headed for Great Falls. There's a military base located there so that makes sense since she says the baby's father is in the military."

"If Stacy can be believed," he said quietly.

Dana mugged a face at him. But telling the truth wasn't one of her sister's strong suits. It bothered him that Dana was defending her sister. He figured the baby had something to do with it. Dana was a sucker for kids.

"Stacy seems different now," she said. "I think it's the baby. It seems to have grounded her some, maybe."

"Maybe," he said doubtfully.

"Go on, you have a murder investigation to worry about instead of me."

"You sound way too happy about that."

LIZA ALREADY HAD THE CRIME scene cordoned off when Hud arrived. He waved to the deputy on guard at the falls parking lot as he got out of his patrol SUV. The coroner's van was parked next to the two police vehicles.

"The coroner just went in," the deputy told him.

He turned on his flashlight and started down the trail. Hud couldn't help thinking about his wife's siblings trying to force her to sell the family ranch. They'd been like vultures, none of them having any interest in Cardwell Ranch. All they'd wanted was the money.

Jordan had been the worst because of his New York lifestyle—and his out-of-work model wife. But Stacy and Clay had had their hands out, as well. Hud hated to think what would have happened if Dana hadn't found the new will her mother had made leaving her the ranch.

He smiled at the memory of where she'd found it. Mary Justice Cardwell had put it in her favorite old recipe book next to "Double Chocolate Brownies." The brownies had been Hud's favorite. Dana hadn't made them in all the time the two of them had been apart. When they'd gotten back together six years ago, Dana had opened the cookbook planning to surprise him with the brownies, only to be surprised herself.

Two of her siblings were back in the canyon? That had him worried even before the call from his deputy marshal that there'd been a murder. And oh, yeah, Liza had told him, Jordan Cardwell was somehow involved.

Now as he hiked into the falls, he tried to keep his temper in check. If Dana's family thought they were going to come back here and upset her—

Ahead he saw the crowd gathered at the top of the falls. He headed for the coroner.

Coroner Rupert Milligan was hugging seventy, but

you'd never know it the way he acted. Six years ago, Hud had thought the man older than God and more powerful in this county. Tall, white-haired, with a head like a buffalo, he had a gruff voice and little patience for stupidity. He'd retired as a country doctor to work as a coroner.

None of that had changed in the past six years. Just as Rupert's love for murder mysteries and forensics hadn't.

"So what do we have?" Hud asked over the roar of the falls as he joined him.

Rupert answered without even bothering to look up. "Single gunshot through the heart. Another through the lungs. High-powered rifle."

"Distance?"

"I'd say fifty yards."

"That far," he said, surprised. The killer would have needed the victim to be out in the open with no trees in the way to make such a shot. Like at the top of a waterfall. "Any idea where the shot came from?"

Rupert had been crouched beside the body. Now he finally looked up. "In case you haven't noticed, it's dark out. Once it gets daylight you can look for tracks and possibly a shell casing. And once I get the body to Bozeman for an autopsy I might be able to tell you more about the trajectory of the bullet. Offhand, I'd say the shot came from the other side of the creek, probably on the side of the mountain."

"So either it was a lucky shot or the killer had been set up and waiting," Liza said, joining them. "The killer either picked the meeting spot or was told where the victim would be."

Rupert shifted his gaze to her and frowned. Being from the old school, the coroner made no secret of the fact that he didn't hold much appreciation for women law enforcement. If he'd had his way, he would have put them all behind a desk.

Hud liked that Liza didn't seem to let him bother her. His deputy marshal's good looks could be deceiving. Small in stature, too cute for her own good and easy-going, Liza often gave criminals the idea that she was a pushover. They, however, quickly learned differently. He wondered if Jordan Cardwell thought the same thing about the deputy marshal. If so, he was in for a surprise.

"Which could mean either that the victim was expecting to meet not only Jordan Cardwell up here, but also someone he trusted," she continued. "Or—"

"Or Jordan told the killer about the meeting," Hud interjected.

Liza nodded and glanced over to the stump where Jordan was waiting. "That is always another possibility."

"One I suggest you don't forget," Hud said under his breath. "If it's all right with you, I'll take our suspect down to the office."

She nodded. "I want to wait for the crime scene techs to arrive."

Hud hadn't seen Jordan for six years. As he walked toward him, he was thinking he could have easily gone another six and not been in the least bit sorry.

"You just happen to come back to the canyon and a man dies," he said.

"Good to see you again, too, brother-in-law. I guess my invitation to the wedding must have gotten lost in the mail, huh?"

"What are you doing here, Jordan?"

"I already told your deputy marshal."

"Well, you're going to have to tell me, too. Let's get out of the woods and go to my office. You have a rifle you need to pick up before we go?"

Jordan gave him a grim, disappointed look. "No, I'm good."

THE DOOR OPENED A CRACK. "Oh, good, you're awake," Stacy said as she peered in at Dana. "I brought you some still-warm chocolate chips cookies and some milk."

"That was very thoughtful of you," Dana said, sitting up in the bed and putting her crossword puzzle aside. Earlier, before her doctor's appointment, Hud had made her a bed in the sunroom so she wouldn't have to go up the stairs—and would be where she could see most of what was going on. She patted the bed, and her sister sat down on the edge and placed the tray next to them.

"I'm just glad you let me stay and help out. It was fun baking with Hank and Mary. They are so cute. Hank looks just like a small version of Hud and Mary is the spitting image of you. Do you know..." She motioned to Dana's big belly.

"No," she said, taking a bite of cookie. "We want to be surprised. Did you find out ahead of time?"

Stacy had cautiously placed a hand on Dana's abdomen and now waited with expectation. The babies had been restless all day, kicking up a storm. She watched her sister's face light up as one of the twins gave her hand a swift kick.

Stacy laughed and pulled her hand back. "Isn't that the coolest thing ever?"

Dana nodded, studying her older sister. Stacy had changed little in appearance. She was still the pretty one. Her dark hair was chin-length, making her brown eyes the focus of her face. She'd always had that innocent look. That was probably, Dana realized with a start, why she'd been able to get away with as much as she had.

"So did you know ahead of time you were having a girl?" she asked again.

Stacy shook her head and helped herself to a cookie. "It was a surprise."

"Speaking of surprises…" She watched her sister's face. "Jordan is in town."

"Jordan?" Had Stacy known? "What is *he* doing here?"

"I thought you might know."

Stacy shook her head and looked worried. "I haven't heard from him since we were all here six years ago." She made a face. "I still feel bad about trying to force you to sell the ranch."

Dana waved that away. "It's history. The ranch is still in the family and it makes enough money that you and our brothers get to share in the profits. You know I think my lawyer did mention that he'd received notice that Jordan was divorced."

"I wonder how much of his ranch profits he has to give to Jill? That woman was such a gold digger." Stacy laughed as she realized the irony. "I should know, huh? Back then I figured if I was going to get married, I might as well get paid for it." She shook her head as if amazed by the woman she'd been. "Have you heard from Clay?"

"No." She helped herself to another cookie and sipped some of the milk. "He hasn't been cashing his checks lately. My attorney is checking into it."

"That's odd," Stacy agreed. "Well, I need to clean up the kitchen."

"Thanks so much for giving the kids their baths and getting them to bed." Mary and Hank had come in earlier to say good-night and have Dana read a book to them before bed. They'd been wearing their footie pajamas, their sweet faces scrubbed clean and shiny. They'd been excited about helping their aunt Stacy cook.

"Thank you so much for all your help," Dana said, touched by everything Stacy had done.

"I'm just glad I was here so I could." She smiled. "I didn't know how fun kids could be."

"Wait until Ella is that age. Mary loves to have tea parties and help her daddy cook."

Stacy nodded thoughtfully. "Let me know if you need anything. Knowing you, I can guess how hard it is for you to stay down like this."

Dana groaned in response. She couldn't stand the thought of another day let alone weeks like this. "Thanks for the cookies and milk. The cookies were delicious."

Stacy looked pleased as she left the room.

Chapter Four

Hud walked out with Jordan to the road, then followed him to the marshal's office. Once in the office he got his first good look at his brother-in-law. Jordan had been only two years ahead of Hud in school, three years ahead of his sister Dana. His brother-in-law had aged, but it hadn't hurt Jordan's looks. If anything the years seemed to have given him character, or at least the appearance of it.

"Why don't you have a seat and start at the beginning?" Hud said dropping into his chair behind his desk.

"I thought Liza was handling this case?"

"*Liza?* You mean Deputy Marshal Turner?" He shouldn't have been surprised Jordan was on a first-name basis with the deputy. He, of all people, understood the charm of the Justice-Cardwell genes. Dana could wrap him around her little finger and did.

"Don't think just because she's a woman that she isn't a damned good marshal," Hud said to his brother-in-law. "She's sharp and she'll nail you to the wall if you're guilty."

"If you have so much confidence in her abilities, then why are you here?"

Hud gritted his teeth. Jordan had always been difficult. At least that hadn't changed. "Several reasons. None of which I have to explain to you. But—" He held up a hand before Jordan could speak. "I will because I want us to have an understanding." He ticked them off on his fingers. "One, I'm still the marshal here. Two, Liza has her hands full up at the site. Three, I want to know what happened on that mountain. And four, your sister is my wife. I don't want her hurt."

With a smile and a nod, Jordan ambled over to a chair and sat. "Dana doesn't have anything to worry about. Neither she nor the ranch is why I'm back in the canyon."

"Why *are* you here?" Hud asked, snapping on the recording machine.

"It doesn't have anything to do with family."

"But it does have something to do with Alex Winslow."

"Alex was a good friend from high school. I didn't kill him." Jordan sighed and looked at the ceiling for a moment.

Hud noticed that he was no longer wearing a wedding ring. He vaguely remembered Dana mentioning that she'd heard Jordan was divorced from his ex-model wife, Jill. The marriage had probably ended when Jordan didn't get the proceeds from the sale of the ranch.

"If Alex was your friend, I would think you'd be interested in helping us find his killer," Hud said. "Not to mention you're neck deep in this. Right now, you're the number one suspect."

Jordan laughed. "Does that work on most of your suspects?" He shook his head. "I came back because Alex called me. He hinted that he might know something about Tanner's suicide but it was clear he didn't want to talk about it on the phone. He said he'd share his theory with me if I came to our twenty-year high school reunion. The next time I talked to him, he sounded scared and wanted to meet at the falls. That's it."

That was a lot. Hud wasn't sure how much of it he believed. But at least he had some idea of what might have brought Jordan back to town—and it wasn't family.

"Tanner Cole committed suicide when the two of you were seniors in high school. Why would that bring you back here after all these years?"

"When your best friend commits suicide, you never stop thinking you could have done something to stop him. You need to know *why* he did it."

"Unless that person leaves a note, you never know. Tanner didn't leave a note, as I recall."

Jordan shook his head.

"Did you talk to Alex before he was shot?"

"As I told your deputy, I heard the shot, he stumbled toward me, there was another shot and he went down. All he said was the word *Shelby*. At least that's what I thought he said." Jordan shrugged. "That was it."

Hud studied him openly for a moment. "Maybe the bullets were meant for you and the killer missed."

Jordan sighed. "What are you insinuating?"

"That maybe Tanner didn't commit suicide. Weren't you the one who found his body?"

Anger fired Jordan's gaze. "He was my *best* friend. I would have taken a bullet *for* him."

"Instead, another friend of yours took the bullet tonight," Hud said. "You're telling me you came all this way, hiked into the falls in the dark, just for answers?"

"Why is that so hard for you to understand?"

"What about Alex Winslow? Don't I remember some falling-out the two of you had before you graduated?"

"It was high school. Who remembers?"

Hud nodded. "Is Stacy in the canyon for the same reason?" Stacy had been in the grade between the two of them.

"Stacy?" Jordan looked genuinely surprised. "I haven't seen or talked to her in years."

"Then you didn't know that not only is she back in the canyon, she also has a baby."

Jordan laughed. "Stacy has a *baby?* That's got to be good. Look, if that's all, I need to get some sleep."

"Once Liza allows you to, I'm sure you'll be leaving. I'd appreciate it if you didn't upset Dana before then. She's pregnant with twins and having a rough go of it."

"I'm sorry to hear that," Jordan said, sounding as if he meant it. "Don't worry, I won't be bothering my sister. Either of my sisters," he added.

"Then I guess we're done here."

A WHILE LATER, DANA HEARD HUD come in. She heard him go upstairs to check on the kids, before coming back down to her room. He smiled when he saw her still awake and came over to her side of the bed to give her a kiss.

"So everything's all right?" he asked.

"I'm the one who should be asking you that. You said there'd been a shooting?"

He nodded. "Liza's got everything under control. The crime techs are on their way from Missoula." He sounded tired.

"Stacy kept a plate of dinner for you. She made chicken, baked potatoes and corn," Dana said. "Then she and kids baked chocolate chip cookies." She motioned to the cookies on the tray next to the bed.

Hud gave her a who-knew-she-could-cook look and took one of the cookies.

Who knew indeed? Dana couldn't believe the change in her sister. She felt horribly guilty for not trusting it. But even Stacy was capable of changing, right? Having a baby did that to a person. But Stacy?

Unfortunately, the jury was still out—given her sister's past.

"Did she mention how long she's staying?" Hud asked, not meeting her gaze.

"She was planning to leave earlier, but I asked her to stay. I'm sure she'll be leaving in the morning."

Hud nodded. She could tell he would be glad when Stacy was gone. Dana couldn't blame him. Her sister had hurt them both. But she desperately wanted to believe Stacy had changed. For Ella's sake.

Unfortunately, like her husband, Dana had a niggling feeling that Stacy wasn't being completely honest about the real reason she'd come to the ranch.

EXHAUSTED, JORDAN WENT BACK TO his cabin, locked the door and fell into bed with the intention of sleeping the rest of the day.

Unfortunately, Deputy Marshal Liza Turner had other plans for him.

"What do you want?" he said when he opened the cabin door a little after eleven o'clock that morning to find her standing outside. He leaned a hip into the doorjamb and crossed his arms as he took her in.

"What do I want? Sleep, more money, better hours, breakfast."

"I can't help you with most of that, but I could use food. I'll buy."

She smiled. "I know a place that serves breakfast all day. We can eat and talk."

"No murder talk until I've had coffee."

"Agreed."

Liza drove them to the upper mountain. The huge unpaved parking lots sat empty. None of the lifts moved on the mountain except for the gondolas that rocked gently in the breeze.

"It's like a ghost town up here," he commented as they got out of her patrol SUV.

"I like the quiet. Good place to talk. Most everything is closed still. Fortunately, there are enough locals that a few places stay open."

The café was small and nearly empty. Liza led him outside to a table under an umbrella. The sun was low to the south, but still warm enough it was comfortable outside. A waitress brought them coffee while they looked at the menu.

Jordan ordered ham and eggs, hashbrowns and whole wheat toast.

"I'll have the same," Liza said and handed back the menu. As soon as the waitress was out of earshot, she said, "You didn't mention last night that you and the victim were no longer friends at the end of your high school years."

"So you spoke with Hud." He looked toward the mountains where snow dusted the peaks, making them gleam blinding bright. "It was a stupid disagreement over a woman, all right? Just high school stuff."

She nodded, not buying it. "What girl?"

"I don't even remember."

Liza's look called him a liar, but she let it go. "I'm still confused why he contacted *you*. He must have had other friends locally he would have talked to."

"Obviously he must have talked to someone locally. One of them knew where he was going last night and killed him." Jordan said nothing as the waitress served their breakfasts. He picked up his fork. "Look, do we have to talk about this while we eat? I feel like I got him killed."

"You can't blame yourself, or worse, try to take the law into your own hands." She eyed him for a long moment. "Why would I suspect that's what you're planning to do?"

He chuckled. "If you talked to my brother-in-law he would have told you that I'm not that ambitious. Anyway, you're the deputy marshal. I'm sure you'll find his killer."

She took a bite of toast, chewed and swallowed before she said, "You contacted Tanner's girlfriend from his senior year in high school."

Jordan took her measure. "Why, Liza, you've been checking up on me. I contacted Shelby before I went up to the falls last night. She said she had nothing to say to me about Tanner. That was high school and so far back, she barely remembers."

"You didn't believe her?" Liza asked between bites.

Jordan laughed. "High school was Shelby's glory days. Just check out our yearbook. She is on every page either as president or queen of something. Not to mention she was dating Tanner Cole, the most popular guy in school. She was in her element. I'd bet those were the best days of her life and that nothing she has done since will ever compare."

Liza considered that for a long moment before she asked, "So you talked to Shelby before last night. Before the only word Alex got out after he was shot was her name?"

"Like I said, she and Tanner dated."

"When you talked to Shelby, did you mention Alex or where you were meeting him?"

He gave her an exasperated look. "Do you really think I'm that stupid? Alex was acting terrified. I wasn't about to say anything until I talked to him."

"And yet you called Shelby."

"Yeah. I just told her I was in the area as if I was here for the twenty-year reunion and worked Tanner into the conversation. I didn't realize then that anything I might do could put anyone in danger, including her."

"That's so noble. But I thought you didn't like her. In fact, I thought you were instrumental in breaking up her and Tanner."

He shook his head and took a bite of his breakfast. "You're determined to ruin my appetite, aren't you?"

"Is it true?"

"I couldn't stand Shelby and that bunch she ran with. But you're wrong. I had nothing to do with breaking her and Tanner up, no matter what Hud thinks, as I'm sure that's where you got your information."

Liza lifted a brow. "You weren't the one who snitched on her?"

"Wasn't me." He met her gaze. "Why keep questioning me if you aren't going to believe anything I say?"

"I don't want you involved in my investigation," she said. "That includes asking about Tanner among your old friends—and enemies."

He smiled. "What makes you think I have enemies?"

She smiled in answer as she smeared huckleberry jam on a piece of her toast.

He watched her eat for a few moments. He liked a woman who ate well and said as much.

"Does that line work on women?" she asked.

He laughed. "Every time."

They finished their breakfast in the quiet of the upper mountain. She was right about it being peaceful up here. He liked it. But once winter came, all that would change. The parking lots would be packed, all the lifts would be running as well as the gondola. The mountain would be dotted with skiers and boarders, the restaurants and resorts full. He recalled the sounds of people, the clank of machinery, the array of bright-colored skiwear like a rainbow across Lone Mountain.

Tanner had loved it when Big Sky took on its winter wonderland persona. He'd loved to ski, had started at the age of three like a lot of the kids who grew up in the shadow of Lone Mountain.

With a start, Jordan found himself looking high up on the peak, remembering one of the last days he and Tanner had skied the winter of their senior year. Tanner had always been gutsy, but that day he'd talked Alex and him into going into an out-of-bounds area.

They hadn't gone far when Tanner had gone off a cornice. The cornice had collapsed, causing a small avalanche that had almost killed him.

"Hey, man. You have a death wish?" Alex had asked Tanner when they'd skied down to find him half-buried in the snow.

Tanner had laughed it off. "Takes more than that to kill me."

"I THOUGHT YOU'D BE HAPPIER down here," Hud said as he opened the curtains in the sunroom. "You can leave the door open so you can see everything that is going on."

Dana shot him a look. Seeing everything that was going on was his not-so-subtle way of saying he wanted her to keep an eye on her sister.

They'd all gathered around her bed after breakfast. Stacy hadn't made any attempt to leave. Just the opposite, she seemed to be finding more things she wanted to do before she and Ella packed for the rest of their trip.

"Is there any chance you could stay another day or so?" Dana asked her now as Stacy picked up her breakfast tray to take to the kitchen.

Her sister stopped and looked up in surprise. Her face softened as if she was touched by Dana's offer. "I'd love to. I can cook and help with the kids. Hud has this murder investigation—"

"My deputy marshal is handling all of that," Hud interrupted, shooting Dana a what-could-you-be-thinking? look. "Plus the crime techs are down from Missoula. I am more than capable of taking care of Dana and the kids and—"

Dana had been holding Ella since finishing her breakfast. She quickly interrupted him. "Stacy, that would be great if you can. I know Hud won't mind the help and I love having you and Ella here."

Her husband sent her a withering look. She ignored it and looked instead into Ella's adorable face.

"Is Auntie Stacy going to stay, Mommy?" Mary asked excitedly.

"Yes, for a few more days. Would you like that?" Both children cheered.

"Auntie Stacy is going to show us how to make clay,"

Hank said. "You have to put it in the oven and then paint it."

Stacy shrugged when Dana looked at her. "I found a recipe on the internet. I thought they'd like that."

"That was very thoughtful," she said and shot her husband a see?-everything-is-fine look. "I know Hud will want to check in with the murder investigation, and there are animals to feed."

He tried to stare her down, but Dana had grown up with three siblings. Having to fight for what she wanted had made her a strong, determined woman.

"Fine," Hud said as he left the room. "Stacy, if you need me, Dana has my number. I have animals to feed."

"He'll check in with Liza," Dana said. "He can pretend otherwise, but he won't be able to stay away from this case."

"Are you sure it's all right if I stay?" Stacy asked. "Hud doesn't seem—"

"He's just being territorial," she said. "He can't stand the idea that anyone might think he can't take care of his family." Dana reached for her sister's hand and squeezed it. "I'm glad you and Ella are here."

LIZA FIGURED JORDAN CARDWELL had lied to her at least twice during breakfast.

"I need to know everything you can remember that led up to Tanner's death," she said when they'd finished their breakfast and the waitress had cleared away their plates and refilled their coffee cups.

The scent of pine blew down on the breeze from the mountain peaks. She breathed in the fall day and pulled out her notebook. They still had the café deck to themselves and the sun felt heavenly after so little sleep last night.

"We were seniors." Jordan shrugged. "Not much was going on."

"Who did Tanner date after his breakup with Shelby?"

"A couple of different girls."

"Who was he dating in the weeks or days before he died?" she asked.

"Brittany Cooke." The way he said it gave him away.

"You liked her?" she asked with interest.

His shrug didn't fool her.

"You used to date her?"

He laughed, meeting her gaze. "You got all that out of a shrug?"

"Who were *you* dating at the time?" she asked.

"I don't see what—"

"Humor me."

"I can't remember."

She laughed and leaned back in her chair to eye him. "You don't remember who you were dating the spring of your senior year? Give me a break."

"I wasn't dating anyone, really. It's a small community, cliques. There weren't a lot of options unless you dated someone from Bozeman. I was just anxious to graduate and get out of here."

"Shelby and Brittany were in one of these cliques?"

"Not Brittany. Brittany and Shelby got along, but she was never really one of them. But Shelby, yeah. She was the leader of the mean girls—you know the type. Too much money, too much everything."

Liza knew the type only too well. "So what happened when Brittany went out with Tanner?"

"I'm sure Shelby would deny it, but her and her group of friends closed Brittany out."

"What did Tanner think about that?"

"He thought it was funny. Believe me, that wasn't why he killed himself. Don't get me wrong, Tanner liked Shelby. He went with her a lot longer than any other girl. But once he found out she'd been trying to get pregnant to trap him, it was all over. He wasn't ready to settle down. He'd worked two jobs all through high school while getting good grades so he could do some of the things he'd always wanted to do. Both of us couldn't wait to travel."

"And get out of the canyon," Liza said.

"Tanner not as much as me. He would have come back to the family ranch. He was a cowboy."

"He wasn't from Big Sky resort money?"

"Naw, his folks have a ranch down the canyon. They do okay, just like everyone else who still ranches around here. As my sister is fond of saying, it's a lifestyle more than a paying career. Tanner *loved* that lifestyle, was happiest in a saddle and not afraid of hard work."

"He sounds like a nice, sensible young man."

"He was." Jordan looked away toward the mountains for a long moment. "He worked a lot of odd jobs throughout high school. That's how he ended up at that cabin on the mountain. He talked his folks into letting him stay there because it was closer to school. He traded watching the landowner's construction equipment for the small cabin where he lived that spring."

"He didn't want to live at home?"

Jordan grinned. "Not his senior year. His parents were strict, like all parents when you're that age. Tanner wanted to be on his own and his folks were okay with it."

"So who were the mean girls?"

"Shelby, the leader. Tessa, her closest ally. Whitney. Ashley. They were the inner circle."

"And Brittany?"

"She was always on the fringe. Last I heard Brittany had married Lee Peterson and they have a bunch of kids. I think I heard they live in Meadow Village. Shelby married Wyatt Iverson. She'd started dating him after she and Tanner broke up. Wyatt's father was a contractor who built a lot of the huge vacation homes. It was his maintenance cabin where Tanner stayed with his equipment." He stopped, a faraway look coming to his gaze. "Shelby has a yoga studio near the Gallatin River."

For a life he'd put behind him, Jordan certainly knew a lot about the players, Liza thought as she closed her notebook.

Chapter Five

Yogamotion was in a narrow complex built of log and stone, Western-style. Liza pushed open the door to find the inside brightly painted around walls of shiny mirrors.

According to the schedule she'd seen on the door, the next class wasn't for a couple of hours. A lithe young woman sat behind a large desk in a room off to the side. She was talking on a cell phone, but looked up as the door closed behind Liza.

"You should be getting the check any day. I'm sorry, but I have to go," she said into the phone and slowly snapped it shut, never taking her eyes off the deputy marshal.

"Shelby Iverson?"

As the woman got to her feet she took in Liza's attire, the boots, jeans and tan uniform shirt with the silver star on it. "I'm Shelby *Durran-Iverson*."

"Liza Turner, deputy marshal." Big Sky was small enough that Liza had seen Shelby around. The canyon resort was situated such that there were pockets of development, some pricier than others depending on where you lived.

Shelby lived in a large single-family home on the

north side of the mountain on the way to Mountain Village, while Liza lived in a condo in Meadow Village. She and Shelby didn't cross paths a lot.

"I'd like to ask you a few questions," the deputy said.

"Me?" The catch in her throat was merely for effect. Shelby Durran-Iverson had been expecting a visit from the marshal's office. Everyone within fifty miles would have heard about Alex Winslow's murder at the falls last night. Word would have spread through Big Sky like a fast-moving avalanche.

Liza had to wonder though, why Shelby thought *she* would be questioned. "It's about the shooting last night."

"I don't know anything about it," she said.

"But you knew Alex."

"Sure. Everyone from around here knew him."

"You went to high school with him?" Liza asked pulling her notebook and pen from her pocket.

"Do I need a lawyer?"

"You tell me. Did you shoot Alex?"

"No." Shelby sounded shocked that Liza would even suggest such a thing.

"Then I guess you don't need a lawyer. I just need to ask you a few questions so I can find the person who did shoot him."

"I still can't see how *I* can help." But she motioned Liza to a chair and took her own behind the desk again. Liza could tell that Shelby was hoping to learn more about the murder, getting more information out of her than she provided.

Settling into a chair across the desk from her, Liza studied Shelby. She was a shapely blonde who looked as if she just stepped out of a magazine ad. Her hair was pulled up in a sleek ponytail. Everything about her seemed planned for maximum effect from her makeup to her jewelry and the clothes on her back. She wore a flattering coral velvet designer sweatsuit that brought out the blue of her eyes and accentuated her well-toned body.

"I understand you used to date Tanner Cole," Liza said.

"*Tanner?* I thought you were here about Alex?"

"Did you date Alex, too?"

"No." She shook her head, the ponytail sweeping back and forth. "You're confusing me." She flashed a perfect-toothed smile, clearly a girl who'd had braces.

"I don't want to confuse you. So you dated Tanner how long?"

She frowned, still confused apparently. "Till just before Christmas of our senior year, I guess."

"But the two of you broke up?"

"I can't understand how that—"

Liza gave her one of her less-than-perfect-toothed smiles. She'd been born with a slight gap between her front teeth that her parents had found cute and she had never gotten around to changing. "Humor me. I actually know what I'm doing."

Shelby sighed, making it clear she had her doubts about that. "Fine. Yes, I dated Tanner, I don't remember when we broke up."

"Or why?"

The yoga instructor's eyes narrowed in challenge. "No."

"Here's the thing, I'm trying to understand why Tanner killed himself and why now one of his friends has been murdered."

"I'm sure there is no possible connection," Shelby

said with a mocking laugh as if now she knew Liza didn't know what she was doing.

"So Tanner didn't kill himself over you?"

"No!"

"So you weren't that serious?"

Shelby fumbled for words for a moment. "It was high school. It seemed serious at the time."

"To you. Or Tanner?"

"To both of us." She sounded defensive and realizing it, gave a small laugh. "Like I said, it was *high school.*"

Liza looked down at her notebook. "Let's see, by that spring, Tanner was dating Brittany Cooke? Wasn't she a friend of yours?"

Shelby's mouth tightened. "Tanner was sowing his oats before graduation. I can assure you he wasn't serious about Brittany."

"Oh? Did she tell you that?"

"She didn't have to. She wasn't Tanner's type." Shelby straightened several things on her desk that didn't need straightening. "If that's all, I really need to get back to work."

"I forgot what you said. *Did* you date Alex?"

"No, and I'd lost track of him since high school."

"That's right, he'd moved down to Bozeman and had only recently returned to Big Sky for the class reunion?"

"I assume that's why he came back."

"You didn't talk to him?" Liza asked.

Shelby thought for a moment. More than likely she was carefully considering her next answer. If Liza had Alex's cell phone in her possession, she would know who he called right before his death—and who'd called him.

"I might have talked to him since I'm the reunion

chairwoman. I talked to a lot of people. I really can't remember."

"That's strange since you talked to Alex five times in two days, the last three of those calls just hours before he was killed."

Shelby didn't look quite so put-together. "I told you, it was about the reunion. I talked to a lot of people."

"Are you telling me he didn't ask you about Tanner's alleged suicide?" Liza said.

"*Alleged* suicide?"

"Apparently, Alex had some questions about Tanner's death."

Shelby shook her head. "I might have heard that, but I wouldn't have taken anything Alex said seriously." She leaned forward and lowered her voice even though they were the only two people there. "I heard he had some sort of breakdown." She leaned back and lifted a brow as if to say that covered it.

"Hmmm. I hadn't heard that." Liza jotted down a note. "Whom did you hear this from?"

"I don't—"

"Recall. Maybe one of your friends?"

Shelby shook her head. "I really can't remember. I'm sure you can find out if there was any truth to it."

Liza smiled. "Yes, I can. What about Brittany?"

"What about her?" Shelby asked stiffly.

"Do you still see her?"

"Big Sky is a small community. You're bound to see everyone at some point," Shelby answered noncommittally. "She and her husband, Lee Peterson, own a ski shop up on the mountain. Now I really do need to get to work," she said, rising to her feet.

"Did you see Tanner the night he died?"

"No. As you are apparently aware, we had broken up. He was dating Brittany. If anyone knows why he killed himself, she would, don't you think?"

"Even though she and Tanner weren't that serious about each other?"

Shelby's jaw muscle bunched and her blue eyes fired with irritation. "If she doesn't know, then who would?"

"Good question. Maybe Alex Winslow. But then he isn't talking, is he?" Liza said as she closed her notebook and got to her feet. "One more question. Why would the last word Alex Winslow would say be your name?"

All the color washed from her face. She sat back down, leaning heavily on her desk. "I have no idea."

AFTER BREAKFAST, JORDAN WENT back to his cabin and crashed for a while. He figured Liza would be keeping an eye on him. Not that he knew what to do next. He couldn't just hang out in this cabin, that was for sure. But he'd been serious about not wanting to put anyone else in danger.

When he woke up, he realized he was hungry again. It was still early since the sun hadn't sunk behind Lone Mountain. According to his cell phone, it was a quarter past three in the afternoon.

He found a small sandwich shop in Meadow Village, ordered a turkey and cheese and took a seat by the window overlooking the golf course. Lone Mountain gleamed in the background, a sight that brought back too many memories. There'd been a time when he'd told himself he'd left here because he didn't want to be a rancher. But coming back here now, he realized a lot of his need to leave and stay gone had to do with Tanner's suicide.

When the waitress brought out his sandwich, he asked if he could get it to go. He followed her to the counter and was waiting when he heard a bell tinkle over the door and turned to see someone he recognized coming through.

With a silent curse, he put a name to the face. Tessa Ryerson. She had already spotted him and something about her expression gave him the crazy idea that she didn't just happen in here. She'd come looking for him.

Before he could react, the waitress brought out his sandwich in a brown paper bag and handed it to him. He dug out the cost of the sandwich and a generous tip and handed it to the server, before turning to Tessa.

She had stopped just a couple of feet from him, waiting while he paid. When he turned to her, he saw that she looked much like she had twenty years ago when the two of them had dated. She wore her light brown hair as she had in high school, shoulder length and wavy, no bangs. A hair band held it back from her face.

She seemed thinner, a little more gaunt in the face, than she had the last time he'd seen her. He recalled that she'd always struggled to keep her weight down. Apparently, she'd mastered the problem.

He couldn't help noticing that her ring finger was bare. Hadn't he heard that she'd gone through a bad divorce from Danny Spring? Two years ahead of them in school, the guy had been a jerk. Jordan recalled being surprised when he'd heard that she'd married him.

"Jordan," Tessa said a little too brightly. "Imagine running into you here."

"Imagine that," he said, now sure the only reason

she'd come in here, crazy or not, was to see him. So
did that mean she'd followed him? Or had she just been
looking for him?

"Oh, are you getting your sandwich to go?" she
asked, sounding disappointed as she glanced at the bag
in his hand as if just now noticing it. "I missed lunch
and I hate eating alone. Would you mind staying?"

How could he say no even if he'd wanted to? Anyway, he was curious about what she wanted. "Sure, go
ahead and order. I'll get us a table."

"Great."

He took a seat away from the girl working behind the
counter, positioning himself so he could watch Tessa
while she ordered. She dug nervously in her purse, paid
for a small salad and a bottled water, then joined him
at the table.

"So you came for the reunion," she said, smiling as
she unscrewed the lid on her water bottle.

He smiled at that and dug his sandwich out of the
bag and took a bite.

"Wow, it's been so long."

"Twenty years," he said between bites.

"I guess you heard about Danny and me." She sighed.
"But I've put it behind me."

Too bad the look in her eyes said otherwise. He suspected the slightest thing could set her off if asked about
her marriage. Unfortunately, he could remember how
he was right after Jill had left him. He didn't want to
go there again.

"So wasn't that awful about Alex?" she said. "Were
you really there?"

He gave her points for getting right to what she really

wanted to talk to him about. He nodded and took another bite of his sandwich. She hadn't touched her salad.

"When I heard, I just couldn't believe it. How horrible. Do they know who shot him?" she asked when he didn't answer. "I heard it could have been a stray bullet from a hunter."

"Really?" he said. "I heard it was murder. Someone wanted to shut Alex up."

"Who told you that?" she cried.

He said nothing for a moment, letting her squirm. "The state crime lab trucks have been up at the falls since last night looking for evidence to track them to the killer. I thought you would have heard."

Tessa fiddled with her water bottle, looking worried. "Why would anyone want to kill Alex?"

He shrugged. "Probably because he'd been asking a lot of questions about Tanner's suicide. But you'd know better about that than I would."

"Me?"

"I'm sure Alex talked to you." He wasn't sure of anything except that he was rattling her. "If you know something, I'd suggest you talk to Deputy Marshal Liza Turner. Alex was murdered and there is an investigation into Tanner's death, as well. It's all going to come out."

"I don't know *anything*." She squeezed her plastic water bottle so hard it crackled loudly and water shot up and out over the table. She jumped up and grabbed for a stack of napkins.

He watched her nervously wipe up the spilled water, almost feeling guilty for upsetting her. "Then I guess you have nothing to worry about. But I wonder if Alex said the same thing."

"This is all so upsetting." She sounded close to tears.

He reached across the table and put a hand on hers. "Tessa—"

"Please, don't," she said, snatching back her hand. "I told you. I don't know anything."

He put down his sandwich to study her. Why had she come looking for him? Why was she so scared? "You and Shelby have always been thick as thieves. What don't I know about Alex's death? Or Tanner's, for that matter."

She shook her head. "How would I know? Shelby wasn't even dating Tanner then."

"No, but she'd conned you into breaking up with Alex to go out with me. I thought you were just playing hard to get when you wanted to always double date with Brittany and Tanner. I should have known Shelby put you up to spying on him."

"I don't know what you're talking about," she said. "But I do remember you didn't mind double dating. It was Brittany you wanted to be with. Not me." She got to her feet, hitting the table and spilling some of her salad.

"Brittany," he said under his breath. "Thanks for reminding me of that prank you and your friend Shelby pulled on her." It was straight out of a Stephen King novel.

Tessa crossed her toned arms over her flat chest, her expression defiant. He'd expected her to stomp off, but she didn't. Whatever the reason that she'd wanted to see him, she hadn't got what she'd come for apparently.

That spring of their senior year was coming back to him after years of fighting to forget it. Hadn't he had a bad feeling he couldn't shake even before Alex had called him? "Did Shelby send you to find me?" He let out a laugh. "Just like in high school. What is it she wants to know, Tessa?"

"I have no idea what you mean."

He laughed. "Still doing her dirty work even after all these years."

Tessa snatched up her water bottle from the table with one hand, the untouched salad with the other. "I know what you think of me."

"I think you're too smart to keep letting Shelby run your life."

She laughed at that. "Run my life? Don't you mean *ruin* my life? She practically forced me to marry Danny Spring. It wasn't until later that I found out her husband was trying to buy some land Danny owned and thought my marriage would get it for Wyatt." She smiled. "It did."

"Then what are you doing still being friends with her?" he demanded.

"*Seriously?* Because it's much worse to be Shelby's enemy, haven't you realized that yet? My life isn't the only one she's destroyed. Clearly, you have forgotten what she's like."

"No, I don't think so. I know what she did to Tanner."

"Do you?" she challenged.

"She got pregnant to trap him into marrying her. If she hadn't miscarried, he probably would have married her for the kid's sake." Something in Tessa's expression stopped him. "She did have a miscarriage, didn't she? Or did she lie about that, as well?"

Tessa looked away for a moment.

Jordan felt his heart drop. *My life isn't the only one she's destroyed.* The thought came at him with such force, he knew it had been in the back of his mind for a long time.

"She didn't do something to that baby to get back at Tanner, did she?" he asked, voicing his fear.

"I have to go," Tessa said, glancing toward the parking lot.

He followed her gaze, seeing her fear as a white SUV cruised slowly past. He recognized Shelby Durran-Iverson behind the wheel. She sped up when she saw Tessa hurry out of the sandwich shop, barely missing her as she drove away.

Jordan stared after both of them for a moment before he wrapped up his sandwich. He'd lost his appetite. Worse, he wasn't sure what his best friend would have done if he'd found out Shelby hadn't miscarried early in the pregnancy, but waited as long as she could, then aborted his baby to hurt him.

He realized it was possible Tanner really had killed himself.

Chapter Six

The ski shop Brittany Cooke Peterson and her husband Lee owned on the mountain was still closed for the season.

But Liza found her at the couple's condo in Meadow Village. Brittany answered the door wearing a black-and-white polka-dot apron over a T-shirt and jeans. Her feet were bare and her dark hair in disarray. She brushed a long curly lock back from her face, leaving a dusting of flour on her cheekbone. In the background a 1960s hit played loudly. As Brittany's brown eyes widened to see the deputy sheriff at her door, Liza caught the warm, wonderful scent of freshly-baked cookies.

"Don't touch that pan, it's hot," Brittany said over her shoulder after opening the door.

"Did I catch you in the middle of something?" Liza asked facetiously.

Brittany laughed. "Not at all."

"Mommy, Jake stuck his finger in the icing," called a young female voice from the back of the large two-story condo.

Brittany wiped her hands on her apron. "Come on in. We're baking iced pumpkin cookies."

Liza followed the young woman through a toy-cluttered living room and into a kitchen smelling of cinnamon and pumpkin.

Three small children balanced on chairs around a kitchen island covered in flour and dirty baking bowls and utensils. One of the children, the only boy, had icing smudged on the side of his cheek. Brittany licked her thumb pad and wiped the icing from the boy's face, took an icing-dripping spoon from one girl and snatched a half-eaten cookie from the other girl as if it was all in a day's work.

The two girls who Liza realized were identical twins appeared to be about five and were wearing aprons that matched their mother's. The boy had a dish towel wrapped around his neck like a bandana. He was a year or so younger than the girls.

"You'd better have a cookie," Brittany said as she finished slipping warm ones from a cookie sheet onto a cooling rack.

Liza took one of the tall stools at the counter, but declined a cookie.

"Just a little icing on them, Courtney," her mother said to the girl who had the spoon again and was dribbling thin white icing over each cookie as if making a masterpiece. The other girl watched, practically drooling as her sister slowly iced the warm cookies. "Okay, enough sugar for one day. Go get cleaned up." They jumped down and raced toward the stairs. "And don't argue!" she called after them.

With a sigh, Brittany glanced around the messy kitchen, then plopped down on a stool at the counter and took one of the cookies before turning her attention on Liza. "Sure you don't want one?" she asked between bites. "They aren't bad."

"They smell delicious, but I'm fine."

"You didn't come by for cookies," Brittany said. "This is about Alex, isn't it?" She shook her head, her expression one of sadness. "I heard it was a hunter."

"A hunter?"

"You know, someone poaching at night, a stray bullet. It had to be. No one would want to hurt Alex. He was a sweetheart. Everyone liked him."

"Not everyone," Liza said.

Brittany turned solemn. "So it *was* murder. That's the other rumor circulating this morning." She shook her head.

"Any idea who didn't think he was a sweetheart?"

"No one I can think of."

"What about Tanner Cole?"

Brittany blinked. "Even if he came back from the dead, he wouldn't have hurt Alex. They were friends."

Liza smiled. She liked the woman's sense of humor. "Do you know why Tanner killed himself?"

"No. I suppose someone told you that Tanner and I were dating at the time." Brittany chuckled as she realized whom. "Shelby. Of course."

"She did mention that if anyone knew, it would be you. Did Tanner seem depressed?"

"Far from it. He was excited about graduating. He had all these plans for what he was going to do. I think he already had his bags packed."

"He was planning to leave Big Sky?"

"Oh, yeah. He'd been saving his money for years. He wanted to backpack around Europe before college. He had a scholarship to some big college back east."

"What about you?"

"I was headed for Montana State University."

"Weren't you upset that he was leaving?"

She shook her head as she helped herself to another cookie. Upstairs, Liza could hear the kids squabbling over the water and towels. "It wasn't like that between me and Tanner. I liked him. A lot. But I knew from the get-go that it wasn't serious."

"Had it been serious between him and Shelby?"

Brittany stopped chewing for a moment. She sighed and let out a chuckle. "If you talk to Shelby it was. She was planning to marry him, apparently. She loved his parents' ranch and used to talk about when she and Tanner lived on the place, what their lives were going to be like."

"She must have been upset when he broke it off and started dating you."

Brittany laughed. "Livid. But Tanner told me he'd just gone through a scare with her. She'd apparently gotten pregnant."

"On purpose?"

"Tanner thought so. He said he'd dodged a bullet when she miscarried…" Brittany seemed to realize what she'd said. "So to speak. Anyway, he didn't trust her after that, said he didn't want anything to do with her. They broke up right before Christmas. She'd been so sure he would be putting an engagement ring under the tree for her."

"How could Shelby have thought that was going to happen?" Liza asked. "Surely she knew what Tanner was planning to do once they graduated."

"Sure, she knew, but Shelby was so used to getting what she wanted, I think she'd just convinced herself it was going to happen."

"Maybe she thought a baby would be the tipping point," Liza suggested.

"And it probably would have been. Tanner loved kids. He wanted a bunch when he settled down. If she had been pregnant, I still don't think he would have married her, but he would have stuck around to help raise his child. He was that kind of guy. But he was over Shelby. Nothing could have made him go back to her."

"Did she know that?" Liza asked.

Brittany broke a cookie in half and played in the icing for a moment. "I think she did. She really was heartbroken. She cried hysterically at the funeral. I'd never seen her like that. I actually felt sorry for her."

"But you didn't feel sorry enough not to go out with Tanner."

Brittany shrugged. "It was high school. Tanner asked me out. He was a nice guy and a lot of fun. Shelby knew it wasn't serious. She didn't blame me."

"But she did Tanner?"

Brittany smiled. "Let me put it this way. If Shelby was the kind to make voodoo dolls and stick pins in them, she would have had one with Tanner's name on it. But she moved on quick enough. Tanner was barely in the ground before she was dating Wyatt Iverson. One thing about Shelby, she seems to bounce back pretty fast."

"Wyatt Iverson of Iverson Construction?" Liza said. "Isn't that the same construction company that Tanner was working for at the time of his death?"

Brittany nodded and got up to go to the bottom of the stairs to yell up at the kids to quit fighting. When she came back she began to clean up the kitchen. "Wyatt was four years ahead of us in school, so I didn't really know him. But later that summer his father went bankrupt, shot Harris Lancaster and went to prison. Malcolm was never the same after that, I guess. He died in a boating accident. At least that's what they called it. He drowned up on Canyon Ferry. Everyone suspected he killed himself. I've gotten to know Wyatt a little since then. He never got over what happened with his father. That's one reason he's worked so hard to get the construction company going again." She looked up. "Sorry, that's probably a whole lot more than you wanted to hear."

"You like Wyatt."

Brittany smiled at that. "*Like* might be a little strong. He and Shelby are cut from the same cloth. Both go after what they want and the rest be damned." She frowned. "Why all the questions about Tanner?"

"Tanner was Alex's friend."

"And now they're both dead," Brittany said with a nod.

"With all Tanner's plans, he doesn't sound like someone who would commit suicide before graduation. Was anything else going on in his life that you knew of? Maybe with his parents, his friends?"

Brittany shook her head. "His parents are still happily married and still live on the ranch. His friends were fine—well, that is, they were until last night." She sighed. "There was the vandalism, though."

"Vandalism?" Liza asked.

"Tanner was staying in the cabin at the construction site in payment for watching over Malcolm Iverson's equipment. There was a party at the cabin one night. The next morning, Malcolm discovered his equipment had been vandalized. Tanner blamed himself."

"Enough to kill himself?"

"I didn't think so at the time. Wyatt didn't even blame Tanner. The party hadn't been his idea in the first place. Tanner was really responsible, but everyone showed up with beer and things must have gotten out of hand. But who knows. Maybe Tanner was taking it harder than any of us knew. Wyatt talked his father into letting Tanner stay at the cabin even after the vandalism. So I really don't think that had anything to do with Tanner's death."

"Well, thank you for the information," Liza said.

"It's kind of strange though. I heard Jordan Cardwell was back in the canyon—and that he was at the falls when Alex was shot?"

"Why is that strange if they were friends?"

"Because he and Alex had a huge falling-out the night of the party."

Liza felt her pulse quicken. "Over what?"

"I never knew. I just remember Tanner refused to take sides. He said they'd work it out."

"Did they?"

"Not that I know of. Jordan left right after graduation and seldom came back. I'm not sure he and Alex ever spoke again."

"Could it have been over a girl?"

Brittany laughed. "Isn't it always?"

"So who would that girl have been?"

"If I had to guess, I'd say Tessa Ryerson. Shelby's BFF."

Liza laughed. "Best friend forever? Is that still true?"

Brittany nodded and crossed her fingers. "Shelby and Tessa, they're like this and always have been. I was surprised when Jordan went out with Tessa since he never could stand Shelby."

DANA HAD DOZED OFF FOR A WHILE, she realized. She woke to find Hud lying on the bed next to her. Listening, she could hear the sound of their children's voices coming from the kitchen along with that of her sister's. She placed a hand on her stomach, felt her two babies and tried to relax. Nothing seemed to be amiss and yet, when she'd awakened…

"What's wrong?" she asked, turning her head to look at her husband.

Hud was staring at the ceiling. "You're going to think I'm crazy."

"I've never thought you were anything but completely sane in all instances," she joked.

"I'm serious," he said, rolling over on his side to look at her.

She saw the worry etched in his handsome face. "What?"

"You aren't going to want to hear this."

"Hud!"

"Something's wrong," he said. "I feel it."

She sighed. "Your marshal intuition again?" She felt her eyes widen, her heartbeat kicking up a notch. "About the murder investigation?"

"It's your sister."

She groaned and, shaking her head, turned to look at the ceiling. "What are you saying?"

"Have you noticed the way she is with the baby?" he demanded, keeping his voice down even though the bedroom door was closed.

Dana hadn't noticed. Usually when her sister brought the baby in, she would hand Ella to her to hold.

"It's as if she has never changed a diaper," Hud was saying.

"She's probably nervous because you're watching her. She's new at this."

He shook his head. "She stares at Ella, I swear, as if she's never seen her before. Not just that," he rushed on. "She arrived with hardly any clothes for the baby and when she came back from buying baby food, I asked her what Ella's favorite was and she said carrots. You should have seen her trying to feed Ella carrots—"

"Stop. Do you realize how ridiculous you sound?" She'd turned to look at him again. "I repeat, what are you *saying?*"

Hud clamped his mouth shut for a moment, his eyes dark. "Okay, I'll just say it. I don't think that baby is hers. In fact, I don't even think the baby's name is Ella. That baby quilt has the name Katie stitched on it."

"Okay, you are *crazy,*" Dana said. "The quilt is probably one she picked up at a secondhand store or a friend lent it to her."

"A friend? Has she received even one phone call since she's been here?" He shook his head. "No, that's because your sister doesn't have friends. She never has."

"You don't know that she hasn't made friends the past six years."

"How could she? She moves around all the time. At least that's her story. And what does she do for money, huh?"

"She didn't go to college or learn a trade so of course she has a hard time supporting herself." Dana knew she was grasping at any explanation, but she couldn't stop herself. "One look at Stacy and you can see she doesn't have much. It's probably the best she can do right now. And you know babies can change their food likes and dislikes in an afternoon. As for diapering…"

Hud shook his head stubbornly.

"Is she helping with the kids?"

"Sure, she seems right at home with a four- and five-year-old." He sighed. "I still have a hard time trusting Stacy."

"I know. She stole five years from us, breaking us up with one of her lies so I understand why you would question everything about her now." Dana didn't want to admit that she had felt the same way around her sister. But when she saw her sister with Ella—

"Okay," Hud said. "After dinner I might check in with Liza and see how the investigation is going." He placed a large hand on her belly and waited for their twins to move as if needing reassurance.

She could see that it was hell for him having a murder investigation going on while he was home playing Candy Land and Old Maid. But she saw something else in his expression, as well. "You're going to your office to do more than check in, aren't you? You're going to investigate my sister."

"I just want to do some checking on her. Just to relieve my mind."

She knew there would be no stopping him no matter what she said. "I want to get to know my niece. After everything that has happened between us and Stacy, it wouldn't take much for us to never see her or Ella again."

"If Ella isn't her baby—"

"You're wrong. So go ahead and see what you can find out."

He bent down to kiss her before getting to his feet. "You're probably right about everything."

Dana nodded as he left the room. But she hated that she didn't feel sure about anything right now. To make matters worse she was trapped in bed, her children were out making clay with a woman who her husband thought might be a kidnapper and meanwhile, her brother Jordan was involved in a murder case.

All she needed right now was for her younger brother, Clay, to show up.

Her babies moved. She splayed her fingers over them, whispered that she loved them and did her best not to cry.

Chapter Seven

Jordan hadn't been back to the cabin long when he heard a knock at his door. He put his unfinished sandwich in the small kitchenette refrigerator, then peeked out the window. He was in no mood for company.

"You've been holding out on me," Liza said when he finally opened the door.

He'd let her knock for a while, then had given up that she wasn't going to take the hint and leave him alone. He was in no mood after his run-in with Tessa and no longer sure about Tanner's death any more than he was Alex's.

"I beg your pardon?" he said.

"Tessa Ryerson Spring. You dated her at the same time Tanner was dating Brittany."

He sighed and stepped back to let Liza in, not wanting to discuss this on the cabin stoop. "I'd forgotten I dated her."

"Uh-huh." The deputy marshal came into the small cabin and looked around. "Why did you and Alex fight over her?"

Jordan shook his head and laughed. "I don't recall."

She smiled. "Try again. It sounds as if it was quite the fight. Didn't speak to each other for years. Does that refresh your memory?" She sat down on the end of his bed and crossed her legs, leaning back on her hands, her gaze on him.

"Make yourself comfortable," he said sarcastically.

"I thought this might take a while."

He sighed and pulled out a chair from the small table that constituted the dining room. He straddled it and leaned his arms on the back as he looked at her. The woman was like a badger burrowing into a hole.

"Fine. It isn't something I like to talk about but since you're determined... Shelby talked Tessa into breaking up with Alex and going out with me so we could double date with Tanner and Brittany."

"Tessa was a spy?"

He nodded.

"But it doesn't explain why you dated Tessa. Or does it?" She grinned. "Brittany. You wanted to be close to her. Wow, what a tangled web we weave."

"Happy? When I found out what Shelby had done, I told Tessa off." He shrugged.

"Which explains why you and Alex got into a fight over her how exactly?"

"I might have called her some names. Alex took offense. When I told him how far Tessa would go to do Shelby's dirty work, he took a swing at me. I swung back. We were in high school. Stuff like that happened."

"Alex had forgotten all about it when he called to talk to you about Tanner?"

Jordan shrugged. "I assume so."

Liza got to her feet and walked around the cabin for a moment. "You all talk about high school as if it was kid stuff." She let out a chuckle. "You forget. *I* went to high school."

"That doesn't surprise me," Jordan quipped.

"Then this probably won't, either. I let mean things happen to other students. No, worse than that, sometimes I was part of those things. I ran into one of the girls who was terrorized recently. She told me that she still has scars from the way she was treated."

He said nothing, afraid she'd been that girl. Liza would have been just different enough that he suspected she hadn't been in a group like Shelby's. He'd sensed a rebellious spirit just under her surface, a fire that the girls who followed Shelby didn't have.

She suddenly turned to face him, her expression angry and defiant. "Don't tell me that what happened in high school didn't matter. It mattered to Tanner and now I believe it has something to do with Alex Winslow's death, as well. What I'm trying to understand is what *happened*."

"You and me both," he said, feeling guilty because he'd been one of the popular kids. In his teens he hadn't given much thought to those who weren't. "If it helps, I saw Tessa today." He held up a hand before she could berate him for getting involved in her investigation. "*She* sought me out. I went to get a sandwich and she came in. She either followed me or had been looking for me."

"What did she want?"

"I don't know. Maybe just information about Alex's death. I thought at first Shelby had sent her. But then Shelby drove past and Tessa got all scared and left."

"What did you tell her?"

"She asked why anyone would want Alex dead. I said it could have something to do with him asking around about Tanner's death."

The deputy sheriff let out an unladylike curse.

"I wanted to see her reaction."

"And?"

"It spooked the hell out of her. She knows something. When I was talking to her I had a thought. If Tanner *did* kill himself, it would have had to be over something big. What if Shelby didn't have a miscarriage? What if she lied about that, maybe as a test to see if Tanner loved her, who knows?"

"What are you suggesting, that she was never pregnant?"

"No, that she aborted the baby," he said. "That she did it out of meanness to get back at him. To hurt him in a way that would haunt him to his grave."

Liza said nothing for a few moments. "You think that little of Shelby?"

He met her gaze and held it. "Tessa is her best friend. She knows the truth. I also think she's scared of that truth coming out."

"Wait, even if you're right and Shelby did do something to get back at Tanner, that wouldn't be something that she'd kill Alex to keep secret."

"Couldn't it? Shelby is all about getting what she wants, whatever it takes, and Tessa and her other minions have always followed her blindly."

"You don't think they'd draw the line when it came to out-and-out murder?" Liza demanded.

"Not if they had something to do with Tanner's death. What's another body if Alex was getting too close to the truth?"

Liza nodded. "So your graduating class from Big Sky was small, right?"

Jordan reached behind him to pick up the crumpled

piece of paper he'd left on the table. "This is the list of people who RSVP'd that they would be attending the reunion this weekend," he said, handing it to her. "I marked the other two girls who ran with Shelby in high school. Ashley and Whitney."

Liza considered the wrinkled-up paper in her hand, then looked at him quizzically.

"I had to dig it out of the trash before I flew out here. I wasn't planning to attend—until Alex called. Then I was curious about who was coming."

"Let me guess," Liza said. "You're planning on going to the reunion now?"

He smiled. "Not without a date. What do you say? Come on, this way you can get to see all the players in their natural habitat."

Liza actually seemed at a loss for words for a moment. "I feel like you're asking me to the prom."

"If you're expecting a corsage, a rented limo, champagne and a fancy hotel room afterwards..." He saw her expression and stopped. "You didn't go to prom?"

"I'm not wearing a prom dress," she said, ignoring his question.

"Just don't wear your silver star or your gun," he joked, hating that he'd been right. She was one of the girls who'd been tormented by girls like Shelby and Tessa.

LIZA STOOD IN FRONT OF HER closet. She hated to admit how few dresses she owned—and what she did have were old and out of style, though hardly worn. Worse, she hated that she cared what she wore to the reunion.

She'd been a tomboy, so dresses had never really appealed to her. Add to that her profession, she'd had little need of anything besides jeans and boots.

"I don't know what I'm going to wear," she said when Dana answered the phone. "I know it doesn't matter. It's not like it's a date."

"No, going out with a suspect probably couldn't be called a date," her boss's wife agreed with a chuckle. "Come over. You're welcome to dig through my closet. I'll call Hilde. She's more girlie than either of us. She'll help."

"Thanks," Liza said, relieved. She definitely needed help.

"How is the investigation going?" Dana asked.

Liza knew Dana must be bored to tears now that she was being forced to stay in bed. "Slowly." She didn't want to admit that it brought up a lot of high school memories, ones she thought she'd left behind when she'd graduated.

"And Jordan?" Dana asked.

She didn't know how to answer that. "He's fine. Actually, I get the feeling he's changed. Don't worry," she said quickly. "If he hasn't, I'll be the first to know. He's still a suspect."

"But you don't think he killed Alex Winslow."

"No. I think he really did come back to find out what happened to his friend Tanner. It's looking like he had reason to be concerned."

Dana was silent for a moment. "Tell him to stop by, if he wants to."

"I will. I'll drop by later this afternoon for the clothing search." In the meantime, she thought, closing her closet door, she wanted to pay Tessa Ryerson Spring a visit.

DANA COULDN'T HELP THINKING of Jordan and half wishing she hadn't told Liza to have him stop by. Feeling the babies kick, she willed herself not to worry about Stacy or her brother. Instead, she put in a quick call to Hilde, who, of course, was delighted to help with Liza's clothing dilemma.

"I'll gather up some dresses and bring them over later," her best friend said. "Can I bring you anything?"

"Maybe some needlepoint from the store?" Dana suggested, cringing since the mere thought had always given her hives.

"Oh, girl, you really are bored to tears!" She laughed as she hung up.

After she'd found her mother's will and got to go back to ranching, Dana had become a silent partner in Needles and Pins, the small sewing shop she and Hilde had started in Meadow Village. She'd never been the one who sewed. That had been Hilde. But Dana had always loved working with her best friend in the shop.

She missed it sometimes. Not that she and the kids didn't often stop in to visit. Mary and Hank loved all the colorful bolts of fabric and Hilde always had some fun craft for them to do.

"Look what we made, Mommy!" Mary and Hank cried in unison now as they came running into the bedroom. They held up the clay figures, and Dana praised them for their imagination and their choice of multiple bright colors.

Behind them, Stacy stood in the doorway looking on with what appeared to be contentment. Dana had been watching her sister all day. She hated letting Hud's suspicions cloud her forgiving thoughts about Stacy. She'd missed having a sister all these years. Not that she and Stacy had been close like some sisters. There were no tea parties, doll playing or dressing up for pretend weddings.

Stacy had done all those things, but Dana had been an outside kid. She loved riding her horse, climbing trees, building forts. Two years older, Stacy had turned up her nose at most things Dana thought were fun and vice versa.

"Okay, let's clean up our mess," her sister told the kids. "I think that's your daddy who just drove up."

As they scampered out of the room, leaving a couple clay figures beside her bed to keep her company, Dana waited expectantly for Hud. She knew where he'd gone and what he'd been up to—running a check on her sister. A part of her feared what he might have discovered.

She listened. The moment he came in the house, Mary and Hank were all over him. He played with them for a moment, and, like her, praised everything they'd made before coming into the bedroom. When he closed the door, she knew the news wasn't going to be good.

LIZA COULDN'T SHAKE the feeling that Jordan was right about the two deaths being connected. While anxious to talk to Tessa Ryerson Spring, she went to the office and pulled out the Tanner Cole investigation file. There wasn't much in it since the coroner had ruled the death a suicide.

The incident had happened back up the North Fork where the victim had been staying in a cabin. His body had been found hanging from a tree limb in sight of the cabin, a rope noose around the victim's neck. There was evidence of a log stump having been dragged over under the limb of the tree. When the body was found, the stump was on its side, a good foot from the dead man's dangling boots. Cause of death was strangulation.

The victim was found by Jordan Cardwell, who'd gone looking for Tanner when he hadn't shown up for school.

Attached were a half dozen black-and-white photographs taken at the scene. She flipped through them, noticing that the tree where Tanner was found hanging was next to a fire ring. She could see that there were dozens of footprints around the scene, no doubt because the area had been used for a party. Other stumps had been dragged up around the campfire area. Numerous discarded beer cans could be seen charred black in the firepit.

As she started to put the file back, something caught her eye. The investigating officer had been Brick Savage—Hud's father.

HUD SMILED SHEEPISHLY at his wife after closing the door. She was watching him expectantly. He wished she didn't know him so well sometimes. Walking over to the bed, he bent down and, touching her cheek, kissed her. "You get more beautiful every day."

She swatted his hand playfully as he drew back. "If you think you can charm me—"

He laughed as she moved over to let him sit on the edge of the bed next to her. "Just speaking the truth." She *was* beautiful. The pregnancy had put a glow in her cheeks and her eyes. Not that she wasn't a stunner anytime. Dana had always smelled of summer, an indefinable scent that filled his heart like helium. He counted his blessings every day he woke up next to her.

"Okay, charmer, let's hear it," she said. "With you being so sweet, I'm guessing it's bad news."

He shook his head. "Am I that transparent?"

"Hud," she said impatiently.

"I didn't find out much. There wasn't much to find out. Apparently, she doesn't have credit cards or even a checking account."

"She's in the process of moving and not having credit cards is a good thing."

He sighed, seeing that she was determined to think the best. But then, that was Dana. But with her family, their history proved out that he definitely had reason to be suspicious. He knew she wanted to believe that Stacy had changed. He did, too. He was just a whole lot more skeptical than Dana.

"A tiger doesn't change its spots," he said.

"Isn't it 'a zebra doesn't change its stripes' and what does that even mean?" she demanded.

"I had a look in her car last night after everyone went to bed. If she's moving to Great Falls, she sure didn't pack much." He held up his hand. "I know. She apparently doesn't have any money. But she gets the check from the ranch profits."

"You know that isn't enough to live on."

"Well, you'd think she would have had a job for the past six years."

"Stacy didn't go to college so more than likely she can't make much more than minimum wage."

He shook his head. "I could find no employment in her past."

"So she worked off the books somewhere. Or maybe the baby's father has been taking care of her and now she can't work because she has a baby to raise."

Yeah, Hud thought. That's what had Dana so desperate to believe Stacy had changed. That baby. Ella was cute as a bug's ear. No doubt about that. Just the thought of Stacy raising the child, though, terrified him.

"So that's all you found," Dana said.

He nodded. "No warrants or outstanding violations." No missing kids on Amber Alert who matched either the name Katie—or Ella's description.

"So there is nothing to worry about."

"Right." He just wished he could shake his uneasy feeling.

"And don't you go interrogating her," Dana said. "Give her the benefit of the doubt. She is in absolute awe of that baby. She couldn't be prouder of Ella. It's the first time I've seen my sister like this."

He nodded, not wanting to argue with her. He needed to keep Dana in this bed for their twins' sake. Placing a hand on her stomach, he felt their babies move. It had a calming affect on him. Just as being here with his family did.

But in the other room he could hear Stacy with the kids. Something wasn't right with her story. Call it his marshal intuition. But Stacy wasn't telling them the truth. And as much as he hated to think it, whatever she was lying about, it had something to do with that precious baby.

TESSA RYERSON SPRING didn't answer her phone so Liza drove over to the house. Getting out of the patrol SUV, she walked past the garage, noting that at least one vehicle was inside, before she rang the doorbell.

She had to ring it four times and knock hard before Tessa appeared. She'd wrapped a towel around her head and pulled a robe on, no doubt hoping Liza would think she'd been in the shower.

"I'm sorry," she said, looking more than a little flustered. "Have you been standing here long?"

Long enough. "Mind if I come in for a moment? Or you can come down to the office? Which works better for you?"

"Actually, I was just…" Tessa gave up and said, "I suppose I have a few minutes." She stepped aside to let Liza in. "I should make some coffee."

"No, thanks. Why don't we sit down for a minute." She could tell that Tessa wanted something to occupy herself. Jordan was right about one thing. Tessa was nervous and clearly afraid.

"This won't take long," Liza assured her.

The woman finally perched on the edge of the couch. Liza took a chair across from her. Like many of the residences at Big Sky, the decor was made to look like the Old West from the leather furniture to the antler lamps. The floor was hardwood, the rugs Native American, the fireplace local granite.

Tessa straightened the hem of her robe to cover whatever she was wearing beneath it, then fiddled with the sash.

"I'm here about Alex Winslow's death."

"Oh?" Her smile was tentative. "Why would you want to talk to *me?*"

"You were a friend of his in high school."

"Yes, but that was twenty years ago."

"But you talked to him recently. The calls were on his cell phone," Liza said.

Tessa's eyes widened with alarm. Her hand went to her forehead as if suddenly struck with a migraine.

Clearly she hadn't expected anyone to know about the calls.

"I'm curious what you talked about," Liza said.

After a moment the woman pulled herself together. "I'm sorry. I'm just upset. I heard he was murdered?"

"So what did you talk about?"

"The reunion. Shelby must have told him to call me. I'm in charge of the picnic on Sunday. It's going to be at the top of the gondola. Weather permitting, of course." Her smile was weak, nervous. She worked at the robe sash with her fingers, toying with the edges.

"You and Alex dated in high school."

She nodded. "For a short while."

"But you were close?"

"I'm not sure what you mean."

"I mean Alex trusted you. He would have confided in you."

"I don't know what you're asking."

"He would have told you if he had some reason to suspect that Tanner Cole didn't kill himself." The statement had the effect Liza had hoped for.

Fear shone in the woman's eyes. Her hand went to her throat. Jordan was right. She knew *something*.

"Had you ever been up to the cabin where Tanner was staying that spring before high school graduation?" Liza asked.

"I might have."

"With Alex?"

"Maybe. I really can't remember."

"Do you knit?" Liza asked.

"What?"

"I wondered if you knitted because this case started like a loose thread in a sweater. At first it was just a small problem, but once it started unraveling…" She shook her head. "Alex started it unraveling. Now it's going to come apart. No doubt about it."

Tessa managed a smile. "That's an odd simile."

"Metaphor," Liza said. "It's a metaphor for murder. Alex was just the beginning. As this unravels, more people are going to die. Because even though you believe you can keep this secret, whoever killed Alex is afraid you can't. You see how this works? You just can't trust each other anymore and when push comes to shove…"

"I'm sorry, deputy," Tessa said, getting to her feet. "I have no idea what you're talking about and I'm running late for an appointment. She held her head in a regal manner. Liza got a glimpse of the girl Tessa had been when she and Shelby and the others had been on the pinnacle of popularity and thought nothing could bring them down. But as they all seemed fond of saying, "that was high school." This was real life.

"Think about it, Tessa. If they think you're the weak link, they'll attack you like rabid dogs." Liza rose. "I'll see myself out."

Chapter Eight

Jordan hadn't seen his father since the last time he was in Montana. They talked once in a while by phone, but they really didn't have much to say to each other.

For a long time Jordan blamed his mother for the divorce, believing she cared more about the ranch than she did her husband. There was probably some truth in that. But the divorce wasn't all her fault. She hadn't driven his father away. Angus Cardwell was more than capable of doing that himself.

He found his father at Angus's favorite watering hole, the Corral, down the canyon from Big Sky. Angus had been one handsome cowboy in his day. It was easy to see even now why Mary Justice had fallen in love with him.

Unfortunately, Jordan's mother had loved ranching and her husband had loved bars and booze. The two hadn't mixed well. Angus had taken the healthy settlement Mary had offered him and had left amicably enough. He'd made the money last by working an odd job here and there, including cash he and his brother made playing in a Country-Western band.

Most of the time though, Angus could be found on a

bar stool—just as he was now. And most of the time his brother Harlan would be with him—just as he was now.

"Well, look what the cat dragged in," Angus said as Jordan made his way down the bar toward them. Like all out-of-the-way Montana bars, everyone had looked up to see who'd come through the door. Angus and Harlan were no exceptions.

"Hey, Bob," his father called to the owner as he slid off his stool to shake Jordan's hand and pound him on the back. "You remember my eldest."

Bob nodded, said hello and dropped a bar napkin in front of an empty stool next to Angus. Uncle Harlan nodded his hello and Angus patted the stool next to him and said, "What would you like to drink, son?"

Jordan wasn't in the mood for a drink, but he knew better than to say so. Angus took it personally when anyone wouldn't drink with him—especially his son. "I'll take a beer. Whatever's on tap."

Bob poured him a cold one and set it on the napkin, taking the money out of the twenty Angus had beside his own beer.

"What are you doing in Montana?" Uncle Harlan asked.

"I was just asking myself that same thing," Jordan said and took a sip of his beer. He could feel his father's gaze on him. News traveled fast in the canyon. Angus and Harlan would have heard about the shooting night before last.

He braced himself for their questions. To his surprise, that wasn't the first thing his father wanted to know.

"Been to see your sister yet?" Angus asked.

"Not yet. I wasn't sure Dana would want to see me."

"You know better than that." He took a drink of his beer. "That is, unless you're going to try to hit her up for money. No one will want to see you in that case."

Jordan shook his head. "I'm not here looking for money."

"In that case," his father said with a laugh, "you can buy the next round."

Two beers later Jordan asked his father if he remembered when Tanner Cole died.

Angus nodded solemnly. "He hung himself up by that construction site. I remember he was staying up there because there'd been some vandalism."

"There'd been some before Tanner moved into the cabin?" Jordan asked in surprise.

Angus nodded. "Couldn't prove who did it, but Malcolm Iverson was pretty sure it was his competitor, Harris Lancaster, trying to put him out of business. So he hired the kid to keep an eye on things."

Jordan hadn't known about the earlier vandalism or that Iverson had suspected Harris Lancaster.

"Malcolm probably couldn't have survived financially the way things were going even if his equipment hadn't been vandalized a second time," Uncle Harlan said. "Your friend must have taken it hard, though, since everyone blamed it for forcing Iverson into bankruptcy. Apparently, he'd let his equipment insurance lapse."

"How did I never hear this?" Jordan said.

"You were a senior in high school," his father said with a laugh. "You had your nose up some girl's skirt. You were lucky you even graduated."

"Tanner never said anything about this," he said more to himself than to his father and uncle.

Angus tipped his beer up, took a swallow, then turned his gaze on his son. "You can't blame yourself. Malcolm had no business hiring a kid to watch over his equipment. I'm just sorry you had to be the one to find your friend like that."

Jordan nodded, remembering the day he'd gone up to the construction site looking for Tanner. He'd been worried about him since it wasn't like Tanner to miss school.

He'd never forget parking and walking up the road to find the front door of the cabin open. He'd called Tanner's name and gotten no answer and yet, his friend's pickup had been sitting next to the cabin.

One glance and he'd seen that it was empty. He'd heard the creaking sound and at first thought it was a tree limb scraping against another limb.

It wasn't until he turned toward the fire pit where the party had been held the night of the vandalism that he saw the shadow. A breeze had stirred the pines, making the shadow flicker over the dead campfire. He'd called Tanner's name again, then with a sinking feeling he'd followed the creaking sound until he saw what was casting the long shadow over the fire ring.

He would never forget the sight of his best friend hanging from the tree limb.

Jordan took a drink of his beer, cleared his throat and said, "I never believed that Tanner killed himself. I knew he blamed himself for the vandalism because of the party up there that night, but now with Alex murdered... I have to find out what really happened."

"If I were you, I'd stay out of it," Angus said, looking worried. "Two of your friends are dead. Whatever's going on, you might be next."

LIZA HAD TO ADMIT IT. She was having fun. She and Dana had hit it off from the first time they'd met and Hilde was a whole lot of fun.

"Oh, you have to try this one," Hilde said as she pulled a black-and-white polka-dot dress from the huge pile she'd brought. "It's one of my favorites."

They'd been laughing and joking as Liza tried on one dress after another. Hilde had kidded Dana after exploring her closet and deeming it probably worse than Liza's.

"You cowgirls," Hilde said. "Jeans, jeans, jeans. Don't you ever just want to show off your legs?"

"No," Liza and Dana had said in unison.

The polka-dot dress was cute and it fit Liza perfectly. "Do you think it's *too* cute? Maybe it's not dressy enough," Liza asked.

"Come on, this is Montana, no one dresses up," Dana said.

Hilde rolled her eyes. "Sweetie, this is Big Sky and all the women will be dressed to the nines. The men will be wearing jeans, boots and Western sports jackets, but for these women, this is a chance to pull out all those expensive clothes, bags and high heels they're just dying to show off."

"Then I'm wearing this," Liza said, studying her reflection in the mirror. She loved the black-and-white polka-dot dress. "This is as dressy as this cowgirl is going to get."

Dana laughed. "Good for you."

As Liza changed back into her jeans, boots and uniform shirt, Dana said, "So have you seen my brother?"

She shook her head. "Not since earlier. I haven't had a chance to talk to him, either."

"He is still a suspect, right?" Hilde asked, sounding worried.

Liza realized that her two friends were worried about her being taken in by Jordan. She had to smile, warmed by their concern.

"I hope I don't have to remind you that he was best friends with both Tanner and Alex and now they're both dead," Hilde said. "I grew up around Jordan. He always had a temper." She shot a look at Dana, who nodded, though with obvious regret.

"People change," Liza said, instantly regretting coming to Jordan's defense. She saw Hilde and Dana exchange a look. *"What?"*

"It's Stacy. I think *she's* changed," Dana said.

"You *hope* she's changed," Hilde corrected.

"Hud told me he was doing some checking into her past," Liza said. "I assume he didn't find anything."

"That's just it, he found nothing and that has him even more worried," Dana said. "Him and his marshal intuition."

Liza laughed. "Don't be joking around about our intuition." She'd been a green deputy six years ago, but Hud had taken her under his wing after seeing what he called an instinct for the job. Now he trusted her to handle this investigation and that meant everything to her.

The three women visited for a while longer, then Liza said she had to get moving. "The cocktail party and dinner is tonight. I've studied up on the players. Jordan had a list of those attending. Surprisingly, or maybe not, all eight of the Big Sky senior graduates will be up at Mountain Village tonight. Everyone but Alex and Tanner, that is." It was a small class twenty years ago. Although they attended high school down in Bozeman, they wanted their own reunion up here. Only in the past few years had Big Sky gotten its own high school.

"Just be careful," Dana said. "I know a few of those women." She pretended to shudder. "They're vicious."

"I don't think they're that bad," Hilde said. "I work out at Yogamotion. They're nice to me."

This time Dana and Liza exchanged a look. Hilde was petite, blonde and lithe. She would fit right in.

Dana reached for Liza's hand and squeezed it. "Just don't forget that one of them could be a killer."

JORDAN HAD SPENT THE REST of the afternoon writing down everything he could remember about his senior year of high school, especially what might pertain to Tanner and Alex.

The trip down memory lane had exhausted him. When he glanced at his watch, he'd been shocked to see how late it was. He quickly showered and changed and drove over to pick up his date.

What surprised him was the frisson of excitement he felt as he rang Liza's bell. He realized with a start that he hadn't been on a real date in years. Since his divorce he'd stayed clear of women.

When he'd left the canyon, he'd shed the cowboy side of him like an old snakeskin. He'd wanted bright lights and big city. He'd wanted sophistication. He'd kicked the Montana ranch dust off his boots and hadn't looked back.

That was how he'd ended up married to Jill. He'd been flattered that a model would even give him a sec-ond look. She'd been thrilled that he came from Montana ranch stock, saying she was bored with New York City–type men.

What he hadn't realized was that Jill thought he had money. She'd thought the ranch was the size of Ted Turner's apparently and couldn't wait to get her hands on the funds it would bring in once it sold.

He'd gotten caught up in trying to make her happy, even though she'd quit modeling the moment they were married and spent her days spending more money than he could make on Wall Street.

Now he could admit that he had become obsessed with keeping her. Although he hadn't acknowledged it to himself back then, he'd known that if he ran out of money, Jill would run out on him.

And she had—just as Dana had predicted. He hadn't wanted to hear it six years ago. Hell, he didn't like to think about it even now. The truth hurt. He'd fought back, of course, driving an even wider wedge between himself and his younger sister.

When Dana had discovered their mother's new will in that damned cookbook at the ranch house, Jill had realized there would be no ranch sale, no gold at the end of the rainbow, and she'd split. In truth, she'd already had some New York male model lined up long before that.

It had been some hard knocks, but he felt as if they had maybe knocked some sense into him. He saw things clearer than he had before. Mary Justice Cardwell had tried to instill values in her children. He'd rejected most of them, but they were still at his core, he thought as he rang Liza Turner's doorbell again.

When the door opened, he was taken completely off guard by the woman standing there. Liza took his breath away. She was wearing a black-and-white polka-dot dress that accentuated curves he'd had no idea were beneath her uniform. Her beautiful long curly hair had been pulled up, wisps of curls framing her face and she smelled heavenly.

"Wow, you look killer," he said when he caught his breath.

"So to speak," she said, sounding embarrassed as she quickly stuffed her gun into her purse. "My feet already hurt in these shoes."

He smiled at her. "You can kick them off the minute we hit the dance floor."

"Dance floor?" she asked, cocking an eyebrow.

"Didn't I mention I do one hell of a two-step?"

She took him in, her gaze pausing on his cowboy boots.

"Dana had a box of my clothes dropped off at the cabin," he said, feeling sheepish. It was so like Dana to be thoughtful. He'd found the boots as well as a couple of dress Western shirts and a Western-cut sports coat. He'd been surprised when everything still fit.

"You are a man of many surprises," she said, sounding almost as if she meant it.

He laughed. "You haven't seen anything yet." As he walked her to his rental SUV, he breathed in her scent, thinking he couldn't wait to get this woman in his arms on the dance floor.

DANA SUCKED ON HER BLEEDING finger. Needlepoint wasn't for her, she decided after jabbing herself another time. She surveyed her stitches and cringed. As Stacy came into the bedroom, she tossed the needlepoint aside, glad for an interruption.

Earlier, Mary and Hank had come in and colored

with her before their naps. She missed holding them on her lap, missed even more riding horses with them around the corral. All these beautiful fall days felt wasted lying in bed. But Hud had promised to take both kids out tomorrow.

As Stacy came over to the side of her bed, Dana saw that her sister had the cookbook open to their mother's double chocolate brownies.

"Is it all right if I make these?" Stacy asked.

They were Hud's favorite. That's why Mary Justice Cardwell had tucked her new will in her old, worn and faded cookbook next to the recipe. She'd wanted Dana not only to have the ranch—but the man she loved beside her.

"Sure. Hud would like that," Dana said, disappointed she couldn't even do something as simple as bake a pan of brownies for her husband.

"Mother used to make them for Dad, remember? Do you ever see him?"

"On occasion. Usually a holiday. He and Uncle Harlan keep pretty busy with their band." And their drinking, but she didn't say that.

Stacy nodded. "I might see them while I'm here. Maybe tomorrow if you don't mind me leaving for a little while in the morning?"

"Stacy, you don't need to ask. Of course you can go. Hud will be here."

"I suppose I know where I'll find Dad. Would you mind keeping Ella? I won't go until I put her down for her morning nap. I don't want to take her to a bar."

"I would be happy to watch her. You can bring her in here for her nap. She'll be fine while you're gone."

Stacy smiled, tears in her eyes, and gave Dana an

impulsive though awkward hug. "I've missed you so much."

"I've missed you, too."

Her sister drew back, looking embarrassed, grabbed the cookbook and left. In the other room, Hud was playing fort with the kids. She could see a corner of the couch and chairs pulled into the middle of the room and covered with spare blankets.

Hud caught her eye. He smiled and shrugged as if to say, maybe she was right about her sister. Dana sure hoped so.

LIZA BRACED HERSELF AS JORDAN ushered her into the lodge at Mountain Village for the Friday-night dinner and dance. Tomorrow there would be a tour of Big Sky and a free afternoon, with the final picnic Sunday.

A room had been prepared for the reunion party that impressed her more than she wanted to admit. A DJ played music under a starry decor of silver and white. The lights had been turned low, forming pockets of darkness. Candles flickered at white-clothed tables arranged in a circle around the small shining dance floor.

A few couples were dancing. Most were visiting, either standing next to the bar or already seated at the cocktail tables.

"Hilde was right," Liza whispered. "I *am* underdressed." The women were dressed in fancy gowns and expensive accessories. The men wore jeans and boots and Western sports jackets, looking much like Jordan.

"You look beautiful, the prettiest woman here," Jordan said, putting his arm around her protectively.

She grinned over at him. "You really can be charming when you want to, Mr. Cardwell."

"Don't tell Hud," he said. "I've spent years cultivating his bad opinion of me. I'd hate to ruin it with just one night with you." He put his hand on her waist. "Let's dance." He drew her out on the dance floor and pulled her close. She began to move to the slow song, too aware of her dance partner and his warm hand on her back.

Jordan *was* full of surprises. He was light on his feet, more athletic than she'd thought and a wonderful dancer. He held her close, the two of them moving as one, and she lost herself in the music and him as she rested her cheek against his shoulder. He smelled wonderful and she felt safe and protected in his arms. The latter surprised her.

The night took on a magical feel and for the length of several Country-Western songs, she forgot why she and Jordan were here. She also forgot that he was a murder suspect.

When the song ended, she found herself looking at him as if seeing him for the first time. He appeared completely at home in his Western clothes. They suited him and she told him so.

He smiled at that. "I thought I'd dusted the cowboy dirt off me when I left here. My mother used to say this land and life were a part of me that I could never shed." He quickly changed the subject as if he hadn't meant to tell her those things. "Looks like everyone is here except for Tessa, Alex and Tanner. That's the nice thing about having a small graduating class. They're fairly easy to keep track of. Shall we get a drink?"

They'd done just that by the end of the next song when Shelby took the stage. She gave a short speech, updating anyone who didn't know about the members of the class, announced who had come the farthest, who had changed the most, who had the most kids.

"I thought we should have a few minutes of silence for Alex," she said at the end. "Since he can't be with us tonight."

Liza spotted Tessa, who'd apparently just arrived. There was chatter about the murder around the tables, then everyone grew silent. It seemed to stretch on too long. Liza found herself looking around the room at the graduates.

She quickly picked out the main players Jordan had told her about. Shelby and her husband, contractor Wyatt Iverson; Tessa, who'd come alone; Whitney Fraser and husband and local business owner, Von; and Ashley Henderson and husband, Paul, had all congregated to one area of the room. Ashley and her husband and Whitney and hers appeared to be cut from the same cloth as Shelby and Wyatt. Brittany Peterson and husband Lee were visiting at a table of former students who were no longer Big Sky residents.

As Liza took them all in, she knew that what she was really looking for was a killer.

Wyatt Iverson was as handsome and put-together as his wife, Shelby. Liza waited until he went to the bar alone before she joined him.

"Wyatt Iverson? I don't think we've met. I'm Liza Turner—"

"Deputy marshal in charge of the Alex Winslow case," he said with a wide smile. "I know. I checked. I wanted to make sure someone capable was on the case. I heard great things about you."

"Thank you." She recalled a rumor going around that Wyatt was considering getting into national politics.

Right now he served on a variety of boards as well as on the local commission. Wyatt was handsome and a smooth talker, a born politician and clearly a man with a driving ambition. He'd brought his father's business back from bankruptcy and made a name for himself, not to mention a whole lot of money apparently.

Shelby joined them, taking her husband's arm and announcing that dinner was being served in the dining room. "Everyone bring your drinks and follow me!" Ashley and Whitney fell into line and trailed after Shelby, just as Tessa did, but according to Jordan they'd been doing that for years.

To no one's surprise, Shelby had distributed place cards around a long table. Liza was surprised to see that she and Jordan were near the center, with Tessa and Brittany and her husband, Lee, at one end and Shelby's inner circle at the other.

She noticed that Tessa seemed surprised—and upset—when she found herself at the far end of the table. Clearly Tessa had done something Shelby hadn't liked. Either that or Shelby was sending her friend a message. If Shelby had anything to do with Alex's murder and Tessa knew about it, Liza feared that Tessa might get more than banished at the reunion dinner table. Whatever had Shelby upset with her could get Tessa killed just as it had Alex.

Chapter Nine

Jordan could have wrung Shelby's neck even before dinner was served. They'd all just sat down when Shelby insisted everyone go around the table and introduce their dates and spouses before dinner was served.

When it came Jordan's turn, he squeezed Liza's hand and said, "This is my date, Liza Turner."

"Oh, come on, Jordan," Shelby said. "Liza Turner is our local deputy marshal and the woman in charge of investigating Alex's murder." She smiled as she said it, but Jordan couldn't miss the hard glint in her eyes. "So, Deputy, tell us how the case is going."

"It's under investigation, that's all I can tell you," Liza said.

Shelby pretended to pout, making Jordan grit his teeth. "Oh, we were hoping as Alex's friends we could get inside information."

Jordan just bet she was. Fortunately, the staff served dinner and the conversations turned to other things.

"How have you been?" Brittany asked him. She was still as strikingly beautiful as she'd been in high school, but now there was a contentment about her.

"Good. You look happy," he said, glad for her.

"My life is as crazy as ever with three small ones

running around and…" She grinned. "Another one on
the way. Surprise!"

"Congratulations," Jordan said, meaning it. She
didn't seem in the least bit upset to be seated away
from Shelby and her other classmates. Unlike Tessa,
who hadn't said a word or hardly looked up since sitting down.

Everyone offered their congratulations to Brittany,
including Shelby, who seemed to have her ears trained
on their end of the table.

"How many does this make now?" she asked.

"Four, Shelby," Brittany said, smiling although Jordan could tell Shelby irritated her as much as she did
him.

Shelby pretended shock. "I think you get the award
for most children and also our Look Who's Pregnant!
Award."

Jordan glanced over at Liza. He knew she was taking all of this in. Like him, he was sure she'd noticed
the way Tessa had been acting since they'd sat down.
Also, Tessa had been hitting the booze hard every time
she could get the cocktail waitress's attention.

Jordan couldn't have been happier when dessert was
finally served. Shelby had been running the dinner as
if it was a board meeting. He noticed that, like Tessa,
Shelby had been throwing down drinks. Just the sound
of her voice irritated him. He was reminded why he
hadn't wanted to come to his reunion.

"Jordan, what was the name of your wife, the one
who was the model?" Shelby asked loudly from the
other end of the table.

He didn't want to talk about his marriage or his
divorce. But he knew Shelby wasn't going to let it go.

"Jill Ames. She was my *only* wife, Shelby," he said and felt Liza's calming hand on his thigh.

"Jill Ames is *gorgeous.* What were you thinking letting her get away?" Shelby said and laughed. She gave Liza a sympathetic look. "Jill Ames would be a hard act to follow."

"Shelby, you might want to back off on the drinks," Brittany said, throwing down her napkin as she shoved to her feet. "Your claws are coming out." She shot Jordan and Liza an apologetic look and excused herself before heading for the ladies' room. Shelby glared after her for a moment, then followed her.

LIZA WAITED UNTIL SHELBY disappeared down the hallway before she, too, excused herself. She was within ten feet of the ladies' room door when she heard their raised voices. She slowed, checked to make sure there was no one behind her, before she stepped to the door and eased it open a few inches. She could see the two reflected in the bathroom mirrors, but neither could see her.

"How dare you try to embarrass me," Shelby screeched into Brittany's face.

"Embarrass *you?* Seriously, Shelby?" Brittany started to turn away from her.

Shelby grabbed her arm. "Don't you turn your back on me."

"Touch me again and I'll deck you," Brittany said as she jerked free of the woman's hold. "I don't do yoga every day like you, but I do haul around three kids so I'm betting I'm a lot stronger and tougher than you are. I'm also not afraid of you anymore."

"Well, you should be."

"Are you threatening me?" Brittany demanded as

she advanced on her. "This isn't high school, Shelby. Your reign is over." She turned and went into a stall.

Shelby stood as if frozen on the spot, her face white with fury as Liza stepped into the ladies' room. Seeing the deputy marshal, Shelby quickly spun around and twisted the handle on the faucet, hiding her face as she washed her hands.

Liza went into the first stall. She heard Brittany flush, exit the next stall and go to the washbasin. Through the sound of running water, she heard Shelby hiss something.

"Whatever, Shelby." Brittany left, but a moment later someone else came in.

"Aren't you talking to me? What's going on?" Tessa whined, sounding like a child. "Are you mad at me? I don't understand. I haven't done *anything*."

She was sure Shelby was probably trying to signal that they weren't alone, but Tessa was clearly upset and apparently not paying attention.

"I told you I wouldn't say anything. You know you can trust me. So why are you—"

"Tessa, this really isn't the place," Shelby snapped.

"But all evening you've—"

Liza had no choice but to flush. As she opened the stall door, both Tessa and Shelby glanced in her direction. "Ladies," she said as she moved to the sinks and turned on the water.

"I could use some fresh air," Shelby said. "Come outside with me for a minute." She smiled as she took Tessa's arm and practically dragged her out of the bathroom.

Liza washed her hands, dried them and then stepped out. She could see Shelby and Tessa on the large deck in what was obviously a heated discussion. She watched them for a moment, wishing she could hear their conversation, but having no way to do that went back to the table and Jordan.

"Everything okay?" he asked quietly.

She smiled at him. "Great."

"I love your dress," Brittany said.

Liza laughed. "That's right. You like polka dots. I remember your apron." Liza liked Brittany. She could see why Jordan had had a crush on her in high school. Probably still did.

With dinner over, everyone began to wander away from the table and back into the first room where the music was again playing.

Liza pulled Jordan aside and told him what she'd overheard.

"So basically you just wanted to let me know I was right about Tessa," Jordan said, grinning.

"Apparently, you can be right once in a while, yes." She smiled back at him, realizing he was flirting with her again and she didn't mind it.

A few moments later Shelby came back in from the deck. She put her game face on again and breezed by them, already dancing to the music before she reached the dance floor. But she didn't fool Liza. Shelby was trying hard to hide whatever was really going on with her and Tessa.

"I'm going to talk to Tessa," Liza said. "Save me a dance."

As JORDAN LEFT THE DINING ROOM and joined the others, he spotted Shelby talking to her other two cohorts. Ashley and Whitney could have been sisters. They were both brunettes, both shapely, both pretty—at least from a distance. He knew his perception of them had been poisoned a long time ago.

He liked to think all of them had changed, himself included. But he could tell by the way Ashley and Whitney were listening to Shelby that they still followed her as blindly as they had in high school. It made him sad. Brittany had grown up, made a life for herself and seen through Shelby. But apparently Brittany was the only one who'd made the break from Shelby's control.

"Jordan, do you have a minute?"

He turned to find Paul Henderson, Ashley's husband. Paul had been two years ahead of them in school. "Sure," he said as Paul motioned to the empty lobby of the lodge.

"I hope I'm not speaking out of school here," Paul said. "But there's a rumor going around that Alex was asking about Tanner before he was...killed. I figured if you really were with him at the falls, then he must have talked to you."

"We didn't get a chance to talk," Jordan said, wondering if Paul had any information or if he was just fishing.

"Oh." He looked crestfallen.

"*You* talked to him?"

Paul nodded and met Jordan's gaze. "I wasn't sure if I should tell the deputy marshal."

"What did Alex tell you?"

He hesitated for a moment, then said, "Alex asked me if I remembered the party Tanner had that night at the cabin, the night the equipment was vandalized?"

Jordan nodded. He vaguely remembered the party. He'd drunk too much and, after his fight with Tessa, had left early with some girl from Bozeman who he couldn't even remember. "Were you there?"

"No. I was grounded from the past weekend. He was asking if I knew where Shelby was that night."

"Shelby?"

"He wanted to know if Ashley had been with her."

"And was she?"

"That's just it. I told Alex that I thought she was because she called a little after two in the morning. She'd been drinking. We argued and I hung up. The next day when I asked her where she'd been the night before, she swore she didn't go to the party. But Alex said something about some photos from the party that night that proved not only were Ashley and Whitney there, but Shelby and Tessa were, too."

"Why was he interested in photos of the party?" Jordan asked.

Paul shrugged. "That's just it. I can't imagine what some photographs of a high school kegger twenty years ago could have to do with anything. That's why I haven't said anything to the deputy marshal."

"Did you ask Ashley about them?"

"She still swears she wasn't at the party that night, but…" He looked away for a moment. "I'd like to see those photos. Alex seemed to think there was something in them that could explain why Tanner is dead."

"I'll mention it to the deputy marshal," Jordan said. "She might want to talk to you."

Paul looked relieved. "I didn't know if I should say anything, but I'm glad I did. Okay, back to the party huh?" He didn't look as if he was enjoying the reunion any more than Jordan had enjoyed dinner.

The only thing that kept Jordan from calling it quits was the thought of another dance with Liza.

TESSA STOOD AT THE DECK railing, her back to the lodge. She looked cold and miserable and from the redness around her eyes, she'd been crying.

Liza joined her at the railing. "Shelby's trying to bring you back under control, you know."

Tessa glanced over at her and let out a laugh. "I'd pretend I didn't know what you were talking about, but what would be the use?"

"Talk to me, Tessa. Tell me what Shelby is so terrified I'll find out?"

Tessa hugged herself and looked away. A breeze whispered in the nearby pines. Earlier it had been warm. Now though, the air had cooled. It carried the promise of winter. Closer, Liza could hear the muted music from inside the lodge. The party was resuming. She was betting that Shelby wouldn't leave Tessa out here long. If Liza didn't get the truth out of her quickly—

A door opened behind them. "Tessa?" Whitney called from the open doorway. "Shelby needs your help with the awards."

"I'll be right there," she said over her shoulder and started to turn toward the lodge.

"Tessa," Liza said, feeling her chance slipping through her fingers. She was genuinely afraid for Tessa. For some reason, the woman had been cut from the herd. Liza feared for the woman's life.

"Let me think about things. Maybe I'll stop by your office Monday."

Liza nodded. The one thing she'd learned was when to back off. "I can help you."

Tessa laughed at that and looked toward the lodge. "I'm not sure anyone can help me," she said and pushed off the railing to go back inside.

Liza bit down on her frustration. Tessa needed her best friend's approval. But surely she was tired of playing Shelby's game.

Telling herself this night hadn't been a total waste, Liza waited for a few moments before going back inside. The moment she saw Jordan, she thought, no, this night had definitely not been a waste.

He stood silhouetted in the doorway, reminding her that she'd come with the most handsome man at the party. Suspect or not, Jordan Cardwell was a pretty good date, she thought as he drew her into his arms and out on the dance floor.

Out of the corner of her eye she saw that Shelby had Tessa in the corner. Liza meet Tessa's gaze for a moment before the woman shoved away from Shelby and dragged Wyatt Iverson out on the floor to dance with her.

"You might want to talk to Paul Henderson," Jordan said, as they were leaving the reunion party a few dances later. "Apparently, Alex asked him about the party at the cabin that night. Alex thought there were photographs taken at the party that might have something to do with Tanner's death."

"Photographs?" Liza asked. She'd settled into the SUV's passenger seat, still feeling the warmth of being in Jordan's arms on the dance floor. She'd had fun even though she hated to admit it since she was supposed to be finding a murderer.

"Paul wasn't at Tanner's kegger, but he seems to think Ashley might have gone and lied about it."

"And how does all of this lead to Alex's death?" she asked, wanting to hear Jordan's take on it.

"Tanner was staying in a cabin up on the mountain to keep an eye on Iverson Construction equipment," he said as he drove. "He throws a party, the equipment gets vandalized, he gets in trouble. Malcolm Iverson, who is on the edge of bankruptcy, believes his competitor Harris Lancaster is behind the vandalism in an attempt to take over his business. Malcolm goes gunning for him, shoots Harris accidentally and goes to prison for a couple of years. When he gets out, he drowns in a boating accident." He looked over at her. "These things have to be connected and if there really are photographs from Tanner's party, then maybe they tie it all together—and explain why Tanner is dead."

"Tanner sounds like such a sensible kid," Liza said. "Why would he throw a party at the cabin with the construction equipment nearby?"

"He swore he didn't. People just started showing up. So he went with it. But after the equipment was vandalized, he felt horrible about it." He shrugged as he drove down the mountain. "I know he blamed himself."

"Was Tanner drinking a lot that night?"

Jordan sighed. "I don't know. I got drunk and left with some girl."

"So if these photographs exist, then they might not just show who was there and with whom, the photographer might have captured the vandalism on film."

"That's what I was thinking, and if Ashley's father, Harris Lancaster, was behind it, he would have good reason not to want the photographs to surface and so would Ashley."

Liza thought of the suicide scene photos in Tanner's

file, the campfire ringed with rocks, the charred beer cans, all the tracks at the scene. "If Harris was questioned about the vandalism, there should be something down at the office in the file."

"Both Malcolm Iverson and Harris Lancaster are the kind of men who would have taken the law into their own hands," Jordan said. "And so are their sons. I doubt either of them reported anything."

"I think I should talk to Harris Lancaster," Liza said.

"Let me go along. Just to make sure you're safe. Truth is, Lancaster is the kind of man who won't take a female deputy seriously. No offense."

"Oh, none taken," she said sarcastically. "But you've done enough, thanks. So what do you have planned tomorrow?"

He'd grinned over at her. "Worried about me?"

"Tell me I don't have any reason to be."

"Look, I'm touched but—"

"It isn't personal, so save it," she said quickly. "I have one murder on my hands, maybe two. I don't need you adding another one for me to solve."

"Don't worry, Deputy. I have no intention of getting myself killed. I'll watch my back. You do the same."

She nodded. "I'm driving up to West Yellowstone to see Brick Savage. He was the investigating marshal on Tanner's death."

"I need to go see my sister. But maybe I'll see you later tomorrow? How about dinner?"

She shook her head. "I don't think that's a good idea."

"I get it. You're afraid that over dinner I might charm you into thinking I'm harmless, if you weren't careful."

"You aren't that charming and you're far from harmless."

He grinned at that. "I'm going to take that as a compliment."

"I was sure you would."

As he drove toward her condo, he said, "Seriously, watch your back tomorrow."

WHEN THEY REACHED LIZA'S CONDO, Jordan insisted on walking her to her door.

"This really isn't necessary," she said, shaking her head at him as she dug for her key. He saw the glint of her weapon in her purse along with her badge. For a while on the dance floor, he'd forgotten she was a deputy marshal. She was merely a beautiful woman in his arms.

"A gentleman always walks his date to the door."

"This isn't a date."

"Because I'm a suspect?"

She looked up from searching in her purse for her key. He'd noticed that she'd suddenly become ill at ease when he'd driven up in front of her condo. Now she froze as he moved closer until they were a breath apart.

"Do you really think I'm dangerous?" he asked.

Her laugh sounded nervous. "Absolutely."

"Well, date or not, I had fun with you," he whispered and kissed her gently. She still hadn't moved when he drew back to look into her beautiful green eyes.

He knew he should leave it at one quick kiss, turn and walk away, but there was something so alluring about her that he gripped her waist and pulled her to him. This time he kissed her like he'd wanted to since the day he'd seen her sitting astride her horse, watching him from the darkness of the trees. There'd been something mysterious and sensual about her even when he'd realized who she was.

Now she melted into him, her hands going to his shoulders, her lips parting, a soft moan escaping from deep within her.

He felt his own desire spark and catch flame. It had been so long since he'd felt like this, if he ever had before. Liza was slight in stature, but had curves in all the right places. There was something solid and real about her. He couldn't help thinking how different she was from his ex, Jill. Jill ate like a bird. If she'd consumed even a portion of the food Liza'd had tonight at the dinner, she'd be anxious to get inside the condo and throw it all up. He'd gotten so sick of her constant dieting and complaining about the way she looked.

Liza was so different from any woman he'd ever known. She knew who she was and what she wanted. She looked perfect as she was, felt perfect. He wanted to sweep her into his arms, take her inside and make love to her until daylight.

AT THE SOUND OF A VEHICLE coming up the street, Liza pushed back from the kiss as if coming up for air. She was breathing hard, her heart pounding, desire making her blood run hot.

As a white SUV slowly drove past, she saw the woman behind the wheel and swore.

"Shelby," she said, mentally kicking herself for not only letting this happen but also wanting it to.

Jordan turned to watch the vehicle disappear down the street. "Sorry."

It was bad enough that a lot of people didn't think a woman could do this job. She'd only made it worse by letting someone like Shelby see her kissing Jordan Cardwell.

"I should never have gone to the reunion dinner with you," she said.

"You were working."

"That kiss wasn't work."

"No," he said and grinned at her.

"Go home," she said.

He raised both hands and took a step back. "You want to pick me up at the cabins or should I meet you tomorrow to—"

"I already told you. I can handle this without your help."

He stopped. "Liza, I'm not giving up until Alex's killer is caught."

"It's too dangerous."

He studied her for a moment. "Too dangerous for who?" he asked, stepping to her again. He cupped the side of her face with one of his large hands. She was surprised to feel the calluses. Taking his hand, she held it to the light.

"I thought you worked on Wall Street?" she asked, hating the suspicion she heard in her voice. Worse, that Jordan had heard it.

"I used to. I quit. I've been working construction for a few years now."

"Do you even live in New York City?"

He shook his head. "Why are you getting so upset?"

"Because I've run background checks on everyone involved in this case—except *you*."

"Because you know I didn't kill Alex."

"Do I?" She glared at him, although it was herself she was angry with.

He held up his hands again. "I'm sorry if one little kiss—"

"It wasn't one little kiss," she snapped and closed her eyes as she realized what she'd said. The kiss had shaken her. Worse, it had sparked a desire in her for this man, of all men.

"Run your background check. Do whatever it is you have to do," he said as he took a step away. "I have nothing to hide. But know this. That wasn't just some little kiss for me, either. If I had my way, I'd have you inside that condo and I'd be taking off your clothes right now. Good night, Deputy Marshal. I had a nice time. You make a nice date."

With that, he turned and walked to his vehicle while she stood trembling on the condo stoop thinking about what he'd said. Imagining the two of them tearing at each other's clothing. She knew that if he had taken her inside, they would have never made it to the bedroom.

As he drove away, she stood breathing in the cold night air, trying to still the aching need inside her. She'd always prided herself on her strength and determination. Nothing had kept her from realizing her goal to get where she was now. That had meant not letting a man either slow her down or stop her dead in her pursuit.

She wasn't going to let Jordan Cardwell ruin not just her reputation, but her credibility as a deputy marshal. The realization that she wanted him as much as he wanted her shocked her. No man had ever interested her enough for the problem to come up before. She reminded herself that Jordan was a suspect.

After a moment she dug into her purse until she found her key. With shaking fingers, she unlocked the door and stepped inside.

Even before she turned on the light, she knew something was terribly wrong. Someone had ransacked her
condo.

She stood staring at the mess, trying to make sense
of it. Why would someone do this? Her heart began to
pound. This felt as if it was a warning.

Or had someone been looking for something and
not finding it, just decided to tear the place up? Were
they looking for the photographs Alex had been asking about?

Either way, she felt as if she'd gotten the message.
Unfortunately, she'd never been good at heeding these
kinds of warnings.

If anything, she was more determined than ever to
solve this case and get Jordan Cardwell off her suspect list.

Chapter Ten

Saturday morning after cleaning up her condo, Liza drove up the canyon. It was one of those amazing Montana fall days. The sky was robin's-egg blue and not a cloud was in sight. The deciduous trees along the river glowed in bright blinding golds and deep reds next to the dark green of the pines.

At the heart of it all was the Gallatin River, running clear and beautiful, as it wound through the canyon and rocks. Harris Lancaster lived in a large modern home that looked as if it had been picked up in some big city and accidentally dropped here by the river.

His wife answered the door and pointed Liza toward a building a ways from the house. She followed a graveled path to the door and knocked.

Harris was a big burly brisk man with a loud deep voice and piercing gray eyes. Liza tried to imagine him in the very feminine furnishings of the house she'd glimpsed before his wife had closed the door.

His office looked like him, large and messy. The space was taken up by everything from dirty outdoor clothing and piles of papers and building plans to equipment parts and an old couch that Liza suspected he probably slept on more often than not. Given the pristine look of the house and Malcolm's wife, Liza doubted he was allowed to set foot inside it.

He cleared off an old wooden chair, motioned her into it and took a seat behind his cluttered desk. "So what's this about?" The office smelled of cigar smoke.

"I want to talk to you about Tanner Cole," Liza said.

"Who?"

"He worked for Malcolm Iverson twenty years ago when he was in high school."

He laughed. "*Seriously?* I can't remember who works for me right now, why would I remember who worked for Malcolm?"

"Tanner committed suicide twenty years ago after Malcolm Iverson's construction equipment was vandalized. It was just days before Malcolm shot you and went to prison."

He shook his head. "I try not to think about any of that."

"Tanner was in the same class as your daughter Ashley. He lived in a cabin near the construction site. Malcolm held Tanner responsible, but ultimately, he believed you were behind the vandalism that forced him into bankruptcy."

He scoffed at that. "Malcolm didn't know anything about running a business. He spent too much time in the bar. But I had nothing to do with vandalizing his equipment. He was just looking for someone to blame. Anyway, I heard the vandalism was kid stuff. You know, sugar in the gas tanks, broken and missing motor parts. Pure mischief. That's what happens when you get a bunch of drunk kids together."

"Or it was made to look like kids did it," she noted, but Harris Lancaster didn't seem to be listening.

"I do remember something about that Tanner boy now that you mention it. Ashley was real upset. We all were," he added. "Tanner's family has a ranch on the way to West Yellowstone. Too bad, but I don't see what any of that has to do with me."

"You benefited by Malcolm going broke."

He shrugged. "Maybe, at the time. But there was plenty of work to go around. His son and I are competitors, but we aren't shooting each other and we're both doing quite well."

He had a point. Maybe his problems with Malcolm and vice versa had nothing to do with Tanner's death. Maybe it had been guilt. Or maybe there were some photographs somewhere that told a different story.

JORDAN PULLED UP OUT IN FRONT of the house where he'd been raised. He sat for a moment just looking at the large two-story house. The other day when he'd come into town, he'd driven in from the other side of the ranch to make sure no one was at home before he'd come down to borrow a hat.

At least that had been his excuse. He'd wanted to wander around the house without anyone watching him. He knew his sister would think he was casing the joint, looking for valuables he could pawn or sell on eBay.

He and Dana had always butted heads, although he wished that wasn't the case. He'd always respected her. She worked harder than anyone he knew and made the rest of them feel like slackers.

Even after the good luck he'd had after Jill had left, he still felt like he could never measure up to Dana. Now as he opened his car door and climbed out, he half expected Dana to meet him on the porch. Possibly with a shotgun in her hands. Then he remembered that Hud had said she was pregnant with twins and having a hard time.

At the door, he knocked. It felt strange to knock at a door he'd run in and out of for years.

To his surprise, Stacy opened the door. He'd thought she was just passing through. But then again that would explain the beater car with the California plates he now saw parked off to the side. He hadn't even noticed it he'd been so busy looking at the house.

"Stacy," he said, unable to hide his surprise.

"Jordan?" She put a lot into that one word.

"It's all right. I didn't come by to cause trouble. I just wanted to see my sister. Sisters," he corrected. "And my niece and nephew."

"Nieces," she said and stepped back to let him come in.

"That's right. Hud said you have a baby?"

"Don't sound so surprised." Stacy studied him for a moment. "I'll see if Dana is up to having company."

"I'm not company. I'm *family*."

She lifted an eyebrow as if to say, "Since when?"

As if *she* should talk, he thought as she headed for the downstairs sunroom that had been their parent's bedroom, then their mother's and now apparently Dana's.

"Where are the kids?" he called after Stacy.

She shot him a warning look. "Down for their naps."

"Sorry," he whispered. He stood in the doorway, afraid to step in and feeling badly that it had come to this.

Stacy returned a moment later. She didn't look happy. "Dana isn't supposed to be upset."

"Thanks for the warning," he said and stepped across the living room to the doorway Stacy had just come from.

He stopped the moment he saw Dana. She looked beautiful, propped up against an array of pillows. Their gazes locked and he stepped the rest of the way into the room, closing the door behind him.

"Hey, sis," he said.

"Jordan." She began to cry.

With a lump in his throat at her reaction, he closed the distance and bent down to hug her awkwardly. "Are you all right?" he asked pulling back to look at her. "You look...beautiful."

"I thought you were going to say...big," she said laughing and crying as she wiped at her eyes. "It's the hormones," she said pointing at her tears. "I cry over everything."

"That explains it. For a minute there I thought you might have missed me," he said as he pulled up the chair next to the bed.

She stopped drying her tears to meet his gaze. "You seem...different."

He smiled. "Oh, I'm still that stubborn, temperamental brother you remember. But maybe some of the hard edges have gotten knocked off."

Dana nodded. "Maybe that's it. Hud told me why you were in town."

"I didn't think you wanted to see me or I would have come by sooner."

"You're my older brother."

"Exactly," he only half joked.

The bedroom door opened. Stacy stuck her head in.

"I think I'll run that errand I told you about yesterday. The kids are still down. Should I move Ella?"

"No, I'll have Jordan bring her in before he leaves."

Stacy looked to her brother as if she wasn't sure that was a good idea.

"I haven't dropped a baby all day," he said.

"And Hud should be back any minute," Dana said to reassure her sister.

Stacy mugged a face at him and closed the door. He listened to her leave. But it wasn't until they both couldn't hear her old beater car engine any longer before they spoke.

"I did a lot of soul searching after everything that happened," he said. "I'm sorry."

"Me too."

"I went up to the cemetery and saw Mom the first day I got here. I borrowed a hat. Nothing else," he added quickly.

"Jordan, this ranch is your home too."

"I know, sis," he said putting a hand on her arm. "Mom always thought I'd come back and want to help you ranch."

Dana chuckled at that. "She said Stacy and Clay were gone, but you...well, she said there was ranching in your blood."

"Yeah. So tell me what's going on with you."

She placed her hands over her huge stomach. "I'm on bed rest with these two for the last weeks. I'm going insane."

He laughed. "I can imagine. And Stacy is...?"

"She's been great. Mary and Hank adore her."

"Mary and Hank. I can't wait to meet them."

"You should come back for dinner tonight," Dana said.

He shook his head. "Not sure that's a good idea given the way your husband feels about me, not to mention everything else going on right now."

"I wish you would. At least once before you leave," Dana said, tearing up again.

"You and your hormones." He got up and hugged her again. Straightening to leave, he asked, "So where's this baby I'm supposed to bring you before I leave?"

At the sound of the front door opening, Dana said, "Sounds like Hud's home. You'll have to come back to meet Ella."

"I'll try. You take care of yourself and your babies." As he opened the door, he came face to face with his brother-in-law again. "I was just leaving and no, I didn't upset her."

Hud looked past him to Dana. "What is she crying about then?"

"It's just the hormones," Dana said.

Jordan shrugged. "Just the hormones."

As he left, he found himself looking toward the barn, remembering his childhood here. Amazing how the place looked so different from the way he remembered it the last time he was here. Had he really tried to force his sister into selling it, lock, stock and barrel?

He felt a wave of shame as he walked to his rental SUV and climbed inside.

"WHERE'S STACY?" HUD ASKED as he stuck his head in the bedroom door later.

Dana saw that he had Ella on one shoulder. She realized she'd fallen asleep after Jordan had left and had awakened a few moments ago when she'd heard the baby cry.

"She said she wanted to go see Angus," Dana said groggily as she pulled herself up a little in the bed. "She said she wouldn't be gone long." Glancing at the clock beside her bed, she was shocked to see what time it was. "She hasn't come back?"

Hud shook his head. "I just changed Ella. I was going to heat some formula for her." He sounded worried.

Past him, Dana could see that it was dark outside. She felt a flutter of apprehension. "Stacy should have been back by now. Here, I'll take the baby. Call my father. Maybe they got to visiting and she just lost track of time."

"The kids and I are making dinner." Hud handed her Ella. "They ordered beanie wienies."

"Sounds great." She could smell the bacon and onions sizzling in the skillet. But her gaze was on the baby in her arms. Ella smiled up at her and she felt her heart do a somersault. Stacy was just running late. She probably didn't remember how quickly it got dark this time of year in the canyon.

A few minutes later, Hud came into the bedroom. "I called your father. He hasn't seen Stacy."

She felt her heart drop, but hid her fear as the kids came running in excitedly chanting "beanie wienies."

Hud set up Mary and Hank's small table in the bedroom so they could all eat dinner with her. The beanie wienies were wonderful. They finished the meal off with some of the brownies Aunt Stacy had made.

"Is Auntie Stacy going to live with us?" Mary asked.

"No, she's just visiting," Dana told her daughter. There was still no sign of Stacy. No call. Dana found herself listening, praying for the sound of her old car coming up the road. But there was only silence. "I'm not sure how long your aunt can stay."

Hank looked over at Ella who was drooling and laughing as she tried to roll over on the other side of the bed. "She can't leave without her baby," he said. "Can she?"

She shot Hud a look. Could Stacy leave without her baby?

"I'm going to call Hilde and see if she can come over while I go look for Stacy," Hud said. "I called Liza but she's in West Yellowstone. Apparently, she went up there to talk to my father about the case she's working."

Dana nodded, seeing her own worry reflected in his face.

"I'll call you if I hear anything." Big Sky was relatively small. Stacy couldn't have gone far. Unless she'd changed her mind about seeing their father and gone into Bozeman for some reason. But she'd said she would be back before Ella woke up from her nap. What if something had happened to her sister?

Trying to rein in her fear, Dana told the kids to get a game for them all to play.

"Ella can't play, Mommy," Mary cried. "She'll eat the game pieces."

"No, Ella will just watch," she told her daughter as she fought the dread that Stacy hadn't changed at all.

In that case Dana hated to think what that might mean. That Stacy wouldn't be back? Or worse, she'd left her baby. If it was her baby.

Chapter Eleven

Jordan felt at loose ends after leaving his sister's. On impulse he drove as far as he could up the road to the construction site where he'd found Tanner that horrible morning twenty years before.

The road was now paved and led up to a massive home. He could tell from the looks of it that the owner wasn't around and probably didn't come up but for a few weeks in the winter and summer.

The house had been built on a cleared area high on the mountain where the construction equipment had been parked twenty years ago. The small log cabin where Tanner had lived was gone. So was the campfire ring. Nothing looked as it had except for the tree where he'd found Tanner hanging that spring day.

There was also no sign that this was the spot where his best friend had taken his life. No log stumps. No rope mark on the large old pine limb. Nothing left of the tragedy even on the breeze that moaned in the high boughs. Jordan doubted the place's owners knew about the death that had occurred within yards of their vacation home.

He felt a sadness overwhelm him. "Why, Tanner? Why the hell did you do it?" he demanded as he looked up at the large limb where he'd found him. "Or did you?" He feared they would never know as he looked again at the dried-pine-needle-covered ground. Did he really think he was going to find answers up here?

Too antsy to go back to his cabin, he drove up the canyon. When he saw his father's truck parked outside The Corral, he swung in. He found his father and uncle sitting on their usual stools at the bar.

"Son? I thought you would have left by now," Angus Cardwell said. "Bob, get my son a beer."

Jordan noticed there were a few men at the end of the bar and several families at the tables in the dining area eating.

Angus slapped his son on the back as Jordan slid onto a stool next to him. The bar smelled of burgers and beer. Not a bad combination, he thought, figuring he understood why his old man had such an infatuation with bars.

"What have you been up to?" Uncle Harlan asked him.

"My twenty-year class reunion," he said, figuring that would suffice.

"You actually went to it?" his father said with a laugh.

"I went with the deputy marshal."

Both older men hooted. "That's my son," Angus said proudly.

Jordan had known that would be his father's reaction. It was why he'd said it. He was just glad Liza hadn't been around to hear it.

The draft beer was cold and went down easy. Heck, he might have a burger while he was at it. He settled in, listening to the watering hole banter, a television over the bar droning in the background.

"Your deputy figured out who killed that man at the falls?" his uncle asked him.

"Not yet, but she will," he said with confidence.

His father smiled over at him and gave him a wink. "That's really keeping you in the canyon, ain't it?"

Jordan smiled and ordered burgers for the three of them.

Later when he drove back to Big Sky and stopped by the Marshal's Office, he was disappointed to learn that Liza hadn't returned from West Yellowstone. He thought about what his father had said about his reasons for staying around. If he was being honest with himself, Liza definitely played into it.

LIZA FOUND BRICK Savage sitting on the deck of his Hebgen Lake home. She'd heard stories about him and, after he'd ignored her knocks at his front door, braced herself as she approached his deck.

"Mr. Savage?"

He looked up, his gaze like a piercing arrow as he took in her uniform first, then studied her face before saying, "Yes?"

"I'm Deputy Marshal Liza Turner out of the Big Sky office. I'd like a moment of your time."

"You have any identification?" His voice was gravelly but plenty strong.

She pulled her ID and climbed a couple of steps so he could see it.

He nodded, amusement in his gaze. "Deputy Marshal. Times really have changed. I heard my son left you in charge of the murder case."

"That's correct."

"Well, come on up here then," Brick said and pushed himself up out of his chair. He was a big man, but she could see that he used to be a lot bigger in his younger days. There was a no-nonsense aura about him along with his reputation that made her a little nervous being in his company.

He shoved a chair toward her as she reached the deck and waited for her to sit before he pulled up a weather-grayed log stump and settled himself on it.

"I hate to take your chair," she said, wondering about a man who had only one chair on his deck. Apparently he didn't expect or get much company. Did that mean he didn't see much of Hud and family?

"So?" Brick said as if his time was valuable and she was wasting it.

"I want to ask you about Tanner Cole's death. He was a senior—"

"I know who he was. Found hanging from a tree up on the side of the mountain overlooking Big Sky twenty-odd years ago," Brick said. "What do you want to know?"

"Was it a suicide?"

He leveled his gaze at her. "Wasn't it ruled one?"

"At the time. Is it possible Tanner had help?"

"It's always possible. Was there any sign of a struggle like scratches or bruises? Not according to the coroner's report but if you did your homework, you'd already know that. As for footprints, there were a lot of them. He'd had a beer bash, kegger, whatever your generation calls it. He'd had that within a few days so there were all kinds of tracks at the scene."

She knew all this and wondered if she'd wasted her

time driving all the way up here. Past him she could
see the deep green of the lake, feel a cold breeze coming off the water. Clouds had already gathered over
Lion's Head Mountain, one of the more recognizable
ones seen from his deck. Add to that the sun had already gone down. As it was, it would be dark before
she got back to Big Sky.

"I can tell you this, he used his own rope," Brick said.

She nodded. "What about Jordan Cardwell?"

"What about him?"

"You found him at the scene. Is there any chance—"

"He didn't kill his friend, if that's what you're asking."

"You're that sure?" she said, hearing the relief in her
voice and suspecting he did too. She'd started to like
Jordan, suspect or not. She knew it was a bad idea on
so many levels, but there was something about him...

"What did you really come up here to ask me?" Brick
demanded.

"I guess what I want is your gut reaction."

"My gut reaction isn't worth squat. Do I think he
killed himself?" The former marshal shrugged. "Strangulation takes a while. Gives a man a lot of time to re-
consider and change his mind, but with all his body
weight on the rope, it's impossible to get your fingers
under the rope and relieve the pressure."

She looked at him in surprise. "Are you telling me
he—"

"Changed his mind and clawed at the rope?" He nodded.

"Why wasn't that in the coroner's report?"

"It's not uncommon. But also not something a family member ever wants to know about. I would imagine Rupert wanted to spare them any more pain."

Liza shook her head. "But couldn't it also mean that Tanner Cole never meant to hang himself? That someone else put that rope around his neck?"

"And he didn't fight until that person kicked the log out?" Brick asked. "Remember, there were no defensive wounds or marks on his body."

"Maybe he thought it was a joke."

The elderly former marshal studied her for a moment. "What would make you let someone put a noose around your neck, joking or otherwise?"

That was the question, wasn't it?

"You think he killed himself," she said.

He shrugged. "Prove me wrong."

HUD SPENT A GOOD TWO HOURS canvassing the area for his sister-in-law before he put out the APB on her vehicle. He checked with the main towing services first though, telling himself her car could have broken down. All kinds of things could have happened to detain her— and maybe even keep her from calling.

But after those two hours he knew in his gut that wasn't the case. Stacy had split.

At the office he did something he'd hoped he wouldn't have to do. He began checking again for kidnappings of children matching Ella's description and realized he needed to narrow his search. Since Stacy was driving a car with California plates...

He realized he should have run her plates first. Feeling only a little guilty for having taken down her license number when he'd first become suspicious of her, he brought up his first surprise.

The car had been registered in La Jolla, California—but not to Stacy by any of her former married names or her maiden name of Cardwell.

The car was registered to Clay Cardwell—her brother.

He picked up the phone and called the family lawyer who was handling the dispersing of ranch profits to Dana's siblings.

"Rick, I hate to bother you, but I need to get a phone number and address for Dana's brother Clay. I understand he's living in La Jolla, California."

Rick cleared his voice. "Actually I was going to contact Dana, but hesitated when I heard she's on bed rest at the ranch pregnant with the twins."

News traveled fast, Hud thought. "What's up?" he asked, afraid he wasn't going to like it.

"Clay. He hasn't been cashing his checks. It's been going on for about six months. I just assumed he might be holding them for some reason. But the last one came back saying there was no one by that name and no forwarding address."

Hud swore under his breath. Six months. The same age as Ella. Although he couldn't imagine what the two things could have in common or why Clay hadn't cashed his checks or how it was that his older sister was driving a car registered to him.

"I think we need to find him," Hud said. "I'd just as soon Dana didn't know anything about this. Believe me, she has her hands full right now. One more thing though. Stacy. Did she give you a new address to send her checks?"

"No. She's moved around so much, I wait until I hear from her and usually send them general delivery."

"Well, could you do me a favor? If you hear from her, call me."

"I thought she was here in the canyon."

"She was, but right now she's missing and she left a small…package at the house."

IT WAS DARK BY THE TIME LIZA drove past the Fir Ridge cemetery, climbed up over the Continental Divide and entered Gallatin Canyon.

This time of year there was little traffic along the two-lane road as it snaked through pines and over mountains along the edge of the river.

She kept thinking about what Brick Savage had told her. More to the point, the feeling she'd had when she'd left him. He'd challenged her to prove Tanner Cole had been murdered. No doubt because he knew it would be near impossible.

And yet if she was right and Alex's murder had something to do with Tanner's death, then the killer had shown his hand.

Pulling out her phone, she tried Hud's cell. In a lot of spots in the canyon there was no mobile phone service. To her surprise it began to ring.

"Marshal Savage," he snapped.

"Sorry, did I catch you at a bad time?" she asked through the hands-free speaker, wondering if he was in the middle of something with the kids.

"Liza. Good. I'm glad you called. Did you get my message?"

She hadn't. Fear gripped her. Surely there hadn't been another murder. Her thoughts instantly raced to Jordan and she felt her heart fall at the thought that he might—

"It's Stacy," he said. "She left the house earlier. No one has seen her since. She hasn't called. I've looked all over Big Sky. She left the baby at the house."

"What?" It took her moment to pull back from the thought of another murder. To pull back from the fear and dread that had had her thinking something had happened to Jordan. "Stacy wouldn't leave her baby, would she?"

"Knowing Stacy, I have a bad feeling the baby isn't even hers."

Liza was too shocked to speak for a moment. "You think she...stole it?"

"Something is wrong. I've suspected it from the get-go. Dana was hoping I was just being suspicious because it's my nature, but I'd been worried that something like this would happen. I didn't want Dana getting attached to that baby, but you know Dana, and Ella is adorable, if that is even her name."

"Oh, boss, I'm so sorry."

"So you spoke to my father?" Hud asked.

"He was the investigating officer at Tanner Cole's suicide."

"What did he tell you?"

"That it was Tanner's rope."

Hud let out a humorless laugh. "That sounds like Brick. Have you met him before?"

"Never had the honor. He must have been a treat as a father."

"You could say that." He sighed. "Look, Hilde's at the house. I'm going to make another circle through the area to look for Stacy before I go home."

"I'm about twenty minutes out. Do you want me to stop by?"

"If you don't mind. I know you're busy with this murder case…"

"No problem. I'll see you soon." She snapped the phone shut, shocked by what he'd told her. She was so deep in thought that she hadn't noticed the lights of another vehicle coming up behind her.

She glanced in the mirror. One of the headlights was out on the approaching car. That struck her about the same time as she realized the driver was coming up too fast.

She'd been going the speed limit. By now the driver of the vehicle behind her would have been able to see the light bar on the top of her SUV. Only a fool would come racing up on a Marshal's Department patrol car— let alone pass it.

And yet as she watched, the driver of what appeared to be an old pickup swerved around her and roared up beside her.

Liza hit her lights and siren, thinking the driver must be drunk. She glanced over, saw only a dark figure behind the wheel wearing a black ski mask. Her heart jumped, but she didn't have time to react before the driver swerved into her. She heard the crunch of metal, felt the patrol SUV veer toward the ditch and the pines and beyond that, the river.

She slammed on the brakes, but was traveling too fast to avoid the truck crashing into her again. The force made the vehicle rock wildly as she fought to keep control. The tires screamed on the pavement as the SUV began to fishtail.

Liza felt the right side of the vehicle dip into the soft shoulder of the highway, pulling the SUV off the road. She couldn't hold it and felt her tires leave the pavement. A stand of trees blurred past and then there was nothing but darkness as she plunged over the edge of the road toward the dark green of the river.

Chapter Twelve

Hud was headed home when he heard the 911 call for an ambulance come over his radio. His heart began to race as he heard that the vehicle in the river was a Montana marshal's patrol SUV.

He threw on his siren and lights and took off up the canyon toward West Yellowstone. As he raced toward the accident, he called home, glad when Hilde answered the phone.

"Tell Dana I'm running a little late," he said to Hilde. "Don't act like anything is wrong." He heard Dana already asking what was going on. Hilde related the running a little late part.

"We're just fine," Hilde said.

"It sounds like there's been an accident up the canyon," he told her. "It's Liza. I don't know anything except that her car is in the river. I don't know how long I'm going to be."

"Don't worry about us."

"Is it my sister?" Dana demanded in the background.

"I heard that. Tell her I haven't found Stacy. I'll call when I have news. I just don't want Dana upset."

"Got it. I'll tell her."

He disconnected and increased his speed. Liza was

like family. How the hell did she end up in the river? She was a great driver.

As he came around a bend in the windy road, he saw her patrol SUV among the boulders in the Gallatin River. Some bypassers had stopped. Several of the men had flashlights and one of them had waded out to the patrol vehicle.

Hud parked, leaving his lights on to warn any oncoming traffic, then grabbing his own flashlight, jumped out and ran toward the river. As he dropped over the edge of the road to it, he recognized the man who was standing on the boulder beside Liza's wrecked vehicle.

"Jordan?" he called.

"Liza's conscious," he called back. "An ambulance is on the way. I'm staying with her until it gets here."

Hud would have liked to have gone to her as well, but he heard the sound of the ambulance siren and climbed back up the road to help with traffic control.

All the time, though, he found himself wondering how Jordan just happened to be on the scene.

"WHAT'S HAPPENED?" DANA demanded the moment Hilde hung up. "Don't," she said before Hilde could open her mouth. "You're a terrible liar and we both know it. Tell me."

"He hasn't found your sister."

She nodded. "But something else has happened."

"There's been an accident up the canyon. He needed to run up there."

Dana waited. "There's more."

"You're the one who should have gone into law enforcement, the interrogation part," Hilde said as she came and sat down on the edge of the bed. On the other side of Dana, baby Ella slept, looking like an angel. Hilde glanced at the baby, then took Dana's hand as if she knew it was only a matter of time before her friend got the truth out of her. "Hud didn't know anything about the accident except that Liza is somehow involved."

"Oh, no." Her heart dropped.

"Now don't get upset and have these babies because Hud will never forgive me," Hilde said quickly.

Dana shook her head. "I'm okay. But I want to know the minute you hear something. Are you sure you can stay?"

"Of course."

"You didn't have a date?"

Hilde laughed. "If only there were more Hudson Savages around. All of the men I meet, well...they're so not the kind of men I want to spend time with, even for the time it takes to have dinner."

"I *am* lucky." Dana looked over at Ella. "What if Hud is right and Ella isn't Stacy's baby?"

"Where would she have gotten Ella? You can't just get a baby off eBay."

"She could have *kidnapped* Ella. You know Stacy."

"I'm sure Hud checked for any kidnapped babies six months old with dimples, blond hair and green eyes," Hilde argued.

"Yes, green eyes. You might have noticed that all the Justices have dark brown eyes and dark hair, including Stacy."

"Maybe the father has green eyes and Stacy carries a green-eyed gene. You don't know that Ella isn't Stacy's."

"No," Dana admitted, but like Hud, she'd had a bad

feeling since the moment Stacy had arrived. "I think Stacy only came here because she's in trouble and it has something to do with that poor little baby."

"You think that's why she left Ella with you?"

Dana fingered the quilt edge where someone had stitched the name Katie. "I wish I knew."

JORDAN WOKE WITH A CRICK in his neck. He stared down at the green hospital scrubs he was wearing for a moment, confused where he was. It came back to him with a start. Last night his clothes had been soaking wet from his swim in the river. He'd been shivering uncontrollably, but had refused to leave the hospital until he knew Liza was going to be all right.

That's how he'd ended up in scrubs, he recalled now as he sat up in the chair beside Liza's bed and smiled at the woman propped up staring at him now.

"What are you still doing here?" she asked, smiling.

"I *was* sleeping." He stood up, stretched, then looked to see what she was having for breakfast. "You haven't eaten much," he said as he took a piece of toast from the nearly untouched tray.

"I'm not very hungry."

He was famished and realized he hadn't eaten since yesterday at noon. "How are your ribs?" he asked as he devoured the piece of toast.

"They're just bruised and only hurt when I breathe."

"Yep, but you're breathing. Be thankful for that."

Liza nodded and he saw that her left wrist was also wrapped. Apparently, it was just badly sprained, not broken. His big worry, though, had been that she'd suffered internal injuries.

Apparently not, though, since all she had was a bandage on her right temple, a bruised cheek and a scrape on her left cheek. She'd been lucky.

"So what did the doctor say?" he asked.

"That I'm going to live."

"Good."

She looked almost shy. "Thank you for last night."

He shrugged. "It's wasn't anything. I just swam a raging river in October in Montana and clung onto a slippery boulder to be with you." He grinned. "I'm just glad you're all right." He'd been forced to leave the room last night while Hud had talked to her, but he'd overheard enough to more than concern him.

"You said last night that someone forced you off the road?" he asked now. "Do you remember anything about the vehicle?"

She narrowed her gaze at him and sighed. "Even if I knew who did it, I wouldn't tell you. I don't want to see you get killed."

He grinned. "Nice that you care—"

"I told you, I don't have time to find your killer, too."

"Why would anyone want to kill me? On second thought, scratch that. Other than my brother-in-law, why would anyone want me dead?"

"Hud doesn't want you dead."

"He just doesn't want me near my sister."

"Can you blame him?"

"No," he said with a sigh. "That's what makes it worse. I would be the same way if someone had treated my wife the way I've treated my sister." He looked away.

"Do you mean that?"

He grinned. "Do you question everything I tell you?"

"Yes."

He laughed and shook his head. "I've been more

honest with you than I have with anyone in a very long time. Hud doesn't want me near you, either." He met her gaze and saw something warm flash in her eyes.

"I talked to the investigating officer in Tanner's death yesterday before the accident," she said, clearly changing the subject. "He cleared you as a suspect, at least in Tanner's death."

"Did Brick Savage tell you what I did the day I found Tanner?"

"I would assume you were upset since it was your best friend."

"I broke down and bawled like a baby until Hud's old man kicked me in the behind and told me to act like a man. He said I was making myself look guilty as hell." He chuckled. "I took a swing at him and he decked me. Knocked me on my butt, but I got control of myself after that and he didn't arrest me for assaulting an officer of the law so I guess I respect him for that."

Liza shook her head. "Men. You are such a strange breed. I think it would have been stranger if you hadn't reacted the way you had."

He shrugged. "Tanner left a hole in my life. I've never had a closer friend since. Sometimes I swear I can hear his voice, especially when I do something stupid."

She smiled. "So he's still with you a lot."

"Yeah. You do know that when I say I hear him, I don't really *hear* him, right?"

"I get it."

"I didn't want you to think I hear voices. It's bad enough you still see me as a suspect."

She nodded slowly. "I mean what I said about wanting you to be safe. You need to keep a low profile."

"How can I do that when I have a reunion picnic to go to this afternoon?"

"You aren't seriously planning to go?"

"What? You don't think I can get another date?" he joked.

"What do I have to do to make you realize how dangerous this is?"

His expression sobered. "All I have to do is look at your face and think about where I found you last night."

"You could be next," she said quietly. "What time is the picnic?"

"The doctor isn't going to let you—"

"What time?" she demanded.

"One."

"I'll be there."

He grinned. "Good, I won't have to find another date." He wanted to argue that she needed to stay in bed. He couldn't stand the thought that she was now a target. Last night when he'd seen her car in the river— Just the thought made it hard for him to breathe even now.

He barely remembered throwing on the rental car's brakes, diving out and half falling down the bank to the river. All he could think about was getting to her. The moment he'd hit the icy water of the Gallatin, he'd almost been swept away. He'd had to swim to get to her, then climb onto a large slick boulder to reach the driver's-side door.

At first he'd thought she was dead. There was blood from the cut on her temple.

Impulsively, he reached for her hand now. It felt warm and soft and wonderfully alive. He squeezed her hand gently, then let it go.

"Unless you need a ride, I guess I'll see you at one on the mountain then," he said and turned to leave.

"Liza isn't going anywhere, especially with you," Hud snapped as he stepped into the hospital room. "I'll speak to *you* in the hall," he said to Jordan.

Liza shot him a questioning look. Jordan shrugged. He had no idea why his brother-in-law was angry with him but he was about to find out.

"Later," he said to Liza and stepped out in the hall to join Hud.

The marshal had blood in his eye by the time Jordan stepped out into the hall. "What were you doing at the accident last night? Were you following Liza?"

He held up his hands. "One question at a time. I had tried to call her. I knew she'd gone up to West Yellowstone to talk to your father. I got tired of waiting for her to return and drove up the canyon. I was worried about her."

"Worried about her?" Hud sighed. "And you just happened to find her?"

"The other driver who stopped can verify it."

"Did you pass another vehicle coming from the direction of the accident?"

"Several. A white van. A semi. An old red pickup."

"The red pickup. Did you happen to notice the driver?"

He shook his head. "I just glanced at the vehicles. I wasn't paying a lot of attention since I was looking for Liza's patrol SUV. You think the truck ran her off the road."

Hud didn't look happy to hear that Jordan knew about that. He ignored the statement and asked, "Where is Liza going to meet you later?"

"At the reunion picnic up on the mountain."

"Well, she's not going anywhere." Hud started to turn away, but swung back around and put a finger in Jordan's face. "I want you to stay away from her. I'm not sure what your game is—"

"There's *no* game. No angle. Liza is investigating Alex Winslow's murder. I've been helping her because I know the players and I think it is somehow tied in with Tanner's death."

"That better be all there is to it," Hud said and started to turn away again.

"What if that isn't all it is?" Jordan demanded, then could have kicked himself.

Hud turned slowly back to him. "Like I said, stay away from Liza." With that, he turned and pushed into his deputy's room.

"Tell me you weren't out in the hall threatening the man who saved me last night," Jordan heard Liza say, but didn't catch Hud's reply, which was just as well.

He collected his clothes at the nurse's station, changed and headed for the canyon and Big Sky. Now more than ever he wanted to get to the bottom of this. Someone had tried to kill Liza. He didn't doubt they would try again.

But what were they so afraid she was going to find out? He suddenly recalled something he'd overheard Hud say to his deputy marshal last night at the hospital. Something about her condo being ransacked. Someone thought she had something. The alleged photographs?

LIZA COCKED HER HEAD at her boss as he came around the end of her bed. "Well?" she asked.

He gave her a sheepish look. "You don't know Jordan like I do. He's...he's..."

"He's changed."

Hud shook his head. "I really doubt that he's changed any more than his sister Stacy."

"Talk about painting them all with the same brush," she said.

"Look, I don't want you getting involved with him."

Liza grinned. "I'm sorry, I must have misheard you. You weren't telling me who I can get involved with, were you, boss?"

"Damn it, Liza. You know how I feel about you."

She nodded. "I'm the most stubborn deputy you've ever had. I often take things in my own hands without any thought to my safety. I'm impulsive, emotional and driven and I'm too smart for my own good. Does that about cover it?"

"You're the best law officer I've ever worked with," Hud said seriously. "And a friend. And like a real sister to my wife. I just don't want to see you get hurt."

She smiled. "I can also take care of myself. And," she said before he could interrupt, "I can get involved with anyone I want."

He looked at his boots before looking at her again. "You're right."

"That's what I thought. Did you bring the information I asked for?" she asked, pointing to the manila envelope in his hand and no longer wanting to discuss Jordan.

Truthfully she didn't know how she felt about him— waking up to see him sleeping beside her hospital bed or being in his arms the other night on the dance floor.

"I brought it," Hud said with a sigh. "But I don't

think you should be worrying about any of this right now. How are you feeling?"

"Fine," Liza said, reaching for the manila envelope and quickly opening it.

"There are Alex's phone calls over the past month as well as where he went after arriving at Big Sky."

Liza was busy leafing through it, more determined than ever to find out who'd killed him—and who'd tried to do the same to her the night before.

"Alex was in the middle of a contentious divorce?" she asked, looking up in surprise from the information he'd brought her. "He had a *wife?*" When she'd notified next of kin, she'd called his brother as per the card in his wallet.

"Her name is Crystal."

"A classmate?"

Hud nodded. "But not from Big Sky. She lived down in Bozeman."

"What was holding up the divorce?" Liza asked.

He shook his head and had to take a step back from the bed as Liza swung her legs over the side and stood up. *"What are you doing?"*

"I'm getting up. I told you, I'm fine. Just a little knock on the head and a few cuts and bruises and a sprained wrist, but it's my left wrist, so I'm fine. All I need is a vehicle."

He shook his head. "I can't allow—"

"You can't stop me. Someone tried to *kill* me. This has become personal. Not only that, you need to stay close to home," she said as she rummaged in the closet for her clothes. "No sign of Stacy yet?" He shook his head. "What about the baby?"

"The lab's running a DNA test. We should be able

to tell if the baby is Stacy's by comparing Ella's DNA to Dana's. Liza, you're really not up to—"

"Could you see about my clothes?" she asked, realizing they weren't anywhere in the room. Her clothes had been wet and the nurses had probably taken them to dry them. "Stubborn, remember? One of the reasons I'm such a good law officer, your words not mine." She smiled widely although it hurt her face.

He studied her for a moment. "Clothes, right. Then get you a vehicle," he said, clearly giving up on trying to keep another woman in bed.

DANA WATCHED HILDE TRYING to change Ella's diaper until she couldn't take it anymore. "Give me that baby."

Hilde laughed. "You make it look so easy," she said, handing Ella to her.

Ella giggled and squirmed as Dana made short work of getting her into a diaper and a sleeper. Hud had come in so late, Hilde had stayed overnight and gotten someone to work for her this morning. He'd promised to be back soon.

"I'm just so glad Liza is all right," she said as she handed Ella back to Hilde. Through the open bedroom door she could see Mary and Hank playing with a plastic toy ranch set. She could hear them discussing whether or not they should buy more cows.

"Me, too," Hilde said. "Fortunately, Liza is strong."

"Hud's worried now that she and Jordan might be getting involved."

Hilde arched an eyebrow. "Really?"

"I have to admit when Jordan stopped by, he did seem different. But then again I said Stacy had changed, so what do I know? I can't believe we haven't heard anything from her. What if she never comes back?" Dana hadn't let herself think about that at first, but as the hours passed... "Did she leave anything else besides Ella and the baby's things?"

"I can check. She was staying in the room I slept in last night, right?"

"I would imagine Hud already checked it, but would you look? That should tell us if she was planning to leave the baby all along or if something happened and she can't get back."

Hilde jiggled Ella in her arms. "Watch her for a moment and I'll go take a look." She put the baby down next to Dana on the bed. Ella immediately got up on her hands and knees and rocked back and forth.

"She is going to be crawling in no time," Dana said with a smile. Stacy was going to miss it. But then maybe Stacy had missed most of Ella's firsts because this wasn't her baby.

Hilde returned a few minutes later.

"You found something," Dana said, excited and worried at the same time.

"You said she didn't have much, right?" Hilde asked. "Well, she left a small duffle on the other side of the bed. Not much in it. A couple of T-shirts, underwear, socks. I searched through it." She shook her head. "Then I noticed a jean jacket hanging on the back of the chair by the window. It's not yours, is it?"

"That's the one Stacy was wearing when she arrived."

"I found this in the pocket."

Dana let out a surprised groan as Hilde, using two fingers, pulled out a small caliber handgun.

ALEX WINSLOW'S WIFE, CRYSTAL, lived up on the hill overlooking Bozeman on what some called Snob Knob. In the old days it had been called Beer Can Hill because that was where the kids used to go to drink and make out.

The house was pretty much what Liza had expected. It was huge. A contentious divorce usually meant one of three things. That the couple was fighting over the kids, the pets or the money. Since Alex and Crystal apparently had no children or pets, Liza guessed it was the money.

She parked the rental SUV Hud'd had delivered to the hospital and walked up to the massive front door. As she rang the bell, she could hear music playing inside. She rang the bell a second time before the door was opened by a petite dark-haired woman with wide blue eyes and a quizzical smile.

"Yes?" she asked.

Liza had forgotten her bandages, the eye that was turning black or that all the blood hadn't completely come out of her uniform shirt.

She'd felt there wasn't time to go all the way back to Big Sky to change. Her fear was that if she didn't solve this case soon, someone else was going to die.

"Crystal Winslow? I'm Deputy Marshal Liza Turner. I need to ask you a few questions in regard to your husband's death."

"*Estranged* husband," Crystal Winslow said, but opened the door wider. "I doubt I can be of help, but you're welcome to come in. Can I get you something?" She took in Liza's face again.

"Just answers."

Crystal led her into the formal living room. It had

a great view of the city and valley beyond. In the distance, the Spanish Peaks gleamed from the last snowfall high in the mountains.

"How long have you and Alex been estranged?"

"I don't see what that has to do—"

"Your *estranged* husband is dead. I believe whoever murdered him tried to do the same to me last night. I need to know why."

"Well, it has nothing to do with me." She sniffed, then said, "A month."

"Why?"

For a moment Crystal looked confused. "Why did I kick him out and demand a divorce? You work out of Big Sky, right? I would suggest you ask Shelby."

"Shelby Durran-Iverson?"

She nodded, and for the first time Liza saw true pain in the woman's expression—and fury. "I knew he was cheating. A woman can tell. But *Shelby?* I remember her from high school. People used to say she was the type who would eat her young."

"That could explain why she doesn't have any children," Liza said. She still felt a little lightheaded and knew this probably wasn't the best time to be interviewing anyone.

"Did Alex admit he was seeing Shelby?"

Crystal gave her an are-you-serious? look. "He swore up and down that his talking to her wasn't an affair, that he was trying to get her to tell the truth, something involving Tanner Cole."

"You remember Tanner?"

"He hung himself our senior year. I didn't really know him. He was a cowboy. I didn't date cowboys. No offense."

Liza wondered why that should offend her. Did she look that much like a cowgirl?

"I think your husband might have been telling you the truth. I believe he was looking into Tanner's death."

"Why would he do that?"

"I was hoping you could tell me since I suspect that's what got him killed."

"You don't know for sure that he wasn't having an affair with Shelby though, right?"

"No, I don't. But Alex mentioned to other people that he felt something was wrong about Tanner's suicide, as well. He didn't say anything to you?"

"No."

"Do you or your husband own any weapons?"

Crystal looked appalled. "You mean like a Saturday night special?"

"Or hunting rifles."

"No, I wouldn't have a gun in my house. My father was killed in a hunting accident. We have a state-of-the-art security system. We didn't need *guns*."

Liza nodded, knowing what that would get Crystal if someone broke into the house. She could be dead before the police arrived. "Alex didn't have weapons, either?"

"No. I still can't believe this was why Alex was spending time with Shelby."

"Did she ever call here?"

Crystal mugged a face. "Shelby said it was just to talk to Alex about Big Sky's reunion plans. They wanted their own. Ours wasn't good enough for them."

Liza could see that Crystal Winslow had been weighted down with that chip on her shoulder for some time.

"But I overheard one of his conversations," she said

smugly. "Shelby was demanding something back, apparently something she'd given him. He saw me and said he didn't know what she was talking about. After he hung up, he said Shelby was looking for some photographs from their senior year. He said she was probably using them for something she was doing for the reunion."

"You didn't believe him?"

"I could hear Shelby screeching from where I was standing. She was livid about whatever it really was."

"Did he send her some photos from high school?"

"I told you, that was just a story he came up with. He had some photographs from high school. I kept the ones of me and gave him the rest."

"Where are those photos now?"

"I threw them out with Alex. I assume he took them to his apartment," she said.

"Do you have a key?"

"He left one with me, but I've never used it." She got up and walked out of the room, returning a moment later with a shiny new key and a piece of notepaper. "Here's the address."

Liza took it. "Was that the only Big Sky friend who contacted Alex?"

"Right after that was when Alex started driving up to Big Sky and I threw him out."

"What made you suspect he was seeing Shelby?" Liza asked.

For a moment, Crystal looked confused. "I told you—"

"Right, that a woman knows. But how did you know it was *Shelby?*"

"After Tanner broke up with her in high school, she

made a play for Alex. He was dating Tessa Ryerson before that. The two of them got into it at school one day. That's when he and I started dating."

"Did he tell you what his argument with Shelby was about?"

She shrugged. "Eventually everyone has a falling-out with Shelby—except for her BFFs." She made a face, then listed off their names like a mantra. "Shelby, Tessa, Ashley, Whitney and Brittany."

Liza noted that Brittany was on the list. "When did Alex and Shelby have the falling-out?"

Crystal frowned. "It was around the time that Tanner committed suicide. After that Alex hadn't wanted anything to do with her. That is until recently."

Liza could tell that Crystal was having second thoughts about accusing her husband of infidelity.

"You said your father was killed in a hunting accident. Did you hunt?"

"No. Alex did and so did his friends," she said distractedly.

"What about Shelby?"

"She actually was a decent shot, I guess, although I suspected the only reason she and her friends hunted was to be where the boys were." Her expression turned to one of horror. "You don't think Shelby killed Alex, do you?"

Chapter Thirteen

Dana stared at the sleeping Ella as her husband updated her on Liza's condition. She'd had a scare, but she was going to be fine. In fact, she'd already checked herself out of the hospital and was working.

"You didn't try to stop her?" Dana demanded of her husband.

He gave her a look she knew too well.

"All right, what did you find out about Stacy?" she asked and braced herself for the worst.

"There is really nothing odd about her having Clay's car," she said when he finished filling her in. "Obviously they've been in contact."

"It wouldn't be odd if Clay had been cashing his checks for the last six months," Hud said. "Why would he be driving an old beater car if he had money?"

"Maybe it was a spare car he let Stacy have," she suggested.

Hud rolled his eyes. "It is the only car registered to your brother. Nice theory." He instantly seemed to regret his words. "I'm sorry. I'm not telling you these things to upset you. On the contrary, I know you'll worry more if I keep them from you."

"Which proves you're smarter than you look," she

said, annoyed that he was treating her as if she was breakable. "The babies are fine. I'm fine. You'd better not keep anything from me."

He smiled. "As I said…"

"So you can't find Clay or Stacy."

"No. But I've put an APB out on Stacy's car. It was the only thing I could do."

"Something's happened to her," Dana said. "She wouldn't leave Ella." When Hud said nothing, she shot him an impatient look. "You saw how she was with that baby. She loves her."

"Dana, we haven't seen your sister in six years. She doesn't write or call when she gets pregnant. She just shows up at the door with a baby, which she then leaves with us. Come on, even you have to admit, something is wrong with this."

She didn't want to admit it. Maybe more than anything, she didn't want to acknowledge that Stacy could have done something unforgiveable this time. Something that might land her in prison.

"What do we do now?" she asked her husband.

"I've held off going global with Ella's description, hoping Stacy would show back up. But Dana, I don't think I have any choice."

"You haven't heard anything on the DNA test you did on Ella and me?"

"I should be hearing at any time. But if the two of you aren't related, then I have to try to find out who this baby belongs to—no matter what happens to Stacy."

LIZA DROVE TO THE APARTMENT address Crystal Winslow had given her. She used the key to get into the studio apartment. As the door swung open, she caught her breath and pulled her weapon.

The apartment had been torn apart. Every conceivable hiding place had been searched, pillows and sofa bed sliced open, their stuffing spread across the room, books tossed to the floor along with clothing from the closet.

Liza listened, then cautiously stepped in. A small box of photographs had been dumped onto the floor and gone through from the looks of them. She checked the tiny kitchen and bath to make sure whoever had done this was gone before she holstered her weapon and squatted down to gingerly pick up one of the photographs.

It was a snapshot of Jordan Cardwell with two other handsome boys. All three were wearing ski clothing and looking cocky. She recognized a young Alex Winslow and assumed the other boy must be Tanner.

A curtain flapped loudly at an open window, making her start. Carefully, she glanced through the other photographs, assuming whatever the intruder had been looking for wasn't among these strewn on the floor.

It took her a moment though to realize what was missing from the pile of photos. There were none of Crystal. Nor any of Shelby or the rest of her group. That seemed odd that the women Alex had apparently been close to were missing from the old photographs. Nor were there any wedding pictures. Crystal had said she'd taken the ones of her. But who would have taken ones of Shelby and the rest of the young women he'd gone to school with in the canyon?

Rising, Liza called it in to the Bozeman Police Department, then waited until a uniformed officer arrived.

"I doubt you'll find any fingerprints, but given that Alex Winslow is a murder victim and he hasn't lived here long, I'm hoping whoever did this left us a clue," she told the officer. "I've contacted the crime lab in Missoula. I just want to make sure no one else comes in here until they arrive."

As she was leaving, Liza saw an SUV cruise slowly by. She recognized Crystal Winslow behind the wheel before the woman sped off.

JORDAN HAD JUST REACHED the bottom of the gondola for the ride up the mountain to the reunion picnic, when he spotted Liza.

She wasn't moving with her usual speed, but there was a determined look in her eye that made him smile.

"What?" she said when she joined him.

"You. After what happened, you could have taken one day off."

"I'm going to a picnic," she said. "I'm not even wearing my uniform."

She looked great out of uniform. The turquoise top she wore had slits at the shoulders, the silky fabric exposing tanned, muscled arms as it moved in the breeze. She wore khaki capris and sandals. Her long ebony-dark hair had been pulled up in back with a clip so the ends cascaded down her back. For as banged up as she was, she looked beautiful.

"I'm betting though that you're carrying a gun," he said, eyeing the leather shoulder bag hanging off one shoulder.

"You better hope I am." She laughed, but stopped quickly as if she was still light-headed.

"Are you sure you're all right?" he whispered, stepping closer.

"Dandy."

Past her, he saw Whitney and Ashley. Neither looked in a celebratory mood. When they spotted the deputy marshal, they jumped apart as if talking to each other would make them look more guilty.

"This could be a fun picnic," he said under his breath.

A few moments later Brittany arrived with her husband and small brood. Jordan was taken back again at how happy and content she looked.

I want that, he thought as his gaze shifted to Liza.

As their gondola came around, they climbed in and made room for Whitney and Ashley, who'd come up behind them. Both women, though, motioned that they would take the next one.

"I'd love to know what they're hiding," Jordan said as he sat across from the deputy marshal. The gondola door closed then rocked as it began its ascent up the mountain. He had a view of the resort and the peaks from where he sat. And a view of Liza.

He could also see the gondola below them and the two women inside. They had their heads together. He wondered at the power Shelby still held over these women she'd lorded over in high school. Did anyone ever really get over high school?

"There's something I need to ask you," Liza said, drawing his attention back to her, which was no hardship. "How was it that you were the first person on the scene last night?"

He smiled, knowing that Hud was behind this. "I got worried about you and I wanted to see you. I drove up the canyon thinking I could talk you into having dinner with me. Another car had stopped before I got there. I was just the first to go into the river." He hated that she was suspicious of him, but then again he couldn't really blame her.

"Did you see the pickup that forced me off the road?"

He nodded. "But it was just an old pickup. I was looking for your patrol SUV so I really didn't pay any attention."

She nodded. "I'd already told you I wasn't having dinner with you."

He grinned. "I thought I could charm you into changing your mind." He hurried on before she could speak. "I know you already told me no, but I thought we could at least pick up something and take it back to my cabin or your condo."

"You just don't give up, do you?"

"Kind of like someone else I know," he said and smiled at her. "I didn't have any ulterior motives. I've given this a lot of thought. Somehow, I think it all goes back to that party Tanner had at the cabin that night and the vandalism."

"And the photographs?" she asked.

He nodded. "I wish I'd stayed around long enough that night to tell you who took them."

They were almost to the top of the gondola ride. Off to his left, he saw where the caterers had set up the food for the picnic.

The gondola rocked as it came to a stop and the door opened. Jordan quickly held the doors open while the deputy marshal climbed out, then he followed, recalling what he could of that night, which wasn't much.

LIZA HOPED THE PICNIC WOULDN'T be quite as bad as the dinner had been. Jordan got them a spot near Shelby and the gang on one of the portable picnic tables that had been brought up the mountain.

"*Whatever* happened to you?" Shelby exclaimed loud enough for everyone to hear when she saw Liza.

While everyone in the canyon would have heard about her accident, Liza smiled and said, "Tripped. Sometimes I am so clumsy."

Shelby laughed. "You really should be more careful." Then she went back to holding court at her table. The usual suspects were in attendance and Tessa had been allowed to join in.

Liza watched out of the corner of her eye. Shelby monopolized the conversation with overly cheerful banter. But it was as if a pall had fallen over her group that not even she could lift.

After they ate, some of the picnickers played games in the open area next to the ski lift. When Liza spotted Tessa heading for the portable toilets set up in the trees, she excused herself and followed.

Music drifted on the breeze. A cloudless blue sky hung over Lone Peak. It really was the perfect day for a picnic and she said as much to Tessa when she caught up with her.

"Deputy," Tessa said.

"Why don't you call me Liza."

The woman smiled. "So I forget that I'm talking to the *law?*"

"I'm here as Jordan Cardwell's date."

Tessa chuckled at that, then sobered. "What happened to you?"

"Someone tried to stop me from looking into Alex's and Tanner's deaths."

The woman let out a groan.

"I was hoping you would have contacted me to talk," Liza said. "I can see you're troubled."

"Troubled?" Tessa laughed as she glanced back toward the group gathered below them on the mountain.

Liza followed her gaze and saw Shelby watching them. "We should step around the other side."

Tessa didn't argue. As they moved out of Shelby's sight, Tessa stopped abruptly and reached into her shoulder bag. "Here," she said, thrusting an envelope at the deputy marshal. "Alex left it with me and told me not to show it to anyone. He said to just keep it and not look inside until I had to."

Liza saw that it was sealed. "You didn't look?"

Tessa shook her head quickly.

"What did he mean, 'until you had to'?"

"I have no idea. I don't know what's in there and I don't care. If anyone even found out I had it…"

"Why did he trust *you* with this?" Liza had to ask.

Tessa looked as if she wasn't going to answer, then seemed to figure there was no reason to lie anymore. "I was in love with him. I have been since high school. Shelby always told me he wasn't good enough for me." She began to cry, but quickly wiped her eyes at the sound of someone moving through the dried grass on the other side of the portable toilets.

Liza hurriedly stuffed the envelope into her own shoulder bag.

An instant later Shelby came around the end of the stalls. "Are they all occupied?" she asked, taking in the two of them, then glancing toward the restrooms.

"I just used that one," Liza improvised. She turned and started back down the hillside.

Behind her she heard Shelby ask Tessa, "What did she want?"

She didn't hear Tessa's answer, but she feared Shelby wouldn't believe anything her friend said anyway. Tessa was running scared and anyone could see it—especially Shelby, who had her own reasons for being afraid.

Liza thought about the manila envelope Alex had left in Tessa's safekeeping. What was inside it? The photographs that Shelby had been trying to get her hands on? Liza couldn't wait to find out.

HUD HAD PUT A RUSH ON ELLA'S relational DNA test. He'd done it for Dana's sake. He saw that by the hour she was getting more attached to that baby. If he was right and Stacy had kidnapped it, then Dana's heart was going to be broken.

He was as anxious as she was to get the results. Meanwhile he needed to search for Stacy as he continued to watch for possible kidnappings on the law enforcement networks.

So far, he'd come up with nothing.

He found himself worrying not only about Stacy's disappearance, but also everything else that was going on. He'd done his best to stay out of Liza's hair. She could handle the murder case without him, he kept telling himself. Still, he'd been glad when Hilde had called and said she could come stay with Dana if he needed her to.

His phone rang as he paced in the living room. He'd never been good at waiting. He saw on caller ID that it was Shelby Durran-Iverson.

"Marshal Savage," he answered and listened while Shelby complained about Liza. It seemed she'd seen the deputy kissing Jordan. Hud swore silently. He had warned Liza about Jordan, but clearly she hadn't listened.

"Deputies get to have private lives," he told Shelby.

"Really? Even with the man who was with Alex when he was murdered? I would think Jordan Cardwell is a suspect. Or at least should be."

It was taking all his self-control to keep from telling Shelby that she was more of a suspect than Jordan was.

"I'll look into it," he said.

"I should hope you'd do more than that. Isn't fraternizing with a suspect a violation that could call for at least a suspension—if not dismissal?"

"I said I would look into it." He hung up just as a car pulled up in front of the house. With a sigh of relief, he started to open the door to greet Hilde when he saw that it wasn't her car. Nor was it Stacy's.

When he saw who climbed out, he let out a curse. Before he could answer the door, his phone rang again. Figuring to get all the bad news over with quickly, he took the call from the lab as he heard footfalls on the porch and a tentative knock at the door.

"Hud, who is that at the door?" Dana called.

He listened to the lab tech give him the news, then thanked him and, disconnecting, stepped to her bedroom doorway.

"What is it?" she demanded. "Was that the lab on the phone?"

He nodded. "Ella *is* your niece."

Dana began to cry and laugh at the same time as she looked into Ella's beautiful face.

There was another knock at the door.

"Is that Stacy?" she asked, looking up, her eyes full of hope.

He shook his head. "I wish," he said and went to answer the door.

Chapter Fourteen

"Clay?" Dana said as her younger brother appeared in the bedroom doorway, Jordan at his heels.

"Hi," he said shyly. Clay had always been the quiet one, the one who ducked for cover when the rest of them were fighting. "Jordan told me you're pregnant with twins. Congratulations."

"Jordan?" she asked, shooting a look at her older brother. "Clay, what are you doing here?"

"I called Clay at the studio where I knew he was working," Jordan said.

"The studio let me use the company plane, so here I am," Clay said.

"Tell me what is going on. Why haven't you cashed your checks for the past six months and why does Stacy have your car?"

"Easy," Hud said as he stepped into the room. He gave both her brothers a warning look.

She didn't look at her husband. Her gaze was on her younger brother.

"I've been in Europe the past six months, then I changed apartments and forgot to put in a change of address," Clay said. "That's why I haven't cashed my checks. As for the car, I wasn't using it, so I told Stacy she could have it. I'm working for a movie studio in L.A. so I have a studio car that picks me up every morning."

"I'm glad things are going well for you," Dana said. "But you know what's going on with Stacy, don't you?"

"All I know is that she said she needed to get here to the ranch and could she borrow my car," Clay said. "So where is she?"

"That is the question," Hud said next to him. "She seems to have disappeared."

"Well, if you're worried because she has my car, it's no big deal."

"It's not the car that we're worried about," Dana said. "She left her baby here."

"Her *baby?*" Clay said. "Stacy has a baby?"

At the sound of another vehicle, Hud quickly left the room. Dana assumed it would be Hilde, but when he returned, he had Liza with him.

"You've met my brother Clay," Dana said.

Liza nodded. "Looks like you're having a family reunion."

"Doesn't it though," Hud said under his breath.

"Yes, all we need is Stacy," Dana said. "And a larger bedroom." She saw a look pass between the deputy and her husband. "I know that look. What's happened?"

"I just need to talk to the marshal for a few moments," Liza said. "But I'm going to need Jordan." He nodded and stepped out of the room with her and Hud, closing the door behind them.

"I can't stand being in this bed and not knowing what's going on," Dana said.

Clay was looking at the baby lying next to her. "Is that Stacy's?"

"Yes," Dana said with a sigh as Ella stirred awake.

At least Stacy hadn't kidnapped Ella. This little baby was Dana's niece. But where was Stacy? And did whatever Liza needed to talk to Hud and Jordan about have something to do with her sister or the murder?

"I THINK YOU'D BETTER SEE these photographs," Liza said to Hud the moment the bedroom door closed behind him. "Tessa gave them to me. She said Alex had left them in her safekeeping."

"Alex *trusted* Tessa?" Jordan said. "He had to know how close she was to Shelby."

"Obviously Alex trusted her not to give the photos to Shelby," Hud said and gave Jordan a how-did-you-get-involved-in-this-discussion? look.

"Tessa and Alex had a history," Liza said and told them what Crystal Winslow had told her. "She thought Alex was having an affair with Shelby, but I think it might have been Tessa. The two of them were dating in high school when Shelby broke them up so Tessa could spy on Tanner, right, Jordan?" He nodded and she continued. "That's a bond that Alex and Tessa shared against Shelby. With Tessa's marriage over and Alex's apparently not going well, they reconnected."

Hud looked through the photos then reluctantly handed them to Jordan. "You know the people in the photos?" he asked his brother-in-law.

Jordan nodded. "So someone took photos of the party. This can't be enough to get Alex killed over."

She waited until Jordan had finished going through the photos before she took them back, sorted through them until she found the two she wanted, then produced a magnifying glass from her pocket. "Check this out."

They all moved over to the table as Liza put the large

magnifying glass over the first photograph. "You can clearly see Malcolm Iverson's construction equipment in the background. But look here." She pointed at a spot to the left of one of the large dump trucks.

Jordan let out a surprised, "Whoa. It's Shelby."

Liza moved the magnifying glass to the second photo and both men took a look.

"Shelby vandalized the equipment," Jordan said. He let out a low whistle and looked at Liza. "You can clearly see Shelby dressed in black, dumping sugar into one of the two-ton trucks' gas tanks. If these photographs would have come out back then, she could have gone to jail."

Liza nodded. "Shelby has every reason in the world not to want these photographs to ever see daylight. She's married to the man whose father she bankrupted by vandalizing his construction equipment. The rest is like knocking over dominos. She vandalizes the equipment, Malcolm Iverson blames Harris Lancaster and shoots him, Malcolm goes to prison, then gets out and mysteriously dies in a boating accident."

"She didn't pull this off alone," Jordan said.

"No," Liza agreed. "In these two photos you can see Whitney and Ashley are keeping everyone's attention on them at the campfire," she said as she showed them two other photographs of the girls pretending to strip to whatever music was playing.

"Where was Tessa?" Jordan asked.

"With Tanner in the woods," Liza said and sifted through the photos until she found one of Tanner and Tessa coming out of the woods together.

Jordan let out a low whistle. "Shelby thought of everything."

"She just didn't realize that someone was taking photographs of the party," Liza said.

"I wonder where the negatives are. Alex wasn't dumb enough to trust Tessa completely. So who has the negatives?"

"Jordan has a point," Liza said.

Hud looked at his brother-in-law. "You should have gone into law enforcement."

Jordan smiled. "I'm going to take that as a compliment."

"I'm sure Hud meant it as one," Liza said.

"If Alex had the goods on Shelby and was blackmailing her, then why ask around about photos that were already in his possession? Or hint that Tanner's death wasn't a suicide?" Hud asked.

"Maybe he just wanted to shake up those involved. Or shake them down. What I'd like to know is who took the photos," Jordan said.

She looked over at him. "I just assumed Alex did since he isn't in any of them. Was he at the party that night?"

Jordan shrugged. "He was earlier."

"So these could merely be copies of photographs taken at the party," Hud said. "Which means there could be more than one person shopping the photos. That is what you're getting at, right, Deputy? Blackmail? For the past twenty years?"

Liza shook her head. "At least Alex hasn't been blackmailing Shelby for twenty years that I can find. I got his bank records for the past two years faxed to me. He made his first deposits only four months ago. Nine thousand dollars each month. He must have known that anything over ten thousand dollars would be red flagged by the bank."

"Why wait twenty years if he was going to blackmail Shelby?" Hud asked.

"I suspect that when his wife threw him out—along with all his stuff including some old photographs from high school, he hadn't looked at them in years," Liza said. "When he did, he saw what we're seeing and, since he already had reason to hate Shelby over the Tessa deal, decided to blackmail her."

"And she killed him," Jordan said.

Hud sighed. "Can we prove it?"

"Not yet," Liza said as she sorted through the photographs. "But I overheard Shelby on the phone with a creditor saying the check was in the mail. I asked around. Yogamotion has been having trouble paying its bills the past few months, but Hilde says it is packed for every class and it isn't cheap to join."

"So have you talked to Shelby yet?" Hud asked.

She shook her head. "There's something else you need to see." She pointed to a figure in the shadows of the pines at the edge of the campfire in one of the photographs.

"Stacy?" Hud said after taking the photo from her and using the magnifying glass to bring his sister-in-law's face into focus. He groaned and looked at Jordan.

"She wasn't there when I left," he said, holding up his hands. "It never dawned on me that she might have been at the party. We never went to the same parties or hung with the same crowd, so I have no idea what she was doing there."

"This could explain why Stacy came back to the canyon," Hud said with a curse.

"Maybe it is just bad timing on her part." Liza tapped

the photo. "But Stacy knows who was taking the photographs. She's looking right at the person with the camera."

"Which means she also knew there were photographs taken of the party that night."

"HUD?"

"Dana, what is it?" he cried, hearing something in his wife's voice that scared him. He rushed to the bedroom door to find Clay holding Dana's hand. Ella was crying.

"Can you take Ella? She needs a bottle," Dana said.

He tried to calm down. "That's all?" Then he saw his wife grimace. "What was that?" he demanded as Liza volunteered to take the crying baby and get Ella a bottle. Jordan had moved to the side of Dana's bed.

"A twinge. I've been having them all day," Dana admitted.

"Why didn't you tell me?" he demanded.

"Because I didn't want to worry you." She cringed as she had another one, this one definitely stronger from her reaction.

"I'm calling the doctor," he said and started to turn from the crowded room.

Hud hadn't heard a car drive up let alone anyone else enter the house so he was surprised to turn and see Stacy standing in the doorway of Dana's bedroom.

Maybe more shocking was how bad she looked. Both eyes were black and the blood from a cut on her cheek had dried to a dark red. Her hair was matted to her head on one side with what Hud guessed was also blood.

Dana let out a startled cry when she saw her sister.

"I wasn't completely honest with you," Stacy said in a hoarse voice as she stumbled forward.

That's when Hud saw the man behind her, the one holding the gun.

"Just get the baby," the man ordered Stacy, jabbing her in the back with the barrel of the gun. "Then we won't be troubling you people any further."

Stacy moved toward the bassinet that had been brought in next to Dana's bed. She leaned over it, gripping the sides.

Hud saw the bruises on her neck and noticed the way she was favoring her left side as if her ribs hurt her. He looked at the man in the doorway still holding the gun on Stacy.

"What's this about?" he asked the man, trying to keep his tone calm while his heart was pounding. Dana was in labor. He needed to get her to the hospital. He didn't need whatever trouble Stacy was in right now.

"Didn't Stacy tell you? She made off with my kid."

"She's my baby, too, Virgil," Stacy said, still staring down into the crib.

Hud remembered that the crib was empty because Liza had taken the baby into the kitchen with her to get her a bottle.

"He took Ella away from me," Stacy said, crying.

"Her name isn't *Ella*," Virgil snapped. "I told you I was naming her after my mother. Her name is Katie, you stupid b—"

"He took her from me right after she was born and has been raising her with his girlfriend," Stacy said through her tears. "He would only let me come see her a few times."

"Because you'd make a crappy mother. Letting you even see her was a mistake," the man spat. "Now get the damned baby and let's go."

Even the thought of this man taking Ella made Hud

sick to his stomach. But he couldn't have any gunplay around Dana, especially since his own gun was locked up like it always was when he was home with the kids.

Dana still kept a shotgun by the kitchen back door though, high on the wall where the kids couldn't reach it, but handy for adults. He wondered if Liza had heard Stacy and the man come in, if she had any idea what was going on?

Stacy turned her head, her gaze locking with Hud's, as she pleaded for his help.

"Let me get the baby for you," Hud said and stepped to the bassinet.

LIZA HAD BEEN HEATING A BOTTLE of formula for Ella when she heard the door open, then close softly. She listened, drawn by the faint sound of footfalls crossing the living room to Dana's door.

She peered around the corner in time to see the man with the gun. Her heart leaped to her throat. She was out of uniform, her weapon was in the car and she had a baby in one arm. She carefully opened the door of the microwave before it could ding and looked at Ella. The baby grinned at her and flapped her arms.

"I'm going to have to put you down. I need you to be really quiet," Liza whispered. She looked around for a place to put the baby and decided the rug in front of the sink was going to have to do. Carefully, she put down the baby. As she was rising, she saw the shotgun hanging high on the wall over the back door.

Knowing Dana, the shotgun would be loaded. All she could do was pray that it was since she wouldn't have the first idea where to look for shells. She could hear Ella babbling on the rug behind her and trying to snake toward her.

Hurry. She reached up on tiptoes and eased the shotgun off its rack. Trying not to make a sound, she cracked the gun open. Two shells. She dearly loved Dana who knew there was nothing more worthless than an unloaded shotgun.

Ella was watching her expectantly as she crept to the kitchen doorway. She could see the man with the gun, but she could hear voices coming from Dana's bedroom. Normally, she was cool and calm. It was what made her a good cop. But so much was riding on what she did now, she felt the weight of it at heart level.

She had no idea what she would be walking into. No idea who the man was or why he was in this house with a gun. Moving along the edge of the room to keep the old hardwood floor from creaking, she headed for the bedroom doorway.

"Come on, hurry it up. Give me the baby," snapped a male voice she didn't recognize. "We don't have all day."

Liza was next to the doorway. She could see the man holding the gun. He had it pointed at Stacy who was standing next to Hud beside the empty bassinet. Hud had his hands inside the bassinet. He appeared to be rolling up Ella's quilt.

Taking a breath, she let it out slowly, the same way she did at the gun range just before she shot.

Then she moved quickly. She jammed the barrel of shotgun into the man's side and in clear, loud voice said, "Drop the gun or I will blow a hole in you the size of Montana."

The man froze for a moment, then slowly turned his

head to look at her. When he saw her, he smiled. "Put down the shotgun before you hurt yourself, little lady."

"There's something I wasn't honest with you about either," Stacy said turning from the bassinet. "My brother-in-law is a marshal and that woman holding a shotgun is a deputy. She will kill you if you don't drop your gun."

"But I'll kill you first," he snarled and lifted the gun to take aim.

Liza moved in quickly, slamming the barrel hard into his ribs as Hud threw Stacy to the floor. Her momentum drove the man back and into the wall. She knocked the pistol from his hand, then cold-cocked him with the shotgun. As his eyes rolled back into his head, he slid down the wall to the floor.

Hud already had the man's gun and bent to frisk him, pulling out his wallet. "Dana, are you all right?" he asked over his shoulder. Liza could hear Stacy sobbing.

"I'm fine," Dana said.

The marshal rose. "I'll get my cuffs." He was back an instant later and had the man cuffed. Liza hadn't taken her eyes off their prisoner. She'd seen his hand twitch and knew he was coming around.

"Stacy, Ella is in the kitchen on the floor," Liza said over her shoulder.

"I'm not leaving without my baby," the man screamed at Stacy as she hurried past her and into the kitchen. "I'll kill you next time. I swear, I'm going to kill you."

Hud hauled him to his feet. "You aren't going anywhere but jail. You just threatened to kill my sister-in-law in front of a half dozen witnesses."

"I'll take him in," Liza said. "You take Dana to the hospital. I heard her say her water just broke." As she led him out of the house, Liza began to read him his rights.

Chapter Fifteen

After booking Virgil Browning, Liza was just in time to catch Shelby as she was coming out of Yogamotion. She had a large bag, the handles looped over one shoulder, and seemed to be in a hurry. As Liza had walked past Shelby's SUV, she'd noticed there were suitcases in the back.

"I'm sorry, we're closed, Deputy," Shelby said. "And I'm in a hurry."

"You might want to open back up. Unless you want to discuss why you were being blackmailed at your house with your husband present."

All the color washed from the woman's face. She leaned into the door as if needing it for support. "I don't—"

"Don't bother lying. Alex would have bled you dry since his wife was taking everything in the divorce, right? He needed money and he had you right where he wanted you. *Of course,* you had to kill him."

"I didn't kill Alex." When Liza said nothing, Shelby opened the door to Yogamotion and turned on the light as they both stepped back inside.

Liza saw the sign that had been taped to the door.

Closed Until Further Notice. Shelby was skipping town, sure as the devil.

"I swear I didn't kill him," she said as they went into her office and sat down. "Why would I kill him? I had no idea who was blackmailing me," Shelby cried.

Liza studied her face for a moment, trying to decide if she was telling the truth or lying through her teeth.

"So how was it you made the payment if you didn't know who was blackmailing you?"

"I sent ten thousand dollars in cash to J. Doe, general delivery in Bozeman each month."

"You were that afraid of the truth coming out?" Liza had to ask.

"How can you ask that?" Shelby cried. "It wasn't just the vandalism. Wyatt's father lost his business, went to prison and probably killed himself, all because of what I did." She was crying now, real tears.

"You had to know it would eventually come out."

She shook her head adamantly. "It would destroy my marriage, my reputation, I'd have to leave town. Wyatt has said if he ever found out who did that to his father, he'd kill them."

Liza felt a chill run the length of her spine. "Maybe he's already killed. Didn't he blame Tanner for what happened?"

She quit crying for a moment and wiped at her tears, frowning as she realized what Liza was saying. "Yes, he blamed Tanner, but he wouldn't..." The words died off. "Tanner killed *himself.*"

"Did he? Was Wyatt jealous of your relationship with Tanner?" Liza saw the answer in the woman's expression. "Tanner was supposed to be watching the equipment, right?"

"No, Wyatt wouldn't..." She shook her head. "He's had to overcome so much."

"Does he know about the blackmail?"

"No, of course not."

But Liza could see the fear in the woman's eyes. "If he found out that you were being blackmailed and thought it was Alex Winslow behind it, what would your husband do?"

"He couldn't have found out," she said. "If he knew, he would have left me."

Liza thought about that for a moment. "What if you weren't the only one being blackmailed?"

Shelby's head came up. "What?"

"Has your husband been having similar financial problems to yours?" Liza asked.

"It's the economy," Shelby said. "It's not..."

"Because he's been paying a blackmailer just like you have?"

"Why would he do that?" Her eyes widened and Liza saw that, like her, Shelby could think of only one reason her husband might be paying a blackmailer.

"Oh, no, no." She began to wail, a high keening sound. "He wouldn't have hurt Tanner. Not Tanner." She rocked back and forth, hugging her stomach.

"I have to ask you," Liza said. "Were you ever pregnant with Tanner's baby?"

Her wailing didn't stop, but it slowed. She shook her head, before she dropped it into her hands. "I didn't want him to leave Big Sky after graduation. I thought that if he married me I could say I had a miscarriage. Or with luck, I could get pregnant quickly."

"Where is your husband?" Liza asked her.

"He's been out of town, but I expect him back to-night."

"That's why you were leaving. You're afraid your husband has found out."

Shelby didn't have to answer. The terror in her eyes said it all.

"I'd tell you not to leave town," Liza said, "but I'm afraid that advice could get you killed tonight."

Shelby's cell phone rang. She glanced at it. "I need to take this."

As Liza was walking away, she heard Shelby say, "I'm so sorry." She was crying, her last words garbled but still intelligible. "Really? Just give me a few min-utes."

AFTER LEAVING THE RANCH, Jordan drove around aim-lessly. His mind whirled with everything that had hap-pened since his return to the canyon.

Foremost was Alex and Liza's blackmail theory. Alex had always resented the rich people who came and went at Big Sky—but especially those who built the huge houses they lived in only a few weeks each year.

So had Alex blackmailed Shelby for the money? Or for breaking him and Tessa up all those years ago?

But was that what had gotten him killed? As much as he disliked Shelby, he couldn't imagine her actually shooting Alex. True she used to hunt, maybe still did, and hadn't been a bad shot. And she was cold-blooded, no doubt about that.

It just felt as if there had to be more.

Both Hud and Liza had warned him to leave town and stay out of the investigation. He couldn't, even if he wanted to. Driving past Yogamotion, he saw that the lights were out. There was a note on the door. Getting out, he walked to the door. Closed Until Further Notice.

He pulled out his cell phone and tried Shelby's house. No answer. Then he got Crystal Winslow's number from information and waited for her to pick up.

"Hello?"

"Crystal, you probably don't remember me, I'm Jordan Cardwell."

"I remember you." Her voice sounded laced with ice.

"I need to ask you something about Alex. I heard he majored in engineering at Montana State University. Is that how he made his money?"

"He was a consultant. He worked for large construction projects like bridges and highways and some smaller ones that I am only now finding out about."

He heard something in her voice, a bitterness. "Smaller jobs?"

"Apparently, he was working for Shelby Iverson and had been for years. Her husband signed the checks, but I'm betting she was behind it. He must have thought I was so stupid. What could Iverson Construction need an engineer consultant for? They build houses."

"Crystal, how often did they hire Alex?"

"Every month for years."

"Twenty years?"

"All these years." She was crying. "That bitch has been…playing my husband like a puppet on the string."

More likely it was Alex playing her. So he had been blackmailing not Shelby, but Wyatt since Tanner's death and hiding it as work-related payments. No wonder Liza hadn't found it.

As he told Crystal how sorry he was and hung up, he wondered how Wyatt had been able to hide this from

Shelby all these years. With building going crazy at Big Sky until recently, maybe it hadn't been that much of a strain on Wyatt.

He would ask Wyatt when he saw him. Which would be soon, he thought as he parked in front of the Iverson mansion on the hill. The place looked deserted. As he started to get out a big black SUV came roaring up.

WYATT IVERSON LOOKED HARRIED and dirty as if he'd just been working at one of his construction sites. He had a cut on his cheek that the blood had only recently dried on and bruises as if he'd been in a fist fight. "If you're looking for Shelby, she's not here."

"Actually, I was looking for you," Jordan said, not caring what had happened to Wyatt Iverson or his wife. "Have a minute?"

"No, I just got home. I've been out of town."

"This won't take long," Jordan said, following him up the steps to the front door and pushing past him into the large marble foyer. "I just need to know how you killed Tanner Cole. I already suspect *why* you did it, misguided as it was." Through an open doorway he saw a large bedroom with women's clothing strewn all over the bed and floor. Shelby either had trouble finding something to wear tonight or she had hightailed it out of town.

"I really don't have time for this," Wyatt said behind him.

He got as far as the living room with its white furniture he would bet no one had ever sat on, before he turned to look into the other man's face. Wyatt was magazine-model handsome, a big, muscled man, but Jordan was sure he could take him in a fair fight.

Unfortunately, when he saw the gun in Wyatt Iverson's hand, he knew he wasn't going to get a chance to find out.

"You want to know how your friend died?" Wyatt demanded. "I told him that everything was going to be all right. That he shouldn't blame himself for my father's construction equipment being vandalized. He'd already had a few drinks by the time I got to the cabin." Wyatt stopped just inches from Jordan now.

"Tanner felt horrible about what had happened, blamed himself," he continued, a smirk on his face. "I suggested we have more drinks and bury the hatchet so to speak. By the time we went out by the fire pit, he was feeling no pain. I kept plying him with booze until he could barely stand up, then I bet him he couldn't balance on an upturned log. You should have seen his expression when I put the noose around his neck."

Jordan knew the worst thing he could do was go for the gun. Wyatt had the barrel aimed at his heart and, from the trapped look in the man's eyes, he would use it if provoked. But seeing that Wyatt Iverson felt no remorse for what he'd done and realizing the man was ready to kill again, Jordan lunged at the gun.

Wyatt was stronger than he looked and clearly he'd been expecting—probably hoping—Jordan would try something. The sound of the gunshot ricocheted through the expanse of the large living room, a deafening report that was followed by a piercing pain in Jordan's shoulder.

Wyatt twisted the gun from his fingers and backhanded him with the butt. Jordan saw stars and suddenly the room started spinning. The next thing he knew he was on the floor, looking up at the man. His shoulder hurt like hell, but the bullet appeared to have only grazed his skin.

"You lousy bastard." Jordan struggled to get up, but Wyatt kicked him hard in the stomach, then knelt down beside him, holding the gun to his head.

"Your friend knew he deserved it. I told him how my old man had let his insurance on the equipment lapse, how this would destroy my family and your friend Tanner nodded and closed his eyes and I kicked the log out."

"You *murdered* him," Jordan said between clenched teeth.

"He got what he deserved."

"He didn't deserve to die because of some vandalized equipment even if he had been responsible. Shelby set up Tanner that night—from the party to the vandalism—to get back at him. It was that old story of a woman scorned."

With a start Jordan saw that this wasn't news. Wyatt had known. "How long have you known that you killed the wrong person? Then you killed Alex to keep it your little family secret and end the blackmail?"

"*Alex?* I didn't kill Alex."

Jordan started to call the man a liar. But why would he lie at a time like this when he'd already confessed to one murder? With a jolt, Jordan realized that Wyatt was telling the truth. He didn't kill Alex. *Shelby.* No wonder she'd taken off. Not only would it now come out about her vandalizing the Iverson Construction equipment, but that she'd killed Alex to keep the photographs from going public.

"Where's your wife, Iverson?" Jordan asked through the pain as Wyatt jerked him to his feet and dragged him toward the front door with the gun to his head.

"Have you known all along it was her? No? Then you must be furious. Did you catch her packing to make her getaway?" Jordan had a thought. "Does she know that you killed Tanner?"

Wyatt made a sound that sent a chill up Jordan's spine.

He thought about the cut and bruise on Iverson's cheek, that harried look in his eye—and the dirt on him as if he'd been digging at one of his construction sites. "What did you do to her?" he demanded. "You wouldn't kill your own wife!"

"One more word and I'll kill you right there," the man said as he pulled him outside to the rental car. He reached inside and released the latch on the hatchback.

"You're going to kill me anyway. But you have to know you can't get away with this." He felt the shove toward the open back of the SUV just an instant before the blow to his head. Everything went dark. His last clear thought was of Tanner and what he must have felt the moment Wyatt kicked the log out from under his feet.

LIZA CALLED HUD'S CELL ON HER way to the Iverson house.

"How is Dana?" she asked first.

"In labor. We're at the hospital and they are making her comfortable. They're talking C-section, but you know Dana. She's determined she's going to have these babies the natural way."

"Give her my best. Did you get a chance to ask Stacy about Tanner's party?" she asked as she drove toward the mountain and the Iverson house.

"She was pretty shaken up after what happened and I got busy, but she's standing right here. I'll let you talk to her since I have to get back to Dana." He handed off the phone.

A moment later a shaky-voiced Stacy said, "Hello?"

"I need to know about the party Tanner Cole had at the Iverson Construction site twenty years ago."

"What?"

"You were there. I've seen a photograph of you standing around the campfire. I need to know who shot the photos. Come on, Stacy, it wasn't that long after that that Tanner died. Don't tell me you don't remember."

"I remember," she said, sounding defensive. "I was just trying to understand why you would ask me who took the photos. I did. It was my camera."

"*Your* camera? Why were you taking photographs at the party?"

"Jordan. I wanted to get something on him," she said. "He was always telling on me to Mother."

Blackmail, great. Liza sighed. "If it was your camera, then how is it that there's a photo of you?"

Silence then. "Alex Winslow. He wanted to borrow the camera for a moment. I made him give it back—"

"By promising to get him copies," Liza finished.

"Yes, how did you—"

"Do you still have the negatives?"

"I doubt it. Unless they're stored in my things I left here at the ranch."

"Let me talk to Jordan," Liza said, feeling as if all the pieces of the puzzle were finally coming together.

"Jordan? He's not here. He asked me who took the photos, then he left, saying he'd come by the hospital later."

"Do you know where he went?" Liza asked, suddenly worried.

"He said something about blackmail and the other side of the coin."

Ahead, Liza saw the Iverson house come into view in her headlights. "If you see him, tell him to call my cell." She gave Stacy the number, then disconnected as she pulled into the wide paved drive.

Parking, she tried Jordan's cell phone number. It went straight to voice mail. She left a message for him to call her.

The Iverson house could only be described as a mansion. But then Wyatt Iverson was in the construction business. Of course his home would have to be magnificent.

Liza got out and walked up the steps to the wide veranda. She rang the doorbell, heard classical music play inside and was reminded of Crystal Winslow's house down in Bozeman. It wasn't anywhere as large or as grand.

Liza thought about an old Elvis Presley song about a house without love. Or honesty, she thought as she rang the bell again.

Getting no answer, she checked the five-car garage. There was a large ski boat, a trailer with four snowmobiles and the large black SUV, the same one Liza had seen Wyatt Iverson driving the night of the reunion dinner.

He'd returned home. So where was he? And where was Jordan? She tried his cell phone again. As before, it went straight to voice mail.

Something was wrong. She felt it in her bones. If Wyatt Iverson had returned, where else might he have gone? She recalled overhearing Shelby say what sounded like she was going to meet someone. Was she stupid enough to agree to see her husband? If so, where would they have gone if not their house?

Yogamotion was her first thought. But she'd seen Shelby hightail it out of there. Was it possible Wyatt had taken another vehicle? She thought about Jordan. What if he'd come up here as she suspected?

She didn't want to go down that particular trail of thought. Maybe Wyatt Iverson had gone by his construction office. Unlike his father, Wyatt kept all his equipment under lock and key at a site back up Moonlight Basin.

She hurried to her rental SUV and, climbing behind the wheel, started the engine and headed for Moonlight Basin. All her instincts told her to hurry.

Chapter Sixteen

Jordan came to in darkness. He blinked, instantly aware of the pain. His wrists were bound with duct tape behind him. More duct tape bound his ankles. A strip had been placed over his mouth. He lay in the back of the rented SUV. Outside the vehicle he heard a sound he recognized and sat up, his head swimming. Something warm and sticky ran down into his left eye. Blood.

Through the blood he looked out through an array of construction equipment. He couldn't see the piece of equipment that was making all the noise, but he could see a gravel pit behind the site and catch movement.

Now seemed an odd time to be digging in a gravel pit. Unless, he thought with a start, you wanted to bury something.

Jordan knew he was lucky to be alive. He'd been a damned fool going to Iverson's house unarmed. What had he hoped to accomplish? The answer was simple. He'd wanted to hear Wyatt Iverson admit to Tanner's murder. He'd also wanted to know how he'd done it.

So he'd accomplished what he'd set out to do—a suicidal mission that had been successful if one didn't take his current predicament into consideration.

Hurriedly, he began to work at the tape on his wrists.

There were few sharp edges in the back of the SUV. Nor could he get the door open thanks to child locks. In frustration at modern advances, he threw himself into the backseat and was headed for the front seat to unlock the doors, when he heard it.

The noise of the running equipment had dropped to a low purr.

Jordan felt around quickly for a sharp edge. He found it on the metal runner of the front passenger seat and began to work frantically at the tape. Whatever Wyatt Iverson had been up to, he'd stopped. Jordan had a bad feeling that he'd be coming for him any moment.

The tape gave way. He quickly peeled the strip from his mouth then reached down to free his ankles.

The back door of the SUV swung open and he was instantly blinded by the glaring beam of a heavy-duty flashlight.

"Get out," Iverson barked.

Jordan saw that the gun was in the man's other hand and the barrel was pointed at him. He freed his ankles and did as he was told. As he stepped out, he breathed in the cold night air. It made him shiver. Or it could have been the sudden knowledge of what Iverson planned to do with him.

Standing, he could see where the earth had been dug out in a long trench. There was already one vehicle at the bottom of the trench. He recognized Shelby's expensive SUV.

"Get behind the wheel," Iverson ordered, and holding the gun on him, climbed in behind him in the backseat.

Jordan could feel the cold hard metal of the gun barrel pressed against his neck.

"Start the car." Iverson tossed him the keys.

His hand was shaking as he inserted the key. The engine turned right over even though he was wishing for a dead battery right then.

"Now drive through the gate to the back of the property. Try anything and I'll put a bullet into your brain and jump out."

Jordan drove through the gate and down the path that led to the gravel pit and ultimately the trench Iverson had dug for Shelby—and now him. He realized there was only one thing he could do. Iverson would have him stop at the high end of the trench. He would get out and send Jordan to his death—either before he buried him at the bottom of the trench or after.

He hit the child locks so Iverson couldn't get out and gunned the engine. He would take Iverson with him, one way or the other.

As the Iverson Construction site came into view, Liza noticed that the large metal gate hung open. She cut her headlights and slowly pulled to the side of the road.

It wasn't until she shut off her engine and got out that she heard the sound of a front-end loader running in the distance. Drawing her weapon, she moved through the darkness toward the sound.

She'd just cleared the fence and most of the equipment when she saw an old red pickup parked back between some other old trucks. She could see where the right side of it was all banged up. Some of the paint of the patrol SUV was still on the side. It was definitely the pickup that had run her off the road.

Ahead she heard a car start up. She could make out movement in the faint starlight. She hurried toward it, keeping to the shadows so she wasn't spotted.

But the car didn't come in her direction as she'd thought it would. Instead, it went the other way. In its headlights she saw the gravel pit and finally the trench and the front-end loader idling nearby.

To her amazement the vehicle engine suddenly roared. The driver headed for the trench.

Liza ran through the darkness, her heart hammering, as the vehicle careened down the slope and into the narrow ditch. She reached the fence, rushed through the gate and across the flat area next to the gravel pit in time to see the lights of the vehicle disappear into the trench.

Her mind was racing. What in the—

The sound of metal meeting metal filled the night air. She came to a skidding stop at the edge of the trough and looked down to see two vehicles. Smoke rose from between their crumpled metal, the headlights of the second one dimmed by the dirt and gravel that had fallen down around it.

She waited a moment for the driver to get out, then realizing he must be trapped in there, the trench too narrow for him to open his door, she scrambled down into the deep gully, weapon ready.

As she neared the vehicle, she recognized it. The rental SUV Jordan had been driving. Her pulse began to pound. Jordan did crazy things sometimes, she thought, remembering how he'd swum out into the river to be with her while she waited for the ambulance to arrive.

But he wouldn't purposely drive into this trench, would he? Which begged the question, where was Wyatt Iverson?

"COME ON, BABIES," DANA SAID under her breath and pushed.

"That's it," her doctor said. "Almost there. Just one more push."

Dana closed her eyes. She could feel Hud gripping her hand. Her first twin was about to make his or her way into the world. She felt the contraction, hard and fast, and pushed.

"It's a boy!" A cheer came up at the end of the bed. She opened her eyes and looked into the mirror positioned over the bed as the doctor held up her baby.

A moment later she heard the small, high-pitched cry of her son and tried to relax as Hud whispered that they had a perfect baby boy.

Dr. Burr placed the baby in Dana's arms for a moment. She smiled down at the crinkled adorable face before the doctor handed the baby off to the nurses standing by. "One more now. Let's see how that one's doing."

Dana could hear the baby's strong heartbeat through the monitor. She watched the doctor's face as Dr. Burr felt her abdomen first, then reached inside. Dana knew even before the doctor said the second baby was breech.

"Not to worry. I'll try to turn the little darling," the doctor assured her. "Otherwise, sometimes we can pull him out by his feet. Let's just give it a few minutes. The second baby is generally born about fifteen minutes after the first."

Dana looked over at her son now in the bassinet where a nurse was cleaning him up. "He looks like you," she said to her husband and turned to smile up at him as another contraction hit.

LIZA REACHED THE BACK of the car. She could hear movement inside. "Jordan!" she called. A moment later the back hatch clicked open and began to rise. She stepped to the side, weapon leveled at the darkness inside the SUV, cursing herself for not having her flashlight. "Jordan?"

A moan came from inside, then more movement.

"Liza, he has a gun!" Jordan cried.

The shot buzzed past her ear like a mad hornet. She ducked back, feeling helpless as she heard the struggle in the car and could do little to help. Another shot. A louder moan.

"I'm coming out," Wyatt Iverson called from inside the SUV. "I'm not armed."

"I have him covered," Jordan yelled out. "But you can shoot him if you want to."

Liza leveled her weapon at the gaping dark hole at the back of the SUV. Wyatt Iverson appeared head-first. He fell out onto the ground. She saw that he was bleeding from a head wound and also from what appeared to be a gunshot to his thigh. She quickly read him his rights as she rolled him over and snapped a pair of handcuffs on him.

"Jordan, are you all right?" she called into the vehicle. She heard movement and felt a well of relief swamp her as he stumbled out through the back. "What is going on?"

"He planned to bury me in this trench," Jordan said. "I think Shelby is in the other car. I suspect he killed her before he put her down here."

Wyatt was heaving, his face buried in his shoulder as he cried.

"Can you watch him for a moment?" Liza asked, seeing that Jordan was holding a handgun—Wyatt's, she assumed.

She holstered her own weapon and climbed up over the top of the SUV to the next one. Dirt covered most of the vehicle except the very back. She wiped some of the dirt from the window and was startled to see a face pressed against the glass.

There was duct tape over Shelby's mouth. Her eyes were huge, her face white as a ghost's. Blood stained the front of her velour sweatshirt where she'd been shot in the chest at what appeared to be close range since the fabric was burned around the entry hole.

Liza pulled out her cell and hit 911. "We'll need an ambulance and the coroner." She gave the dispatcher directions, then climbed back over the top of Jordan's rental SUV to join him again.

Wyatt was still crying. Jordan, she noticed, was more banged up than she'd first realized. He was sitting on the SUV's bumper. He looked pale and was bleeding from a shoulder wound.

"Come on, let's get out of this trench before the sides cave in and kill us all," she said. "Are you sure you're all right?"

He grinned up at her. "Just fine, Deputy," he said, getting to his feet. "I sure was glad to see you."

As she pulled Wyatt to his feet and the three of them staggered up out of the hole, she smelled the pine trees, black against the night sky. The air felt colder as if winter wasn't far behind. She looked toward Lone Peak. The snow on the top gleamed in the darkness. Everything seemed so normal.

The rifle shot took them all by surprise. Wyatt suddenly slumped forward and fell face-first into the dirt. Jordan grabbed her and knocked her to the ground behind one of the huge tires of a dump truck as a second shot thudded into Wyatt's broad back.

Liza rolled and came up with her weapon. She scrambled over to Wyatt, checked for a pulse and finding none, swore as she scrambled back over to Jordan out of the line of fire. She could hear the sound of sirens in the distance. It was too dark to tell where the shot had come from.

But over the high-pitched whine of the sirens, she heard a vehicle start up close by. "Stay here," she ordered Jordan and took off running toward her SUV.

A SECOND SON WAS BORN seventeen minutes after the first. Dana began to cry when she saw him.

"Identical twin boys," Dr. Burr told her. "Congratulations."

Hud hugged her. "We really have to quit doing this," he whispered. "I can't take it."

She laughed through her tears. No one was more fearless than her husband, but she knew what he meant. Her heart had been in her throat, afraid something would go wrong. She couldn't bear the thought of losing her babies.

"You did good," the doctor said, squeezing her hand. "Do you have names picked out yet?"

Dana shook her head and looked to Hud. "I have a couple of ideas though."

He laughed. "I'm sure you do. I'd better call everyone."

"You mean Liza," she said. "You haven't heard from her?"

He checked his phone. "No."

She could tell he was worried.

"Jordan left without telling anyone where he was going, but everyone else is out in the hall waiting for the news."

"Go do whatever it is you have to do, Marshal," she said, smiling. "But let me know when you hear from Liza—and my brother."

He grinned at her. "It's going to be so nice to have you back on your feet."

LIZA REACHED HER PATROL SUV just moments after seeing a set of headlights coming out of the pines in the distance. Jordan was hot on its heels. He leaped into the passenger seat as she started the engine. She hurriedly turned around and went after the killer.

The other vehicle was moving fast. She saw the headlights come around as the vehicle hit the narrow strip of pavement, the driver almost losing control.

Liza followed the other vehicle headed down the mountain. The road was treacherous with lots of switchbacks. She had to assume whoever had killed Wyatt knew the road. But the driver was also running scared.

She glanced over at Jordan. He needed medical attention. "You should have stayed back there to wait for the ambulance," she said as she managed to keep the vehicle in front of her in sight. "Call and tell the ambulance to wait in Meadow Village. The coroner might as well wait, too."

"See, you would have missed my company if I hadn't come along," he said. "And Wyatt wasn't great company when he was alive, let alone dead."

She shot him another look, worried that he might be hurt worse than she thought. "Did he say anything about why he killed Shelby?"

"We didn't get to talk much. He knew she vandalized his father's equipment. I don't think he took it well. He swore he didn't kill Alex. But he killed Tanner and Alex has been blackmailing Wyatt for years, writing it off as a business expense."

Liza suspected that whoever had killed Alex

Winslow had just killed Wyatt Iverson as well, but why? Shelby was dead. So who had just shot Wyatt?

"All of this started because Shelby was going to force Tanner into marriage, one way or the other," Jordan said. "When he broke up with her, she vandalized the construction equipment he was responsible for to get even with him. She hadn't given a damn whose equipment it was. Ironic it turned out to be her future father-in-law's. And look where the repercussions of that one malicious act have landed us all."

The vehicle ahead swung through a tight curve, fishtailed and for a moment Liza thought the driver would lose control and crash. She could make out a figure behind the wheel, but still couldn't tell who it was. All the SUVs looked similar.

Liza knew who wasn't behind the wheel of the car in front of her. Shelby was dead. So was Malcolm Iverson and his son Wyatt. Alex had found the photographs and gotten himself killed when he'd blackmailed Shelby— her husband. She'd been so sure that Wyatt had killed Alex because of it. Alex had somehow figured out that Wyatt had killed Tanner.

Now she suspected that the last piece of the puzzle was in that SUV ahead of her. Whoever had shot Wyatt Iverson must have shot Alex. But why? Was it possible Alex had been blackmailing someone else?

Ahead she caught a glimpse of the lights of Meadow Village. She was right behind the vehicle in front of her. The driver didn't stand a chance of getting away.

She thought about the photos and tried to remember if there was anything else in them. "That one photograph," she said more to herself than to Jordan. "Wasn't it of Tanner and Tessa coming out of the woods?"

"Like I said, Shelby thought of everything."

"Including making her best friend go into the woods with Tanner?"

Jordan let out a curse. "I never could understand why Tessa did what Shelby told her to. She said Shelby even talked her into marrying Danny Spring, when apparently she has always been in love with Alex."

Liza felt a chill race up her spine. "But Alex had these photographs. He would have seen Tessa coming out of the woods with Tanner."

"What are you saying?" Jordan asked.

"Alex would have known just how far Tessa would go to protect Shelby. So why give her the photographs for safekeeping?"

"That's what I said. Unless he *wanted* her to look at the photos. But once she did, why wouldn't she destroy them to protect Shelby?"

"Because she was through protecting Shelby," Liza said. "Shelby had finally done something that she couldn't forgive. Alex's estranged wife believed Alex was having an affair with *Shelby.* I suspect Tessa thought the same thing."

"That would have been the last straw for Tessa. She would have felt betrayed by all of them."

"You're saying if Tessa found out, it would have been the last straw."

Ahead the SUV fishtailed on one of the turns and Liza had to back off to keep from hitting it.

"Tessa. She's in that car, isn't she?" Jordan said. "She used to go out shooting for target practice before hunting season with Shelby and the rest of us. She always pretended to be a worse shot than Shelby, but I always suspected she was better and just didn't dare show it.

She's been hiding her light under a bushel for years, as my mother used to say."

"Not anymore," Liza said as the vehicle ahead of them went off the road on the last tight turn. It crashed down into the trees. Liza stood on the brakes. "Stay here or I'll arrest you!" she shouted to Jordan and jumped out.

With her weapon drawn she hurried to where the SUV had gone off. She hadn't gone far when she heard the shot.

Liza scrambled down into the trees, keeping out of the driver's sights until she finally reached the back of the vehicle. She saw that just as she'd suspected, Tessa was behind the wheel. There was a rifle next to her, the barrel pointed at her. She was bleeding heavily from the crash and the gunshot wound to her side, but she was still breathing.

Liza quickly called for the ambulance. "Just stay still," she told Tessa. "Help is on the way."

Tessa managed a smile. "There is no help for me. Is Wyatt dead?"

"Yes."

"And Shelby?"

"She's dead, too."

Tessa nodded. "Good. They all ruined my life."

"Why kill Alex, though?" Liza asked. "I thought you loved him?"

Tessa got a faraway look in her eyes. "Alex was the only man I ever really loved. I thought he loved me but he was only using me. He said he forgave me for the past, but he lied. He used me just like Shelby and Wyatt used me." She smiled sadly. "They all used me. But I showed them. I wasn't as good at playing their games, but I was always a better shot than any of them."

Epilogue

The hospital room was packed with well-wishers, flowers, balloons and stuffed animals. Dana looked around her and couldn't help the swell of emotion that bubbled up inside of her.

"It's the hormones," she said as she wiped her eyes.

Clay and Stacy had brought Hank and Mary to the hospital to see their new little brothers.

"Hank wants to name them after his horses," Stacy told her. "Mary wanted to name them after her dolls." Stacy looked stronger. Hud had promised her that Virgil would never bother her again. Apparently, there were numerous warrants out on him, including the fact that he'd broken his probation. So added to the latest charges, Virgil would be going back to prison for a very long time.

Dana watched her elderly ranch manager make his way through the crowd to her. Warren Fitzpatrick was as dried out as a stick of jerky and just as tough, but he knew more about cattle than any man she'd ever known. He'd also been there for her from the beginning. As far as she was concerned he was a permanent fixture on the Cardwell Ranch. She'd already promised him a spot in the family cemetery up on the hill.

He gave her a wink. "That's some cute little ones. I just had a peek at them down the hall. Goin' to make some fine ranchhands," he said with a chuckle. "I've got a couple of fine saddles picked out for them. Never too early for a man to have his own saddle."

She smiled up at him. It was the first time she'd ever seen a tear in his eye.

Her father arrived then with a giant teddy bear. "How's my baby girl?" he asked. She'd always been his baby girl—even now that she was the mother of four and only a few years from forty.

"I'm good," she said as she leaned up to hug him. He put the bear down and hugged her tighter than usual.

"I was worried about you," he whispered.

"I'm fine."

"Yes, you are," he said, smiling at her.

Then Uncle Harlan came in with the second giant teddy bear and her father grinned, knowing that she'd thought he'd forgotten she was having twins.

Her father-in-law called. Brick Savage had been sick for some time, but he promised to make the trip down from his cabin outside West Yellowstone to see his new grandsons soon.

"I think we should all leave and let her get some rest," Hilde said to the crowd of friends and family.

"I agree," Hud said. He looked exhausted and so did Liza, who'd stopped in earlier. It had been a shock to hear about the deaths up on the mountain and Tessa Ryerson Spring's involvement. Tessa had died before the ambulance got to her.

Jordan had stopped by earlier, his shoulder bandaged. Dana had hugged him for a long time after hearing what he'd been through. Both he and Liza were lucky to be alive.

Dana noticed that they had left together. She smiled to herself. There was nothing like seeing two people falling in love.

Now as everyone said their goodbyes with Stacy and Clay taking Hank and Mary home, she finally relaxed. Everything was turning out just fine. Stacy had her baby—and a job working for Hilde at Needles and Pins.

"I want to stay around, if that's all right," her sister had said. "I want Ella to know her cousins."

Dana couldn't have been happier. Clay, though, said he would be returning to Hollywood, but that he would come visit more often.

And Jordan, well, Liza was right. Jordan *had* changed. Love did that to a man, she thought, studying her own husband as he came back into the room pushing two bassinets.

"I thought you'd like to see your sons," he said. "Isn't it time you told me what names you've picked out? I know you, Dana. Or do you want me to guess?"

She merely smiled at him.

Hud laughed and shook his head. "You do realize what you're doing to these two innocent little boys by naming them after our fathers, don't you?"

Dana nodded. "I'm giving them a little bit of family history. It isn't just about the ranch. It's about the lives we've carved out here."

Hud looked into the bassinets. "Angus?" he asked as he picked up one of their sons. "And Brick?" He handed her both infants. "So when is the building going to start on the new house?" he asked as he climbed up in the bed beside her and the babies.

"What new house?"

"Jordan's. You know he's staying."

"Did he tell you that?" she asked, unable to keep the hope out of her voice.

Hud gave her a disbelieving look. "You know darned well he is. I wouldn't be surprised if you haven't already picked out a spot on the ranch for him and Liza to live."

"You're taking this pretty well," Dana noted.

He chuckled at that. "Your mother always said Jordan would be back. Stacy, though, I think even that would have surprised your mother."

Dana nodded. "Mom did know her children. She always knew that one day you and I would be together. Mary Justice Cardwell was one smart woman."

"So is her youngest daughter," he said and kissed her.

LIZA REINED IN HER HORSE and looked out over the canyon. The day was warm and dry, possibly one of the last before winter set in. A light breeze stirred the fallen aspen leaves and sighed through the pine boughs.

Jordan brought his horse up beside hers.

"It's beautiful, isn't it?" she said.

"Yes. Beautiful."

She heard something in his voice and looked over at him. He was grinning at her and not looking at the view at all.

"She is *very* beautiful."

"You know you can't charm me," she said, embarrassed. No one had ever told her she was beautiful before. Cute, maybe. Unusual, often. But not beautiful. It wasn't even the word that warmed her to the toes of her boots, though. It was the way he looked at her. He made her *feel* beautiful.

She thought of the scars she'd carried since high school. This case had brought back those awful years, worse, those awful feelings about herself. It had also brought Jordan back to the canyon, a surprise in so many ways.

"You think I'm trying to charm you?" He chuckled as he swung down from his horse.

Before she knew what was happening, he cupped her waist with his large hands and pulled her off her horse and into his arms.

"No, Miss Turner, quite the opposite," he said, his lips just a breath away from hers. "You're the one who's charmed me. All I think about is you. You're like no one I've ever known. I'm under your spell."

She shook her head and laughed softly.

"I'm serious, Liza. You have me thinking crazy thoughts."

"Is that right?"

"Oh, yeah. I've been thinking that I want to stay here and work the ranch with my sister. How crazy is that? Worse, right now, I'm thinking there is only one thing that could make this day more perfect."

She grinned at him. "I'm afraid to ask."

"I'm the one who is afraid to ask." He dropped to one knee. "Marry me and make an honest man out of me."

"Jordan—"

"I know this seems sudden. We should probably at least go on a real date where I'm not just another one of your suspects."

"Be serious."

"I am. I've fallen hopelessly in love with you. Say you at least like me a little." Jordan looked into her wide green eyes and thought he might drown in them. "Just a little?"

"I like you."

He grinned.

"A lot. But marriage?"

"Yes, marriage because I'm not letting you get away, Deputy, and I can't stand to spend another day away from you. I'd marry you right now, but we both know that my sister Dana isn't going to allow it. She's going to insist on a big wedding at the ranch. But that will give us time to go on a few dates. So what do you say?"

Liza's laugh was a joyous sound. "What can I say but yes."

He laughed and swung her up into his arms, spinning them both around. As he set her down, he kissed her, then he drew back to look into her lovely face. Their gazes locked. Electricity arced between them, hotter than any flame.

"I suppose we should wait until our wedding night," he said ruefully.

"Not a chance," Liza said, putting her arms around him. "I can think of no place more wonderful to make love to you the first time than up here on this mountain."

THE WEDDING OF JORDAN CARDWELL and Liza Turner was a glorious affair. Hud and Clay gave Liza away, and stood up with Jordan. Hilde and Dana were Liza's attendants. Hilde had made Liza's dress, a simple white sheath that made her feel like a princess.

The ceremony was short and sweet and held in the large house on the ranch. Stacy baked the wedding cake and the kids helped decorate it. There were balloons and flowers and music. Jordan's father and uncle came with their band to play old-fashioned Country-Western music for the affair.

Neighbors and friends stopped throughout the day to offer felicitations. Even Brick showed up to congratulate them on their wedding and Liza on solving the Tanner Cole case.

The murders and deaths had rocked the small community. Only a few people knew the story behind them and the twisted motives of those involved.

Fall and winter had come and gone. Jordan had been right about Dana insisting on a big wedding. It was spring now. The canyon was turning green from the tall grass on the ranch to the bright leaves on the aspen trees. Work had begun on a ranch house up in the hills from the main house for the two of them.

Liza had never been so happy. She had loved this family even before she fell in love with Jordan. Now she was a part of it. Raised as an orphan, she'd never known this kind of family. Or this kind of love.

Construction on their house on the ranch wasn't quite done, but would be soon. In the meantime, the two of them had been staying in Liza's condo and dating.

Jordan had insisted on a honeymoon. "Hawaii? Tahiti? Mexico? You name it," he'd said.

But Liza didn't want to leave Montana. "Surprise me," she'd said. "Wherever you take me will be perfect."

"How did I get so lucky?" he asked and kissed her as they left in a hail of birdseed.

She had no idea where they were going. She didn't care. With Jordan she knew it would always be an adventure.

* * * * *

A sneaky peek at next month...

INTRIGUE...

BREATHTAKING ROMANTIC SUSPENSE

My wish list for next month's titles...

In stores from 21st December 2012:

❏ Grayson – Delores Fossen

& Dade – Delores Fossen

❏ Breathless Encounter – Cindy Dees

& Switched – HelenKay Dimon

❏ Cavanaugh's Surrender – Marie Ferrarella

& Montana Midwife – Cassie Miles

❏ Colton Destiny – Justine Davis

Available at WHSmith, Tesco, Asda, Eason, Amazon and Apple

Just can't wait?

Special Offers

Every month we put together collections and longer reads written by your favourite authors.

Here are some of next month's highlights— and don't miss our fabulous discount online!

On sale 21st December

On sale 4th January

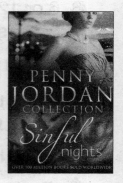

On sale 4th January

Save 20%
on all Special Releases

Find out more at
www.millsandboon.co.uk/specialreleases

Visit us Online

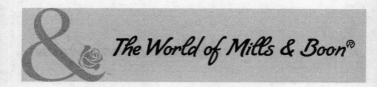